INTERVIEW WITH THE . . .

I lowered my voice. "I'm sure you'd look spectacular without the sunglasses."

She hesitated, then peeled them back and blinked her eyes. She wasn't blind, she wasn't albino, but something struck me wrong. It took a few seconds to puzzle it out: it was dark in the bar, but her pupils weren't even dilated. "Grandmother, what big eyes you have," I said. Something was clicking, but I couldn't put it together.

"They're very sensitive to light," she said with care.

"Grandmother, what fine, white, delicate skin you have."

She smiled wide. "Beauty cream and lots of sleep," she said with utter insincerity.

"Grandmother, what big teeth you have."

She looked at me levelly for a long moment. "They're still growing a little."

It all came together. "I get it—you're a vampire!"

By Robert Frezza
Published by Ballantine Books:

A SMALL COLONIAL WAR

And look for these Del Rey Discoveries . . .
Because something new is always worth the risk!

McLENDON'S SYNDROME

Robert A. Frezza

A Del Rey Book
BALLANTINE BOOKS • NEW YORK

A Del Rey Book
Published by Ballantine Books

Copyright © 1993 by Robert A. Frezza

All rights reserved under International and Pan-American Copyright Conventions. Published in the United States of America by Ballantine Books, a division of Random House, Inc., New York, and simultaneously in Canada by Random House of Canada Limited, Toronto.

Library of Congress Catalog Card Number: 92-97263

ISBN 0-345-37516-5

Manufactured in the United States of America

First Edition: May 1993

For my father, whose Indian name means "Teller of Stories" and who invented Bucky Beaver; and for my mother, who died of cancer while I was writing my first book, in gratitude and with love.

An Unexpected Party;
or, Ill-Met in a Dank Bar

A few tables away, Dinky the piano player was trying to learn "As Time Goes By." He was making a hash of it.

I whipped a Brazil nut out of a bowl and whacked it open with a sap borrowed for the occasion. The bowl was marked with the Prancing Pony Bar and Grill logo on one side and had "Squirrel Food" printed on the other.

A glass of limewater slid across the table, spun around twice, and stopped artistically beside my right hand. " 'Lo, Harry," I said without looking.

Harry, the Prancing Pony's proprietor, leaned across the table, which trembled slightly. He grinned. "Hello, Admiral." Clad from head to toe in Lincoln green, Harry could have passed for the bottom half of a very large tree. Portions of his green suit were covered with leaflike tendrils, which enhanced the effect only slightly.

I pitched the nut at him. "It's Journeyman MacKay to you, O fat innkeeper who only remembers his name because people shout it at him all day."

For some reason, Harry loves this line and encourages me to use it. His face broke out in various interesting directions. "Roger that, Ken." He eased himself into a chair. "How're they cooking?"

I sighed. "They're cooking, Harry. They're still cooking." In three trips to Schuyler's World, I'd spent a fair amount of time in Harry's bar and figured out most of his more obvious peculiarities. I pointed my thumb toward the ceiling. "You know,

Harry. About this 'Admiral' bit—the itinerant ship I have the misfortune to crew is far more likely to be mistaken for orbiting junk than a Navy vessel, and since neither my civilian career as a journeyman spacer nor my military career as a reservist seems to be sprouting jets . . ."

Harry waited expectantly.

I figuratively threw up my hands. "Oh, skip it."

Deep disappointment welled up in Harry's eyes. Harry knows I'm an ensign in the inactive Navy reserve, which probably gives me more social cachet than most of Harry's clientele. Harry likes all things military and enjoys bumping people he likes up a grade or so—in my case from ensign to admiral. Harry is a frustrated jet jockey.

I softened the blow for him. "Tell you what, Harry, I'll roll you double or nothing."

We used his dice, so two limewaters went on my tab. "You shouldn't be so hard on the *Scupper*. She's not so bad," Harry said complacently.

"She's a cut above space debris," I conceded.

He shrugged. "I'm surprised to see you tonight. I thought you said you were heading out."

I waved my hands expressively. "Davie Lloyd Ironsides changed his mind for about the fourth time this week, so we're staying here an extra day or so. Davie Lloyd the Iron-Ass is getting on my nerves a bit more than usual. I keep hoping he'll jam his pipe in the wrong orifice or something to break the monotony."

"I'm glad you decided to drop by. I figured it was going to be a dull night. Nice of you," he said, staring at one patron who suddenly decided that he didn't need a drink right that minute.

"The way I roll, you ought to pay me to stop in," I told him. "By choice, I'd have been in Callahan's Place, swilling your competitor's brew, but Elaine O'Day preempted that watering hole by virtue of seniority, intending to cuddle anything that could walk, fly, or crawl."

"You know, Ken, I always thought torchship crews were supposed to cling like sand in cement," Harry observed.

I shuddered. "You must not remember Elaine. In any case,

my shipmates avoid laying eyes on each other dirtside, and O'Day is not necessarily my first choice as a shift partner."

"Yeah, you mentioned that. She may not even be your second choice," Harry said, apparently recalling some of my pithier comments. "I brewed up a fresh batch of stew. Want some?"

"Uh, no thanks." Harry's son-of-a-bitch stew is made from the parts of a bull the bull can least do without. I took another nut out of the bowl. "Why do you give these things away?"

Harry shrugged elaborately, which caused his foliage to ripple. "The bags to sell them in cost more than nuts do. I make it up on drinks."

"How's business?"

Harry shook his head. "Not even fair. None of the farmers are in town, and there's only one ship in orbit besides yours, one of the Rodents'."

"Rodents?"

"Two lights over. It's listed as Dennison's World. They have a few ships that touch here on their way out." Harry pointed to two dark, fuzzy bowling pins sitting on the other side of the room. "The big one there is a wheel over at the consulate."

It seemed natural to have large furry things sitting around Harry's bar. His hole in the wall looks more like a hole in the ground—he has fake tree roots dangling from the ceiling and mushrooms growing in hanging baskets. "He likes the place?" I commented.

Harry leaned over. "He gets buzzed on honey," he whispered.

"And you charge him double when he does," I replied, and bounced the nut off his chest.

Harry winked and grinned. Harry is an even-tempered guy who wouldn't hurt a fly—unless the fly really deserved it.

"How're things with you?" he asked, but his attention began to wander when a minor disturbance commenced involving a couple of barstools and a good-time girl on the other side of the room.

As Dinky switched to something a little up-tempo, Harry pushed back his chair and reclaimed the sap I'd been using to crack nuts. "Ken, I'm my own bouncer tonight, I've got to run.

Oh, there's a woman, good-looking if you like them thin. She's been asking about you. You must be popular."

"Oh? That's news to me."

"Over there in the dark glasses," he said. He scurried off, pausing on the way to gently swat one enterprising citizen who had absently begun playing mumblety-peg on the table.

Harry keeps the place dark enough for the good-time girls to make a living, so it took me a few seconds to spot her. She was in the corner with a glass a few tables down from the two Rodents. Her hair was ash blond, shoulder-length. She was wearing a large silver butterfly pinned on a black bodysuit and large oval sunglasses, which looked strange even for the Prancing Pony. She was slim and wore black very well—her skin was fair and then some, pure alabaster. A long scar on her left hand made it look whiter by contrast.

The shades were definitely out of place. She must have noticed me staring, because she grinned—lots of teeth, but better proportioned than Harry's.

I knocked back half my limewater and made a wide circuit around the riot, dropping coins in Dinky's jar along the way. When I got to her table, I asked politely, "Hello, bright eyes. Is this seat taken?"

She looked up. "Not at all, spacer."

"Ken," said I, hoping to keep things on a first-name basis. As I parked, Dinky shifted to something slow and romantic.

"Catarina." She had a solitaire layout spread on the table in front of her, and I noticed her butterfly was sprinkled with blue stones.

I'm not real good with snappy pickup lines. She must have seen me hesitate, because she smiled. "Yes, I know I can put the black jack on the red queen, and no, please don't tell me how dangerous it is to fly your ship into a black hole."

Black holes aren't holes, nobody ever flies "into" one, and the procedure is about as dangerous as hopping the shuttle. The line is primarily known for its remarkable effect on vapid young things.

I must have looked hurt, because her smile widened. "Now you're remembering that Harry's idea of a joke is to touch off three kilos of plastique in a commode somebody's using."

I had to grin. "Uh, yeah. I was just thinking that if this blew up in my face I was going to use one of the light-salvage demolition charges to repay Harry in kind."

She chuckled. "Let me buy you another drink."

"Uh, thanks. No." I consider myself a friend of Harry's, and his liquor is strictly for customers—Harry being perennially short of friends and unwilling to place the ones he has at risk.

"Business, then. You're Kenneth MacKay, off *Rustam's Slipper*."

I coughed.

"Occasionally known as the *Rusty Scupper*," she conceded. "You hit Schuyler's World four days ago. Your middle name is Andrew. You have ten months' seniority on a journeyman's rate, a reserve Naval commission, and an identifying mark on your left knee."

I looked down at my knees and then over at the cheatsheet she had spread across hers. "Are my eyes really brown?"

"You've seen *Casablanca*?"

"All four versions, including the one set on the moons of Jupiter. I've seen several versions more than once, *not* including the one set on the moons of Jupiter."

She chuckled again, sweeping up her cards and tucking them away into a little belt purse.

"MacKay am I, off in body and spirit, tonight. What brings you to this locale and sudden interest?" I replied cautiously. "Looking for a ship?"

"Curiously, I am." She was looking at me from behind those thick sunshades.

"Oh, a ship. That lets out the *Scupper*."

She actually thought that was funny. Just then a body came hurtling by our table, closely followed by a flying bowl of stew for emphasis. "Is it like this all the time here?" she asked.

I looked over to where Harry was escorting one citizen to the door and slightly beyond. "I understand around midnight the place gets lively," I said, and added, "Please don't feed me lines like that."

She clinked her glass against mine. "It's a deal."

"What do you plan on shipping?" I asked. The dark glasses

and the way the conversation was becoming unhinged were both bothering me.

"How long do you plan on staying with the ship?" she asked, ignoring my question.

"At least another two months, eleven days, and four hours, but who's counting." I lowered my voice. "I'm sure you'd look spectacular without the sunglasses."

I saw her hesitate. She started to say something, but I shook my head. She peeled them back and blinked her eyes. She wasn't blind, she wasn't albino, but I sure bring home weird ones. Still, she had a great deal more about her than any other patron of Harry's, and I was about to cast my line when something struck me wrong.

It took a few seconds for me to puzzle it out. I wouldn't buy a suit in the light Harry keeps in his place, but I could see that the pupils of her eyes weren't even dilated.

I notice things like that. "Grandmother, what big eyes you have," I said. Something was clicking, but I couldn't put it together.

"They're very sensitive to light," she said with care.

"Grandmother, what fine, white, delicate skin you have."

She smiled wide. "Beauty cream and lots of sleep," she said with utter insincerity.

"Grandmother, what big teeth you have," I said waiting for the thought to decrypt before I made too much of an ass of myself.

She looked at me levelly for a long minute. "They're still growing a little."

It all came together. "I get it. You're a vamp!" I edged away delicately.

She made a wry face. "McLendon's Syndrome."

"Like I said, a vampire." Tact is not my strong suit.

She let it go. "How much have you read about McLendon's?"

"Quite a bit, actually." Crewing a torchship eight hours on with Elaine O'Day would induce an illiterate to finish *War and Peace*. "McLendon's is a slow bacillus, like leprosy. For a disease, it's more than slightly unusual. Normal people replace their cells completely for the last time before they hit puberty.

McLendon's germ encourages complete cell replacement at an age when people are old enough to know better.''

"Close enough."

"After the tabloids played it up big, I got interested and read McLendon's paper—I think it was in the *New England Journal of Medicine*. Bits and pieces of it stuck. He wrote the disease up as a veritable fountain of perpetual youth, with a few drawbacks: problems with porphyrins, hypersensitivity to sunlight up to and including skin sarcoids, allergies I wouldn't wish on my ex-wife, a few other things.''

She nodded.

"Although you aren't exactly Count Dracula, or even Vlad Tepes, the revelation does put our relationship in a new light. As I recall, McLendon's bug affects different people to a different degree, and blood was about all some of his subjects could keep down. Reading through the footnotes, I got the impression that one or two of them hadn't been too particular how they got it.''

"And?'' she asked, planting her elbow on the table and leaning her chin on her hand.

"Ah, yeah. I suspect it's my public duty to turn you over to the health authorities,'' I said, trying to sound composed.

My tablemate tilted her head complacently. "I suspect they'd quarantine me forever and you for at least six months.''

"Ah, right. This is Schuyler's World, isn't it?'' There were places I could think of where I'd rather spend six months.

Having heaved an evening's worth of bodies into the street, Harry waltzed by to fill a slight void in the discussion. "How are you two lovebirds doing?''

"You wouldn't believe it if I told you,'' I observed.

Harry winked. "She's good people, Ken. I told her all about you.''

"All?'' I commented.

Harry nodded. "Uh-huh.''

"That I'm beginning to believe. Later, then?''

"Sure, sure,'' Harry said, wandering off with a wave of his hand.

"Harry know you're a vamp?'' I asked Catarina thoughtfully.

"No. To be truthful, you're the first person to spot it.''

"Okay. Well. It was swell talking to you, but I'm allergic to the sight of blood, especially my own, and I think I feel this attack of amnesia coming on. Also, my mother taught me never to talk to people I pick up in bars," I said, beginning to rise.

"You really shouldn't be worried," she said seriously. "Less than three percent of the population has a genetic predisposition for the disease."

"Well, yeah, but McLendon never said which three percent, and I'm not real interested in finding out just how lucky I am."

She took me gently by the wrist with long, slender fingers. "Oh, sit down! I won't bite."

I sat, no tribute to my common sense. "Promise?"

"Promise. Cross my heart and hope to put a stake in it." She tilted her head again. "Tell me about the *Scupper*."

How many vampires have good legs and a sense of humor? I sat. I told. "What would you like to know? The *Scupper* is Kobold class, eleven hundred meters and five holds. She came out of the Blohm und Voss shipyard at Luna nineteen years ago and reached her present exalted state by a process of steady decline. Her skipper, Davie Lloyd Ironsides, picked her up at auction when the Star Lines went spectacularly bankrupt four years ago. Since then, she's been affectionately described as both a hazard to navigation and a bucket of bolts traveling in close formation. We haul general freight nobody wants to places where people might not realize this fact immediately."

Catarina nodded.

I shrugged. "She's competitive on rinky-dink gravity wells like Schuyler's. This particular landfall, we unloaded a few tons of Thai gimcrack appliances to barter for guano and other so-phisticated local manufactures."

"Where's the profit margin in that?" she asked innocently.

"Truth is, there's not much of one. I make more on straight salary as a journeyman than Davie Lloyd takes out of the ship. After we service the loan, we might clear ten dollars a ton."

She smiled very slightly. "Don't the transshipment costs eat you up?"

I shook my head. "To handle low-density bulk cargo, all Schuyler's needs is a platform in stationary orbit, a winch, a pump, and thirty kilometers of frictionless four-centimeter vacuum tubing. With the price of a secondhand chute, it actually costs us more to float our appliances down than it did to suck up a return cargo.''

"Of manure?"

I shrugged again. "It's an even exchange. We knew what we were getting was fertilizer. If the inhabitants of Schuyler's didn't, they'll figure it out quick—which is why I had expected Davie Lloyd Ironsides to have departed here yesterday, if not sooner.''

"What about Davie Lloyd Ironsides?''

"Iron-Ass. Iron-Ass is a pain even when trying to be polite, which is seldom. Davie Lloyd is one of those people who remind you of the flaws in the theory that all men are created equal. The fact that a torchship can pretty well fly herself makes his skill at mismanaging people his most noticeable deficiency. I often elaborate on his shortcomings, mental and moral, for Harry's benefit, which Harry enjoys because he learns new words with which to insult his customers.''

I studied her face. "To ask a delicate question, since a vamp has about as much chance of passing port clearance as an ax-murderer—which you might very well be—how did you get into space? As a class, spacers tend to be stuffy about incurable, unpredictable diseases.''

She reached into the purse around her waist and pulled out a plastic card, then turned her head sideways and let it drift onto the table.

I picked it up. It was a Guild card, a match to my own except for the word "Apprentice" overstamped. She was a spacer. I whistled, long and liquid, and glared at her. "And you asked if the transshipment costs eat you up? Right. How did you get through . . . Oh, hell. Don't tell me.''

She nodded. "Night school.''

"I had to ask. Why space, I ask?''

"I figured it was the perfect profession. No sunshine. Regulated temperature. Quiet, peaceful. Plus the stars overhead—romantic.''

"The living conditions are lousy, the pay is worse, and after six months of standing watches with Elaine O'Day, why, I could just go all dewy-eyed. I take it not everyone agreed it was the perfect profession for you.''

"I didn't have McLendon's when I entered the profession. I did when I got here, which is why I got dumped," she explained.

I opened my mouth and shut it. "I take your point."

She smiled again and then got serious. "Ken, I need a job. I'm not going to rot on this rathole forever."

"No cemeteries?"

"Bad joke. If I don't cash in pretty quick, I'm going to have to turn myself in. I need a ship."

"True enough. The *divertissements* offered by the port and township of Schenectady on the wonderful world of Schuyler's are drinking, fighting, and fornicating, in that order. But why ask me? Why not go to the source direct?"

She smiled yet again, this time a full-magnitude flare, and she held it long enough for me to realize just what an idiotic question it was, coming from someone in the least bit familiar with Iron-Ass. She looked at me long enough to make me appreciate everything that Elaine O'Day was not, then asked, "Any chance, Ken?"

I thought it through for half a moment. "Sorry," I said slowly. "Even if you were desperately interested in helping us haul dung from tedium to ennui and even if our peerless leader was willing to take you, which I much doubt, we're not rated for passengers. We've got a full crew, four guys and four dolls, although it's sometimes difficult to tell which is which. We don't have a place to put you."

"If something did come up, would you put in a word for me?" she pleaded.

The *Scupper* wasn't exactly thrills and spills, but, Elaine notwithstanding, I'd have rather been dipped in goo and left to harden than spent an extra four minutes on Schuyler's World. "I could, but given a choice, Iron-Ass would rather leave me with you than take you with me, if you take my meaning. Also, I doubt we'll be here more than another day."

"I understand." She picked up her Guild card and scribbled her name and a number on the back of a cocktail napkin. "If something does turn up, you'll give me a call?"

I picked it up with two fingers while I tried to remember whether you had to get bit in the neck to catch McLendon's.

"Humor me," she said. "I'm supposed to have second sight. Call it a premonition."

"Well, okay. Tell you what. If the occasion arises, I'll make the pitch for you, just so I don't have to shake on it."

She smiled. I smiled. I looked around the bar and resigned myself to yet another six months of celibacy. On the way out, I dropped another handful of coins in Dinky's jar and said, "Play 'As Time Goes By,' Dinky."

"Again?" he said.

Halfway across the room, my vampire rose to her feet and to the occasion. "You haven't played it the first time, squirt!"

I tipped her a salute and walked.

I hit the little room marked MALE BEINGS and paused on my way out the door to admire Harry's plaque. The Prancing Pony is Number 7 Esquimaux Street, situated between a pawnshop and a Laundromat of ill repute. There's a funeral home on the other side of the pawnshop, and the little plaque says, THE GUY NEXT DOOR GETS THEM COMING AND GOING.

The gay metropolis of Schenectady doesn't exactly sleep, and I hit a few of the all-night places for souvenirs, fruit, and other local manufactures. Somebody on board the *Scupper* had fouled the ship's coffeepot, so I bought a little one for myself and dropped a few coins in one of the sidewalk slot machines to see if my luck could get worse. It did, but not immediately. Four more hours put me sitting next to my shipmate Frido Kundle in Night Magistrate's Court to watch Elaine O'Day cap off an evening.

O'Day can best be described by casting unflattering allusions to the habits and morals of innocent swine. Apparently, Callahan's was a little slow, because she'd tried to take down one unwilling citizen on a tabletop. Even on Schuyler's, that's an indictable offense. If half the police force hadn't been on duty and in there drinking, things might have gotten out of hand. As it was, the place set a new record for broken glass.

Judge Osman, the night court magistrate, was a portly gentleman with pink cheeks and an enormous white mustache, who never stopped smiling all through the testimony. After the ambulatory casualties finished damning Elaine sufficiently, he rapped his gavel twice and folded his hands. "Mistress O'Day, please stand and receive the sentence of this honorable court."

Elaine's defense lawyer stood and nudged her to her feet.

"Mistress O'Day, I find you guilty of the many things with which you have been charged, and of other things besides. I fine you a hundred dollars in local currency for lewd acts, a hundred more for causing a public riot, five hundred for assaulting sundry peace officers in the performance of their estimable duty, and ten for public nuisance which was disrobing prior to committing these aforementioned dastardly acts, said fines to be paid to this honorable court. I also sentence you to pay restitution to the owner of the estimable establishment you defiled and to pay compensation to the unfortunate individuals you injured. Finally, I further sentence you to six months in jail for willful damaging of private property, to give you an opportunity to contemplate the heinousness of your multitudinous offenses. Do you understand this? Very, very good."

Kundle, one of the *Scupper's* two mayflies straight out of basic, turned to me. "I've always wondered how various offenses rate in a place like this. What happens next, Ken?"

"Mistress O'Day, please have your attorney approach the bench," Osman intoned in a singsong monotone.

I whispered to Frido. "Now he suspends the six months, after he gives her a lecture and Elaine makes appropriately contrite noises—her lawyer's already done everything but offer the old darling a bribe in open court."

Elaine could have sounded more contrite. At that point, she blurted out, "You potbellied pig turd!"

Her mouthpiece tried to clamp his hand over her jaws, but the damage was done. It was not the thing to say to a devout Muslim during sentencing. It took the hand-puppet smile off Osman's face and made it turn various pretty colors.

"Oh, no. Saint Nicholas there is going to have a fit," Kundle whispered. I looked down to see if there might be a hole in the floor under my chair. Somewhere on the other side of the courtroom, another of my esteemed shipmates, Annalee McHugh, said in a very loud voice, "Christ, that rips it. It's crispy-critter time! You're toast, Elaine!"

"Bailiff, take the prisoner away to serve her full sentence, and more besides! Court is adjourned," the magistrate said through clenched teeth. He stood up and strode away from the bench with a rustle of black silk. The lawyer, who had sensibly collected his fee in advance, disappeared with equal dispatch.

As they led away my erstwhile partner in chains and scanty attire, Frido said, "Hey, Elaine! Can I use your stereo while you're gone?"

Davie Lloyd Ironsides is tall and square-hewn, like something carved out of balsa with a dull ax. "That's great!" he muttered as we clustered around him. He was so obviously annoyed he almost looked human. "This is just great! The portmaster here is never going to let us lift orbit unless we find someone to replace her."

Next to Ironsides, Rosalee Dykstra said mournfully, "Not even a blind portmaster is going to clear a bucket like ours to ship out shorthanded."

I'd met the portmaster, Commander Hiro, once. He may not have been bright, but he certainly wasn't blind.

"Yeah," Annalee McHugh rasped, "Navy types who get sent to dumps like this do things by the book, unless they want to stay." McHugh is a reserve petty officer second with a sallow, yellowish complexion and a permanent scowl. She looked around the circle from face to face. "Just how are we going to find somebody?"

Dykstra let her mouth hang open, apparently completely overcome by the notion that you could go to jail just for wrecking bars and muscling cops, her favorite pastimes.

The remainder of our Greek chorus was silent.

Our other mayfly was Wyma Jean Spooner. Spooner was a well-nourished woman, and she had on an expression of dumb distress that made her look like something Peter Paul Rubens would have painted when he was tight. Her shift partner, Kundle, merely looked dumb. He grinned. "People like Elaine ought to have a license to be that stupid," he said, which added to the overall effect.

McHugh looked at him. "Christ, if I owned the stupidity franchise for this ship, I'd get rich selling licenses at ten bucks a pop. Hell, Kundle, I'd make you buy two!"

"Will you two stop that! This is serious!" Ironsides roared.

"Twit!" Rosalee Dykstra said under her breath, staring at the spots on the ceiling. I wasn't entirely sure who she was referring to.

The only crew member who wasn't present was Bernie Bobo. "Boo-Boo" was listed on the ship's papers as mate, to the amusement of all concerned. We'd left him as the port watch aboard the *Scupper*. His absence was the only positive factor I could think of.

I glanced around the courtroom and spied my newfound friend in the back, grinning large as life. "Damn, she does have second sight," I muttered. Catching Ironsides's eye, I handed him Catarina's napkin. "Davie Lloyd, by coincidence the lady in the glasses back there is an apprentice spacer, down on her luck and looking for a berth. Allow me to lay on you a proposition, with only one slight catch."

He took the napkin and grunted. Then he handed it back and checked out her legs. "What's the catch?" he grumbled noncommittally, in his most endearing manner.

"She's got McLendon's Syndrome," I said, waiting to hear the pin drop.

"Oh, well. If that's all, it's settled," Davie Lloyd said without a flicker of recognition.

I saw a bunch of heads move up and down. Spooner and Kundle paid tribute to the solemnity of the moment by playing footsie with each other. While I have never been known for underestimating Davie Lloyd's capacity for creative idiocy, it hadn't occurred to me that they might not publish articles on McLendon's Syndrome in the kind of magazines he reads.

McHugh's brows were knit. "Wait a second, how'd she end up here? Is this McLendon's Syndrome contagious or something?" Annalee McHugh may not have been well read, but when they were handing out brains, she was there for somebody's share.

I nodded vigorously. "Or something."

Davie Lloyd frowned, displaying those qualities of leadership which have made him famed throughout the known universe. "Well, MacKay, it was your partner that got canned, so you'll just have to take your chances until we hit Brasilia Nuevo and we can see about getting somebody else."

While I was looking for a MacKay other than me, Annalee McHugh folded her arms and nodded. "Ken, tell her we'll sign her up and get her moving," Davie Lloyd added. "I'm thinking about moving up our departure, and I want her on board the shuttle and checked out to go in an hour. What did you say her name was?"

I glanced down at the napkin, which ripped it. Her full name, neatly inscribed, was Anna Catarina Lindquist, and I was damned if I was going to try to explain a Swedish vampire. As I stood there with my mouth open and my index finger cocked, my shipmates trooped off in a clump.

Catarina appeared by my left shoulder blade. "Hello, Ken. If it's any consolation, the only other Guild member I know of on Schuyler's is doing five to seven years for affray and aggravated maiming, and I really don't think Judge Osman is going to want to make up with your shipmate O'Day for love, or even money."

"You probably got that right. Well, welcome aboard," I said with a general lack of enthusiasm.

She sidled close to add insult to injury. "That's the spirit, Ken. Want to help me with my things?"

I stared at the spots on the ceiling and told her carefully, "It doesn't pay to talk to people you meet in bars. And it especially doesn't pay to talk to vampires you meet in bars. I don't know how you did it, but if I ever find out, I'm going to pound you full of toothpicks."

She brushed a stray lock of hair into place and positively beamed.

"Okay, tell me the truth. Why did you pick me to talk to? Weren't you taking a risk?"

"Calculated risk. Blame it on Harry. He said you were an okay guy for a half striper." She started to slap me on the shoulder and thought better of it. "He also said you can't lie worth a damn and don't like people who can."

That was true enough to hurt. "Remind me to buy Harry some flowers," I said glumly.

"Fair flower never won faint heart?" she offered. The people sweeping up the courtroom stared at us.

"Oh, no. Not a pun. I can't deal with puns," I explained

weakly. "If a pun were humor, it would be the lowest form known to sapient beings."

I could feel her eyes growing bright behind those dark glasses. "You know, I think I'm really going to enjoy this trip, Ken," she said.

As we headed down Cinco de Mayo Avenue to her guest-house, we passed a steady stream of citizens who were starting or finishing their day. It only took a few minutes to pack her out. Turning the corner back onto Esquimaux Street, I almost stopped when I saw two furry beings walking toward us side by side.

They were both dressed in matching collars and cuffs, black morning coats, and gray pin-striped ties and trousers. They both had wraparound sunglasses stuck on their pointed little faces. The tall one was about a meter and a half high and had something that looked like a feather duster precariously balanced on his head. The little one was about half a meter shorter. He had a black bowler hat jammed down around his eyes.

"They look like the two dinks we saw in Harry's bar," I whispered.

"They probably are. Want me to find out?" she whispered back.

"Not really—" I started to say.

She stepped up close and curtsied. "Good day to you. If I may, I am Catarina Lindquist, and my friend is Ken MacKay. You look like the two gentlebeings we noticed last evening in the Prancing Pony, and we were wondering if this were indeed the case."

The tall one lurched a little and straightened his tie. "We were indeed in the Prancing Pony last evening, and that experience we share. Permit me to introduce myself. I am Dr. Beaver, the !Plixxi* ambassador." He introduced the little guy, whose name was something like "Cheeves."

The little Rodent pulled himself up stiffly and said, "I am His Rotundity's body servant and confidential secretary." Cheeves had a staccato, alto voice. Beaver was more of a mezzo-soprano.

"Pleased to meet you," said Catarina, extending her hand.

"The pleasure is mine," Beaver chirped, taking it and bowing, to the extent that you can get a bend in a shape like a beer bottle. "Please, call me Bucky—I insist. Have we made your acquaintance before?"

He turned his head slightly toward Cheeves, who shook his head solemnly.

"Ah, well," he continued, "as the original Bucky says, 'New friends are like sunshine in the morning. They brighten the rest of the day.' We are exceedingly pleased to have made your acquaintance."

"Uh, right. Cheeves and Bucky," I said, trying to figure out if I was supposed to curtsy.

"My dear Ken, is it?" Beaver asked. "While we Rodents, as you call us, are primarily visually oriented, I am adept at deciphering human olfactory cues, and I detect that you have a perplexed smell about you. My nose knows these things."

"Ah, yeah, Bucky," I mumbled. "I was just curious about your names. They don't sound very alien."

"Oh, yes. That. The !Plixxi* language is mostly composed of melodious click-whistles and glottal stops. Humans rarely do justice to its lyric, poetical beauty. Indeed, there are some sounds, like the perfectly charming little hoot-whistle at the end of '!Plixxi*,' that you humans don't seem to make use of at all for some unaccountable reason. It is therefore customary for those of us who deal with humans to pick human names. I myself was fascinated by the complex philosophical and ethical structure underlying the various Bucky Beaver stories, and I decided to choose that name in his honor."

I nodded. It made sense, sort of. There was one Chinese guy I'd shipped with who had told us to call him Sherman. "Sounds like an interesting language," I commented politely.

"Oh, most definitely, friend Ken," Beaver continued. "In English and other human Indo-European languages, the importance of time sense through use of verb tenses and distinctions between inherently stable nouns and transitory verbs make for a truly positive literature. In !Plixxi*, by contrast, case endings are largely dependent on whether the object or action being spoken about can be seen by the speaker and whomever is being spoken to, and whether an action in progress is habitual or brief."

The little guy Cheeves made a slight noise in his throat and pulled out a large pocket watch. When that didn't work, he made a quick but dignified cutting motion across his throat.

"Oh, I had almost forgotten," Beaver said. "We have an appointment this morning to meet with the portmaster, Commander Hiro, and we must hurry or we shall be late. I am pleased, however, to have made your acquaintance, and I hope someday that we might renew it."

"Uh, right" was my contribution to the conversation.

"That isn't very likely," Catarina said. "Ken and I are shipping out today, and it's very unlikely we'll be returning."

"How saddening. But, as Bucky says, 'A moment's pleasurable conversation is a lit beacon on a storm-tossed night.' " He twitched his nose again. "How strange, I detect that you two have been quarreling. Are you married to each other?"

"Ah, no," I murmured.

"Pity. Well, as Bucky says, 'Some people are just too considerate to get married.' Speaking for both myself and Cheeves, I must say that we have been enlightened by making your acquaintance, and I am grieved that our moments together must end so abruptly."

Cheeves tightened his grip on Beaver's elbow, tipped his bowler, and bowed slightly from the hips. With that, they toddled off.

As they walked away, I noticed that the seams on their trousers were slightly split in back, and they had little, vestigial tails, like bears' tails, sticking out. Beaver's tail was wagging.

I looked at Catarina. "Bucky Beaver?"

"Didn't you read Bucky Beaver stories?"

"Sure. I read all eleven volumes, but that was when I was nine years old. I didn't read my horoscope this morning. Was there anything about this in there?"

"I liked the bit with the pocket watch. It reminded me of *Alice in Wonderland*," she said.

I coughed, and as I turned around I almost bumped into a wimpy little guy who came up waving beads in my face.

"Hey, man, you want to buy some beads. Handcrafted, very fine. You feel the texture," he said, passing them under my nose. The guy's hair was cut short, but he had it spiked straight up with mousse. He had on sandals, wing-tip sunglasses, and a purple dashiki that would have gotten him arrested on aesthetic grounds on a civilized world.

"The White Rabbit, and now the Mad Hatter," I said to no one in particular. I was beginning to get absolutely paranoid about sunglasses. "Look, uh, no thanks. I don't want any beads." I put two fingers in his chest to give myself enough room to discontinue the discussion.

The little guy slid right back in. "No, no! These finest kind beads. You a spacechip guy? You look like a spacechip guy. You on your way to catch your chip? You got a pretty lady friend, you need beads. Finest quality, just for you very cheap." He put them around my neck with one fluid motion, and I noticed that he'd been eating onions.

Catarina stood by, making small noises of amusement.

I took the guy by the wrist, pulled the beads off, and slapped them into his palm.

"Yes, I'm a spaceship guy. Yes, I have a ship to catch. No, I don't want beads. Particularly not for this particular lady friend. Especially not from you. Not even for free. Not even if you pay me. Now is not a good time to annoy me. Read my lips. No! Beads!" I wiped my hand on my pants and started to walk away.

The guy began jumping up and down, screaming bloody murder. I looked around for Catarina in time to see her slip behind him and push his shoulders down with her left hand as she pulled his arm into the small of his back with her right. She braced herself with her hip. "All right, Clyde, fun is fun. Now hand the nice gentleman the wallet you're holding."

"Nice lady, I honest don't know what you're talking about . . . Ouch! That hurts," Clyde observed.

"I think it's intended to," I said. "Hey, that looks like my wallet."

Catarina beamed and applied pressure. "Now, Clyde, just hand the gentleman his wallet or we'll see if you can scratch the top of your tiny head from a north-south direction with those clever little fingers."

"My name's not Clyde . . . Ouch!"

"If your name's not Clyde, I suggest changing it quickly," I said, removing the wallet from his limp hand and counting the cash inside.

"Name's Clyde! Happy to meet you gentlepersons! Sorry about the little misunderstanding . . . Ouch!"

The dawn crowd flowed around us, completely unconcerned.

"What's the penalty for pickpocketing here?" I asked Catarina.

"Under Reformed Islamic law, I think the first time, they give you a warning. The second time they cut off your hand. That sound right, Clyde?"

Hunched over, Clyde nodded as vigorously as the circumstances allowed.

"You wouldn't happen to have a prior, would you, Clyde?" Catarina purred.

Clyde was beginning to sweat somewhat. "Yeah, man. They got me. It was a frame, all the way. The cops, they don't like me."

"I understand. Do we?" I asked.

"Hey, man, just one break, that's all I need. You let me go, I walk the straight and narrow all the rest of my days. I never even look at another wallet. Honest, pretty lady friend. You let me go, I even give you the beads. Just one break."

"What do you think?" I asked Catarina.

"Just this once." She propelled him forward with her knee. "Listen, Clyde, the nice gentleman and I are about to catch a ten o'clock shuttle to board the *Rusty Scupper*. If I even see you before we board that shuttle, they're going to call you 'Lefty.' "

"Hey, man, I thank you from the bottom of my heart and the tops of my toes. I thank your mothers and your fathers. I thank your grandmothers' maiden aunts . . ." Clyde said, salaaming in the street.

"Here, take these," I said, scooping up the beads and tossing them to him. "Just keep out of the bottom of my pocket."

We watched Clyde make a rapid disappearance. "I've had weirder days than this, but not sober," I said. "Is it me, or do you attract lunatics?"

Catarina didn't say anything, but she tucked her arm in mine, and we resumed our progress down the street.

"You were pretty good back there. I suspect I'd better be very nice to you. Where did you learn that?"

"Oh, out and about. Can we stop in here? I need to buy a

few things," she said, pointing to one particularly dilapidated shop that was just opening. She managed to spend half an hour in there without buying a thing, but I figured I owed her one. We also stopped off at an all-night florist so I could have them mail Harry a bunch of dead petunias.

. . . And the Bad News Is,
the Captain Wants to Water-Ski

Between Clyde and picking up Catarina's things and making sure the all-night florist didn't bill me for long-stemmed roses, we were the last ones to arrive at the shuttle. Davie Lloyd was waiting by the forward lock, wearing his usual impatient grimace. "Damn it, Ken!" he said. "I thought I told you to be on time!"

"Hey, chill out, dude," the shuttle pilot told him. "You got another fifteen minutes before I start running the meter." Periodically shuttling us down to planets for relaxation and mayhem and back up again costs Davie like hell, but it's guaranteed in our contracts and keeps us from tearing the ship apart.

"What's our hurry?" I asked.

Ignoring me, Ironsides asked Catarina her name and launched into his welcome speech in between glances at his watch as we moved her stuff on board.

"Hello, ah, Lindquist? Welcome aboard. Name's, ah, David Lloyd Ironsides, and I'm the captain. You, ah, know Ken. You're, er, shift-partnered with him."

He rubbed his chin and tried not to look in her eyes. "Ken, ah, told us about your, ah, disorder. Er, we'll be sure you get the finest medical attention when we hit Brasilia Nuevo. Now, there's just a few things I, ah, want to make sure you understand. I run a tight ship and a happy ship. You got a problem, you see Bernie and he'll let me know. All my rules for running the ship are in the Standard Operating Procedure. I want you to read it and memorize it. Ah . . . I don't see a copy here. Where's Bernie?''

Boo-Boo, of course, was still aboard ship where we had left him.

The shuttle pilot studiously ignored us. Annalee McHugh and Rosalee Dykstra were forward with Spooner and Frido Kundle, figuring our ship's departure. My shipmates were not a sociable group at the best of times, but they gave every indication of suspecting one or both of us of carrying plague, which may not have been a bad idea. Dykstra looked up. "Bernie's still on the ship."

"Well, where's a copy of the SOP?"

"Not here. Besides, Bernie hasn't gotten the new one written yet." Dykstra was basically a quiet woman, but she was built like a linebacker, and she didn't take much from Davie Lloyd.

Ironsides pouted. "What do you mean he hasn't got the new one written? Well, what about the old one?"

"That's the one Annalee trashed," Dykstra said. Annalee McHugh grunted something that might have been descriptive.

"Uh, okay. Ah, Ken will tell you what our Standard Operating Procedures are. You and he are the swing watch. Well, ah, like I say, happy to have you on board and if you have any problems, mention it to Bernie." He stumped off to a seat.

McHugh poked her head up. "Don't mind him. He's just ticked off because we're about seventy kilos overweight even accounting for the extra weight of your stuff. We haven't posted a revised watch schedule yet, but you and Ken are going to be the swing watch. You'll have about twenty minutes to freshen up before you're due on." Watches on the *Scupper* were eight hours on, three days out of every four. Swing watch took a stint from whoever was off.

As we buckled in, I told Catarina, "When we get off watch, I'll help you move Elaine's stuff out. Then we can try and fumigate."

She smiled that little crooked smile I was already learning to dread. "As in, 'Many are called, but fume are chosen'?''

I sunk my head in my hands. "Oh, God. That's not even funny."

"I know." She patted my arm. "But it worked."

"Did your shipmates figure out you were a vamp before or after they decided to dump you? While I'm thinking about it, I can't remember what ship you said you were from."

"Actually, Ken," she replied, "I didn't say. And I would just as soon not." This pretty well ended the conversation as the shuttle took off.

We did a standard, fuel-efficient approach. I could see Catarina peering intently at the viewscreen as the *Rusty Scupper* came into view. She wasn't much to look at. They built her to a standard configuration to save on construction costs, and she looked more like a spacegoing shoebox than anything else. Although she'd seen better days, you could still see where Blohm und Voss had ionized the plating to outline the holds. Number One hold was a very small one underneath the crew area. Holds Two, Three, and Five were spaced evenly along the ship's length to carry bulk goods, and Number Four was rigged with subdivisions to carry everything and anything else. The *Scupper* was a tired little lady, and her makeup could have used touching up, but she was home.

When we connected, I showed Catarina to Elaine's sleeping space and left her to try and figure out where to start cleaning.

I took a quick shower. Then, belatedly recollecting everything I'd ever read about vampires, I put on a large crucifix and stopped by the galley for several cloves of garlic.

When I arrived on the bridge, Boo-Boo was gone and Catarina was already checking out the panel. "Welcome, Cinderella. Your carriage awaits," I said, sliding into the other command chair.

"You want me to drive?" she asked. The crucifix caused her to smile. A few short seconds later, the garlic caused her to throw up.

"Sorry," she said, "it looks more like a miscarriage. I didn't think garlic would affect me like that."

"That's okay, I didn't like this shirt much anyway," I said, pulling out a tissue and dabbing at it. Either you trust somebody or you don't. She took the board while I found a place for the garlic and my shirt in the disposal chute.

After we traded off freshening up, I sat back to watch her. She was good, much better than I had expected. A ship handler's job on an older ship is mostly making sure nothing important ceases to function, which can be a little tricky on a bucket like the *Scupper*. It was obvious she knew what she was doing.

"It really does take two people to keep this can functional, doesn't it? Have you thought about putting in Madsens?" she asked as she ran through the preflight check-down.

"We've even thought about doing proper maintenance. What we really need is to tear out what we've got and do a refit."

"And?"

I shrugged. "Davie Lloyd can barely meet operating expenses and make payments on the loan."

"I see. What happens when income ceases to match outlay?"

"I suppose sooner or later something vital is going to break that Davie can't afford to get fixed. I hope I have a new ship by then."

"Oh." She punched up a malfunction check. "Ken, I don't mean to sound critical, but your diagnostics look like they've been put together with paper clips and chewing gum. Although I can't tell for sure, I'd swear your vibration damper is miscycling. Want me to take a look?"

"Sure. You're probably right. We can take it apart after we get out of orbit. It looks like Bernie left everything else green. At least nothing is flashing red, and I don't see anything he fudged. You meet Bernie?"

"Very briefly. He reminds me of a skinny Sancho Panza. He was out of here in a hurry."

"Bernie—alias Boo-Boo—is a hypochondriac. He collects nostrums to cure various imaginary ailments. If his friends think he's psychoneurotic, it's not too difficult to imagine what the rest of us think. He usually has so many imagined ills that I suspect he doesn't take short odds on catching real ones."

"Somebody must have said something on the way up, because he was wearing a white mask and rubber gloves when he scampered off." She checked the power flow. "What do you do for exercise around here?"

"Coincidentally, Number One hold is empty, and it's the exact size for a racketball court. You play?"

"A little," she admitted.

"Well, let's take a shot at it after we get off duty and get your stuff squared away. Watch out here, the thing that looks like it ought to be the thrust fluctuation gauge isn't. Yeah, that's what you're looking for, there. Oh, I ought to warn you, we get together Sundays for dinner.''

She tipped me a one-finger salute in acknowledgment, flashing her scar.

''I've been meaning to ask about your hand. Did you, ah . . .''

''A big fish. I acquired the scar before I caught McLendon's, if that's what you want to ask.''

''It seemed tactless of me to ask. A fish?''

She tightened for a moment and then relaxed. ''A little work for a travel magazine a few years back. I convinced them to let me do a layout on spear fishing by moonlight.''

''That sounds interesting. I didn't realize you were nautically inclined,'' I said, fishing for background.

She looked at me and smiled. ''I suppose I ruined a promising literary career by starting out wrong.''

''How so?'' I asked, snapping up the bait.

''It was a shark and stormy night . . .'' she intoned.

The hair on my arms started to rise. I used to have a cousin living down the street from me who liked to make puns. He moved to Luxembourg when I was twelve, which may have saved his life and kept me from embarking on a brutal life of crime at a tender age.

She stretched and handed me back the panel. ''Ken, I wish you could see the way the muscles in your face just go kind of limp. You know, I really think I'm going to like it here. I brought some chocolate chip cookies—you want a nibble?''

Most of the first week went quietly, at least as far as Catarina was concerned, as we headed for our jump hole to Brasilia Nuevo. Meals turned out to be the biggest problem; McLendon's was an unforgiving bug. Meat, dairy products, and almost anything else worth eating either gave her hives or ended up on the deck. Even slightly overripe fruit made her nauseous. I could empathize; finding Rosalee's leftover Stir Fry Surprise in the refrigerator has much the same effect on me. We had spin and were underweight—a full gravity—or we'd have been cleaning up forever.

Fortunately, she'd stuffed about a hundred kilos of her own provisions in her locker—chiefly chocolate chip cookies and Leopard Milk brand liquid-protein diet supplement—to stretch out the fruit and vegetables we had on board. I was used to cooking for myself, so we managed. She wasn't bad as company, either. It was nice to have somebody on board who could discuss important things, like dinosaurs—although after six months of O'Day I'd have taken a vampire who washed under her arms any day.

Sunday dinner was her first real exposure to the rest of the crew. Davie Lloyd and Bernie had a slightly larger central living area in their cabin than the rest of us so that we could lower from the ceiling a table big enough to gather around. I was chef, as usual, and elected to make pasta. Catarina could manage hers plain with a little oil, and I whipped together a cream sauce with basil for everyone else. I threw in some salad and fresh bread, and a couple of bottles of Merlot wine I'd picked up.

McHugh had the conn. Catarina tried to volunteer; I had to explain that Annalee *really* didn't want to eat with the rest of us.

The remaining five of our shipmates gathered together seemed a little more psychotic than usual. With O'Day gone, I had figured that the air would be a little clearer, but Annalee and Rosalee had had a couple of loud, screaming fights, and Bernie had been skulking about like a whipped dog.

Boo-Boo hadn't been his usual disgusting self. He only tried to feel Catarina up once with his rubber gloves, and he desisted when she bounced his pointed little head off the deckplates. Even Wyma Jean Spooner, normally the cheeriest soul on board, looked as though she'd been crying, although Frido was his normally insufferable self.

Under the circumstances, dinner was more awkward than usual. Ironsides, Boo-Boo, and Dykstra concentrated on chowing down and wouldn't meet each other's eyes, while Wyma Jean picked at her food—which in itself was enough to make me uneasy. Frido was doing all the talking, and most of his remarks were about himself and directed at Catarina.

He started to hit his stride with his third glass of wine.

"Where did you live before you become a spacer?" he asked her.

"Out and about. I was in Aurora, Colorado, for a while. That's in the Greater Denver area," Catarina said, easily reaching for some more salad.

"Nice place," Frido said. Wyma Jean nudged him.

"Colorado? I knew a woman in Colorado once. She owned a cat," Boo-Boo exclaimed to fill the void.

"You know a woman, Bernie? That's unusual," Frido said lightly.

Bernie proceeded to explain. After about ten minutes, Rosalee looked at him with a puzzled expression. "Bernie, nobody gives a rat's ass."

That ended discussion for a while. Bernie went back to shoveling vermicelli.

Catarina was sitting to my left. As she leaned over to adjust her napkin, she whispered very softly, "Are they always this friendly?"

I nodded and watched Frido out of the corner of my eye.

"Hey, Catarina, you sure you wouldn't like a glass of wine?" Frido asked loudly.

"No, I really don't drink anything alcoholic," Catarina said politely.

Frido persisted. "Better for your body, I guess. Hey, do you like working out?" I saw Wyma Jean stiffen.

"No, not really," Catarina said.

"Yeah, I guess you wouldn't want to get muscle-bound like some women I know," Frido said cheerfully.

Rosalee Dykstra developed a crease between her eyebrows. She carefully laid her fork and spoon down on her plate.

"But nobody on this ship," Frido added hastily.

Rosalee nonchalantly picked up her tableware and started eating again.

I had the seat nearest the door. "Well, I guess we're ready for some more pasta. Anybody want anything else?"

"I think we could use some more salad. Here, let me help you, Ken," Catarina said smoothly.

"Hurry back," Frido commented.

"I don't know what's gotten into Frido," I said as we stepped outside. "Overactive hormones, I guess. Rosalee almost put him through a bulkhead, and Wyma Jean is not taking this well at all. I expect him to end up with a plate of spaghetti in his lap any minute now."

"Carrying a congealed weapon," Catarina agreed.

We went into the galley, where Catarina pulled the salad out of the refrigerator while I refilled the pasta bowl. "I can see why Annalee volunteered to take the conn," she commented.

"Oh, Annalee and Rosalee absolutely despise Frido. Anything the two of them have to say to the man they relay through Wyma Jean. In fact, I'm not too sure Annalee likes men very much in general. Sorry you signed on yet?"

She smiled. "No problem, Ken."

As we headed back, it appeared from the silence that the discussion around the table had ended. I caught a glimpse of Frido through the doorway and whispered to Catarina, "Frido must really be guzzling the wine. The whole side of his face is flushed."

"Ken, it's not wine, that's a handprint," Catarina whispered back.

"Well, it wasn't Rosalee, because his head is still attached."

"You know, I was thinking, Catarina," Frido said as we walked in. "I hear you play racketball. I used to be a champion racketball player. I got some pictures I could show you . . ."

"Oh, yeah? You going to show her pictures of your kids, too?" Wyma Jean sneered.

"Hey! They're not my kids!" Frido said to her, obviously stung by the remark.

"That's not what the courts said," Wyma Jean retorted. "It's a pain in the tail keeping your paternity suits straight."

"Look, I didn't want to fight it. Can we drop the subject, huh?"

Bernie kept methodically spooning up pasta. Davie Lloyd opened his mouth sharply to say something, but didn't. Rosalee slapped her napkin down and walked out.

As Wyma Jean's little side discussion continued, Catarina whispered to me, "This is getting somewhat embarrassing. Any thoughts on how to get a message through to Frido? Short of punching him out, I mean."

"I'm not sure he'd catch on if you did punch him out."

She took in the remark and waited for a pause in the discussion, then spoke softly but firmly. "Well, Frido, I'm sure your pictures are nice, but I think the only person I'll be playing ball with around here is Ken." She deliberately laid her hand on my arm for emphasis, and I froze.

Wyma Jean nodded primly, fighting back tears. "I think I've had enough to eat. Thanks for making dinner, Ken." She got up and left. Frido hesitated for a moment and then followed her out.

"I think I've had enough, too. What do you think, Ken?" Catarina winked. "I'm tired. Want to call it a night?"

"Go ahead, Ken. It's okay. Bernie and I will finish up and clean the place," Davie Lloyd volunteered unexpectedly, staring out the door after Frido.

Catarina and I headed back to our cabins, and I collapsed in the little sofa in the common area we shared as the door whisked shut. "Uh, Catarina . . ."

"It was the best thing I could think of to get Frido back in line."

"Oh. Yeah. Look, I'm really sorry about Frido. I don't know what got into him. I know he thinks he's Don Juan, but I've never seen him come on that strong. Wyma Jean's probably going to beat his head in."

"Don't apologize, it's not your fault, and the dinner you made was excellent." Catarina pulled the chair from the desk in her room out into the common area and straddled it. "Sorry I grabbed your arm like that. I was improvising."

"That's okay. It didn't bother me," I lied. "I was just a little startled. I'm not used to having good-looking women grab me." I tried to smile. "Just don't try doing that to Wyma Jean. She swears she's been hearing ghosts in the ventilators."

"How long have you known Frido?" she asked.

"Oh, three or four months, now. We picked up Frido and Wyma Jean together. Why?"

"Oh, no reason," she said, too quickly.

I must have given myself away. She smiled. "I'm sorry. I forgot you don't like people who lie. Let's just say I'm trying to puzzle something out. Well, I'd better get some sleep if we're going to take the midwatch tomorrow.'' She disappeared into her cabin before I could answer.

The first crack in her showed the next day during a dull mid-watch.

The *Scupper* was manifesting the usual crop of deficiencies to keep us occupied. We had a persistent anomaly in the starboard sidejet, and the main computer was having the electronic equivalent of a nervous breakdown trying to trace it. Catarina and I were busy making manual course corrections.

"It's probably picking up a ghost image from one of Annalee's patchwork connections," I said with my nose stuck in a technical journal, marking time until the impeller in the sidejet started screwing off again.

Catarina was seated at the panel, flashing her fingers across it wearing an irritated look. "I know. Shut up and let me repatch it," she told me.

"Coffee?" I asked. I half thought it was that time of the month, so I didn't pay much attention.

She shook her head. She had her hair tied back into a ponytail, which jerked back and forth. Coffee dark was something she could drink some days, and some days not. She had laid out her cards to play solitaire, but had given up a while ago.

"Why don't you try and read some? It'll calm you down so you'll stop fidgeting."

"I want a chocolate chip cookie," I heard her say with a lot more emphasis than a statement like that usually gets.

"Go ahead. You know, the behavior of our motley horde over the last two or three days worries me. I wish I knew what was going on around here. If this keeps up, Davie Lloyd's hair is going to start thinning."

Catarina ignored me. I heard her say, "Damn, I want a cookie!" and looked up absently. "What's the problem with the cookies?" I asked, shutting my manual.

"My cookies are locked up in my cupboard." She walked over and rattled the handle on her bridge locker.

"On this ship, chocolate chip cookies are a good thing to keep under lock and key. So?"

"I can't find the damned key. I've looked everywhere."

I thought for a minute. "Did you leave it out anywhere?"

"It was hanging up right beside the watchlist," she snapped.

I shrugged. "That explains it. No cookies for you. Iron-Ass strikes again. You'll find it there tomorrow with a little note telling you everything you don't want to know about physical security."

"I *want* a cookie." Her eyes narrowed to very thin slits.

"Davie Lloyd had the eight-to-sixteen shift. He's sound asleep by now, dreaming of debentures. Trying to get anything out of him now would be worse than useless." I stuffed the manual back into its shell.

She was twisting a paper clip. "You shouldn't do that," I said. "Boo-Boo counts them every time he comes on watch."

She threw it down hard, and it skidded across the deckplates. "I want a cookie. I want one now. I can smell them in there," she said in a very brittle voice.

"Oh, come on. Those lockers are practically airtight, and with the wrapping they put on cookies . . ." I let my voice trail away because she rattled the handle again and the door came away in her hand. She snatched up a package, ripped it open, and wolfed down three cookies. I waited a couple of minutes. Her eyes softened.

She sighed. "I feel a lot better." She looked at me. "Why are you staring like that?"

"You're not supposed to be able to do that to a locker."

"What? Oh. Did I do that?"

"Yup."

"Oh." She popped another cookie in her mouth and chewed it thoughtfully. "Well, I did want a cookie. I had this incredible craving."

"Do you ever get cravings for anything else, like maybe blood?"

She thought for a minute. "Pickles, sometimes. Gherkin pickles."

I took a good look at the door. The hard plastic had pretty well snapped back into shape, but the lock and one of the hinges looked like sheep dip. "I guess you don't need help opening the jar."

"Hysterical strength, do you suppose?"

"I guess. Let me see if there's an extra hinge in stores. I'd hate to have to try and explain this to Iron-Ass."

"I suppose not. Well, no serious hingery done."

I looked at her.

"You okay, Ken? You could use a little red in your cheeks. You're kind of pale."

That may have been because of the pun, but then again, it may not have. "That's another thing, why don't you wear rouge or something?"

"That hurts, coming from someone who looks like the 'before' portion of a home tanning salon commercial," I told her.

"To hide the tell-pale white? I can't." She touched her cheek. "It just tears up my skin."

I looked at the locker. "Yeah."

"Would you like to play some racketball when we get off watch? I think the exercise will do me some good," she said in her serious voice.

"Sure."

After Frido and Wyma Jean relieved us, we hit the court, where Catarina proceeded to smoke me for the seventh or eighth straight time.

"I hate it when you bounce them off the cracks like that," I commented, pulling off my headband to wipe away the sweat.

"Let's grab a shower and get some dinner. You don't seem real comfortable, Ken. You haven't been saying very much."

"To tell the truth, the thing with the locker really bothered me." I looked at her.

"To tell the truth," she said, staring at the wall, "the thing with the locker bothered me, too."

Dinner was pretty quiet.

Thoroughly Scuppered

I had a troubled sleep that night, so I sat up with a couple of sick friends by the name of Jack and Daniels. I normally don't drink, but I wasn't sure how I felt about anything, particularly Catarina. It seemed like a good idea. I woke up a few hours later when somebody rapped hard on my cubicle door. I crawled in that general direction, saying uncomplimentary things.

Catarina was back, in basic black, fingering her trademark butterfly. "Wyma Jean sounds like she's in trouble," she said. All the cabins on the *Scupper* were laid out with a small central living area and sleeping cubicles on either side. The *Scupper*'s only concession to luxury was private bathrooms for each cubicle. Wyma Jean and Frido were in the next cabin down from ours, on Catarina's side.

I crossed my eyes. "She and Frido make an awful lot of noise when they get together."

"No, this is different. Wyma Jean sounds like she's in trouble. Come on." She took off her shades for emphasis. "I hope whatever you've got isn't catching."

The ship gave a little lurch beneath our feet and I bounced off the door. "Was that me or the ship?"

"The ship. It's that starboard sidejet. We were really rocking about a half hour ago."

"One of these days I want to tear out that impeller." I ran my hand through my hair and sighed. "I had a dream that I was Saint George. I was trying to figure out who the dragon was."

34

She looked me up and down. "You look like your ass is dragon. Saurian you overindulged?"

I let myself sag against the doorframe. "No more," I said. "I'll come quietly. It ought to be educational, anyway."

"Ken, your hair is sticking straight up. And I don't mean to criticize those avocado pajamas of yours, but if either Frido or Wyma Jean have a weak heart—"

I shut my cubicle door in her face, then spent a minute or two trying to drown myself and changed into slacks and an old-fashioned turtleneck. When we got to Spooner and Kundle's door, I looked at Catarina. She gave me the thumbs-up, and I knocked. The response was immediate and loud.

"Did you hear somebody say, 'Frido, get your ragged ass in here!'?" I asked.

Catarina nodded. "A little muffled. I think we'd better go in."

The source of the sound was front and center. Spooner was propped up on the sofa on her belly with a pillow under each knee. She had on leg irons and had her hands handcuffed behind her back. They looked to be a matching set. That was about all she had on.

"Wyma Jean, are we interrupting?" I asked.

"Ken, is that you? Get me loose, my bladder's about to explode. I'm going to kill Frido, leaving me like this!"

"Where is he?"

"He went to the galley to get some coffee and left me. I swear, I swear to God I'm going to slay the maggot!"

"I can't imagine Frido walking away from this of his own free will," I said.

"You're just repressed and frustrated," Catarina countered. "Do you see a key?"

I shook my head.

"The slime took it with him," Wyma Jean volunteered.

"You look for Frido. I'll stay here and make sure he didn't drop it somewhere," I offered.

"Come on, Ken," Catarina said.

We left Spooner. "It's unsanitary. You'd think they'd at least put down a plastic sheet before they started smearing vegetable oil all over like that," I complained.

Catarina smiled. "I was thinking what she needs is an apple to go in her mouth."

"You have a point. There's an ample amount of Spooner, and it's a little disgusting to see it all flopping about unconfined."

"Like I said, you're just repressed." She led me into the galley. Kundle was nowhere to be seen.

The galley was built for economy of space. Most of the cookware was built in to simplify maintenance and storage, since spacers tend to be slobs. You could pull out a little table where four reasonably thin people could sit and rub elbows, but it wasn't exactly a place where you could lose yourself among the tall trees. I reached up and slammed a cabinet shut. "He's not here. There aren't too many places you can hide aboard ship. If he's not on the bridge, he's down in stores."

"Wait a minute." Catarina tilted her head and narrowed her eyes. "Something's not right."

"What?"

"I'm not sure. Just start opening cabinets."

"What am I looking for?" I asked.

"You'll know if you find it," she told me, bending over to check the frying pans.

I started with the sink. Frido was stuffed under it.

The corpse wasn't pretty. His throat had been slashed across. His jaw was sagging, and his eyes were bugging out more than usual. Rigor mortis hadn't settled in. His face was unusually pale, as if most of the blood had been drained from his body; there was a little of it on his shirt. It wasn't immediately apparent where the rest of it had gone. I was uncomfortably aware of Catarina standing behind me.

"He's dead, isn't he?" I heard her say.

I looked at her face out of the corner of my eye. It was taut and immobile. "He's dead, all right. I don't want to move the body until Ironsides sees it. In fact, I'm not real interested in moving the body at all."

We heard Wyma Jean down the corridor. "Have you found him yet? I swear I'm going to slay the maggot!"

I looked at Catarina. "I think somebody beat her to it."

Catarina bent over and put her hand on my shoulder. She was normally careful about that. I jumped a little.

"Ken, I know what you're thinking. I didn't do it. I know I didn't. I think. You didn't kill him, either—I think."

Anyone who could have seen the color in my face would have had serious doubts about my ability to commit murder. "I'd like to know who did," I said, trying hard not to think about the locker.

"Frido was in here to make coffee, wasn't he?"

"Yeah. That's what Spooner said," I answered dully.

She turned her head. "The coffeepot's been washed. Where are the cups?"

I shook my head. She bent over and ran her hand over the floor, picking up a little whitish grit on her fingers and rubbing them together.

"Get Ironsides in here. Let's find the key and get Wyma Jean out of those handcuffs," she said in an unfamiliar voice.

We didn't find the key, and we had a time figuring out how to get Wyma Jean loose. Catarina was inconsiderate enough to throw a sheet over her, which speeded things up. Half an hour later, Ironsides got all of the survivors together in the control room, to break the news to everyone and figure out what to do. Dykstra and McHugh were the last to show, and when I saw the expression on McHugh's face, I knew that Frido wasn't the only one who was having an exciting day.

"Frido put this on the computer! It's all about McLendon's Syndrome!" She waved a piece of printout in her hand.

"What's McLendon's Syndrome?" Spooner asked.

"It's what Lindquist's got. It means she's a goddamn bite-you-in-the-neck vampire," snapped McHugh.

When it rains, it pours. Spooner's tear-filled eyes bulged as she began adding up two and two and came up with some whole number.

"We ought to notify local authorities and place the matter in their hands," Boo-Boo said sonorously. Bernie looks good in a bow tie, owns a cat, and affects a lisp. Even Davie Lloyd let that remark slide.

"Lindquist, I guess we're going to have to lock you up," Ironsides said slowly.

"Hold it. Let me see that printout," I said, taking it out of McHugh's hand.

"What difference does it make? We know she killed Frido," McHugh brayed. "Put her away before she kills somebody else!"

"Frido didn't write this," I said.

"What do you mean, 'Frido didn't write this'? That's his name at the bottom!"

"Whoever did this forgot to erase the time group. It was written less than an hour ago. There's no terminal in the galley. Frido wasn't on the bridge, was he?"

Ironsides and Boo-Boo looked at each other, and neither of them were smiling.

"Wyma Jean, did you see him use the terminal in your room?" She shook he head.

"He didn't use ours, and he didn't use McHugh's," I finished.

"What about the one in stores?" McHugh queried triumphantly.

"One, he didn't have time," I said, counting off fingers. "Two, he was probably already a corpse when this message was written. And three, if you'd read yesterday's log, you'd know the terminal in stores is down and I haven't gotten around to fixing it."

Everybody went silent for a few minutes. The Navy has jurisdiction in admiralty cases. What we needed was a good cop from the Naval Criminal Investigation Branch, but there didn't seem to be one handy. "So if Frido didn't compose this, who did?" I asked.

"Catarina could have written it," Bernie said uncomfortably.

"Agreed. But that would make her either very cunning or extremely stupid."

"Well, it still looks like a vampire killed Frido," Dykstra said doggedly.

"Then why the message?" I asked.

No one seemed to know, which meant someone was being less than candid with me.

"Personally, I think all of us just became suspects," I said.

A captain in space has life-and-death power. A captain in space who chooses to exercise that power had better have a damned good reason if he or she wants to retain his or her license. Ironsides put it to a vote. A motion to lock Catarina up for the duration passed five to two. A motion to lock me up failed, three to four, with Spooner and Dykstra unexpectedly on my side.

"Who's going to bell the cat?" I asked innocently.

Ironsides looked around uncertainly. Bernie looked around to see if his pet was in attendance. Catarina saved them both further embarrassment. "It's all right, Ken. If they think I'm a danger, I'll let them lock me up."

"I just hope everyone remembers that whoever killed Frido will still be walking around," I added, pouring oil on troubled waters.

After I said that, Ironsides looked like he'd been sucking on lemons. He looked worse after I proposed that we appoint a committee consisting of McHugh and myself to look for evidence, which carried, nobody having the nerve to vote against it.

While Ironsides and Dykstra were trying to figure out how to weld a bar across her cubicle door, Catarina and I sat down on her bed to go over what we knew—quietly, to discourage eavesdroppers.

"I'm still not sure which knife was used," I said. "There are three or four hanging up that could have done the job, but they're all where they're supposed to be and wiped clean. How tall would you have to be to stick Frido, do you think?"

"From the angle of the slash, neither Annalee nor Bernie could have sliced him if he were standing up straight. I didn't see any bruises or signs of a struggle."

"I'd like to know why not. I'm wondering why there wasn't blood all over the place. Frido may have been three-quarters craven by nature, but he didn't just hold his neck out over a bowl. Or did he?"

"Let's run through who could have done it. What about Ironsides and Boo-Boo? They were together."

"But not all the time. Over an eight-hour shift, they both would have slipped away from the control room to hit the head or get a cup of coffee three or four times, but trying to pin them down on times would be like trying to nail down whipped cream."

"Annalee and Rosalee?" she asked.

I shrugged. "They can alibi each other by saying they were both asleep in their rooms, but it would take a tactical nuke to wake up Rosalee, and Annalee wears earplugs so she can't hear Rosalee snoring through two doors and a common area. Either one could have left and wiped up Frido. For that matter, either you or I could have slipped away and done the deed." I was thinking about the locker.

"Maybe. I don't think you did—I would have heard you leave. And I don't think I did. Even if I'd gone into some sort of trance state, I would have snapped out of it and found myself standing in the kitchen."

"I feel much better. Well, at least we can eliminate Wyma Jean."

Catarina scratched the back of her neck. "I'm not so sure. I took a good look at those handcuffs before we took them apart. It would have been easy for her to put them on herself."

Outside, Rosalee said, "Hey, Ken! We're almost finished."

"Sure," I said without looking. I told Catarina, "Hell, Boo-Boo's cat didn't knife Frido, and he's about the only one we've eliminated. We're no better off than when we started." I thought for a moment. "If we could only figure out what happened to all the blood."

"The case of the corpuscleless corpse," Catarina replied ingratiatingly. She waited a few seconds, then sank the blade. "Blood will tell."

"I'm swearing off bars," I said. "I'm not swearing off drinking, but I am definitely swearing off bars, and people I meet in bars, particularly vampires. Why do you spend half your time needling me?"

She smiled innocently, ear to ear, a real jet job. "If I needled you all the time, I'd lose the element of surprise."

Outside, I could hear Ironsides cursing loudly as he tried to keep the torch lit. "Ken! Will you hurry up in there? We're going to be done here in a minute!" he bellowed.

"We're busy trying to figure out who killed Frido," I told him.

Catarina's smile faded. "Ken, don't stick your neck out for me."

I gave her a funny look. "Why not?"

She hesitated. "Trust me. When we get to Brasília Nuevo, everything will be all right. Nothing's going to happen to me. At least, nothing that wasn't already going to happen to me," she amended.

"How do you know?" I asked.

Ironsides bellowed again. "MacKay!"

She hesitated again, then shook her head. "Trust me. I just know. Don't stir things up by trying to play private detective."

I shook my head. "Sorry, I guess I'm not very trusting. Besides, I've already gone and stirred things up. I can't very well stop now. And in a way, I feel like we owe it to Frido."

"All right." She patted my cheek. "Just don't go stupid on me. Don't take any chances. I don't want someone to panic and stuff you under the sink, if you understand what I'm saying. Why did you do it? Stick up for me like that?"

"With a smile like that, you have to ask? Besides, you didn't do it. And also, I haven't got very many friends on this bucket," I added softly.

"All right, Ken." She wrinkled her nose. "If you're going to poke around, sometime when you're alone you might want to clean the drains in the galley. I think they might be stopped up."

"Ah, come on, Ken! We're almost finished!" Ironsides yelled.

I nodded slowly and stepped out to see how Davie Lloyd and Dykstra were making out.

"This will hold her," Ironsides grunted as I stepped past him. They'd already cut a slot in the door to pass food through, and they were ready to finish fastening the bar. Davie Lloyd fitted it in place and applied the torch.

The right side of the bar slipped and hit the deckplates with a dull thud. "Perhaps if you tried using just the tiniest bit of solder . . ." I heard Catarina say.

I left them to it and went off to find McHugh, who was wild to start searching. She and I then spent five or six hours poking around everyone's room and generally trying to dig up dirt.

We hit the staterooms first. We started with Boo-Boo's and didn't find much worth mentioning. Boo-Boo had so many little bottles and jars of herbs and medicinal substances that he could have hidden the crown jewels in there, although McHugh made an enthusiastic home-wrecker and absolutely drove Boo-Boo's cat, Sasha Louise Kitty, to distraction. There was nothing peculiar about Ironsides's quarters apart from the mold in the corners.

We hit Dykstra next. The only thing that she had that raised eyebrows was a box of tapes that included things like Camus and Sartre.

As I was rummaging through her lingerie, I asked McHugh, "What are we looking for, anyway?"

She stared back at me as if that were the stupidest statement she'd heard in her life. "Evidence!" she snapped.

"What does evidence look like?" I persisted.

McHugh glared. "How the hell would I know? This was your idea, anyway. Hell, there's nothing here. Let's do Kundle's room next."

We went through Kundle's room thoroughly. We had all seen the diary he kept once or twice. But I didn't find it, and neither did McHugh.

"What have we got so far?" I asked her when we finished with the shelves.

"A leash, a dog collar, a bunch of dirty books, a couple bags of Brazil nuts. Jack-all, the same thing we had an hour ago. What, you fall asleep or something and forget?"

I shrugged. "We've been through the bathroom. The only thing left is his bed."

McHugh looked at it and folded her arms. "I'm not touching it."

"Okay." I stripped it down gingerly and found nothing. The frame was plastic tubing. I put my hand on it to brace myself while I lifted the mattress, and one of the ends felt loose. When I twisted it, it came off. There were half a dozen sacks of white powder stuffed inside. I pulled the top one out and tossed it to McHugh. She hesitated. "What is it?"

"Good question. I don't think it's soap."

She opened the bag, licked her finger, and ran it across the top. "Funny," she said, "it tastes like soap."

It didn't help her complexion, and when I tried it, it didn't do a thing for me either. We stuck the bags in the ship's safe with the rest of the late Frido's effects and jointly came to the conclusion that while we didn't know what was going on, it qualified as evidence. People don't hide things like laundry detergent away for no reason, even slobs like Frido.

The galley was next on our list. I let McHugh poke around the pots and pans while I sat down and tried to figure out what everyone's motives might be.

Dykstra was the least obvious suspect. She had no discernible reason for turning Frido into fricassee, and outwardly she lacked the wit to invent one. Of course, if anyone on the ship had the physical strength to toss Frido up against a wall and stick in a knife, it was her.

McHugh wasn't much better as a suspect. Although McHugh was about nine-tenths ruthless and had very little use for Frido, it didn't feel like her style. Normally, she was about as subtle as a kick in the teeth. I couldn't see her using a knife on Frido. Maybe a chain saw, or a ball peen hammer, but not a knife. Also, having known her for ten months, I couldn't imagine her wasting her career or even the time of day on Frido.

Spooner was probably the best suspect I had, and she puzzled me. She didn't seem like the violent type, but McHugh and I had come across her paraphernalia. Not everyone owns a cat-o'-nine-tails. And her reaction to Frido's demise seemed a little overdone. Having been married once, I knew that people fooling around with each other are not noted for behaving rationally, and neither was Spooner. I marked her up as a maybe.

That left Ironsides and Bernie Bobo. Boo-Boo had the only obvious motive. The little clown had been lusting after Wyma Jean in his little tin heart for months. He had been correspondingly jealous of Frido and everyone else over a meter tall, and he had hidden it about as well as he did anything else. Unfortunately, I had to cross him off because Bernie was so deathly afraid of pointed objects that he ate with plastic utensils.

His buddy Ironsides was the one I wanted to be guilty. He had no apparent morals to speak of—he'd even been a little sweet on O'Day. Unfortunately, his best friend—if he had had one—would have had to admit he lacked the manual dexterity necessary to knife a blind cripple, and it was difficult for me to detect criminal genius in a man who couldn't juggle an eight-person watchlist.

Last on my list, of course, was Catarina, who looked to be either the cause or the catalyst of what had gone down. Things had been pretty quiet until she showed up, and she'd said very little about herself, even to me. Still, while the *modus operandi* had fingerprints and possibly tooth marks all over it, my money said no. If she'd done in Frido intentionally, she'd have made a better job of it, and if she'd done him in in an absentminded way, McHugh's printout was curiously timed.

I hadn't done Frido in, I was pretty sure he hadn't been run over by a train, and we didn't have a butler. I was inclined to clear the cat. Before I could figure out who killed Frido, the question I had to answer was "why?" Frido hadn't had a single enemy, although none of his friends liked him.

I'd reached that point in my analysis and was about to go back and start over when Ironsides stuck his head in and interrupted. "Are you two checking for fingerprints?" he demanded.

Annalee slammed a frying pan down on the counter. "Whose? We all eat in here!"

"Besides, I wouldn't know how," I added. "Why don't you go back out front and steer the ship?"

Davie Lloyd's head disappeared. Boo-Boo stuck his in a minute later. "Ken, can I talk with you in private?"

"Sure, Bernie." I walked out in the corridor with him.

"Ken, I've been hearing noises around the ship the last couple of days." Bernie looked unusually harried. I probably did, too, so I refrained from making any of the obvious retorts.

"Okay," I said cautiously.

"Well, I saw a vampire in a movie turn himself to smoke, and I think that's how Lindquist got in the galley and killed Frido without anyone seeing her." Having vouchsafed this revelation, Bernie looked up at me in a touching sort of way.

"Bernie," I said gently, "things like that don't even happen in movies anymore. Will you please go back to the bridge and help Davie Lloyd steer the ship? Annalee and I can handle this."

"Honest, Ken. I've been hearing things!"

"I'm sure you have. Now, go on back up to the bridge." I turned him around and sent him forward. Then I went back into the galley.

Annalee was perched on a chair, rifling through some cabinets. "What did Bernie have to say?"

"He's been hearing things, too."

"Oh, hell." She looked at me. "That's all we need. Well, I'll be damned if I can find anything in here. You want to check the storeroom?"

"Okay, let's go."

We walked down the corridor together. "Goddamn cat scratched me, did you see that?" McHugh pointed to her wrist.

"I told you, you shouldn't have tried to shave her fur off to see if she had messages tattooed on her skin."

"Well, she could have," McHugh said defensively. She pulled open the door to the storeroom, walked in, and started on the bottom shelves. "Goddamn," she muttered, "I swear somebody's been in here moving stuff around."

"Frido's ghost?" I suggested.

"Cut that out!" she snapped. "I told you Wyma Jean's been hearing things." She turned her head and looked at me funny. "Do you hear somebody breathing?"

"No."

"It's coming from in here. Oh, my God! The ship's haunted."

"McHugh, will you stop that?"

"Ken." She turned pasty white and began inching backward toward the door. "I'm serious. I can hear it. It's coming from in there." She pointed toward a vegetable bin. "Oh, my God! It's moaning."

"McHugh! There is nothing in that bin except turnips." I reached over and wrenched open the door.

"There it is!" McHugh wailed.

I stared in amazement. "Clyde, what are you doing here?"

Clyde the bead vendor was sitting cross-legged on top of a pile of tubers, spooning peaches out of a can. He smiled until he recognized me. "Oh, no. You the fellow with the pretty lady wrestler."

McHugh shifted her weight off her heels and narrowed her eyes. "Say, you don't look like a ghost."

Clyde's eyes went wide. He almost dropped his peaches. "Ghost? Where!"

I took the peaches out of his hand and set them down on the

deck. Then I grabbed him by the arm. "He's no ghost. This little so-and-so tried to pick my pocket in Schenectady," I explained. "He must have stowed away."

"Hey, who are you calling a so-and-so? Ouch!" Clyde protested.

"Take him to Iron-Ass and ask him some questions," McHugh said through clenched teeth as she grabbed Clyde's other arm. We both yanked.

"Hey, stop! Not so rough! Maybe I don't remember so good!" Clyde drew his legs up, so we lifted him and carried him down the corridor to the bridge, where we plopped him into one of the jump seats beside a completely befuddled Ironsides.

"What! Where'd he come from?" Davie Lloyd asked.

"Oh, man. My memory's gone. I don't remember so good," Clyde told him.

"You came out of a vegetable bin, Clyde. Let's start with that," I prompted.

"Bernie, keep your eyes on the control panel," McHugh growled. "You, Clyde, maybe we should break off a few of your fingers to help you remember."

"You are not a very nice lady!" Clyde observed with alarm, which was probably the first completely truthful thing he'd said in a while.

"Who's this guy? What is going on here?" Ironsides asked someone.

"He's a goddamn stowaway, and he probably offed Frido," McHugh said.

"What's a probably offrido?" Clyde asked.

"Huh? Who are you!" Davie Lloyd demanded.

"Me? Hey, man, name's Obediah Witherspoon," Clyde said. He looked at me and added hastily, "But my friends call me Clyde."

"Clyde you are," I said.

"Ken, back there did you say this guy tried to pick your pocket on Schuyler's?" McHugh asked.

I nodded.

"Oh, no!" Clyde volunteered hastily. "Just a misunderstanding. The lady with the blond hair, she got it all straightened out."

Ironsides was still having trouble following the conversation. "Who is this guy?" he asked plaintively.

"He's a stowaway who tried to pick Ken's pocket. He must have slipped on board the shuttle," McHugh explained. "He must have done the job on Frido."

Comprehension dawned in Davie Lloyd's face. "You were the extra seventy kilos on the shuttle!" He waved his fist. "Do you know what you cost me?"

"Hang on, Davie, it's only money. Okay, Clyde, what are you doing on board this ship?" I asked. Clyde hesitated. "Why don't we ask Catarina to come up? It might jog his memory if she explained to him that it's traditional to toss stowaways out the air lock."

"Oh, yeah, man! I remember real good, now!" Clyde said.

The problem rapidly became getting Clyde to shut up. The way he explained it, his little encounter with Catarina and me had left him in a slightly nervous state, and he had subsequently had an unsuccessful business encounter with a large gentleman. The large gentleman was apparently a personal acquaintance of several policemen and was considerably less understanding than Catarina. Feeling the need to take air, Clyde had recollected Catarina mentioning a ten o'clock shuttle which would take him off-planet and had acted promptly.

"I'm just an impulsive guy," he explained.

An hour's worth of questions alternating with threats failed to shake him from his story or turn up more than the usual inconsistencies. Questions concerning Frido met with uncomprehending looks. Bernie kept swiveling his head around to look but sensibly stayed quiet, which would have been out of character had McHugh not been standing within easy reach.

McHugh finally motioned Ironsides and me to step outside in the corridor. She gave us a puzzled look. "Am I missing something? Is this guy for real? I mean the way he talks."

I shook my head. "Not a chance. But I still don't think he killed Frido."

"Well, I think maybe he done it," Ironsides said.

McHugh, who was a less than happy camper, snapped back, "You're as much of a squirrel as he is!"

"I think it's all an act!" Ironsides shouted.

I stepped in front of Annalee so she wouldn't be tempted to take a punch. "Hold it, gang. Let me try something."

I stepped back onto the bridge and propelled Clyde to his feet. "Hi, Clyde, we're going to take a little trip, but not to the air lock just yet."

"Hey, wait, man. Where are we going?" he asked excitedly.

I pushed him down to Frido's cabin, where we had Frido temporarily laid out. McHugh and Ironsides followed.

"Clyde, this is your new cabin," I said, and shoved him in the door to see his reaction. "And this is your new roommate."

McHugh caught on. She threw in, "The guy with his throat cut is the former occupant. Clyde, meet Frido."

My buddy Clyde stiffened in every muscle, matching his stuck-up hair. About two seconds later, he let out a piercing shriek and jumped into my arms. "I never stow away before, I never stow away again. You keep me, I'll be good. Honest, I even muck out your pigs . . ."

I let him drop. When he hit the deck, he began wiping my tennis shoes with his sleeve.

I turned around to stare down Ironsides. "Davie, I'd say his dialogue is corny, but if the man expected to see Frido's corpse, he's a better actor than I'll ever be."

Annalee looked at Ironsides and shook her head.

"All right, you win. He didn't do it," Ironsides said disgustedly. "Let's figure out how to stow Frido in the icebox."

We went back, and McHugh and I finished checking stores. We didn't find anything, and finally gave up. Then we got everybody together again and voted on whether to lock Clyde away, but it was a foregone conclusion—only Bernie's cat was in favor of the idea. Ironsides and Bobo resumed their watch, McHugh and Dykstra went back to bed, and we gave Clyde back his peaches and turned him over to Wyma Jean as a booby prize.

After Annalee shut her door, I stopped by the galley. I shoved myself under the sink, disconnected the piping, and took apart the grease trap.

There was a small wad of hair and other slime, which I sealed away in case somebody was ever in a position to test it. As I was bottling it, something like a small stone caught my eye. I fished it out to hold up to the light.

I whistled softly. Drab and dull, it looked to be an uncut emerald, about five and a half carats. I could have been wrong, but I didn't think so—I'm better with crystalline structures than I am with people. I sealed it away with the hair, stuffed the vial in the bottom of my shaving kit, and went to bed.

Davie Lloyd decided to switch to some sort of four bells, eight bells watch schedule, which would have worked better if we had had a bell. My next watch was bad because I had to take it alone. The one after that was worse, and it blurred into the one after that.

When I got off, I walked slowly to our quarters. "Hello, Catarina. How are you holding up?" I said as I came in and shut the door.

"I'm fine, Ken, really. I've been catching up on my reading. I'm doing better than you." The concern was obvious in her voice.

I'd been spending my free time parked in front of Catarina's door; she was good therapy. I set my chair next to her door and pillowed my head against the bulkhead.

"I'm okay. I'm just tired. Wyma Jean doesn't have time to do the routine stuff before I come on. Let's talk about something other than work." I closed my eyes and listened to the ship's engines rip protons into their constituent fermions.

"You want to argue philosophy again?" she asked, amused.

"No, you absolutely astonished me with how many puns you could make on Spinoza." I turned my head around to stare at the metal bar Ironsides and Dykstra had welded in place. "Catarina, I meant to ask you why you didn't speak up when Davie Lloyd started trying to pin Frido's demise on you."

"I thought it would be safer all around if our 'X' thought I was safely locked up," she said mildly.

"Why? If 'X' bumped you off, what would he, she, or it do for a fall guy?" "X" was what we had started to call our mystery killer.

"Ken, if 'X' bumped you off, what would I do for an alibi?" she asked gently, and I shut up. "Ken, it's okay. Trust me.

Everything will sort itself out when we hit Brasilia Nuevo. Quit poking around."

I shook my head. "Not a chance." I chuckled. "Dykstra's already started calling me 'Inspector Javert.' I guess trust isn't exactly one of my strong points."

"How long were you married, Ken?" she asked quietly.

"Oh, I didn't realize it showed."

"It does. Besides, you've only mentioned your ex-wife six or eight times."

"I did? Careless of me, wasn't it?" I thought for a moment. "It lasted six months. I don't think she actually finished unpacking her stuff."

"I'm sorry."

"Don't be. It's over."

"Is that something you want to talk about?"

"Yes, no, maybe. It doesn't bother me much anymore." I reflected for a minute. "To be honest, I don't have the vaguest idea what went wrong. I thought we were going to make it work. She was an ad exec. She wasn't much to look at—I turned her down the first couple of times she asked me out—but she had energy, if you know what I mean."

"I think so," Catarina said slowly.

"It was funny. When we were going together, every day she'd send me flowers and have a hologram waiting on the machine when I got out of class. She liked the idea I was going to be a spacer."

"And afterward?"

"Well, I graduated and lined up an in-system job, and when I asked her to marry me, she got real strange. I thought she was going to say no, and then she got really enthused. She popped down, got the license, and told me how ready we were to tie our lives together. She had it all figured out."

I could feel Catarina's eyes through the door. "You got married right away?" she asked sharply.

"Four hours later, if you can believe that. I still don't. The honeymoon lasted almost as long. After that, I couldn't do anything right."

Catarina sighed. "It fits the pattern, I think. I've known a few men like that."

"God help them. First she didn't want kids, then she had to have a kid, then she didn't want kids. My mind was so screwed on backward, I almost got grounded. Then I cut back on my hours and started spending more time with her, and things just got worse. Damn it, I don't like being told I can't cook by a woman who can't boil water."

"What did her friends think?"

"God knows; she never let me meet them. Does that fit your pattern?"

"It does. I take it she lied occasionally?"

"Like a cheap rug. About little things. I didn't believe it at first, then I'd get so mad . . ." I stopped and caught my breath. "Would you believe I still get holos from her occasionally?" I shook my head. "It's my own fault, really."

I could hear Catarina chuckle. "Say again?"

"No, really, for being an idiot, not for screwing up the marriage. Actually, for a while I thought it was all my fault. It took a long time to get myself put back together. But I figured out that if you're going to walk the railroad tracks, you ought to know what a train looks like. I ended up dangling from the cowcatcher. What is a cowcatcher, anyway?"

"I saw one in a museum in Baltimore once. It's sort of like a big sleeve to push animals off the tracks with."

"Baltimore? The place in Ireland?"

"No, it's part of Washington."

"Oh, I've been there. That's right by the Naval Academy. How long were you in Washington?"

"Oh, not too long," she said, deftly turning aside my question. "So you went out-system."

"As far away as I could get. Which actually turned out to be pretty far."

"How long has it been?"

"Five years, I guess. I was a mess for a while. What was your excuse for going out-system? I mean, before you became a vamp? God, that was a stupid question, wasn't it?"

There was a knock on the outside door to the corridor, which saved her from having to answer. "Come on in," I said. "It's open."

Clyde bopped on in. "Hey man! You still mad at me?"

"Hello, Clyde. No, it's okay. Where have you been? I haven't seen you."

"Oh, I mostly been helping Miss Wyma Jean. After she explained what happened, I sort of figured you might not want to see me right away."

"You got that straight," I told him.

"I also came by to see Miss Catarina."

"Hello, Clyde," Catarina said through the door. "It's all right. I'm not going to break your arms."

"Uh, thanks!" Clyde fidgeted a little bit. "Miss Catarina, can I ask you a personal question?"

"Go for it."

"Are you really, really a vampire?"

"McLendon's Syndrome. Cross my heart and hope to put a stake in it."

Clyde's eyes lit up. "Wow, man. That's neat! I never been assaulted by a real, live vampire before." He reached around until he found a pocket in that dashiki of his and pulled out a notepad. "Uh, can I have your autograph?"

I closed my eyes. "Later, Clyde?"

Catarina said, "It's okay, Ken. Just slide it through the crooked slot in the door."

Clyde sort of danced up to the door and slid his notepad through. Catarina spent a few minutes writing and then passed it back.

Clyde tucked the notebook away. "Uh, thanks! Sorry I disturbed you, man. Uh, Mr. Ken, do you and Miss Catarina play cards? Miss Wyma Jean thought you might like company."

"What do you think, Catarina?" I asked.

"Sure. Poker or bridge?"

"Bridge," I said.

Clyde sort of shuffled his feet. "Uh, I can't play bridge, man."

"Okay," I said, "poker, then, tomorrow night, but I don't play for money. Besides, you don't have any."

"I've got a box of raisins. We could count them out and use them for chips," Catarina offered.

"Uh, sounds great! I'll tell Miss Wyma Jean." Clyde scurried out the door and shut it.

Catarina started giggling fit to die. It lasted about thirty seconds and then I laid one hand against the door and started in.

"Oh, lord," I said, wiping my eyes, "I can't believe this trip."

"Ken, this has to be a first for me, too. Are you off today?"

I shook my head. "No. Davie Lloyd juggled the watchlist again. He tells me I'm on at twenty-four bells."

"Look, Ken, you need to get some rest."

"You're right. But I really want to talk to some people first."

"All right. But make sure you get a few hours' sack time, anyway. Have a good night. And thanks for telling me about your ex."

"Thanks for listening." I stuck my chair back in my cubicle and went back out into the corridor. Spooner had the conn with Clyde as her gopher, so I stopped off first to see Bernie.

Ironsides was sawing wood in his cubicle, but Bernie was in their common area shooting craps with his cat. Sasha Louise was an old tortoiseshell tabby with cataracts in both eyes. She was apparently too blind to read the spots on the dice, because Bernie was cheating her outrageously.

He poked his head up. "Hello, Ken. What were you cooking for dinner? It smelled pretty good." Bernie's head is too big for his neck. Overall, he looks as though they built him out of spare parts.

"Leg of lamb—freeze-dried—with a bordelaise sauce, and some veggies for Catarina."

"How did it turn out?"

I shrugged. "To tell the truth, I wasn't paying attention."

We chatted. I counted pill bottles. Bernie added another twenty-two million to Sasha's debt and fed her a can of salmon to celebrate. He acted a little nervous, but no more than usual. I found out precisely nothing.

"Well, thanks anyway," I told him. On the way out the door, I stopped. "Hey Bernie, this has nothing to do with Frido, but why are you so scared of getting sick?"

He sat there stroking the cat for a minute. "Ken, if I got sick, who'd take care of Sasha Louise?"

I walked out of there feeling a lot shorter than when I walked in.

McHugh was next on my list. I found her in stores doing a spot inventory, which should have been Davie Lloyd's job. While I respected McHugh's competence, I couldn't say I liked her. Other than Dykstra, I'm not sure who did.

She was curious about Catarina, so I told her a little of what I knew. She kept her eyes half-closed and kept any expression off her face. She'd have made a good poker player.

We talked, and she had a lot to say about Frido, none of it nice. She threw in tidbits about Spooner from time to time, and once or twice I caught her sizing me up, trying to decide what to say. We walked back to her cabin. Rosalee was in their common area doing arm-curls with a set of weights, and she gave us a wave and a grunt as we passed by.

I wasn't especially good at the investigation racket. It didn't take me long to run out of questions, and I found my eyes wandering around McHugh's cabin. Apart from the quick once-over I'd given the place when we were looking for evidence, it was the first time I'd been inside, maybe the first time anyone had been inside other than Dykstra.

All along one wall were framed certificates—good framing, too. They were tacked up in neat rows, Navy promotions up through Petty Officer Second in quick succession, plus a scattering of achievement awards and commendations. Her apprentice and journeyman's ratings were tacked up along with letters of appreciation from previous ships. She'd done well on some good ships.

She must have been watching my eyes, because she didn't even let me get the question out of my mouth. "Get the hell out of here, Ken," she said, looking down at the deckplates. For the first time she put a little emotion into her voice. "Just get the hell out of here."

I went across to visit with Rosalee. She was a big woman in her late thirties, the quietest person on board, and also the largest.

We talked. She switched from lifting weights to knitting, which put me in mind of Madame Defarge. I didn't know that much about Dykstra's private life, but after ten months I couldn't truthfully say that I knew much about any of my shipmates.

She didn't have much to say about anyone, herself least of all, and what she said were neutral things that didn't add up to anything. She didn't ask me any questions, and I didn't volunteer much. It was pretty much a waste of time all around.

Looking around the cabin, I only noticed one thing out of place—a picture of a little girl. "Pretty girl," I said, wondering why I hadn't noticed it when we searched the place.

Rosalee didn't say anything, but she turned her head to look at me. I raised an eyebrow. "How old is she?"

"Nineteen," she said, "a week from Tuesday."

"That's nice," I said lamely. "She really is pretty. Do you have any recent pictures of her?"

For a moment, I thought she was going to put the needle through the wall. She set it down without saying anything and picked up one of her dumbbells. When she let it drop, I saw it bounce. We were lucky we had steel underfoot, and Spooner probably had to do a minor course correction. I just sat there, wondering what it was I was using for brains.

Rosalee finally looked me in the eyes. "If you ever think about getting married again, don't go through with it, Ken. It isn't worth it."

Then she picked up both dumbbells and began doing presses, and I let myself out quietly.

Ironsides was waiting for me out in the passageway, hopping mad. I sympathized—Davie Lloyd was so far out of his depth that you couldn't see the bubbles coming up, and he needed somebody to be mad at.

"Goddamn you, mister," he whispered hoarsely. "You come snooping around here with your nose in the air and your goddamned reserve commission. Well, this is my ship! If your goddamned vampire friend didn't kill Frido, you tell me who did! You hear me, mister, you just tell me that!"

Bernie at least had his cat for company.

I looked Davie Lloyd over for a long minute before I left. He started to shake, and I think for a second he thought I was going to tell him.

I still had six suspects. Seven, if you counted Catarina. Eight if you counted the cat, but the cat still didn't know how to chase her tail without banging her head on the wall.

I stopped by Catarina's door to tell her how my inquiries had gone, and then I crashed for a few hours of sleep.

When I came to and made it up to the bridge, Clyde was just departing. Spooner turned around. Her face was drawn.

"Rough watch?" I asked.

"Hello, Ken. Yeah, she was pretty rough this shift. I don't envy you. The board's green, though; I'm ready to hand over whenever you like."

"Fine." I slid into the seat next to her. "How are things otherwise? Is Clyde working out?"

"He's doing fine." She smiled nervously and brushed her hair back with one hand. "He's been teaching me thieves' cant."

I looked up. "Say what?"

"Oh, he doesn't call it that, he calls it 'dive,' but it's the language thieves use. It's fascinating."

"I suppose," I said. Wyma Jean liked to talk more than most of the people on board, and I usually humored her.

"Oh, don't be so reactive, Ken," she scolded. "Clyde can't help being what he is. It's marvelous just watching him change."

"Nurture over nature," I said, trying not to smile. "All right, I'll give him a chance. I ought to be grateful—the way he dresses, nobody can make fun of what I wear."

"Oh, I don't know," Wyma Jean said, leaving it unclear which part of the statement she disagreed with. "What have you been up to?"

I stared at her bleakly. "Still trying to find a murderer."

I looked away as tears welled up in her eyes. She waved and got up. "See you later, Ken. Have a good watch."

I didn't.

The *Scupper*'s drives and her computer really did desperately need an overhaul. Every so often she'd throw a real fit. Halfway through my watch, she threw one for me. About the second time I had two red lights flashing on the board simultaneously and needed four hands, I began regretting having mouthed off to my previous skipper. It was a long and not very enjoyable watch, and I was thoroughly sorry Catarina wasn't around to help out long before it was over.

Ironsides and Bobo were scheduled to relieve me. They were a few minutes late coming on, and I was unusually annoyed by the time they finally showed. I yelled out the door, "Hey, Davie Lloyd, you ready to take over? Any time, guy."

Ironsides cautiously stuck his head in.

"Hi, Davie Lloyd," I said. "You and your munchkin, get in here. The board is yours, and I've finally got it green. I've already signed the log. There is one thing of interest. We've got a ship coming up behind us at constant boost. She should pass us within the hour."

"A ship?" Ironsides croaked. "What ship?"

"I don't know. Probably an alien. Looks like that Rodent we saw at Schuyler's World. Want me to ask?" Bobo scuttled in from somewhere as I switched on the loud-hailer. "This is *Rustam's Slipper*, Guild registry 19747. Identify yourself, please."

There was no immediate response, so I stood up to make a place for Bernie. "All yours, Davie Lloyd. What's wrong? You're paler than Catarina."

Davie Lloyd looked as though he'd been shaking hands with Frido's ghost, and Bernie suddenly didn't look much better. I eyed both of them and shook my head. There were too many question marks floating about the ship, including uncut emeralds and soap powder.

As I was walking away, we got a response from the other vessel. "Doubles-crossing rat-tes," said something in unusually toneless English.

"Got you pegged, Davie. See you." I chuckled and continued down the passageway. I saw McHugh and Dykstra in the galley consoling Spooner. The cabin doors on either side were wide open.

As I started to shut Spooner's door, a flaming garbage can came whizzing past my eyebrows and disappeared into McHugh's and Dykstra's space. I turned my head in time to see a pretty little sunburst through one of the holes in the side of the ship before vacuum pulled the doors on both sides shut.

Spooner's door took some skin off my hand, but I couldn't complain. I know a missile when I see one close up, and a small distance either way and I'd have been watching the action from outside the ship just long enough to find it uncomfortable.

I felt the ship tremble underneath me. I said something profound, like, "Oh, hell," and took off toward the bridge.

In the second seat, Bobo had his hands held over his face. Ironsides was seated beside him as stiff as wax. The other ship was closing the range, ready to fire more missiles.

The toneless, high-pitched voice from the other vessel came on again. "Dirty, rotten, double-crossing rat-tes. You are toast. Prepare yourselves to die."

I reached over Davie Lloyd's shoulder, slammed the abort, and shoved the ship into full astern. The u-channels dropped into place, and four different things lit up red on the board. As our forward momentum dropped off, the alien ineptly sped on by.

The other craft wasn't a warship, but they had a warship's weaponry. They must have assumed we had protective armor or a protective field; otherwise the missile that had gone past my nose probably would have gone off in my face. Glancing at the board, it looked like maybe another five had slammed through Number Two hold and out the other side.

"Friendly sort, wasn't he?" I said, trying to sound calm. I looked around. "As Butch said to Sundance, who are those guys?"

Nobody volunteered an answer. "Bernie! Davie Lloyd!" I slapped Ironsides once, and he didn't react. McHugh and Dykstra piled onto the bridge, followed by Spooner and Clyde.

"What the hell . . ." McHugh began.

McHugh got a reaction. Patience is not one of her virtues, and she can be fairly direct when she gets excited. Bobo must have seen her cock her fist. He moaned. "The ship shot at us. They tried to kill us!" which may have extended his life expectancy.

"My God. We're dead!" I heard Spooner say. Before she could go catatonic on us, I saw Clyde's hands tighten around her shoulders.

"Is he telling the truth?" McHugh asked.

I said, "There's a certain novelty in it."

"What in hell are we going to do?" McHugh demanded, looking from Ironsides to Bobo. She added pointedly, "There's something my DI always said about wiping windows with soft-boiled eggs."

I had forgotten she was a reserve petty officer second. Something clicked, which probably had a lot to do with the fact I was running on pure adrenaline. "Okay," I said. "Ironsides, as the only reserve Navy officer on this vessel, I'm declaring an insurgency. I'm calling myself to active duty and taking your vessel into service pursuant to paragraph 147.2(a) of General Regulations. Clear out of that chair. Bobo, you too. Dykstra, help move these snow cones."

Dykstra may have been slow, but she wasn't stupid. Ironsides got hauled aside like limp fish.

"McHugh, you're second-in-command, you take Bobo's seat. Dykstra, you and Spooner get everyone out of here, then grab a crowbar. Break Lindquist out and send her up here."

"But the door's welded shut," Dykstra countered.

"I'm sure Davie Lloyd handled the torch with his usual flair, so you've got five minutes. After you spring her, go down and clear the lifeboat."

The bridge emptied. "McHugh, ease the pressure in Number Two hold completely. We're holed, and we must be spilling toad guano all over space."

"Aye-aye, Cap'n. What did the other ship do, overrun us?"

"That they did."

"If the clowns running her had half a brain between them we'd be toad shit ourselves. I'll bet they can decelerate better than us, and they'll be back quick." McHugh felt for the controls.

"Let me think on that. As you were, on Number Two. We're leaking out, and we can't patch the holes. All that stuff is traveling with us at the same velocity and making us easier to spot. Pressurize and dump it instead. It'll form a cloud, and we'll use it for a smoke screen."

"Not Number Two!" moaned Ironsides from the corridor.

McHugh dumped Number Two. "You hear something? We got mice in the wall," she commented.

"Belay that out there!" I yelled. I looked at McHugh. "They've still got electronic eyes. What have we got in Number Three?"

McHugh thought for a second. "Puffed wheat."

"No. What about the auxiliary holds? What's in Number Four?"

"A couple tons of Christmas tinsel."

"That's it, tinsel! Dump Number Four!"

"No, not Number Four!" moaned Ironsides and Bobo in unison from the corridor. I heard Catarina say, "What's happened?" behind me.

McHugh dumped Number Four. Wads of tinsel spun around our axis, looking, I hoped, like the radar reflection of a Kobold-class ship. "Christ," she said. "Guano and tinsel. It's going to look like a Polish Christmas."

I turned to Catarina. "Trouble. There's another ship out there. It looks to be a Rodent merchantman configured as a warship. It's got missiles and probably guns, and we're getting shot at. I've dumped Number Two and Number Four holds to give us a smoke screen. Let me think . . ." I punched some numbers into the ship's computer, called up some figures, and built a quick and sloppy model.

"It looks like you've been pouring soil on troubled waters," Catarina observed. "What can I do?"

"In a minute I'm going to want you in McHugh's place. McHugh, while you were on active duty, you went through Woolmera. Did you go through the Indian's demolition course?"

"Filthy, sexist pig!"

"That's the man. We've got four shaped charges in the locker for clearing obstructions. Think you can rig them into a daisy chain and hook the last one on a fifty-meter line with a half-second delay?"

"Sure, we've got the stuff, but that other ship is not exactly going to sit still and let us hang a charge on her nose. We can't guide the thing, and those charges aren't real big—they're maybe a kilogram apiece."

"That's not what I have in mind. Grab Dykstra and Spooner and rig a hoist. Haul one of the big oxygen cylinders up to the air lock, hang the daisy chain on it, and set the timer for three minutes. When I give you the word, pull the pin and shove it out. And do something about Tweedledum and Tweedledee while you're at it."

Clyde stuck his head in. "I, uh, couldn't help overhearing." He rubbed his fingers on his jacket and blew on them. "I am pretty good with my hands. I could help her."

"Why not?" Catarina said.

"It's your funeral, too. Go, McHugh!"

"Aye-aye, Cap'n," McHugh said, still puzzled, as she hurried off.

Catarina slid into her seat. "Why are they shooting at us?"

"Damned if I know."

"When a warship takes on a merchantman, there are two things the merchantman can hope for: luck and stupidity, or stupidity and luck. Dykstra said you gave Davie Lloyd the heave-ho. How hysterical are you?"

"Not too bad. Considering."

"Look." She pointed to the screen. There were a few hundred little white bags floating among the tinsel and guano. "They must have come out of Number Four."

"Damn if this isn't getting more interesting by the minute."

"That it is. Ken, I hate to be a pessimist, but even if the other guys can't see us through the silver lining in your little brown cloud, the cloud is expanding. I think we're going to have a problem."

"We're wobbling—help steer us straight. I'm thinking one of the u-channels didn't drop in place when I reversed thrust. That's it, good job. Yeah, I know what you mean, but we have a couple things in our favor. One is that they'll be able to see those little white bags, and I'm guessing they're not going to want to shoot indiscriminately if they think they can collect them up."

"Good enough. What's another thing in our favor?"

"I'll let you know when I think of one." I punched the button on the intercom. "McHugh, are you in position?"

"Hell, no!" was the reply.

"Something big and close," Catarina volunteered, tracking our meteor guide.

"Company?"

"Company, it is. We're hit pretty bad. This rust trap isn't in any shape to absorb punishment. What's the plan, Ken?"

"I want a big cloud of guano and oxygen. I want a spark. Ideally, I want there to be a big bang when the cloud blows up."

"Where are we going to be?"

"Far, far away, I hope. Maximum acceleration. I think I see them at about a hundred degrees, paralleling our course."

"That's them. Assuming we don't get shot up before we get far enough to worry about it, what do you call our chance of having the guano and oxygen mixed well enough to go off?"

"As it says in the Bible, slim, son of none."

She looked over, punched up my model, and began working it. "I make it about one in three thousand."

"That sounds about right."

"That's what I thought," she said. "I understand you quoted General Regulations when you took command?"

"I quoted paragraph 147.2(a), which may or may not exist. In brief, my assumption of command was also guano, but it seemed like a good idea at the time. You want to take over?"

"No, you're doing fine."

"Sorry you signed up?"

"I never regret anything that doesn't add up to my waistline." She corrected a power fluctuation. "Scared?"

"Hell, no," I said, putting a brave face on things. "I was scared when the first one came whizzing past my nose. Since then, I've worked my way up to terrified."

"So, while we're waiting, did you figure out who killed Frido?"

"Two votes for you, Annalee says the gimp did it, and nobody else has a clue. I voted for the cat."

She reached out a free hand and tousled my hair.

"Anna Catarina, you know what's really annoying?"

"What?"

"When I reach out to people, I've mostly been counting my fingers to make sure I get all of them back . . ."

"Try not to make this too soppy. Your ex-wife?"

"She's merely illustrative of the general principle. What's annoying is realizing that the best friend I've got is a vampire who's probably an ax-murderer."

She tried to smile. "Ken, for what it's worth . . ." She tweaked my nose. "You're kind of cute."

I thought for a minute, leaned over, and kissed her. "I've been meaning to say this for a while. You're not so bad yourself."

"All this flattery is going to my head. Should we try and surrender?"

I hit the intercom. "McHugh, how's it coming?"

There was a burst of profanity. "Son-of-a-bitching thing is stuck. Give me fifteen minutes."

"We're getting there," Clyde chimed in.

"Where's Iron-Ass?" I asked.

"He's locked himself in the lifeboat," Dykstra reported.

"What's he doing?"

"Wait a minute . . . Spooner says he's in there playing with himself . . . No, sorry. She meant pleading with himself."

"Thanks." I snapped off the intercom.

She smiled. "I deduce."

"You got it. Davie Lloyd is using the radio in there. If they haven't accepted his surrender by now, I don't think they'll bother."

"So what do we do, fly straight and level for fifteen minutes and pray a lot?"

"I'm open to suggestions."

"You really think we're going to make it out of here?"

I was busy trying to figure out how to say what was on my mind without being too messy about it. "No," I said, distracted.

My face must be an absolutely open file. She smiled, put her hand up, and ran it through my hair. "Let me suggest something, then."

We locked the door to the bridge, and it beat hell out of any ideas I had on how to spend my last fifteen minutes. Catarina made me keep one hand close to the board to keep the ship straight, which wasn't fair. It was pretty interesting by the time McHugh called in over the intercom.

"Okay," she said. "Clyde and I have got this thing about as set as it's ever going to be. I hope you know what you're doing."

Catarina and I disengaged. "No, but I was learning fast," I muttered. I looked at her. "Are we set?"

She shrugged. Our little brown cloud was decreasing in density as it grew in size, and it was giving our outline the coverage you'd expect from a wet nightgown.

I snapped on the intercom. "McHugh! Count to thirty aloud, dump it, and don't forget the pin."

The first five numbers she sang out all seemed to start with something that rhymed with "duck."

"I'll boost her twenty seconds after McHugh kicks the thing free," I told Catarina. "You correct with the sidejet that doesn't break down."

"Aye-aye, Captain Bligh."

"Just hold our course steady, Mister Christian, while I give this bucket all I've got."

"Which probably isn't very much just now."

"Okay!" sang out McHugh over the intercom.

"Dykstra, what's Davie saying?" I yelled.

"He's telling them about the bomb!"

"Oh, hell. This is going to be rough."

We waited.

"Boosting," I said. Catarina helped correct our course. "Uh, Catarina—"

She freed a hand and messed up my hair again. "Ken, save the really soppy stuff until we see whether that thing goes off . . . Boost her, they're slowing and firing more missiles! Looks like lasers, too!"

We punched past the tinsel, leaving the alien in the proverbial cloud of dust.

"They're firing everything they've got," Catarina observed. "They're wide to the right."

"Never mind that, can you tell how fast they're dropping off speed?"

A small flash of light hit our rear screen. "It didn't work," Catarina said. The tiny explosion set up swirling eddies of toad dung and tinsel.

"Then we're dead."

"No, wait—between the eddies and the tinsel, their missiles are going every which way. One of them has reversed course, and it looks like it's locked on to them! They're trying to slow and reverse course."

A brilliant flash of light emptied out the rear screen. We left the shock wave far behind. "Not fast enough," Catarina sang out, "how slowly the mighty have fallen."

"Well, I'll be damned," I said with awe, most likely in response to her rejoinder.

"Ken, I don't know how I could have doubted you," Catarina said with just enough feigned honesty to make me feel warm inside.

"We got them. All hands secure from action stations," I said over the intercom. "Splice the main brace."

"Hot damn!" I heard McHugh say.

"Right you are, McHugh." I heard a burst of cheering on the other end. I shut off the intercom and looked at Catarina. "It's a little late to ask, but do you think it would help if I brushed my teeth and took a shower with lots of soap?"

Catarina had to turn her head to hide a grin. "No."

"That's about what I thought. Oh, well. What did McLendon say, three percent of the population is susceptible?"

"You think you might hit the jackpot twice in one day?"

"Three times. How did you catch McLendon's?"

"Either from a doorknob or the stork brung it, I forget which."

"Ask a silly question . . ." I opened up the intercom. "Hey, McHugh, tell Iron-Ass and Boo-Boo to get up here. It's still their watch."

"We'll dig Boo-Boo out and send him on his way. Iron-Ass'll be a while. He has to change his pants."

I turned to Catarina. "Any survivors over there, do you think?"

She shook her head. "Negative. There's nothing on any of the distress bands, and the pieces all look very small."

"All right. We need to do repairs anyway." I opened up the intercom and told everyone, "I'm going to stop our rotation in ten minutes, make sure everything's nailed down." I turned back to Catarina. "This bucket is never going to make it through an escape point in the shape that she's in. How about we go outside and fix holes?"

She smiled and tapped her forehead lightly. "Wholly acceptable. You know we've got ten minutes."

It was closer to twenty before we got started. I figured if I was one of McLendon's three-percenters, it was a little late to start worrying.

The job outside was simple in theory and not particularly difficult in practice. It was just a matter of climbing out, hauling patch plates to the spot, and sealing them in place. After we suited, we clipped our lifelines into place and depressurized the inner air lock, which on a Kobold class is pretty elaborate with a retractable arm and cargo panels. I took along a pry bar, which I didn't need to fix plates. Catarina and I climbed onto the outside of the hull to moor the plates to the side of the ship, and we touched helmets to avoid radio eavesdroppers. "Before we start, do you want to snoop around everyone's cabins, or shall I?" she asked.

"You're reading my mind. I'd like to do Dykstra's and McHugh's cabins. I think I can climb through the hole. I'll take the inner and outer sealant and the torch with me. Give me about ten minutes. Then you shove off with the plates, and I'll help break your descent." She nodded. Although the plates didn't mass much, they were unwieldy.

I launched myself, trusting the line to bring me down on the side of the ship in a parabola. As I pushed off, I thought I saw somebody watching us through the inner air-lock door. A third of the way around the ship, I touched down soft and let out a little slack.

The hole into McHugh and Dykstra's common area was large enough to crawl into. The edges were pretty even, but I was still careful not to tear my suit, which is even worse luck than walking under a ladder. I went looking through Dykstra's cubicle first. I plucked the picture of her kid out of the ether and set it gently aside. A quick search convinced me there was nothing there, so I shifted to McHugh's cabin and used the pry bar to go through the closet. There was a bag of the white powder floating free. I snatched it up and started to work on her desk. I didn't find anything going through her drawers, but I brushed my hand against the lip as I was putting them back, and something came loose. It was half of an old coin embedded in wax, loosened by the vacuum. I stuffed it into my pouch and tugged on the rope to let myself out the way I'd come in.

I stayed. My lifeline came drifting toward me. I reeled it in and tried not to think about what would have happened if I had been out on the hull. The end was cut, probably from inside the air lock. I floated free over to the cabin door and secured myself to the door handle before going outside.

Catarina came over the horizon and touched down. She immediately hugged me tight. It may have been acting on her part, but it felt good. "You left the plates," I said.

"Never mind, Ken. Never mind. We'll get them later." She looked at me. "No jokes about the end of the line. I saw it go past, and my heart almost stopped. It wasn't an accident."

"No." Whoever had a knife was still on the other end and could have just as easily made a clean sweep of it when she launched herself over the horizon after me. I couldn't help thinking she'd risked her life to try and save mine. That is, if she hadn't cut the line. I gave her line a jerk. "This is going to sound mushy, but let's hold hands on the way back. Just in case."

As we were floating through on our short transit, I touched helmets. "I assume you knew where every one of us was the night we met."

"Let me think. You and I spent the evening in the Prancing Pony. McHugh was in the White Hart, Dykstra was in Smade's Tavern, O'Day was in Callahan's Place, and Spooner was in Gavagan's Bar. Ironsides spent the evening in the Vulgar Unicorn."

"I won't ask. The Vulgar Unicorn?"

"It's a little dive off Asprin Street. You can tell the men from the boys by the amount of makeup they're wearing."

"Funny name for a drinking establishment. Bobo never left the ship. That leaves Frido unaccounted for," I pointed out.

"Ken, I'm starting to get slightly worried. Stop playing Sherlock Holmes."

"Sorry, Watson. It's gotten personal. Where was Kundle?"

"Difficult to say. The rest of our merry band filled up all the taverns in town, bar none. Frido left neither ashes nor footprints for me to use your methods on," she said, affecting an English accent. "Criminals these days are so beastly tidy."

"You sound as if you disapprove of the Great Sherlock's methods."

"Sherlock was always so busy solving puzzles that he lost a few criminals and an odd client or two. The problem with the Great Holmes of England is no one really lives in them anymore."

I closed my eyes. "That one was unusually bad, even for you. All right. I'll get off the subject. But what's bothering you?"

She hesitated. "Ken, I don't know how to say this, but while you were checking out McHugh's cabin, I took a look at the latticework. They clipped it pretty thoroughly. There's about a fifteen-meter section that's just gone on this side."

"Oh, God! I didn't think to look."

"There's no way we're going to be able to ride what we have left through a black hole and come out. Do we have any spare lattices?"

I thought. "Just short sections."

"Then we can't repair it. I think we're going to have to turn back to Schuyler's World."

"God, what a mess. This will bankrupt the ship."

"Probably. I don't know Davie Lloyd's finances as well as you do."

"We're going to have enough trouble finding parts and a replacement for Frido on Schuyler's. We might be able to scrape by if we all kick in crew shares, but it's going to be tight. You got any idea why we got shot at?"

"I wish I did. All I have is a long list of questions that will hold until we get back to Schuyler's."

When we touched down, I went over to the intercom. "Where is everybody? Report in!"

Spooner and Clyde were in stores. McHugh was in the galley celebrating. Dykstra was tidying up the lifeboat. Bobo had the bridge, and Ironsides was in his cabin.

"I'll bet none of them have alibis," I told Catarina disgustedly and fingered the intercom again. "Okay, I need everyone to meet me on the bridge in five minutes."

When we got up to the bridge, I let Catarina explain about the lattice, then I explained about the long walk I had nearly taken off a very short pier. I looked from face to face and watched the elation everyone felt disappear.

"But we have to get to Brasilia Nuevo," Ironsides said doggedly. His cheeks had absolutely no color. Bernie was the only one who looked worse.

"Davie, we can't," Catarina told him gently. "Going through a black hole is as safe as riding a bus, but going through without a functioning lattice is about as smart as riding a bus with no brakes. We'll lose profits, but the insurance will cover the damage and the lost cargo.''

Bernie shook his head. "Davie dropped the casualty insurance three months ago.''

I shrugged. "Look, Davie, if you can't get an extension on the loan, maybe we can all kick in six months' pay. But we've got to go back.''

We let Clyde vote, and the vote was six to two in favor of returning. None of the ayes wanted to be stuck on Schuyler's, but none of the ayes wanted to be dead either.

Then I asked a few less-than-polite questions about who had been standing near the air lock. Spooner said that she and Clyde had been in stores the whole time we were out. Judging from the marks she'd left on Clyde, it was possible, but Clyde admitted that they'd been apart for a few minutes. Any one of the others could have done it easily.

Bernie suggested, "Maybe it was an accident.''

Everybody stared at him pointedly until we broke up.

I went back and stared at the sharp spur on the thumb of the mechanical arm. "How long would it have taken, do you think?''

"A minute or two,'' Catarina replied.

"You know, this would make a lousy detective story. In a good story, there are at least one or two people who tell the truth occasionally,'' I remarked.

Bernie wandered by and stopped. "Uh, Ken. I just wanted to tell you . . . uh, that I appreciate what you did.'' He waddled off.

I turned and looked at Catarina. "Do you think he was trying to thank me for saving his life?''

She nodded, and I shook my head in resignation.

I hid the powder in my locker and taped the half coin to the back of my mirror. We went back out about an hour later, with Spooner and Dykstra watching the lock, and patched the holes without incident. After that, Catarina and I both crashed. It had been a hectic day. I slept until my stomach told me it was time to get up.

I usually don't snack, but my stomach had a point. I went down to the galley and began rooting around in my corner of the refrigerator. Some of the stuff had floated free when we stopped spin, and it needed rearranging. I pulled out an apple and was starting to section it when I noticed that there was a little pinhole in the peel staring at me. I cut away a small piece and sniffed.

I'm not good at describing smells, but the apple smelled like almonds. I wrapped it up in foil, stuck it in the freezer, and began examining the rest of my fruit. Two pears and a grapefruit showed obvious signs of tampering. I pitched everything. Somebody wasn't keen on having me finish out the trip.

I started looking through the other stuff and was stopped by a whiff of a peculiar odor. It seemed to be coming from the milk cartons in the back, and I pulled them loose and began examining them, one by one. Two were slightly creased. I opened the first one. It was filled to the top with something red and going bad, and the other was the same.

Whoever had sealed the cartons hadn't done a thorough job. I froze them both without leaving too many fingerprints. Even if Catarina liked blood, this stuff was sour.

I found a short length of pipe and put it in my pocket to carry around. Then I went back to my cabin so I could have a real case of the shakes.

Catarina was waiting and gave me a startled look when she saw my expression. I explained.

"It looks like somebody poisoned my fruit. I've got an apple in the freezer with a pinhole in it that smells like almonds. We've either got a snake or a wicked witch. I also found what looks to be two liters of sour blood, probably Frido's. Am I getting paranoid?"

She thought for a minute. "No, Ken, you're not. Go call Dykstra and have her weld me in." I must have given her a funny look, because she rubbed my cheek. "I'm going back into solitary. We've taken enough chances."

Gradually, it began to make sense. If Catarina was supposed to take the fall for one or more murders, icing her away minimized my chances of acquiring an undeserved halo.

She explained, "This is a rougher trip than I'd planned on, Ken. You're going to join me in finishing it on Leopard Milk and chocolate chip cookies unless you'd like to go the way of all rats and have them try to pin it on me.''

It finally started to make enough sense so that I agreed with her. I nodded and went off to find Ironsides.

To his credit, Davie Lloyd tried to talk me out of walling her up until I explained about the fruit. After that, he didn't make any comment.

I slipped Catarina the emerald and some powder, just in case. Then I watched Rosalee and Davie Lloyd weld her back in. After she was taken care of, Clyde came by and found me.

"What's up, Clyde?" I snapped.

"Rosalee told me what was going on with Catarina." He looked a little sheepish. "Uh, Wyma Jean and I were just wondering if you still wanted to play poker."

I started laughing. I couldn't help it. "I'm sorry, Clyde," I finally said, wiping my eyes. "It's been a rough day. Sure, we'd love to. It'll be a good way to unwind."

Dykstra and McHugh volunteered to take the swing watch from me, and poker turned into a nightly routine on the trip back.

It gave me some insights into my shipmates. I noticed that Clyde's poker was aggressive and methodical. He was also a pretty slick politician—I noticed he was quick to fetch Spooner drinks and otherwise attend to her wants. Spooner was more erratic; sometimes she'd fold quickly, and sometimes she'd hang in well past the point of prudence. She liked the game of baseball. We didn't quite clean out her pile of raisins, but we made a dent. I did okay; I usually dropped a few raisins, but never many.

Catarina was usually the big winner—after all, they were her raisins. She was quiet rather than flashy, but I did notice that once a night she'd bluff me out of my shoes, regular as clockwork, probably for the sheer joy of it—which was not reassuring, given my record.

We let Bernie sit in once with Sasha Louise. Bernie's head looks like it's mounted on a gimbal. His Adam's apple is the ball joint, and it bounces up and down like a racketball when he gets excited, which isn't conducive to successful poker. Bernie lost his raisins quickly, which is pretty much what people have been saying for years.

Periodically, I stopped by the refrigerator to look longingly at the food there. In a day or two, the apple and the blood vanished from the freezer.

I was beginning to wish that Frido had been hit by a train.

Congratulations.
Whom Do You Suspect?

Three days later we began our descent back to Schuyler's World. I managed to get a day off, but the watches were rough on me, and they were also rough on Spooner even though she had Clyde to help. The *Scupper* doesn't fly well one-handed, and she had taken a beating. I suffered through on Leopard Milk and some other tinned stuff. The Leopard Milk actually eased my stomach somewhat.

Ironsides seemed to fade into the woodwork, and Bobo asserted himself more and more. He put out his long-awaited SOP, which eclipsed Number Two hold for sheer volume of manure, and began wearing his mate's cap all over the ship.

As far as finding a culprit, none of my facts seemed to go anywhere.

I spent a lot of free time by Catarina's door, and we talked about things we'd like to do and things in general. I forgave her when she explained that a Chinese voyeur was a Peking Tom. The one about the Chinese voyeur was almost as bad as the one about the carrot. The one about the carrot was "a pretty low hoe."

She could tell when I hit a low spot. The day before we were due to arrive, she asked me softly, "You're pretty down, Ken. What's really bothering you?"

I thought for a minute. "You know, at first, trying to figure out who Frido's murderer was was something exciting. Now, it's just a job, like repacking the starboard impeller."

"That doesn't mean it doesn't need to be done, although I'd rather not have you doing it."

"True. It does need to be done, and I guess I nominated myself to do it. Frido may have been a stupid, clownish, immature louse, but he was still *our* louse, and it's not something we can overlook."

"You've got a cop's mind, Ken. No, it's not something we can overlook. Are you sorry you got involved?"

"No, that's not it. When we get to Schuyler's, they'll figure out who did it and make him or her disappear. That's okay. But then they'll take you off the ship and make you disappear. And Iron-Ass will get himself another loan and hire another Frido and maybe another Elaine, and I'll probably tell him to shove it."

"You'll have Guild out-of-work benefits to tide you over. You'll be stuck on Schuyler's for a while, but you'll get a berth, probably a better one. You're good, Ken. Maybe better than this bucket deserves."

"This is going to sound crazy, but I like it here. It's almost funny, considering how many times I've threatened to quit."

"No, it's not so crazy."

I stuck my hand through the slot and twined it around a couple of her fingers. "Too much cargo in the hold for that. What do you think will happen?"

"To be truthful, I don't think Davie Lloyd is going to be able to get a big enough loan to bail him out of this, certainly not on Schuyler's. I doubt anyone else will try and fix the *Scupper* up."

"So we all might end up on the beach. What will you do?"

"I imagine my choices will be limited. Have you ever thought about a ship of your own?"

"Only about three times a day. I'd walk over hot coals to get one," I admitted. Her hands were warm and on her hand was a heavy seal ring I couldn't recall her wearing.

"It's my old school ring," she said, as if she were reading my thoughts. "Maybe I'll show it to you some time."

I nodded, oblivious to the fact that Catarina was not in a position to witness the gesture. "I'd still really like to solve Frido's murder before we have to turn the case over to the Navy.

All Schuyler's has is a class E naval base, so they're probably not going to be able to do a whole lot with it."

"How big is class E?" she asked innocently.

"I've been wondering what there was you didn't know." I thought for a moment. "A class E has trouble putting together a foursome for bridge. There's a passed-over commander in charge. I met him once, but I've forgotten his name. We'll dump the mess in his lap."

"Ken, I'll tell you this. When we get to Schuyler's World, everything will sort itself out. I can't tell you how or why I know, but trust me."

"Okay, I trust you. Did you knife Frido?"

She chuckled. "No. Did you?"

"It depends on who you talk to. The latest rumor in the corridors is that I bumped off Frido to enjoy the fair Wyma Jean's charms."

"Not a well-founded rumor. Clyde seems to have the inside track." She waited a moment. "Do you want to talk about the rest of it?"

I sighed. "I guess I'm just disturbed that one of my shipmates took a crack at me. Several cracks, in fact. Or maybe it was Clyde, who I'm actually beginning to like."

"I know. It hurts. And you don't even know which one."

We sat there for a few minutes. "Ken, you need to get some sleep," she finally said.

"Right as always. Okay. 'Night."

I had a few tins of sardines I was keeping in her room, where they couldn't be tampered with. She handed one to me and I stopped by the galley to open it, but for some reason they smelled a lot more like sardines than sardines should and I lost my appetite.

As I was standing there, I thought I heard a faint whisper of noise. I peered under the cabinets to find Bobo's cat.

"What are you doing under there, Sasha Louise? Haven't you learned it's dangerous to be wandering around here?"

McHugh, who was about the farthest thing imaginable from a cat person, had played skeet-cat with Sasha a couple of times, and I remembered Spooner telling me that Bobo had accidentally locked her out one night and Frido had spent a few hours following her around with an electric prod.

The cat tensed until she figured out who I was. Then she started licking herself.

"Okay, Kitty, it's your funeral." I noticed she had a little cup suspended around her neck with a little pair of dice in it.

"Want to wager?" I waved the sardine can enticingly, which brought her out double quick with her back arched. "Boy, I wish you could tell me what's going on around here."

I took the dice, flung them against the wall, and immediately crapped out. Snake eyes.

Before I could say anything, she pounced and batted the dice back up against the wall. Her first hit was a natural. After that, her point was six, and it took her a few taps to make it. Then she looked up at me and began licking her paws.

I gave her the can. She went through a couple of sardines the way Sherman went through Georgia, and then she carefully picked the can up with her mouth and trotted off.

"Goddamn," I said to myself. "Maybe the cat did do it."

I stood up and shuffled back to my cabin. Almost as soon as I had the door closed, I heard someone moving in the corridor outside.

"Who is it?"

"Wyma Jean. Please, Ken. Let me come in."

I walked into our common area and opened the door. Wyma Jean was standing outside in a blue silk robe with little dragons on it, so I let her in. Running one-handed watches had affected us differently. I was four kilograms lighter. Wyma Jean ate when she was nervous; she was fast acquiring a permanent case of rosy cheeks and beginning to bulge at the seams. She looked like a blue beluga whale.

"Catarina, Wyma Jean's here!" I called. "Wyma Jean, what can I do for you?"

"I need to talk, Ken," she said breathlessly. She looked around. "Do you always lock your door?"

"Lately, I've fallen into the habit, at least the door to my bedroom," I answered pointedly. "Don't you lock yours?"

"Oh, Ken! Don't shout at me! I can't stand it." She clutched me by the arms, dribbling mascara on my shirt.

"It's okay, Wyma. What's up?"

"I don't know how you stand it. You're different. You're like a machine, somehow."

"Not as different as you might think. It's probably the squeaky moving parts that fool you." I caught a whiff of stale beer. "You're here. What do you want to talk about, Wyma Jean?"

She pulled at my arm. "Not here. Let's go in your room."

I shrugged. "Enter into my parlor," I said, pulling free and sliding inside the door.

I had my souvenirs from the Schenectady market scattered on the desk, and she picked up a green can and began fumbling with it.

"Don't play with it, it's an aerosol and you'll get it all over the place." I took it away from her.

"What is it? I can't read the label."

"The label's in Arabic. Just don't play with the can, or you'll wish you hadn't. Wyma Jean, I don't mean to be rude, but I'm pretty tired. Is everything okay? How's Clyde working out?"

She stiffened. "Oh, damn that little sneak thief! I want you to take him. I want him off my shift. He hides things from me. I don't trust a word he says."

"Are you sure you can handle it alone? You're really not looking very good." Wyma Jean didn't look too steady on her feet, so I steered her toward the bed and pulled my chair over to where I could sit.

She pushed herself on to the bed and let her cheeks sag until the words came dribbling out.

"Ken, I don't know. It's frightening. Everything that's happened frightens me, and I think it frightens everyone else. I know you don't think Catarina killed Frido or did any of the other things, but why can't you just let it lie? You never liked Frido all that much. I was the only one who did, and he was a rat. Just like the other one is."

"Why do you say that?" I asked her. There were two people in this dialogue, but I wasn't sure I was one of them.

That really got to her. She pounded her fists on my pillow. "Oh, Ken! Why do you have to keep asking questions? Don't you think the rest of us have things we don't want people to know about?"

"Hold on. I'm not sure I understand. Maybe it would help you if we talked about it."

I have a talent for saying the wrong thing at the wrong time. She came off the bed with her eyes flashing. "Oh, don't you treat me like a child, Ken MacKay. You've got your vampire, Bernie's got his cat, Davie's got his ship. What about me? What have I got? A thief who doesn't tell the truth! You just tell me how it's going to help any of us to find out who killed Frido."

"Don't you want to see justice done to Frido?"

"Frido was then. This is now."

"I suppose," I said flatly.

That stung her. She stood up and put her hands on the arms of my chair so she could look me eye-to-eye. "Ken, Frido doesn't care anymore!"

I didn't want to say it, but I said it anyway. "But I do."

"Would you say the same thing if you knew that your friend Catarina killed him?"

"Probably. But she didn't."

Wyma Jean looked at me scornfully. "Well, Bernie thinks she did."

I nodded. "Bernie also thinks she turns herself into a pillar of smoke and comes sliding under the door."

She straightened up and closed her eyes. "You know, Ken, I keep thinking about you curled up in here with your books, looking down your nose at the rest of us. Frido was a rat, but at least he was honest about it." Then she sank back down on the bed and burst out crying.

It was a little awkward. I don't carry a handkerchief, and I couldn't very well offer her the corner of my shirt. I walked over and found a box of tissues, paper ones. "It's okay, Wyma Jean. Here."

She took one and dabbed at her eyes. "I'm sorry, Ken. I didn't mean to say that. I'm just so frightened about what's going to happen to us." She burped.

"I am, too. No hard feelings."

I listened for about twenty minutes more and ended up pushing her out the door.

"How'd it go?" Catarina asked after I got her out.

"I had a headache," I told her.

"What do you think?"

"Who knows?" I said. "Either she was being honest, or she needs some more acting courses."

I stretched out for a couple of hours, but I couldn't sleep. I got up and walked down to Ironsides's cabin to rattle his chain. He stuck his head out and looked about the way I felt.

"Davie Lloyd, open up the safe. I want to look through Frido's stuff again."

"What?" Ironsides asked.

"Open up the safe, Davie Lloyd. I want to see Frido's stuff," I said patiently. "I'm half the evidence committee, remember?"

Davie Lloyd puffed out his cheeks and tried to think of a reason to tell me to take it to the toads. Failing in this intellectual endeavor, he put on a bathrobe and walked with me to the bridge. I waved cheerily to McHugh and Dykstra while Davie Lloyd opened the safe. McHugh and Dykstra appeared somewhat surprised to see me.

Frido's stuff was still in the safe. The bags of powder were gone. Ironsides looked nonplussed.

"The white stuff seems to have disappeared," I commented.

"I wonder where it went?" Ironsides said weakly.

"I bet you're going to tell me Bernie has the combination inscribed on his lucky rabbit's foot, if anyone's interested," I added helpfully. "May I have Frido's junk to look at?"

I watched varying emotions pass across his face as he handed me the box. McHugh had her head turned. She started to say something, then bit her lip.

I stalked off to my boudoir, locking the door behind me.

Spread out on the bed to paw through, Frido's prized possessions didn't amount to much. I dismissed the polo shirts and the rest of the fancy clothing. That left junk food, a tawdry book that read like the *Kama Sutra*, another one entitled *De Vermis Mysteriis*, and assorted knicks and knacks. I opened up a bag of genuine Schuyler's World Brazil nuts and trickled them through my hand.

I stopped halfway through. One of the nuts felt smaller and lighter than the others. I looked around for something to crack it open.

The only tools I had handy were a screwdriver and the piece

of pipe I was carrying around in my pocket. I thought for a minute and then put the littlest nut in my pocket to look at in the morning.

I went into the bathroom to shower and shave before I went on watch. With the circles under my eyes, I looked like a raccoon. As I looked in the mirror, I noticed that there was a tiny crack in the bottom left corner.

"I wonder how that got there?" I asked myself. "This is wonderful, the mirror isn't the only thing that's cracked in this room. Not only am I getting paranoid, but I'm talking to myself." I thought for a minute more. "I'm mostly paranoid because someone's out to get me." It made me feel better, and a long shower made me feel better still.

I had the midnight shift. As I went down the corridor, I noticed Sasha Kitty had dropped a hairball by McHugh's door for her to find. Clyde was sitting at the board when I came on the bridge. "Evening, Clyde, how are things?" I asked.

He looked up. "Miss Wyma Jean is awfully mad at me. It looks like I'm on your shift now," he said in a subdued tone of voice.

"What did you do?"

"I don't know, Mister Ken. I just don't know," he said ruefully.

"You can speak English. Wonder of wonders. Stop it with the 'Mister Ken.' Ken is fine."

"Okay, Ken."

"I'm pretty used to running the ship by myself, so if you want to go spend time in the galley, it's all right."

"No, thank you. Miss Wyma Jean has been teaching me a lot about the ship, and I think I can help."

"You want to run through a check?"

"Sure, man." He ran through one. He was painfully slow, but thorough. "All green," he announced.

"Not bad. I'm impressed."

He smiled impishly. "It beats picking pockets."

"You spend your life on Schuyler's World?"

He looked down at the board. "If you don't mind, I'd rather not talk about it. That's how I got in trouble with Wyma Jean."

"Okay," I said, trying not to stare.

I read a manual and watched the board. We talked about thievery a little, and it turned out that Clyde had a simple, home-spun philosophy based on the ancient rule of "finders, keep-ers." The way Clyde explained it, anything that wasn't nailed down was his to find, and anything that could be pried loose wasn't nailed down. We were both laughing fit to die by the time he finished spinning it out. I let him go off for a cup of coffee, which he promptly poured down the drain in the head. "I keep forgetting how bad this stuff is," he said as he emerged, staring at the cup.

"Use my pot. I bought it on Schuyler's."

"When do we arrive there?"

I checked the board. "I'd say another twenty-nine hours in our present, crippled condition."

He slid back into his seat. "Ah, Ken . . ."

"What?" I asked mildly.

"Do you think maybe I could get into the Spacer's Guild?"

"Being realistic, probably not. The entrance boards are pretty tough, and if you have a prior conviction anywhere, you don't qualify. It doesn't make any sense to lie about it, because they'll find out eventually. They do background checks through the navy."

"Oh," he said. He thought about it for a few minutes before changing the subject. "Uh, Ken . . ."

"Sure. What?"

"Ken, Wyma Jean is sensitive about her weight. I don't know if she's ever told you, but she was really fat as a child, and she had to sweat off thirty kilos just to get into Basic."

"No, she never mentioned it. I'll keep it in mind."

"Thanks. She thinks a lot of you—she says you're a real sharp pilot."

"That's nice of her," I said awkwardly.

He stared at the board for a few minutes. "Ken, have you ever run your mouth when you shouldn't have?"

I grimaced. "Plenty of times. I managed to screw up a mar-riage in just six short months. You?"

"It didn't take me anywhere near that long to screw things up," he said, and that was about the last thing I heard from him for the next seven hours.

When I got off duty, I tossed my slacks over the chair, re-locked the bedroom door, and went straight to sleep.

Three or four hours later I dreamed I could hear Catarina calling to me faintly. I woke up when I figured out I couldn't breathe. Air wasn't circulating. There was a faint hiss from the duct.

I managed to snap on the light. I staggered to the door and hit the lock. The door wouldn't open. The electromagnet held firm; the lock was jammed from outside. I slammed my fist hard, which didn't do a thing for the lock or for my fist. Bright flashes clouded my vision.

I needed something to open the lock. The screwdriver was still in my pants, but it took forever to find the pocket. I concentrated on pulling the screwdriver out and grabbing the right end. Then I tried to switch it on.

I heard it buzz, but I couldn't see it spin. The blood was beating in my head and my ears. I tried to slam the business end in the keyhole. I got my left hand once, but struck the lock on the third try. The screwdriver shorted. I let it fall and clawed at the handle, dropping my weight against it.

The door slid open. I collapsed across the threshold, panting. Nothing had ever smelled as sweet. I must have passed out, because I woke up a few minutes later with blood all over my hands and a terrific headache. The common area was empty, but I could hear Catarina shouting and banging her fist on her door.

I was lying half in and half out of my room. "It's okay," I told her weakly. Then I threw up on the carpet and tried to clear away the haze.

"Ken, what happened? Are you all right?"

"Yes. No. Somebody tried to put me to sleep permanently. I cut my hand up." I staggered over to her door and stuck it through the mail slot to let her bandage it.

"Thanks," I said. I let my head clear. After a few minutes, I got up and limped to the outer door. The corridor was empty. I walked down to stores for another screwdriver and used it to unfasten the access panel in the corridor for my air duct.

The cutoff was tripped. A cylinder of carbon dioxide was jammed into the space, hissing away merrily. I grabbed it, slammed the valve shut, and flopped down beside Catarina's door again.

"What happened, Ken?"

"Somebody tried to kill me." I coughed and tossed my head to improve the oxygen flow. "Somebody piped carbon dioxide into my air duct and jammed the lock on my door."

"I heard someone come in. That's why I tried to wake you."

"Do you know who it was?"

"No. Normally, I can recognize footsteps, but whoever it was was trying to be stealthy, and I couldn't tell."

My breathing had returned to normal, although my head still hurt. "I figure once they came back and removed the carbon-dioxide cylinder, the natural assumption would have been that I had kicked off from natural causes." I looked down. "What did you use to wrap my hand?"

"One of my shirts."

I grinned weakly. "It's pretty well ruined. I guess that makes us even on clothing."

I could almost feel her smile through the wall. "At least."

"I think I'll be all right. I doubt whoever tried it will try again tonight."

"I'm going to stay awake and listen just in case. Rest in peace."

I grinned and went back into my cabin. Instead of sleeping, I pulled out the little Brazil nut and worried it open with the broken screwdriver. It split evenly into two halves, which was a little unusual since Brazil nuts are three-sided and I generally have to pound hell out of them to get them open.

I sat and thought about everything: Frido, the alien ship, the coin, the emerald, the paper shoved under McHugh's door, appearing and disappearing blood and powder. I'd managed to accumulate a fair amount of evidence, even though I didn't have the vaguest idea what it all meant, and I was getting pretty tired of having people take cracks at me. Whoever was trying to kill me was getting more sophisticated.

The thing to do was to treat it as an engineering problem. I'd used deductive and inductive logic to isolate the malfunction. I'd run diagnostics. I'd tested subsystems. I'd disassembled and checked everything, and I didn't have an expert I could call in to take the blame.

What engineers do when all else fails is hit the sucker with a bigger hammer. I curled up in my chair for two hours of scheming and then flipped on the intercom.

"Hey, Davie Lloyd, get everyone on the bridge in ten minutes. Everyone. Send Dykstra to help me break Catarina out!"

"Have you gone nuts, MacKay?"

"No. I'm going to show everyone who killed Frido. Get everyone assembled on the bridge, Ironsides. Or else." I flipped off the intercom.

I went over and rapped on Catarina's door. "Come, Watson. The game is afoot. I'm about to show who killed Frido."

Rosalee wandered in, wearing a dirty nightshirt and a hair net, with a crowbar in her hand. She just sort of ripped the retaining bar off, having practiced it once.

"Thanks, Rosalee," I said.

"Don't mention it," she replied, dropping the crowbar and shuffling off to the bridge.

Catarina emerged, dressed in black as usual. Her expression was grave. "Ken, do you know what you're doing?" she asked seriously.

"Sort of," I told her. "You'll not dissuade me, fair damsel, I'm tired of having people try and put me in the meat locker with Frido."

She smiled. "All right, Ken. I'll play. But when is the game not afoot?"

I looked at her for a second.

"When it is ahead," Catarina finished for herself. She patted me lightly on the arm. "Come on, let's get this over with."

Everyone else was gathered on the bridge when we arrived. Spooner had the board. Whoever had designed the *Scupper* had planned for alternate bridge configurations, so with the jump seats folded, we had a fair amount of space to spread ourselves on either side of the command seats. McHugh was standing there in her pajamas with her arms folded, looking less self-assured than usual. Dykstra was standing next to her, closer to the door, with her eyes shut and her chin on her chest.

Bobo was by himself in the corner to Spooner's right, holding

Sasha Louise and looking like a duck that's been hit on the head. As I walked in, Ironsides opened his mouth to say something, then closed it abruptly.

Catarina moved in next to my elbow.

I cleared my throat. "I suppose you're wondering why I've gathered you all here."

"Damn straight," McHugh sneered.

"Well, I'll tell you. I'm tired of having somebody try to kill me, so I'm going to tell you who killed Frido. I intend to reveal a murderer. But first . . . ." I held up two halves of a Brazil nut and then passed them around, making sure to give them to Spooner first.

"Frido left this nut behind. I figured out how to open it. Guess what was inside?" I pulled a small metal cylinder out of my pocket and held it up. "Frido left us a microtape. It was supposed to be his insurance."

I turned on Bernie. "This all came out of your smuggling scheme, didn't it? The white powder was supposed to go to the Rodents, Bernie. Want to tell us what the powder is? No? Well, we'll get to that later. Anyway, Frido was supposed to deliver the powder to the Rodent ship, but it never made it there, did it? Frido hid the powder in Number Four hold and asked for a cut, didn't he? That's why we screwed around on Schuyler's World for an extra two days."

Bernie's Adam's apple started working overtime, which was all the confirmation I needed. "No, no," said Bernie, with a startling lack of originality.

"Frido could've blackmailed you forever, so you shut him up, didn't you? But you made a few little mistakes, Bernie. You let one of the jewels you got from the aliens slip down the drain, and I found it in the grease trap." I held up the little emerald. "You needed somebody to take the fall for killing Frido, and you tried to pin it on Catarina. But you shouldn't have left the printout for McHugh and Dykstra. It pointed directly at you. Who other than our resident hypochondriac would read up on rare diseases?"

"No, no," Bernie moaned.

"You made some other mistakes, Bernie. Somebody used a hypodermic needle to poison my fruit. You're the only person on board who owns a hypodermic needle and has access to poisons. And you shouldn't have gotten rid of the evidence in the safe. You were the one with the combination! Naughty of you to create circumstantial evidence against yourself." I gave everyone present a half second to mention the needles in the ship's medical kit. Nobody did, so I drove on.

"You knew all about the Rodent ship and why they wanted to blow us apart, didn't you, Bernie? That's why you were scared even before they started shooting! You double-crossed them, that's why they wanted to kill us. And you knew about the powder, that's why you didn't want me to dump the holds!"

The real reason Ironsides and Bobo had objected to my dumping the holds was because it represented their profit margin going up the flue, but this was no time to be squeamish.

"Another tip-off, Bernie, was the fact that you were the only one who stayed on board ship while we were at Schuyler's World. That's why you needed Frido to move the dope!"

Unless, of course, the dope wasn't dope or Frido was smuggling it on his own, in which case most of my guesses were wrong, and I was going to come out looking like the south end of a northbound horse.

"No, no . . ." Bernie moaned again. Sasha Louise looked at him and jumped out of his arms to the floor. Cats are fickle.

I moved in close to where I could bore into Bernie's eyes. "About three hours ago, somebody tried to gas me in my room by opening a CO_2 cartridge in the hall access panel. I just figured out that you were the only one who could have been alone in the hall corridor at the right time."

"No, no," Bernie groaned. Out of the corner of my eye I watched Catarina daintily grind her foot into McHugh's instep before she could say something.

"Bernie, Bernie, Bernie . . . You couldn't keep your lies consistent," I said in a gentle voice.

Clyde was standing on Spooner's left with Davie Lloyd. I saw him stifle a grin and quietly move opposite Bernie.

"But your last and biggest mistake, Bernie, was not finding the microtape Frido left." I indulged in a little artistic license. "Frido was no dummy."

Bobo's head started bobbing back and forth.

McHugh glanced at Catarina. "I had a pet lizard that used to do that."

I held up my little metal cylinder. "Frido left this behind in a Brazil nut, and it's going to hang you, Bernie! Are you ready to talk?"

"Yes, yes!" Bernie whimpered. "I did it! I did it all! I bought the plants, I ground them up in the coffeepot while you all were asleep. I know it's wrong and evil to sell Rodent dope, but I had to have the money."

At that point, Dykstra woke up. A light went on in her eyes, and she poked her finger at Bobo's cowering figure. "It was you! That's why the coffee tastes like soapsuds."

"They paid me off in jewels. I gave the powder to Frido to deliver," Bernie whispered, "but he double-crossed me, so I killed him. I knifed him over the sink. I put the blood in the refrigerator to implicate Lindquist and left the printout where McHugh could find it. When Ken started to suspect the truth, I cut his lifeline and poisoned his fruit. Yes, yes, I did it. I did everything."

"The little gimp's been busy," McHugh acknowledged grudgingly.

"God!" Spooner said, turning her head around. "I didn't think anybody talked that way except in movies."

It was a full and open confession. It would have wrapped up the caper, except for the utter implausibility of it all and the pistol Bernie was holding.

"You may have found me out, but I won't stay and face the music. Nobody make any funny moves," Bernie said in what was intended to be a threatening manner. He waved the pistol feebly for emphasis. "As soon as we reach orbit, me and Sasha are going to leave in the lifeboat. Don't anybody try and stop us!"

"Nobody's going to stop you, but you know you'll never get away with this," Ironsides countered.

"You got that straight," Dykstra said. "That cat is probably the brains of the outfit."

"Oh, yes I will," Bobo retorted in what was evidently intended to be a nasty voice.

"How did you kill Frido, Bernie?" Catarina asked, ignoring Ironsides.

"I . . . I picked up the knife . . ." Bernie said in a faintly convincing squeak.

"This is going to be embarrassing," Clyde muttered. "In another five minutes, he'll be confessing to robbing stage-coaches and assassinating Julius Caesar."

"No, Bernie," Catarina said slowly, "you didn't kill Frido. You cut your food with plastic utensils."

"But he just said he did!" roared Ironsides.

"But . . . I . . . I did so kill him, I . . ." Bernie stammered.

"Oh, my God. As if we hadn't had enough flying fertilizer for one trip," Spooner exclaimed.

Taking advantage of Bernie's distraction, I whipped out my little green can and pointed it between his eyes. "Drop the gun, Bernie. Slowly. I've got you covered. Don't make me use this, or your sinuses will never be the same again."

Horror filled Boo-Boo's eyes. "What's that?"

"It's an aerosol spray can. It's filled with noxious gas. You didn't think they made spray cans anymore, did you? I picked it up on Schuyler's World. The bars there get a little rowdy. Wyma Jean, you saw me bring it back, didn't you?"

"Yes, he did, Bernie! He told me it was a souvenir he bought there, but he didn't tell me what it was!" Spooner exclaimed breathlessly.

Bobo let the pistol fall from limp wrist and nerveless fingers.

Catarina moved in and scooped it up. "All right," she said, "the party's over. Ken, what's really in that stupid can?"

I shook it up and moved next to her. "Generic cheese whip. Goat cheese, I think. You want to try some?"

"No." She shuddered, then waved the pistol. "Just drop the can, Ken. Bernie, you didn't knife Frido, did you?" she asked in a sweet voice. "You didn't even hold the knife."

"I . . . did . . ." Bernie exclaimed.

"But he just said . . ." Davie Lloyd roared from the other side of the command seats.

Catarina's voice echoed like a whip crack. "Shut up, Davie! No, Bernie. You didn't kill Frido, because I know who did. You didn't kill him, did you!"

"I'll never squeal!" he squeaked.

Catarina smiled evilly. "That's all right, Bernie. I know you didn't kill Frido, because I did!"

Spooner gasped, and my eyes widened. I had my hand inside my pocket. Gripping my little length of pipe, I whipped it out and smacked it down hard on her wrist. The pistol went flying and skipped past Spooner just as Ironsides blurted out, "Hey! You didn't. I did!"

The pistol bounced off Ironsides's shoes. He bent down and picked it up. Then he pulled another pistol out of his pocket and pointed the two of them at us. "I shouldn't have said that."

Catarina rubbed her wrist and smiled at me. "Ken, you're sweet. I love you dearly. But sometimes you're really stupid."

"But you said—but I thought—" I thumped my head. "Yeah, who am I to think?"

Ironsides was fiercely staring at Bernie. "You idiot! If you had remembered to tape up the box, this would have never happened."

"If you hadn't forgot and screwed up the watchlist so that I had to stay on board ship, I wouldn't have had to ask Frido to deliver your stupid box!" Bobo retorted with venom.

"Oh, be quiet! I got to think!" Ironsides held one hand with a pistol up against his head while he covered us with the other.

McHugh and Dykstra looked at each other. "Oh, Christ!" McHugh muttered. "That rips it."

"I don't understand." Spooner said.

Catarina began to explain. "I was trying to trick Ironsides into making an admission. I haven't been doing so well with this case." She reached up slowly and unpinned her butterfly. She opened the back of it and pulled out a little wafer with a metal shield on it. "It really is all over, Davie. I'm Lieutenant Lindquist, Naval Intelligence, seconded to Naval Criminal Investigation Branch. I am going to ask you to surrender. There isn't any place you can run, and anything you do now will just make it worse."

"Oh, wow!" Clyde said, edging a little closer to Ironsides.

"Oh, my God! We had a cop on board the whole time, and we lock her up!" Spooner observed.

"No! Stay away! I got to think," Ironsides said, pointing both pistols at Catarina and scowling.

"Why don't you tell us what happened, Davie," I said.

"What in hell do you think happened?" he hissed. "I needed somebody to take the box down. Frido was supposed to do it, but Bernie left the box open, and Frido must have figured out what the stuff was. Instead of bringing it along, he hid it, and we couldn't find it. We were going nuts because the Rats were going to cut our throats, and that idiot Frido thought it was just a big joke! When we got him in the galley, I grabbed him and shook him, but the stupid clown just giggled. We had to get the stuff, so I picked up the knife and held it to his throat. I threatened to kill him if he didn't talk, but I didn't mean it. Then the ship started bouncing, so Bernie ran back to the bridge to keep her from going adrift." He looked at the wall. "He just laughed at me. He thought it all was a big joke."

"And?" Catarina asked gently.

"Damn it, I tried to hold him but he slipped when the ship lurched, and I lost him. It was awful! He slipped. I didn't do it, he let his head slip."

"How did you know Catarina was a vamp?" I asked.

"Oh, Christ, you know Bernie. Bernie's afraid of any kind of disease. He looked it up right after she came aboard."

"You sure messed things up," Dykstra said with a trace of pity.

"What the hell was I supposed to do? We were going to lose the note on the ship," Ironsides told her. "We didn't mean any of it."

I looked at Catarina. "You're Navy! Then what you told me was phony. That means you're not a vamp!"

"Sorry, Ken," she said slowly. "I'm afraid that part's true."

I closed my mouth and then turned to Ironsides. "Why did you go after me, Davie?"

Ironsides hung his head. "Damn it, Ken. You were sniffing around. You would have found out. I would have lost my ship, everything. She's all I have."

Bernie just looked down and didn't say a word.

"Why you, Bernie?"

He wouldn't meet my eyes. "I couldn't go to jail and leave

Sasha Louise alone. I just couldn't," he explained, with more nobility than I'd given him credit for.

The damn cat almost did kill me.

"We knew the drugs were moving. We were pretty sure it was this ship. Davie, Bernie, it's over. Just give me the guns, and it'll be all right," Catarina said quietly.

"No!" Ironsides shouted. "We'll take the lifeboat."

"Now, listen. Frido's death was manslaughter, not murder. Don't make things any worse for yourself than they already are," Catarina said. She circled a few steps to her left, cutting Davie Lloyd off from the door. Davie Lloyd began turning in place like a dancing bear, the two snub-nosed six-millimeters in his hands as he tried to cover her.

"It's over, David," she continued in a slow, gentle voice. "Just give me the guns."

"No. Don't make me use these," Davie Lloyd said, his voice fraying.

"Look, David. I won't come any closer. But give me the guns. It's over. You can't lock us all up. And there's no place you can go."

"I'll . . . I'll tell them you all mutinied against me," Ironsides said, trying to work himself up to something.

"It won't wash. Why don't you give the guns to Bernie? Ken and I saved your life. You're not going to shoot us. Besides, they're not going to do you any good. I'm a vamp, remember?" Catarina flashed him a lazy smile. "You need silver bullets."

That froze Davie Lloyd completely.

"Just give Bernie the guns to hold and we'll talk," she urged. Sasha Louise vanished down the corridor, just like a sneaky cat.

Ironsides awkwardly pulled his fingers out of the trigger guards. As he turned to hand them to Bobo, Clyde leaped up gracefully and his right foot swung in a long arc. He caught Davie in the nape of the neck. The pistols went flying one way, and Davie Lloyd dropped as though he'd been kicked in the head, which he had.

"Petty Officer Witherspoon, at your service." Clyde sprung up lightly on his toes as Catarina scooped up the weapons.

A flicker of interest animated Rosalee's face. "That looked like fun. Can you teach me how to do that?"

Clyde smiled and nodded as he leaned over and patted down Ironsides and Bobo.

"This is crazy!" McHugh said. "I'm getting out of here before something else happens." She took off down the corridor. I heard her door open and slam shut.

I turned to Catarina. "You really took a chance with the silver bullet stuff, didn't you?"

"Calculated risk. I really didn't think he'd shoot. Besides, I'm wearing body armor under my clothing, just in case." She looked at me. "Should I ask you about that stupid cylinder you claimed Frido stuffed in a Brazil nut?"

"It's the battery from the coffeepot I bought on Schuyler's."

Clyde—Petty Officer Witherspoon—took three steps toward Spooner, but when he tried to put his arm around her, she jerked away.

Catarina looked down at the floor plates where Bobo was cowering with his head in his hands and Ironsides was rubbing the back of his neck, groaning. "We've got enough evidence for a conviction," she said. "When we make planetfall, hopefully we'll be able to wring enough from these two to identify whoever set the operation up. If they want to salvage anything from the wreckage, they'll spill whatever they know."

"Do I get to be captain again?" I asked. Nobody disagreed. "Clyde, will you and Dykstra weld these guys into their cabins? We'll stick them there."

"Good," Spooner muttered, "that'll get the lying cheat off my bridge."

If this had been a movie, we would have ridden off into the sunset while a couple dozen spear-carriers took care of the details. As it was, Catarina and I stood guard while Clyde marched off to clear everything moderately harmful out of the prisoners' cabin.

The two of them were not particularly effective housekeepers, and he had some tough choices to make distinguishing what had evidentiary value from what was too unsanitary to keep. I suspect he fed a lot of things he didn't want to handle into the disposal chute. It took about two hours to make a jail out of the place.

In the interim, we wrapped Ironsides and Bobo in sticky tape.

I wouldn't have taped them together if they hadn't tried to bump me off a couple of times.

After we got them welded in, we flipped coins to see who collapsed. Catarina and I ended up taking the next watch.

After things quieted down, I made a minor course correction. "Catarina Lindquist, why didn't you tell me you were Navy CIB?"

She smiled. "I wasn't completely sure you weren't in on the scheme. No, that's not true. I didn't trust you to lie convincingly." She turned on a grin and waved a finger. "Remember, you were going to stop swearing."

"Sugar and spice!" I said very loudly. " 'How big is a class E?' You were assigned to break up the smuggling ring, right?"

She nodded. "Right."

"Why you? Why somebody from Naval Intelligence?"

"The CIB boys are a little shorthanded, and they needed some fresh faces to work undercover. Besides, we needed to get the trafficking stopped rather quickly. There are political dimensions to all this that I'd rather not go into."

"All right. What about the crazy stories you and Clyde put together?" I asked.

Clyde walked in, presumably having no better place to be. "Our cover stories? Blame that on sector. The cover story they came up with had us being put off the *Potash and Perlmutter* for causing trouble," he said.

"The *Potash and Perlmutter*? That's old Jackie Stein's ship. I know Jackie, I roomed with his son. Jackie wouldn't do something like that," I exclaimed. "Jackie loves causing trouble."

"Sector missed that. They also missed the fact that the *Scupper* wasn't rated for passengers," Catarina explained. "After talking with Harry, I figured that you would have ripped holes in our covers in about five minutes, so we had to improvise. Did you know that Clyde majored in dramatics? It was actually a lot of fun." She nodded. "I'm still going to strangle a few people when we get back."

"It was still a pretty stupid plan you came up with," I persisted.

"After sector screwed up, we didn't have much choice." Clyde held his hands out in the universal gesture that said, *So sue me.* "We could have done worse. Who knows, maybe in about ten years Wyma Jean will start talking to me again. Besides, everybody we spoke with pretty much said that nobody on this bucket had the sense God gave groundhogs."

I put true feeling into my voice. "Well, thanks a lot!"

"On the whole, our cover wore thin, but it held up better than any man could have expected," Catarina said. A light came into her eyes.

"Oh, no. Sort of like a manhole cover?" I said wearily.

"Not bad, Ken. Not bad at all," Catarina said admiringly. "You recovered pretty well."

Clyde started laughing so hard, he almost fell down.

As the Poles say, "What could Adam have done to God to make Him put Eve in the Garden?"

Errands, and Biting Irony

We pulled into orbit twelve hours later. Catarina locked herself into her cabin and didn't emerge until nearly the last minute to beam a call to the port commander, Commander Hiro. He sent in the marines, both of them, Corporal Sin and Lance Corporal Trujillo. They arrived on the shuttle with a news type—marines never go anywhere without photographers.

Spooner volunteered to take the anchor watch, a little too loudly, and she refused to look at Clyde. Catarina tapped him on the back and shook her head. As the rest of us were about to board the shuttle, Dykstra watched the marines frog-march Bobo and Ironsides through the lock and spoke for all of us. "They're the ones going to jail. Why do I feel like I got screwed?"

I didn't say anything.

Spooner told Bobo, "I'll take care of your cat. I'll treat her like she was my own. Every ship has to have a ship's cat." Bobo thanked her, and for the first time in a while I saw him smile. We ignored the news type.

We also pulled Frido's body out of the freezer. The marines brought a bag to put him in. He was a very stiff stiff.

We drifted down in the shuttle. I looked out at the twinkling lights—both of them—of the city of Schenectady at dusk. Another reporter type in a brown beret and a military van driven by a yeoman named Bunker were waiting for us when we landed. We slid by the reporter and climbed in the van. Clyde and the marines got out at the city jail to unload prisoners. Ironsides wouldn't look me in the eye, but the last thing he said before they put him off was "I'm sorry we tried to do what we did to you, Ken. Now that that's all over, I feel kind of sick about that."

Somehow I did, too. "What about the rest of us?" I asked Yeoman Bunker.

"Sir, I have orders to convey you and Lieutenant Lindquist to see Commander Hiro. I can let the rest of your party off anywhere."

"Veinticinco de Mayo Boulevard and Esquimaux Street!" McHugh said loudly. We let her and Dykstra off there and continued on to the navy base, which turned out to be a building about six blocks away from the port where we'd started. Bunker parked the van and took us into Hiro's office.

The office was nice. You could lose golf balls in the carpeting, and the paneling was real wood. The desk was bigger than the bed I sleep in.

Commander Hiro was seated behind his desk with his feet propped up, studying what looked to be the local equivalent of *The Racing Form*. As we walked in, Bunker cleared her throat, and the paper and the soles of Hiro's feet disappeared quickly.

"Ah, welcome back to Schuyler's World! Please sit down," he said. Catarina and I shook his hand and settled into chairs on the far side of the desk.

"Can I offer you something to drink? Lieutenant Piper brought me the text of your transmission about your, ah, murder and a drug-smuggling operation. And a real ship-to-ship naval encounter!" His eyes started to glow. "I wish I could have been there." As I turned my head to look at Catarina, I heard a quick *whap! whap! whap!* like a couple of people knocking their Academy rings on the desk top.

"My earnest congratulations on a successful conclusion to your operation, Lieutenant Lindquist!" Hiro smiled a toothy smile. "Twenty-three."

"Thirty-four. You're too kind, Commander," she said.

I presumed the numbers designated their respective graduating classes. Regular navy types try not to talk like that in front of strangers, but I made allowances since Hiro had undoubtedly been stuck in this postage-stamp sideshow for what must have seemed like forever.

"And this is Mr. Mickey?" Hiro asked, eyeing me speculatively.

"Ensign MacKay. All the credit belongs to him," Catarina corrected on my behalf.

This time, I got the smile. "Ah, very good, Ensign! What class were you?"

Catarina coughed discreetly. "Naval Reserve."

Hiro lost his smile. The regular navy maintains a certain reserve toward the Reserves. "Ah, well. Good work in any case," he said, turning back to Catarina. "Special performance appraisals? Citations? What medal would you like?"

"Oh, nothing elaborate." She looked at me. "Perhaps a recommendation for a below-the-zone promotion for Ensign MacKay?"

"In the Reserve? No problem. I'll get the sector commander, Captain Crenshaw, to countersign it." Hiro smiled again. The regular navy considers a merit promotion in the Reserves the equivalent of a gilt potato.

"And perhaps also a small monetary award for Ensign MacKay," Catarina added, kicking me in the shin.

"Can I do that?" Hiro asked her tentatively. He looked toward the door. Yeoman Bunker stuck her head in the door and nodded solemnly.

"Under chapter seven of the Narcotics Control Act. It's provided for in the General Regulations. In a case like this where we have one smuggler's vessel destroyed and a second captured, there are excellent precedents. He acted at the risk of his life, I might add. It's all in my report." Catarina kicked me a second time for good measure. Yeoman Bunker nodded.

"Chapter seven, you say." Commander Hiro figuratively scratched his head. "Is it customary?"

"Yes, sir. And I can truthfully say that without Ensign MacKay, we would not have cracked the case the way we did," Catarina said, turning my lower leg into one large bruise as I was about to open my mouth.

Hiro wrinkled his brows in puzzlement. "But—"

"Ensign MacKay was acting in a purely civilian capacity when he helped break up the smuggling ring," Catarina added smoothly. "I was on active service at the time, so it would be inappropriate for me to accept any reward from public monies."

"How much do you think?" Hiro said, stroking his jaw. "Say, a thousand?"

"Make it five."

Hiro glanced at Bunker, who nodded yet a third time. "Well, by damn, we'll do it! Bunkie, draw up the paperwork!"

"Here's my preliminary report; that should finish things," Catarina said, handing over a thick wad of foolscap.

"Splendid. Now may I offer you a drink?" Hiro got up and walked over to a handsome, hand-carved vitrine.

"Does he know you're a vamp?" I whispered.

"He will." She coughed delicately. "I put it in my report. It would have come out anyway."

Standing beside the vitrine, Hiro turned his head around.

"Commander, it's in my report that I have McLendon's Syndrome," Catarina told him. When he blinked, she added, "I'm a vampire."

"Oh," he said. "I suppose I'll have to order you into quarantine. Honor system?"

"Yes, sir. I understand. I will be resigning my commission as soon as I finish wrapping up the loose ends."

What she said hit me like a brick.

"On behalf of the service, I wish to express my deepest sympathy, and I wish you a speedy recovery from your condition," Hiro said unctuously.

Reading my expression, Catarina elbowed me solidly in the ribs.

Hiro was lost in thought for a moment. "Go ahead and stay at our VOQ for now," he said. "It would be too much of a bother to place you in the hospital until we finish wrapping this case up."

He pulled out a bottle of sake and two glasses. After a slight hesitation, he added a third glass and came back our way. I had the distinct impression that he thought my Wavy Navy commission was more of a communicable disease than McLendon's. As he poured out a libation, he asked, "Well, is there any more business to attend to?"

I coughed discreetly. "There is the ship."

Hiro raised his eyebrows slightly as if I'd said something profound, apparently on the theory that it's not how well the horse talks, it's the fact that the horse talks at all.

"Ah, yes. We must convene a court in admiralty." He looked at his watch. "Lieutenant Lindquist, if you feel up to it, we could have it done in time to change for happy hour."

"Mess whites? I'm afraid I didn't bring any. Inconsistent with my cover."

"Then you'll go as my guest. Ensign Mickey, too." Hiro took up a miniature ship's bell and rang it.

"We accept," Catarina said, clamping a hand hard over my wrist before I had a chance to consider anything violent.

"Bunkie? Oh, Bunkie! We're going to have a trial! Draft up some charges."

His yeoman popped her head in. "Anytime you're ready, sir. Shall I bring out your wig and your robe?"

"Yes, I think that's appropriate. Tell Lieutenant Piper she's been detailed as defense counsel and have her confer with her clients. Say, five minutes?" He looked at Catarina—excuse me, Lieutenant Lindquist.

Catarina cut in. "Make it ten. Mister Ironsides sometimes needs to have things explained twice."

"Ten minutes then, Bunkie."

"Aye-aye, sir. They should be finished booking them over at the jail by now. I'll take Lieutenant Piper with me, and she can confer with them on the ride back." Yeoman Bunker took off, and Commander Hiro left to change clothes.

I leaned over and whispered to Catarina. "I don't get it. What's going on?"

"You didn't get any admiralty law at Woolmera, did you? Let me try and explain. A navy court in admiralty can only hear cases brought against ships for breach of contract or for tort actions occurring outside the inner atmosphere. It's really a sensible system; there's no skipper alive who'd want a jury box full of groundhogs deciding whether he clipped the station going past. Too many planets would try and pay their maintenance bills with traffic fines. Commander Hiro is going to try the *Scupper* for freighting contraband. Because Commander Hiro doesn't have jurisdiction to hear the criminal charges against them, Ironsides and Bobo will go back to Earth for trial in a Federal criminal court.''

"But why wouldn't they just deny everything if Commander Hiro can't hear the criminal charges?" I asked.

"Ah! That's what the navy likes to call Catch-22. Nobody ever lies in an admiralty suit, because if you're caught lying, after they finish with your ship, the court has jurisdiction to try you gleefully for criminal contempt. Criminal contempt is good for about five years, your Guild rating gets revoked, and best of all, it counts as a federal conviction for impeachment purposes. When you get to Earth for trial on Federal criminal charges, instead of having a fair to middling chance of beating the rap or at least conjuring a reduced sentence, you have the enjoyable task of explaining to your defense counsel why you can't testify on your own behalf without being crucified.''

Yeoman Bunker walked in a few minutes later, followed by Ironsides, Bobo, and a female lieutenant. Bunker coughed. Hiro hurriedly came back into the room wearing a white wig and black robe, and she intoned, "All rise."

Hiro nodded, sat down in his chair, and began thumbing through his manual. "I declare this court in admiralty to be in session. The Confederation versus *Rustam's Slipper*, Guild registry 19747. Said ship is charged with carrying contraband in defiance of Confederation law." He set the manual down, tilted forward, and looked directly at Ironsides and his defense counsel. "Lieutenant Piper, any motions?"

Piper stood up. She was a tall, thin woman with freckles and that wholesome, freshly scrubbed look the Academy cultivates. "Yes, Your Honor. The libelee would request a continuance."

Hiro swiveled his chair around and began twiddling his thumbs. "Grounds?"

"To retain local civilian counsel."

"Bailiff, are there any civilian attorneys on this dump certified to practice before an admiralty court?"

"Not as of two o'clock today, sir," Yeoman Bunker replied.

Hiro resumed twiddling. "Motion denied. Anything else?"

"In the alternative, we request a continuance to permit the true parties in interest to appear before this court," Piper threw out gamely.

"These true parties are just lienholders, right? Mister Iron-sides there is the registered owner of the ship?"

Piper nodded.

"What else you got?"

"In the alternative, we request a continuance out of consideration for general principles of equity."

"You've had a chance to see Lieutenant Lindquist's report, right? Motion denied. We don't grant the defense continuances in the hope that the witnesses die of old age. Any other motions?"

"Motion for a general dismissal based on striking irregularities in the investigation of this case."

"You going to make an offer of proof?"

"Are you going to enter Lieutenant Lindquist's report into evidence?"

"So noted. Lieutenant Lindquist's report is entered into evidence."

Piper shrugged. "In that case, we have no offer of proof, Your Honor."

"Motion denied. Anything else?"

"Motion for a dismissal based on failure to state a lawful charge."

Hiro turned to Yeoman Bunker. "What about it, Bunkie?"

"Sir, I got the stuff tested as soon as I let Lieutenant Lindquist and Ensign MacKay off. The substance in question is identified by the lab report appended to Lieutenant Lindquist's report. It is a prohibited substance clearly proscribed by clause nineteen of the !Plixxi*an treaty, incorporated by reference. Those are my initials on the chain-of-custody document showing I received the substance directly from Lieutenant Lindquist and handed it directly to the lab technician who administered the test."

I blinked in absolute amazement that she already had it done.

Hiro looked at Piper. "Is that the basis for your motion?"

"Yes, Your Honor."

"Denied. Do we need another lab test, recognizing there's only one lab technician on this planet?"

"No, Your Honor."

"Well, is that it?"

"Yes, Your Honor."

"All right. Does the owner of said vessel wish to make a plea?"

Ironsides looked at Piper, who shook her head from side to side. Ironsides shook his head rapidly from side to side.

"Excellent." Commander Hiro believed in short trials. "Any arguments, Lieutenant Piper?"

"Yes, sir."

Hiro looked at his watch. "We're running late. Bunkie, when's the last time we had a court?"

"A year ago last February, sir."

"Beam, were you planning on giving your widows and orphans argument again?"

Piper nodded.

"Okay, argument by counsel is duly noted. Bailiff, please enter it in the record. This court is ready to render a judgment and declares said vessel to be guilty as charged and decrees said vessel to be confiscated and sold at auction to satisfy any liens or judgments against said vessel, the residue to be applied to the public treasury. The court is now adjourned. Bunkie, clear my courtroom. Lieutenant Lindquist, you and Ensign Mickey please remain. Good job, Beam. Come over and meet our guests."

While Bunkie cleared the courtroom with unseemly haste, Commander Hiro introduced Piper to us. "Beam, this is Lieutenant Lindquist from CIB."

"Catarina, I know," Piper said taking her by the hand.

"And Ensign Mickey." Hiro made a motion with his hand in my direction. "He's a reservist, but go ahead and shake his hand anyway."

"L. J. Piper, call me, Beam, like the writer," Piper said extending a hand. "Pleased to meet you, Ensign." She had a firm grip.

"It's MacKay. Call me Ken." I rubbed my nose. "I don't mean to pry, but how do you get 'Beam' out of L. J.?"

Piper grinned. "Family secret. The day I was born, my father thought he was going to get a boy, and my mother was reading Tarzan. L. J. stands for Liana Jane."

"Leigh-Anna?" I asked.

"No, 'Liana,' as in the vine. I was 'Jungle Jane' all through high school. Call me Beam, or I'll break your kneecaps."

"It's a deal. Pleased to meet you, Beam."

Hiro glanced at his watch. "Well, we wouldn't want to be late. Lindquist, why don't you sign yourself into our Visiting Officers' Quarters. I'll have my chauffeur take you there, and then we'll head on over to the club. Oh, you come, too, Ensign Mickey."

"Visiting Officers' Quarters? Club?" I whispered.

Piper winked. "I have a back bedroom we use as a VOQ, and the Atlantic Hotel has a room they've contracted out as a club in return for social cachet and the chance to keep two sets of books. A lot of the smaller bases do the same. I'm about five minutes from here, and the Atlantic is about a block down the street. Come on, Bunkie should have the car out front waiting for us."

As we walked out to the car, Yeoman Bunker handed me a check for five thousand and a receipt to sign.

You can say whatever you like about the regular navy, they have a certain style.

Bunkie dropped me off at the Atlantic to check in. I really couldn't afford the place, since it didn't look like any of us would be seeing crew shares any time soon, but I figured that with a check for five thousand in my pocket, it would be nice for a few days until I could find something more permanent.

The room wasn't bad. It had interactive TV, one of those beds that try to massage you, and a biofeedback link—about what you'd expect, respectable but nothing spectacular. The bed was a waterbed, of course; solid-construction mattresses are one of those things that really aren't worth trying to ship, although I know a few places off-Earth that buy them just to be fancy. Schuyler's World was apparently not a garden spot for hoteliers—the Atlantic was a nice enough place, but you know they're shaving edges when the Bible and the Koran in your room are on computer.

I found a suit somewhere in my kit, got dressed, and went downstairs. The night clerk at the desk told me he couldn't cash my check, but he gave me credit on the strength of it. Then he rang a bell, and a waitress wearing nothing much steered me in the direction of the Officers' Club.

The O Club turned out to be a nice little room with three tables, one of which had a RESERVED sign on it. Catarina, Hiro, and Piper were waiting when I got there. Hiro raised his glass. "Ensign Mickey, glad you could make it! Oh, waitress! Another round here!" he said jauntily. "Mickey, the !Plixxi* ambassador called, and I invited him to join us. Lindquist tells me you've met."

"Briefly," I said. "Sir, this must be my day for asking stupid questions, but I've been wondering how a backwater world like this rates an ambassador."

"Ah, simple, Mickey! Politics! Politics! The !Plixxi* have an ambassador on Terra, but their representative here, Dr. Beaver, is well connected. As I understand it, it wouldn't do for him to have an inferior rank."

"He's part of the royal family of the major confederation there, and I don't think his father wants him too far away from home," Piper explained. "It makes sense, since most of their trade goes through here. He's very interesting to talk to. I understand he's an idealist of sorts."

"Yeah, I think you could say that," I said.

"What are your plans, Mickey?" Hiro asked, grabbing his drink as it came by and gulping it down.

Catarina smiled before I could answer. "I'm not sure he has any. Ken is on the beach, so to speak. A lot will depend on what happens to his ship—"

"She's even more of a wreck than usual, and for the time being she belongs to the Navy," I interjected.

Hiro frowned, trying to remember if a civilian was allowed to interrupt a lieutenant.

"If *Rustam's Slipper* is tied up here any length of time, Ensign MacKay and his shipmates will have to find other berths, which will be difficult," Catarina explained tactfully.

Hiro frowned again, then nodded at the logic of it.

"What is it we're drinking?" I asked, changing the subject.

"Martini, Mickey. Martini. Properly chilled, of course. The only civilized drink," Hiro said, snapping his fingers. "Oh, waitress! Another round of four here, please. I keep forgetting you're not academy, Mickey. Well, no harm in that. Some of my best friends never went to the academy. In fact, I married a woman who never went to the academy!" He looked down at his watch. "Beaver should be here any minute. I told him six-fifteen. Why don't you three youngsters chat while I hit the head. Give my regards to Dr. Beaver if he shows up before I return." Hiro marched off.

"Is he like this all the time?" I asked.

"As long as he doesn't get excited," Piper explained. "I expect you will have trouble finding a berth. There isn't a lot of ship traffic through here. Have you been here before?"

"This is my third trip, so I'm practically a native," I told her.

She nodded. "Schuyler's World just isn't an ideal place for distressed spacemen. Catarina mentioned that you're staying here at the Atlantic. Where are the rest of your shipmates?"

"Well, Annalee McHugh and Rosalee Dykstra are taking rooms down at the Prancing Pony, and they may take up bartending. Wyma Jean Spooner has the port watch. She's somewhere over-head reading romance fiction. Petty Officer Witherspoon is staying here, although he's not part of our crew, strictly speaking." Clyde was upstairs mooning into his beer.

"Last, but not least, Commander Hiro just packed your clients off to jail," Catarina added.

Piper smiled, then rubbed her chin. "Ken, I'm trying to remember, wasn't there another member of your crew?"

"Elaine O'Day, but one of the local magistrates sent her up when we were here a few weeks ago."

"Elaine broke out of jail," Catarina said seriously. "Yeoman Bunker told me while I was transmitting my report."

"I was wondering whether Bobo and Ironsides would end up in her cell. I figured it would either be poetic justice or cruel and unusual punishment. How did she get loose?"

"The usual. They let her out on work release. Like everybody else on work release, she disappeared. The locals probably figure it's cheaper than keeping her in jail and having to feed her. I'm not sure they're looking for her very hard."

"The wicked flee where no man pursueth. I'd have to agree with the part about feeding her. What's the problem?" I asked.

"Oh. Now I remember," Piper said. "She's sworn to get even with you and the rest of your ship's crew for cutting her adrift."

"It's not as if she left us a great deal of choice. How serious is she?" I asked.

"I read that she cut her wrist and wrote the message on the wall of her cell in blood," Piper said.

"That sounds sufficiently serious. Just a nasty suspicion, but you wouldn't happen to have exerted an influence on the judge who sentenced her, would you, Catarina?"

Catarina smiled a wicked smile. "Merely hypothetically, does five hundred in small bills qualify as influence?"

"God, were we outbid. Pretend I didn't ask. Merely hypothetically, I didn't think that the Criminal Investigation Branch did that sort of thing."

"Merely hypothetically, I would mention that I'm Naval Intelligence, seconded to CIB. In NI, we're accustomed to accomplishing the mission and worrying about the details later."

"Oh. Would Elaine be in a hypothetical position to find out?"

"I asked the docket clerk to mention the courtroom betting line, which might have influenced some of her remarks to Judge Osman. I would say that she has a strong suspicion," Catarina admitted. "We were improvising."

Piper rolled her eyes.

As Commander Hiro came over to rejoin us, the waitress escorted two stumpy beings in pinstripes over to our table. Dr. Beaver was in the lead. "Cheeves, how fortunate we are! Commander Hiro and Lieutenant Piper, how good to see you! And friend Ken and friend Catarina, what a joyous occasion this truly is!" he exclaimed, squinting in the bright candlelight.

They bowed low and then sat down across the table from Catarina and me. Hiro stood up and shouted, "Oh, waitress! Two honey-on-the-rocks, please!"

"I hadn't realized it when I spoke to you last," Beaver continued, "but I understand that friend Catarina has been cooperating with our government in a very delicate investigatory matter."

Cheeves whispered in his ear.

"It seems that there has been a problem with the smuggling

of pernicious drugs," Beaver said. "As Bucky says, 'It is a matter requiring our utmost vigilance to prevent great harm.' "

Catarina caught my eye and nodded. "I'm not sure if Commander Hiro mentioned this, but the !Plixxi* ship that was in port at the same time we were was implicated. They fired upon us without warning and succeeded in damaging our ship quite severely. Thanks to Ken's able ship handling, we were able to thwart their efforts until they destroyed themselves with an errant missile. I deeply regret that there were no survivors."

"Oh, dear! How dreadful," Beaver exclaimed. "I did not realize. Cheeves had the afternoon off, and perhaps I should have dealt with the mail. Well, as Bucky says, 'a clean mind and a strong heart weather every storm.' "

Cheeves whispered in his ear. Beaver stood up. "If you will excuse us for one short moment." The two of them went off to another table and began an animated discussion that sounded like a tape being played too fast.

Piper said something that occupied Hiro's attention, so I leaned over to whisper to Catarina. "That's just what I need. Homespun philosophy from something that looks like a melon with hair."

"Ken," she purred, "he does not! Look at those eyes, he looks just like a little collie!"

"He looks like a rat with a glandular problem," I whispered, scenting danger.

Catarina's eyes lit up. "Let's say we'll split the difference. We'll call him a cross between the two, sort of a Melancholy Baby."

I lowered my voice even further. "All right. I surrender. I'll behave, but I want you to know that was twice as low as a snake can go."

"Why, Ken," she said mildly, "that was very good."

Beaver and Cheeves returned, and Hiro broke off his discussion with Piper to listen. "It appears that the matter is even more serious than I could possibly have imagined," Beaver stated. He reached into his waistcoat and pulled out a hologram of a Rodent with a funny-looking mustache. "I regret that the captain of the vessel you engaged was my demi-brother Adolf. He always was a very peculiar child."

"Adolf?"

"He always wanted to go off and be a soldier and conquer something, in a small way. I'm surprised to see him commanding a ship—Genghis was always more the naval type—but Adolf and Genghis were always close, so I suppose that it's the personal element."

"Do you have other brothers?" Hiro asked.

"Two. Demi-brothers, actually. Surviving ones, that is. Cain and Mordred. Cain is the eldest behind Genghis, although he is not in the line of succession. He and Father had a falling-out some time ago. Mordred is the baby of the family."

"Did Cain's falling-out with your father involve any bloodshed?" Catarina asked.

"Well, something of the sort," Bucky admitted airily. "That was when Father decided it might be good to have me go off-planet and get in some diplomatic experience."

"Great family you got there," Piper said under her breath.

"I admit we all have our little differences, but what family doesn't?" Beaver said. "I shall have to acquaint Father with this news, and I suppose I shall have to go into formal mourning."

Cheeves whispered in his ear. Beaver nodded slowly, looking thoughtful, as well as shaggy. "Cheeves tells me that it would be prudent to consult with my government before discussing the matter further, but I look forward to meeting you again very soon, and as Bucky says, an anticipated meeting with friends is a reward for a day diligently spent." He and Cheeves got up, bowed, and left.

I looked over at Hiro, who was obviously in shock, and asked Catarina, "Did he just say we blew away Rodent royalty?"

Catarina nodded. "This could be a problem."

"We've got a wrecked ship, half of our crew is in jail or should be, most of us are broke, and now we have diplomatic problems," I said, "not to mention Elaine."

"Well, look at the bright side," Piper rationalized. "Things could be worse. Think of the alternatives."

"What alternatives?" I asked.

"We could be dead," Catarina explained.

"Commander Hiro and I really should be getting back, but I'd like to thank you for joining us, and I hope that we can all get together again, sometime," Piper said gracefully, helping a somewhat stricken Hiro to his feet.

"Beam, I have a key, and some things to do, so don't wait up for me. Have a good night!" Catarina said.

"Good night," I said mechanically. As soon as they were gone, I looked at Catarina. "I'm not sure what I've gotten myself mixed up in, but the last time I had fun, it was different somehow. What are your plans?"

"I'm going over to the jail now and see if I can persuade Davie Lloyd and Bernie to sing for their supper."

"So late?"

"Too much sun bothers me, or have you forgotten? I'm going to try to get as much done at night as I can. Beam said she'd check into finding some spare lattices for you tomorrow."

"That's good, but I'm not sure how it's going to help. It just hit me that my ship belongs to the Navy."

"Don't worry, Ken. Everything will work out."

"Yeah, I know. 'Trust me,' you said."

She patted my cheek and gave me a kiss. "You got it. Get some sleep and I'll talk to you tomorrow. You have Piper's phone number?"

"It should be listed."

"Okay. Good night."

I went up to my room. Before I went to sleep, on impulse I called room service and had a dozen roses sent to Miss Catarina Lindquist at 147 McKnew Street. While I was at it, I had them send a dozen dead ones over to Harry at the Prancing Pony.

The next morning, I got some oatmeal in the restaurant downstairs and called Piper to ask what the plan was for the day.

"Hello, Ken. Catarina's still asleep. You want me to wake her?"

"No, don't bother her. What are your plans?"

"I have to stop in at the office, and I want to check on those lattices your ship needs. You want me to drive you around later?"

"Sure, when can you get free?"

"How about I meet you for lunch? If Catarina's up and about, I'll pick her up, too." She laughed. "This is the most excitement we've had here in months. Usually, I spend most of my morning on correspondence courses and the crossword puzzle. Anything you need?''

"I need to go cash my check, so maybe I can walk over to a bank and do that now. I'm also thinking that since I'm going to be here for a while, I ought to schedule a dental appointment. It's been a while since I've had my teeth checked.''

She thought for a minute. "Dr. Denis is under contract to the Navy, he's not too bad. He might be able to squeeze you in. He might be the provider under your Guild insurance. Or do you still have Guild insurance?''

"Listen, your client may have been stupid enough to drop the ship's hazard insurance, but even Davie Lloyd is sharp enough to figure that if he drops our health benefits, he's going to wake up sucking vacuum the minute the rest of us find out. I'll give the dentist a call. Can I meet you in the lobby at noon?''

"Sounds fine, and I'll tell Catarina you called.''

"Thanks.''

I punched up Dr. Denis in the directory and called his office to make an appointment. The first thing he had was three-fifteen, and I took it.

The next thing I needed was a bank.

The day clerk was a little guy with a wispy mustache and a semidetached stomach who was busy counting room keys. I noticed his lips were moving. "Is there a bank near here where I can get a check cashed?'' I asked him.

He looked up and blinked. "Sure, sir. The Second Bank of Schenectady is a couple blocks away. In fact, just about everything in Schenectady is a couple blocks away. When you step out the door, go right out here on Ocean and turn left when you see Veinticinco de Mayo Boulevard.'' He looked past me, and his eyebrows curled. "Or is it left on Ocean and right on Veinticinco? I get these things so confused. Maybe I ought to call them.'' He made a dive for the phone on the desk.

A lot of people think that your typical pioneer on a new world is a truly noble soul, one of mankind's best and brightest, striding off to seek truth and opportunity while yearning to be free.

Noble souls tend to grade out at about two percent of the colonial population. Most of mankind's best and brightest stay home and tell each other how great it would be to be a pioneer while they're busy racking up a pile. The other ninety-eight percent of the people who go out to new planets tend to be screwups. Schuyler's World is not a garden spot, and may have gotten more than its share.

The desk clerk got the phone in one hand, and his eyebrows made another U-turn. "Uh, sir—you wouldn't happen to know the phone number there, would you?"

I waved him off. "Thanks, don't bother calling. It's okay, I'll find the place. Did you have trouble landing a job here?" I asked him conversationally.

"Oh, yes, sir! There must have been fifty applicants for my position. Fortunately, my cousin's the junior assistant night manager . . ."

I stepped outside, mentally flipped a coin, and headed right on Ocean.

Land around Schenectady was cheap, so the town was a little spread out. Some of the construction was brick and stone, but the majority of the buildings were one- and two-story plastic prefabricated frames. Plastic prefabs are cheap and reasonably temporary, and look it. Most of the ones in Schenectady could have used a good scrub; judging by the particolored stains, whatever passed for fruit bats found the eaves a handy place to digest dinner.

Ocean Avenue itself had waist-high trees with greenish gray fronds planted down the center meridian strip. They seemed to be fairly well fertilized. Schuyler's World was still a raw, frontier planet, but Schenectady was going to be a lot less raw when the town council put in storm drains.

Right on Ocean turned out to be a good guess. The bank was easy to find—it was the biggest thing around. People prefer putting their money in bank buildings where other people can't get at it very easily, and bankers pretty much have the same attitude.

I walked inside and got in line for the teller. Banks may have machines for entering deposits, machines for accepting loan applications, and machines for giving investment advice so that people can take a flyer on the ponies, but when it comes to handing out sums of money to strangers, I've noticed they like to add what they call "the personal touch." The teller was a cute brunette with braces. I handed the girl my check, and she asked me if I had an account there. I didn't, so she went back to show it to the manager.

The manager came out a moment later. He was a thin guy with capped teeth. "Welcome, sir, to the Second Bank of Schenectady, where the customer is always right, and may I help you, sir?"

"Ah, yeah. I have a government check here I'd like to cash, and I'd like to do a funds transfer from my permanent account."

He looked at the check. "Mr. MacKay, is it? You're from *Rustam's Slipper*? Have you been served?"

"That's me. Yes, I'm being served. The lady here was just helping me."

"Oh," he said. He handed me back the check and folded his hands together. "I'm so sorry, Mr. MacKay, but we can't accept this."

"What?"

"I do hope you'll stop by, again, and remember sir, at the Second Bank of Schenectady, the customer is always right."

"Now, wait just one minute here! This is a federal government check. I am not going to leave—"

"Ah, Bruno, could you come out here, please?" He turned his head, and a man stepped out with arms as thick as my thighs and knuckles level with his kneecaps.

The manager smiled. "Bruno, Mr. MacKay was just leaving; would you please see him to the door? Mr. MacKay, I am sorry that I couldn't be of more assistance, but I certainly trust you'll come back and bank with us again. Remember, at the Second Bank of Schenectady, the customer is always right."

"Ah, thanks. It's all right, Bruno, I can find the door." I walked out and headed back to the Atlantic, where my buddy the day clerk was waiting.

"Mr. MacKay, welcome back! How was your trip to the bank?"

"Putrid," I said briefly.

He blinked at me with a myopic look that meant he'd lost count of the keys and would have to start over. "Oh, well, I'm glad. Uh, sir, there's a lady waiting to see you in the lounge."

"Oh, sure. Which way?"

"Right down there, sir," he said, pointing.

I went down the steps into the lounge. The maitre d' was off somewhere, and the only booth that was taken was filled by a thin woman with curly hair and a turned-up nose. She was wearing a brown raincoat and a matching felt beret, and she had a big leather bag sitting on the bench beside her. She waved. "Hey, MacKay! Over here!"

I pointed. "I remember you. You're the reporter I stiffed at the airport yesterday. The desk clerk told me there was a lady looking for me in here. Did you see her?"

She nodded vigorously, which made the artificial flowers on her beret bounce up and down. "Bubbles at the desk meant me. Get over here. I'm Lydia Dare from the *Schenectady Post-Dispatch* and Channel 2 News—'People You Can Turn On.' I don't give up easy when there's a story to write. I've heard all about you and the Rodent ship." She held out one hand, which I ignored, and pushed a minicamera in my direction with the other. "Can I call you Ken? Tell me, Ken, what was it like?"

I held up my hand. "Slow up. Are we being recorded?"

She looked puzzled. "Of course. Why?"

"Just curious. Well, it was nice meeting you. See you around."

"Hey, where do you think you're going?" She planted her free hand on the table and started to rise.

"Out the way I came in," I said, heading for the door.

"You can't do that! I've got a deadline!"

"Watch me." I stopped and turned around. "My mother taught me not to molest children or associate with reporters. I'm not sure she distinguished between the two." I wiggled my fingers. "So, bye."

I left her sputtering something that I probably wasn't old enough to hear. Bubbles eyed me sympathetically as I came out.

"I'm not doing so well today," I explained.

"There's some mail here for you, sir. Maybe that'll cheer you up!" He rummaged under the counter and pulled out two fat letters.

"I wonder who these are from?" I said as I tore the first envelope open and looked inside. "What the heck is this?"

He reached up and pulled the corner down. "Hmmm, looks

like a court summons. My cousin got one when he ran into a fire hydrant. You don't know my cousin, do you?''

"No, can't say I do." I ripped open the other one and compared the two documents.

"The only person I know who drives worse than he does is his sister—''

"Uh, thanks," I said. "I've got to run."

Piper walked in to save me. I handed her the letters. "Beam, thanks for coming early! I'm being sued. Twice. You have some legal training."

Piper took the papers from me and glanced at them. "It says here you're being sued. Twice."

"Thanks for telling me that."

"The first one is by the Second Bank of Schenectady as the authorized representative for Galactic Life and Casualty. Galactic apparently holds the policy for Little Benny Finance Company, who's the mortgage-lender on the Rodent ship you popped off. The second one is from First National Bank of Schuyler's as the authorized agent for the J. T. Pollard Fertilizer and Feed Company. First National is suing Ironsides and each crew member individually for fraud, deceit, mopery, and dopery. They want to hold you all jointly and severally liable."

"What does that mean?" I asked.

"It means they don't care who they get their money from," Piper explained.

"I was just over at the Second Bank of Schenectady, and they wouldn't cash my check. Does that have anything to do with this?"

"Probably."

"Can they do that? I mean, is it legal?" I asked her.

Piper gave me a pitying look. "What do you mean, 'Is it legal?' These are banks. Of course not." She added, "Just remember, the first rule of law is that anybody can always sue for anything, and they usually do. If it makes you feel any better, in my opinion the second suit has no legal basis, and the first one is completely meretricious."

I gave it a few seconds and gave up. "Beam, I hate to have to ask, but what does 'meretricious' mean?"

She pursed her lips. "Well, it comes from the Latin word

meretrix, which means 'prostitute.' Does that suggest anything?''

"Thanks. What you said is good, right?"

"Well, you still may have a problem. I doubt that either Second Schenectady or First National would be willing to cash your check without trying to offset it against what they claim you owe."

"So I found out. Well, where's another bank?"

She rubbed her chin. "I'm not sure. Those are the only two banks I can think of on the whole planet. There is no First Bank of Schenectady."

"Absolutely swell. You mean I have a five-thousand-dollar check that I effectively can't cash?"

"That about covers it. You still have to declare the money on your taxes. You want to borrow a few hundred until you can pay me back?"

"Thanks, I may have to." I looked at her. "Why are you being so nice to me?"

"I'm Class of Thirty-four, too. I've known Catarina for ages. She asked me to keep you out of trouble, even if you are Navy Reserve."

"Do they train you all to be this sneaky?"

"It comes natural. You want to give Catarina a call? She should be up by now. She had a long night."

I walked over to the phone and punched the call in. "Hello, Catarina, you there?"

"Hello, Ken. Everything all right?"

"No. Actually, nothing's going right. You sound awful."

"I feel awful. I had a really severe allergic reaction to something I drank, and my head is splitting. I'm of two minds about going outside in the shape that I'm in. What are you doing?"

"Reading the want ads in the *Schenectady Post-Dispatch*. None of the banks will cash my check. They're suing us for umpteen million, and I don't have the damnedest idea why I feel so cheerful. What about you, how's the case going?"

"Down a drainspout," she answered.

"What's wrong? Won't Ironsides and Bobo talk?"

"Oh, they talked their fuzzy heads off, at least about the smuggling. They just didn't know anything. Whoever set up their little drug-running enterprise used drops and telephone messages. Ironsides and Bobo don't even know who they were dealing with. I can't even tell you whether it was a human. Piper's put in a petition to have mental evaluations done on them.''

"Most people in prison are mentally defective. How else would cops catch them? So where do we go from here?''

"Ken, truthfully, I don't know." She sounded tired. "I'm not sure where I go with it. This investigation of mine is really interfering with your life, isn't it?''

"Well, the last time I spoke to McHugh and Dykstra, the general consensus seemed to be that Ironsides and Bobo did everything they confessed to, and that I'm a horse's ass for proving it. I wouldn't have missed a moment, though, and with my talent, I could have screwed up my life just as thoroughly without any help from you.''

That got a slight chuckle out of her. "Thanks for the flowers.''

"No problem. When am I going to see you?''

"You're in the Atlantic? Look for me in the lobby around six.''

Piper and I grabbed some lunch. Then we walked around to a couple of places to find some lattices and didn't.

Crossing back over Ocean Avenue to where she was parked, I nearly got run over by a car with a bumper holo of a cat holding a sign reading, HAVE YOU HUGGED YOUR CAT TODAY?

I hopped back on the sidewalk. "He drives the way Davie Lloyd flies.''

"Transmission holograms are getting cheaper and better every day," Piper observed.

"Maybe that's what I ought to go into, marketing holos of cats. Holos have all the advantages of live cats and none of the disadvantages," I said, stepping back out into the street.

"I have the feeling that there's some angle you're missing. I'd work on it a little more.''

"Maybe we could rig it so they irritated people every twenty minutes, like real cats.''

Despite the glowing WALK pictogram, another car came whizzing by and almost clipped me. I got the distinct impression that on Schuyler's World, traffic signals were considered optional.

"Or maybe I could set up a driving school," I said. "There seems to be a need."

"They were probably just making aesthetic statements about the way you're dressed."

I stopped in the middle of the street. "I don't see why you all pick on what I wear. I am dressed perfectly fine," I exclaimed, holding my arms out. Another car came skimming past, a look of panic on the driver's face. "I like wearing solid, basic colors, like green and blue."

Some of the people walking by looked over, mildly interested. Piper grabbed me by the arm and yanked me the rest of the way. "They're fine colors, Ken, just not together. Oh, there's a bakery—you want to stop and get something?"

She bribed me into good behavior with a chocolate croissant, then said, "We still have another hour until your dental appointment. If you want a lawyer, I know one who might be able to help."

"Is he any good?" I asked.

"I didn't say that. However, he's close, he gives free initial consultations, and he's the only lawyer I can think of who has any interest in admiralty law, at least the only one not in jail."

The shyster in question, Jimmy Omura, P.A., turned out to be a stubby guy with a baggy suit. He started getting excited when I explained my predicament and showed him the writs.

"This is fascinating. This is absolutely fascinating," he said, pacing the carpet and gesticulating. "This is a lot more fun than helping people cheat on their taxes! As I see it, this is a perfect General Average case. There's never been one in space before, you know. This is fascinating."

Some people are not meant to wear clothes off the rack. When he raised his arms, most of his jacket followed, which gave him a distinctly hunchbacked look.

"What is a 'General Average' case?"

"Oh, General Average is a universal principle of maritime law, you know, boats and things? It's, uh, illustrated by the Rhodian dictum that if merchandise is thrown overboard to lighten the ship, the loss occasioned for the benefit of all must be made good by the contributions of all. The fascinating thing is that it's never been applied to space before. The principles are the same, so it should.''

I looked at Piper, who shrugged helplessly. I tried to bring Omura closer to the planet I was sitting on. ''I don't know that dumping cargo to lighten a spaceship would help a whole lot. Mr. Omura, let's backtrack for a minute—what is Rhodian law?''

''Oh, you know. Rhodian sea law, from the Greek city-state of Rhodes, sixth century B.C. or thereabouts. Simply fascinating!''

''Oh. That's what it is,'' I said in a very small voice.

''Fascinating stuff, really. It's amazing how advanced those Greeks were in some respects. Of course, the quote I just gave you is merely illustrative of modern General Average law, it's vastly more complicated than not. Vastly . . .'' He waved both of his hands.

''I see.''

''This will be a first! And, of course, the rest of the case is just dripping with wonderful, unresolved issues. We have criminal misconduct on the part of Captain Ironsides, piracy on the part of the ship from Dennison's World with no clear !Plixxi* third party left alive enough to join in any action, seizure by the Navy—not to mention an unlawful assumption of command by you. It simply astounds me that all this is wrapped around a perfectly splendid General Average case. Two banks, three insurance policies—why, this could litigate for years! It could go to the Confederation Supreme Court!''

''The Supreme Court. Do you have a railroad on this planet?'' I asked, holding my head. ''I'd like to go lie down on the tracks for a while and wait for a train.''

He pursed his lips. ''I really can't say for certain. I don't do ground-transportation cases.''

''Uh, let's talk about my case some more. If it goes to trial, who wins?'' I glanced over at Piper and made circular motions with my finger in close proximity to my temple.

''Oh, the judge will tell us that. That's what he's there for, isn't he?'' He reached over and pulled out a reader. ''Let's look in 41 Interstellar Jurisprudence 3rd and see what we have here under *Indemnity*. I'll have my secretary type up a representation form. Oh, I can't wait to file motions!''

"Uh, thanks," I said, looking at the heel of Piper's boot, which was delicately poised to grind my toe into the carpet. "I need to think this over. I'll get back with you."

We stepped outside into the sunlight. "Aside from you and Catarina, the last forty-eight people I've met, worked with, or tried to pick up have uniformly had difficulty navigating through doors and around corners. Is it me?"

"You probably attract them. Birds of a feather and that sort of thing." She left me to hang for a second or two and then asked demurely, "You were expecting sympathy?"

"Class of Thirty-Four, huh?"

She dropped me off at Dr. Denis's just in time for my dental appointment. The receptionist was buffing her nails when I walked in. She had her hair cut shorter than mine and wore a stone like the rock of Gibraltar on her left hand.

"I'm Ken MacKay. I'm here for my appointment."

She tapped the mouse on her computer. "You're a spacer? Please fill out this form, and write your Guild number in at the top. If there are copayments involved, we'll have to ask you to give us a check made out on an account at a local bank or pay in cash. Is that okay?"

"Uh, sure. Cash, then."

"That'll be fine, and if you'll please have a seat, Dr. Denis will see you in a few minutes."

I sat down, completed the form, and pawed through a stack of six-year-old magazines. At the exact moment I found one worth reading, Dr. Denis's assistant, a tired-eyed woman with red hair, called me back.

"Mr. MacKay? I'm Janis. Dr. Denis is ready for you."

"Call me Ken. Pleased to meet you. You look like you're ready to go home. Am I your last appointment?"

"You sure are. Then it's heavy Heineken time for me." She looked at me sympathetically. "Relax. I can see your pulse jumping from here."

"I'm just nervous because people have been trying to kill me," I lied.

She lifted her head as she sat me in the chair. "Have you been here before?"

"No. Why do you ask?"

"Your face looks familiar. Oh, I remember. You were the one on the newscast." She giggled. "Should I call you Captain Teach?"

"Who?"

"You know, the pirate!"

"*What?*"

"I always watch Lydia's newscasts. She's demanding a full and open investigation into your acts of piracy. She sure has a temper! I'm glad she's not mad at me. You look better in person. Should I ask you for your autograph?"

"What? No!" I shut my eyes. "Swell."

"Usually there isn't any news, so Lydia has to make some up. Things would get pretty dull around here otherwise." She giggled. "Well, if you'll just sit back, I'll let you down and we'll get started. Oh, does this mean you're going to make your copayment in pirate treasure?"

"No," I mumbled. I looked over at her tray and pointed. "What's that?"

"That? That's a needle. It's for anesthesia."

"Don't you have an anesthesia machine?"

She shook her head. "There's nobody in Schenectady who can do the maintenance."

"Swell. I'm back in the Dark Ages."

She giggled, then she stuck her head down the hallway. "Dr. Denis, we're ready here."

A few minutes passed. "Dr. Denis, I said we're ready!" she called again. A minute or so later, she cupped her hands and yelled, "Menace! Will you get in here!"

"Swell," I said.

Doctor Denis appeared. "Pleased to meet you, Mr. MacKay." He shook my hand. "Now, you're here—"

"Just for a checkup," I said hastily.

"All right, then. We'll do an ultrasound to see if you have any decay, and then we'll do some cleaning and scaling. Open your mouth wide and bite down on these so we get a good clear picture."

I bit down on the pieces of plastic that he stuffed into my mouth, and they bit back.

"This will only take a moment." He giggled, which sounded better coming from his hygienist.

I started counting to sixty.

"Ah," he said, looking at his screen, "your teeth are lovely. No sign of decay, and not a trace of inflammation around your gums. It appears all we need is a little light cleaning and scaling. Oh, may I take another picture? I collect teeth of interesting people, and yours have such nice, long roots."

"I exercise them by biting people who want to take pictures of me," I told him, trying to whisper with my mouth full of plastic.

"No?" Dr. Denis sounded disappointed. "Oh, well. You know, that picture of you on the news looked exactly like you. Just relax, now, and remember this won't hurt a bit. Janis, would you please turn the music out there up?"

The song was "Why Do Fools Fall in Love, and Why Do Dentists Lie?"

At six, I found Catarina sitting in the hotel lobby. "Hi, how do you feel?"

"Better. Better than you look. You depressed?"

"The press has me depressed. Is that the line I'm being set up for?"

"You're getting better at this. Did you notice the pickets outside?"

"Oh, no!" I rushed over to the window and pressed my face against the glass. Five people were marching around in a circle carrying signs. "Who are they?"

"The Animal Rights Support League," Catarina explained. "Did you see the signs?"

" 'Rats are Man's Best Friends,' and 'Rodents Need Love Too—Shoot People, Not Rats.' I'd give them an A for effort and a C for content."

"I talked with them on the way in. They're very well-meaning and very confused. Also, all three members of the local chapter of the Associated Civil Liberties Union held a press conference to announce they're filing a lawsuit against you."

"What! For what?"

"They're still working on that, but they're sure you must have violated somebody's civil rights."

"Why me? Why not Davie Lloyd? He's the one who smuggled drugs and knifed Frido."

"Ken, Davie Lloyd is a criminal defendant—he's got rights." She chuckled. "Seriously, Beam tells me that you've gotten caught up in the local politics. There's a bill in the legislature to allow importation of Rodent agricultural labor. Since every action in politics that doesn't involve giving away free money has an equal and opposite reaction, the local unions and the local bigots have formed a coalition to 'Keep Schuyler's World White, Black, and Yellow.' The other side is gunning for you."

I sighed. "I don't suppose it would help if I made a public statement that some of my best friends are Rats when they're not shooting at me."

"Trust me. It wouldn't help." Catarina parked her elbow and put her chin up. "Complicated?"

"I could have some safe, dull job, like wrestling alligators or defusing live ordnance."

She nodded. "Some people are just lucky."

"How about we dodge the press and the pickets and go do something?"

"Look, Ken, I've lost most of the day being sick. I need to spend some time on the computer running down leads. Maybe we could get together tomorrow."

"Okay, that's fine."

She left, and I took a walk out to the Prancing Pony. Harry had a new sign: PLEASE DON'T SHOOT THE PIANIST. HE'S DOING THE BEST HE CAN. He had made Rosalee his new night bartender, which left him time to supervise his clientele and avert the more obvious forms of mayhem.

Schenectady's men liked their women—well—hefty, and I could tell from the shiner one guy was sporting that Rosalee had already caught on to the finer points of her job. I waved to her and then spotted a couple of familiar shapeless shapes hunched over a table. The taller one waved back at me.

"Friend Ken, it is indeed a pleasure. Fortune has blessed us and paved the roadway beneath our feet! Come, join us!"

"Dr. Beaver. I'm surprised you're still talking to me," I exclaimed.

"Oh, tush! Ken, you know I would never allow mere politics, particularly sibling politics, to interfere with my friendships. As Bucky says, 'Friendship, once gained, is greater than gold or bills of credit.' "

Cheeves chimed in, "What His Rotundity is attempting to imply is that his demi-brothers have a distressing propensity to shorten each other's life spans, and this situation is not precisely unique."

"Indeed, I sometimes ask what's one demi-brother, more or less. The succession quarrel seems to be heating up this year, eh, Cheeves? What does this make, three brothers and a couple of cousins?"

"More or less," Cheeves agreed. "Friend Ken, His Grace believes that his demi-brother Genghis contrived to place demi-brother Adolf in an embarrassing position, so he does not see any need to blame you at all."

"Oh, indeed. I'm sure that you were merely doing your duty as you saw it, and, as Bucky says, 'Right thinking sometimes requires forceful action.' Since Father announced his imminent retirement a few years ago, it seems as though every month there's another funeral to attend. Such a beastly bother! Friend Ken, I forget—just how long is a month? Is it thirty days or thirty-one?"

"Yes," I said.

He twitched his nose. "I understand from friend Catarina that you disarmed two armed ruffians in succession on board your ship. I am most impressed by your fortitude in handling dangerous situations so deftly."

"If I were any defter, I'd merely be clumsy," I said ruefully, and gave them an edited version of the day's events.

"Well," Beaver commented, "I must say it sounds like you have had a very trying day. Still, as Bucky says, 'Tomorrow is always better because it means you lived through today.' "

I spent a few idle seconds puzzling this one through and changed the subject. "Dr. Beaver—"

"Oh, please, friend Ken, call me Bucky!"

"Uh, Bucky, I've been meaning to ask why the original Bucky Beaver is so popular on your world."

"Ah, friend Ken! An insightful question! I believe that it is the crystal clarity of Bucky's moral philosophy that is so appealing. The intellectuals find it all the rage."

"But the Bucky Beaver stories are kind of . . . simple stories, aren't they?" I said, trying to find a polite way to say they were simpleminded.

"Oh, tush, Friend Ken. Tush! Their depth is incredible. I myself don't fathom half of it. Why, take the incident in 'Bucky Beaver Meets Bun Rabbit' where Bucky takes a respite from his labors to do good in order to mail a postcard to his friend Woody Chuck. The deceptively simple act of mailing a postcard obviously symbolizes Bucky's internal struggle over whether to lay down his burden, as Su-jen points out in his commentary. Bucky's triumph over his own doubts assured by that one apparently insignificant act, he strives on."

Cheeves dipped his nose in his honey.

I was obviously out of my depth. "I always sort of thought that maybe he just wanted to say hello."

"Friend Ken!" Beaver observed sadly, waggling a digit in the air. "You've obviously grasped the inconsistency, in a fumbling way, of course, but you fail to take it to its logical conclusions—you really should read Su-jen. Hypothetically, why would the author inject such a transparently trivial irrelevancy into such a profound work. On the surface, it in no way advances the plot. It is the deeper, psychological meaning which stands out. I am saddened, because unless you strive to plumb the hidden depths of these majestic tales with the wellsprings of your soul, you will not grasp the full richness that Bucky represents. Time will bring you to a fuller understanding. Don't you think, Cheeves?"

"I, myself, sometimes find the commentaries inspiring," Cheeves admitted.

I thought for a minute. "Ah, Bucky, if Bucky Beaver stories are such a hot thing on your planet, how is it that you were allowed to pick the name?"

Beaver looked somewhat crestfallen—which is to say the feather on his hat drooped. "I tell you in confidence, friend Ken, I owe it to my father's influence. It would not have been decorous to allow a commoner, however exalted, to bear the name, but I am still troubled that it was I, admittedly unworthy, who was selected.''

Cheeves pulled out his pocket watch and opened it. As Beaver opened his mouth to continue, I saw one of Cheeves's eyes shoot open.

Bucky took the hint. "Oh, dear me. Friend Ken, I enjoyed our discourse immensely, but I fear the press of time must draw me away. As Cheeves has reminded me, your little encounter has created some work for us back at the embassy. I sincerely hope to continue our discussion under less adverse circumstances. Until then, as Bucky says, 'A ray of sunshine should guide your way.' ''

As he and Cheeves waddled out the door, Harry came over to fill the void. "Hey, Admiral! How's business? I heard all about your little shoot-out in space. Anything you want is on the house.''

"No, thanks. I'm fine. How much did McHugh and Dykstra tell you?''

"Most of it. You going to tell me about the battle? God, I wish I'd been there!''

"I wish you'd been there, too.'' I thought for a moment. "Maybe another night, if you don't mind. I'd just as soon not talk about it.''

"No problem, Ken. I understand. Say, did you hear the joke about the cart horse named Absence that kept getting lost?''

" 'Absence makes the cart go wander'?''

"You heard it.''

"Sorry, Harry. Somebody got to me first.''

"Well, then, did you hear the one about—''

" 'Old whine in new bottles'?''

Harry's brows knitted. "How did you guess?''

"I think I'm getting psychic in my old age,'' I said with a straight face. "Have you seen Catarina?''

"She was here a little earlier. She told me you might not want to talk about the battle just yet. Well, I understand. Keep giving them hell, Ken!'' He punched me lightly on the shoulder and headed off.

I rubbed the sore spot and wandered over to the bar. Rosalee poured me out a limewater and tried spinning the glass so it stopped in front of me. I caught it before it went off the end.

"Hi, Rosalee, how're things?"

Somebody down at the other end of the bar yelled for a beer, which she sort of slung at him as a graceful way of suggesting it wasn't polite to interrupt a conversation. "Things here are okay. Bed, board, salary, and tips—I guess I can't complain. Whenever Harry yells, I just tell him to go stuff it. He likes that." She picked up a static cloth and began wiping glasses. "If you're wondering whether I'm mad at you, I'm not," she added after a minute or two. "Things could have worked out better, but you know how that goes. You know, I even sort of miss that slimeball Frido."

"Let's not get too carried away with nostalgia," I cautioned. "Has Lydia Dare been by here to interview you?"

Rosalee nodded. "She's been by. I said I'd give her an enema with her camera if she came back."

"Lydia seems to be having trouble putting together a story."

I noticed a couple of dejected-looking customers trying to work up enough courage to order drinks. Rosalee flipped her static cloth up on her shoulder. "Ken, I've got to get back to work."

"Thanks, Rosalee. Enjoy your evening." I polished off my limewater and decided to call it a night. About three blocks from the hotel, it started raining, which meant that my luck was holding. When I got back, I finally remembered the question I wanted to ask Rosalee, which was how often you had to water the mushrooms in the baskets behind the bar.

Before I went to sleep I called the local library on impulse and scrolled up some poetry books on the monitor—some Yeats, some A. E. Housman, a little John Donne. It's amazing how much you forget if you get away from it.

Piper phoned the next morning, and I went down to wait for her in the lobby. My buddy the hardworking desk clerk was scanning the newspaper in slow motion. "Are the pickets gone?" I asked.

"Sure, they knocked off when the cameras left and haven't been back." He reluctantly began sorting through the mail. "Did I tell you my brother-in-law got interviewed once?"

"You must have," I said, looking for the bathroom or some other place to hide.

His brother-in-law made the nightly news for raising miniature pigs and dressing them up. Bubbles assured me that pigs were actually very intelligent animals—much smarter than dogs. That made sense; I even knew a dog that liked reporters.

I almost kissed Piper when she walked through the door five minutes later.

"Hi, Beam. Where's Catarina?" I asked, dropping Bubbles in the middle of a long sentence.

Piper pulled off her navy cap and brushed back her short hair. "I let her off at the installation before I swung by to collect you."

"How is she?"

"Still sick as a dog, but she'll be okay. She didn't have any luck trying to piece together who set up the smuggling operation. She's plugging away, but it looks like this one will take a while to crack."

"Good. I mean, about her being okay. I've been thinking, it doesn't make much sense to go look for lattices because whoever ends up with the *Scupper* is probably not going to want to fix her up."

"Probably not," Piper agreed, a little hastily. "Have you thought about what you're going to do?"

"No, but I can't afford to stay here. Can you think of a place?"

"There are cheaper places down the street. Why don't you check with Witherspoon—he found an apartment, and he might want a roommate."

As we walked out to her car, I told her, "I ran into Ambassador Beaver last night."

She smiled. "Did you ask him all about Bucky Beaver?"

"Well, yeah. I just didn't understand the answer."

"Ken, Rodents love Terran literature, but they don't understand the sex—not that humans do either. Bucky Beaver is very big. I understand they've printed nine editions of the collected works plus several compendiums. On the finer points, there are several competing schools of scholars."

I gazed heavenward. "Swell."

"Don't write them off as feebleminded," she cautioned as

we got in and pulled away from the curb. "I've talked to quite a few of them. Once you get past the stuffiness, every last one of them has a quirky sense of humor buried someplace. They surprise you."

"Even Ambassador Beaver?"

She waved a finger that wasn't gripping the steering wheel. "Just keep an open mind, Ken."

"Are you suggesting the Bucky Beaver cult is a planetwide joke?"

"Or worse. Nobody who's studied the Rodents is really sure."

"How are they set up politically?" I asked, trying to digest this.

"Well, it's difficult to describe. Think of it as feudal anarchy. It's actually kind of a touching story of how local boy makes good with unwitting help from pink, yellow, and brown aliens. The first contact ship ran into Beaver's grandfather. Most of the planet was semi-industrial then, and he was running one of the less primitive societies as its semihereditary caudillo."

"Is this the usual story?" I asked. The Contact/Survey Corps are the Navy's missionaries. On average, the Contact boys are noble, kindhearted, and puppy-dog eager to uplift their fellow beings—the kind of people you'd like to get into a poker game. Intelligent beings aren't that common in the universe, but a few of the more sophisticated races have played absolute hell with the Contact boys.

"The usual," Piper explained. "Grandfather figured out how to talk to the Contact boys long before they figured out how to speak Rodent and sold them the usual bill of goods."

"What did they give him? Guns?"

"Not guns. Not even the Contact boys are that stupid. Besides, it's illegal. They did give him industrial technology that they *thought* he had, and what they thought was a *small* Confederation developmental loan. To prime the pump, so to speak. Grandfather turned out to be the original John D. Rockefeller in a furry suit, and the developmental loan he negotiated was approximately equal to the Gross National Product of any two of his competitors. The rest is history. He didn't conquer the planet so much as buy it. Politically, the place is still pretty chaotic, but economically the planet is locked up. The old boy's son—Beaver's father—has a dozen marriage alliances and three digits in every pie that has a crust and berries."

"What does Bucky think of his father?"

"Oh, he's all right. Dr. Beaver doesn't talk about him much. He managed to outlive all his siblings and most of his descendants, which means he's not an idiot, although he's still an industrial pirate at heart. Fortunately, he's not as sharp as Bucky's grandfather was, otherwise he'd probably own Earth by now. He's getting pretty old, though, and the family faction fights are ferocious. Dr. Beaver is the pacifist in the family, and I understand he got shipped out here to keep him out of the line of fire. Here we are—why don't you stow your duffel bag in the trunk?" Piper slid the vehicle into a parking space.

Catarina was waiting for us, dressed in black silk from head to foot to protect herself from sunburn. "Come on in, Ken. We were just about to auction off the *Scupper* in Commander Hiro's office."

"So soon?" I asked.

"Yeoman Bunker did the public announcements yesterday while we were still in orbit. She thought it would save time."

"I see."

There were about a dozen people seated in Hiro's office. The auctioneer was a cadaverous guy in a black suit, and he was already beginning to announce the rules of the auction as we walked in.

"Ladies, gentlemen, and other beings, for a valid auction, there must be three registered bidders and three responsive bids. The bidding will commence at four thousand, this sum to cover port fees, court costs, and auction fees against the vessel. Subsequent bids must be in multiples of five hundred. The person whose bid is highest must present cash or a certified bank check amounting to not less than twenty-five percent of his or her bid at the conclusion of the auction, and must pay the remainder in cash or by means of a certified bank check within twenty-four hours. The successful bidder will acquire complete and clear title to the vessel and its present cargo, subject to the settlement of four complete crew liens and one partial crew lien outstanding."

One of those crew liens was mine. I hoped for Ironsides's

sake that they gave him the death penalty—there were banks on three worlds holding what was now unsecured paper, and they were going to be very upset.

The auctioneer continued. "The cost is one hundred to register as a bidder, and ten to reserve a place as a spectator, the sums collected to go to the Navy Welfare Fund. I would ask all persons who have not already registered or secured a place to leave at this time."

I turned to Catarina. "I guess we've got to go."

She laid a gloved hand on my arm. "No, I already signed you and Beam up. You ought to stay and see the show."

"Well, okay. I guess I ought to see who my new owner is going to be." I'd never seen a ship auctioned off, and I was interested in seeing who would bid. A small tear came to my eye. Watching them knock down the old bucket was like seeing them foreclose the mortgage on Grandma's farm.

"I shall begin the bidding." The auctioneer took a deep breath and began a quick patter. "Four thousand, do I hear four thousand?"

One little guy I didn't recognize in a suit and a beard raised a finger.

"I hear four thousand, do I hear four thousand five hundred, do I hear four thousand five hundred?"

"Somebody might actually get a bargain out of this," I whispered to Catarina. "The wheat in Number Three is worth about four times that much if somebody can figure out how to get it to market."

The auctioneer must have seen somebody signal because the next thing I heard was "I hear four thousand five hundred, do I hear five thousand, do I hear five?"

Catarina made a fist with the arm nearest me and held it level with her stomach. She then slapped it firmly with her free hand, propelling the point of her elbow squarely into my short ribs and jarred me somewhat. I started.

"That's five thousand to the man in dark blue and pale green, registered bidder number three. That is five thousand going once."

Looking around, I saw the little guy who had opened the bidding sneaking out the door with his beard in his hand. I also noticed that I was the only person in the room wearing dark blue and pale green.

"Going twice . . . And this auction concludes. The vessel and its cargo is sold to bidder three for the sum of five thousand. Please give your cash or certified check to the cashier. Thank you all."

The reward check was burning a hot little hole in my pocket.

"Congratulations, Ken," Piper said, pumping my arm up and down.

I reached down and pulled my reward check out of my pocket. "Listen, Beam . . ."

Piper smiled. "It's a Navy check, and this is a Navy auction."

Catarina was standing next to me, brushing open her veil, and I noticed Yeoman Bunker and moved in next to her. "I don't know what to say," I told them. What are you supposed to say when your friends set you up for your own good? I thought for a moment. "What's a ship like the *Scupper* usually *run*, a couple or three hundred thousand?"

Piper shrugged.

"About that," Catarina said.

"So I got a real bargain. Weren't there any other prospective bidders?"

"Well," Catarina said airily, "there were a couple of people who were interested, but we talked to them."

"Oh," I said, "what did you tell them?"

"We pointed out a few obvious problems, the crew liens that had to be satisfied, the holes in the hull, the fact that a new lattice will have to be freighted in," Catarina explained. She looked at me. "Beam and I did some more calling around to try and locate one last night."

"Not to mention the fact that the ship needed a new computer and has operated at a loss for the last three years," I said agreeably. "So I now own a wrecked ship with no prospect of repairing her?"

"Free and clear," Piper chipped in. "More or less."

"Well, I suppose I could always try and sell her for scrap if all else fails," I said lightly. A little voice inside me was saying, *You'd rather cut off your left arm at the navel.* "I don't suppose anyone has any ideas on where I'm going to find the cash to fix her up?'' Somewhere in my stomach was that feeling you get when your friends have given you a helpful shove off the diving board and you're wondering if there's water in the pool.

"Oh, something will turn up," Catarina said, winking at me. "Trust me."

As I say, there's a certain style to the Regular Navy. "Well, we've got a couple of hours until Frido's funeral. Let's go celebrate." I offered each of them an arm.

"We really ought to stop by the Rodent embassy instead," Catarina said. "Beam spoke with Cheeves. The mailship is due in tomorrow, and it wouldn't hurt to make sure Bucky's father views our little run-in with Adolf in the best possible light."

"Not a bad idea. How often does the mailship come through here?"

"It makes a monthly circuit. It stops here, loops over to Dennison's World, comes back, and then continues on to either Brasilia Nuevo or Esperanza, depending on the schedule," Piper explained. "It's the Foxtrot Echo 7—'Fast Eddie.' ''

I nodded. "I know Fast Eddie. We hit a lot of the same planets."

I opened the door for Catarina, and she cursed softly as she stepped out into the sunshine.

"I'll polarize the windows," Piper offered as we climbed into the vehicle.

"Thanks, Beam, I appreciate that," Catarina replied.

"How did you end up with McLendon's, anyway?" Beam asked.

"I'll tell you later. Ken's not old enough to hear this story."

"Maybe when I'm ninety," I suggested.

"That sounds about right," Catarina said.

At the embassy, Cheeves was waiting for us at the gate with—so help me—a parasol. "I thought that this might be most appropriate for the lady," he explained.

I gave him a look, but Catarina took it in stride. Inside, the !Plixxi* embassy was tastefully furnished, mostly with Early American beanbag stuff.

"His Rotundity," Cheeves said deferentially as he led us into the drawing room.

"Ah, friend Ken, friend Catarina, friend Beam, welcome."

Dr. Beaver stood up from behind a knee-high table and solemnly shook each of our hands. "Cheeves and I were just discussing the implications of what has transpired."

"Refreshments for the ladies and gentlemen?" Cheeves inquired.

"Honey and water is fine for us all," Catarina said.

With a nod of approval, Cheeves disappeared.

"Where is the rest of the staff?" I asked.

"Actually, Cheeves and I are here by ourselves for the time being," Beaver said jovially. "The First and Second Secretaries fought the most ridiculous duel a few weeks ago—it was entirely against my precepts and the wisdom of Bucky, as I told the survivor before I put him on a ship and sent him back to Papa. And we had to get rid of the last set of servants—I don't mind them skulking about searching for things that my demi-brothers can use against me, but I insist that they refold clothes neatly when they paw through them. It will probably be another month or two before we can get replacements. Until then, Cheeves and I will just have to soldier on as best we can."

Cheeves appeared among us a moment later with large and very square glasses of amber liquid.

I took mine gingerly. The technique seemed to be to cup the glass in both hands and stick your nose in.

"Anyway," Beaver said, motioning Cheeves to pull up a beanbag and join us, "Cheeves is absolutely insistent that he go back on the mailship and give a personal account of what transpired with poor Adolf's ship. He seems to think that if he does not, my other demi-brothers might try to make Papa think that there was something improper about it. Can you imagine?"

"Well, it seems like a very good idea for Cheeves to go back," Piper said carefully. "Just to make sure there are no misunderstandings."

"Oh. Well." Beaver seemed nonplussed. "Papa was always rather sweet on poor Adolf and tended to overlook his less obvious shortcomings. Still, his guilt in the matter seems so apparent that I thought a simple report would explain things perfectly." He twitched his whiskers, which was apparently the Rodent equivalent of a wink. "We had such fun composing it.

It was so much more interesting than the usual dry economic stuff we usually have to deal with.''

"Still, I think it would be much nicer if your father got a personal account rather than just a dry report," Catarina said. "I'm sure it would comfort him in his grief."

"But, dash it all, it would be such an inconvenience not to have Cheeves here," Beaver said diffidently.

"If I may insist, sir, the delicate political situation at home requires my presence," Cheeves remonstrated. "I feel that it would be most beneficial if I were to personally bring the details of Prince Adolf's unfortunate demise to your dread and august father's attention."

"Oh, nonsense, Cheeves! We need to work out all the details first. You know there's nothing Papa hates more than loose ends. We still don't know who masterminded the drug operation. We'll send Papa a full report, and you can catch next month's mailship and explain everything to him. I quite don't know how I should manage without you here."

"Are you quite sure, sir?"

"Quite sure, Cheeves. I would be utterly lost here without you," Beaver said firmly.

"Very good, sir," Cheeves said in a squeaky but distinctly glacial tone of voice.

"I've been wondering, could Adolf have run the smuggling operation?" I blurted out.

Beaver stroked the ends of his whiskers. "Well, I had a very high regard for my dear, departed demi-brother, but his mental capacity was not . . . well . . . oh, you tell them, Cheeves!"

"What Dr. Beaver is trying to say is that there is a very low probability that Prince Adolf is the criminal mastermind you are seeking," Cheeves translated with unruffled composure. "He exhibited difficulty operating complicated modern devices such as doorknobs."

"A birdbrain like Davie Lloyd?" I asked.

Cheeves ruminated over this. "Perhaps a very small bird, sir."

"We've considered that hypothesis and discarded it, Ken," Catarina said. "Unfortunately, the investigation is still hung out to dry, with no real leads and no clues." She gave me her "don't mess with me" smile and added, "Clues-pinned."

Beaver appeared to be lost in thought. "A mystery, a true mystery. What was it that Bucky said about mysteries? 'They hone the keen edge of one's intellect.' "

"I believe he was referring to the *New York Times* crossword puzzle, sir," Cheeves interjected.

"No matter. Friend Ken, I understand that you are helping friend Catarina with the investigation. I hope that both of you are able to visit my planet to pursue your inquiries. I think that it would be perfectly splendid if you could be my guests!"

"Dr. Beaver, hypothetically, in case your father takes this wrong, what's the penalty for helping blow away the flagship of your merchant navy and sending Prince Adolf to his just rewards?" I asked warily.

"Oh, ritual castration, I'm sure, but I hardly think it will come to that."

"Maybe a visit would be a good idea in about five or ten years," I said, tugging hard on my belt loops. "I hesitate to ask, but are you absolutely sure that it wouldn't be a good idea to send Cheeves? Uh, what would Bucky say? Cheeves, can you help me out?"

" 'Moral fortitude sometimes requires great sacrifice,' " Cheeves interjected smoothly.

"Oh, drat it!" Beaver stroked his whiskers again. "It's so tiresome to have to waste Cheeves's talents on political sorts of things, and I would miss him unbearably." He slapped what could have been his knee. "It's so hard to make decisions like this. I understand there's a new miniseries coming on, 'Jude of the D'Ubervilles.' "

"I could arrange for carry-out popcorn, sir."

"It's not the same, Cheeves," Beaver said stiffly.

Cheeves reached into a waistcoat pocket for his ace in the hole. "Sir, I should mention that friend Ken has been earnestly searching for lattices for his vessel. He is, as I understand it, quite bereft without them. I believe that I would be able to locate some if you would allow me to return. I have even taken the liberty of preparing a contract for him to sign."

"Cheeves, why didn't you mention this earlier?" Bucky

scolded. "Politics is one thing, but a gesture of friendship is quite another. Of course, you shall go without delay!"

"Very good, sir," Cheeves said in a distinctly warmer tone of voice. "I shall extend your profound condolences to help your father bear up."

"Yes, yes, Cheeves. Stiff upper lip, and all that," Bucky said impatiently.

"My cranial anatomy makes it somewhat difficult for me to comply with your wishes, sir."

"Do your best, Cheeves, and hurry back. I shall miss you for as long as you are away!"

"Thank you, sir. I shall miss you as well. I shall endeavor to justify your confidence in me."

"I have utmost confidence, Cheeves. You are a veritable wizard at these political things."

"I admit to some small study of the habits of my species, and strive to be of service," Cheeves said modestly. I saw him put his hands up against the sides of his head. I didn't understand what was going on until I saw Catarina's eyes gleam.

"You pull habits out of Rats?" she asked.

"Where's the contract? Give me a pen. I'll sign!" I said quickly.

Cheeves and Catarina exchanged significant glances. "Penitant, are you?" she said.

Beaver's whiskers twitched, and he chimed in, "A penetrating analysis. Ink-cisive!"

Catarina responded, "Merely inst-ink-tive, Doctor. Some of us are born with the write stuff for good punmanship."

Piper started grinning and slapped me firmly between the shoulders to clear whatever was causing me to choke.

"Ah, pardon me, my dear friend Ken," Beaver said, pulling something that looked like a tablecloth on a chain out of his pocket and mopping his brow. "I was caught up in the rapture of exchanging discourse with another scholar of your language. Friend Catarina, I did not realize you had hidden talents!"

I groaned very softly.

"We should discourse on the nature of puns at another time, perhaps," Catarina suggested diplomatically.

"If I may, sir," Cheeves interjected, "I will go pack my things."

Beaver nodded contentedly. "Well, now that we've settled business, would you three consider staying for lunch? I have some new lines of philosophical inquiry that I would like to try out on friend Ken. As you know, we Rodents normally refrain from eating meat, but I do believe Cheeves could whip up a fricassee of lizard parts."

"Perhaps a small salad instead," Catarina said, studying my face. "We have a funeral service to attend this afternoon for Ken's shipmate, Frido Kundle, and we are fasting."

After we ate, Piper drove us over to the funeral parlor on Esquimaux Street. They do nice cremations, and Harry had gotten us a reduced rate. They had a pretty display set up for Frido, with his urn set up in a niche beside a silk wall hanging and a sprig of white plumeria.

Annalee, Rosalee, Harry, and Clyde were all waiting when we arrived. I was surprised to see Harry—I wasn't aware that he even knew Frido. Clyde, of course, had made Frido's acquaintance after Frido was already dead, which was probably a wise move on his part.

Clyde spotted us as we walked in and slipped up beside me. "I understand you're looking for a place to stay. I've got room."

"Thanks, Clyde. I appreciate that."

We couldn't afford to shuttle Spooner down for the ceremony, so we let Rosalee do the reading. The only religion Frido had was sex, so we'd decided to open things with a passage from the *Kama Sutra* and a moment of silent reflection.

Rosalee yawned her way through it—it had apparently been a lively night at the Prancing Pony—but she put some real feeling into it, which was nice.

Harry started weeping halfway through. For reasons which may or may not have had anything to do with the solemnity of the occasion, nobody made any smart remarks. When Dykstra finished and lapsed into repose, I put an arm over as much of Harry's shoulder as I could reach. "Hey, big guy. What's the problem?"

"It's just not right," Harry insisted, wiping his eyes.

I blinked. "Come again? I missed something."

"I mean, Frido died in combat. Well, not really, but I mean, you had a battle on the trip, and he got killed, maybe not in that order, but it was almost like he died in combat. He should have gently slid over the side of the ship sewed up in sailcloth with a grapeshot at his feet, like they used to do during the age of fighting sail," Harry said dreamily.

I wasn't the only one he lost. "Say what? Fighting what?" McHugh rasped.

"We don't have any grapeshot," Rosalee observed. "We don't even have a cannon." Rosalee was inputting data faster than she was writing it to disk.

"You know, wouldn't it be nice if you could have let Frido float free in space forever, gently resting in the great ethereal void? Instead of locking up his ashes in a coffee can," Harry persisted.

"Yeah, we should have made that goddamn Kundle into an orbiting road pizza," Annalee said succinctly.

"I don't know, anything as big as a body would be a navigation hazard," Rosalee said.

Catarina jerked her head to signal me.

"What's the deal, Harry. You're not usually this gloomy," I said slowly.

"Ah, well, it's . . . It's Frido. He didn't exactly die in battle, but it's sort of like the same thing."

It was becoming obvious that this discussion had a great deal more to do with Harry's state of mind than it did with Frido.

"Harry—" I started to say.

"Well, damn it, Ken! I got kicked out of the Navy before I ever did anything. What do I do? I tend bar," Harry moped.

Clyde gave him a sympathetic look.

"Noble profession," Rosalee said without intending any irony.

"You don't know what it's like," Harry said gloomily while we all stood around and fidgeted.

"And we don't want to find out," Annalee said under her breath. "Can we get this over with?"

They'd selected me to do the eulogy because Wyma Jean was in orbit and most everyone else was in jail. There isn't much you can say about somebody whose ambition in life was to be stunt man in a porno film, but I gave it my best shot.

"Dearly beloved, we are gathered here to mark the passing of our shipmate Frido Kundle. I didn't know Frido long, or well. None of us did. None of us tried to. He wasn't particularly intelligent . . ." I was having trouble reading my notes.

"He was dumb as a post," Rosalee said in her sleep.

"He had children and loved life. He wasn't particularly nice as a person, but he was ours. He has a family somewhere, and they probably deserved him, and we probably did, too. And if we helped to make him what he was . . ." I faltered.

Catarina picked up the thread. "I hope we do better if the opportunity comes along again. Thanks, Ken."

And that was it. Clyde nodded again, and Rosalee lifted her chin and opened her eyes. Annalee stood there with her arms folded, defiant to the last. By custom, Frido's ashes would ride out free aboard the next mailship back to his family.

I think it was the sort of ceremony Frido would have liked. And when it was over, two cops were waiting there to arrest me.

The tall one spoke. "Uh, Mr. MacKay?"

"That's me," I replied. "What can I do for you?"

"Uh, sir. We have orders to take you in." He let his hands rest on his gun belt, and his partner sucked in his breath.

"That's not quite what I had in mind when I asked what I could do for you. You boys want to tell me why?" Although I was learning to take little things like this in stride, I still got that feeling you get when you're out in a boat and you feel water in your shoes.

"Well, sir. We have instructions to hold you as a material witness on suspicion of piracy," the short one explained.

I shook my head. "That doesn't even make sense." Noticing that there was blockage on the line, my shipmates gathered around.

The tall cop slapped his gloves against his free hand. "That's what they wrote down, and we got to bring you in. I guess the sheriff thinks you're a dangerous criminal, like the lady on the news said."

For some reason, this all seemed perfectly normal. "Catarina, I think I need help."

Catarina lifted her veil. "Piracy is a federal crime. Your local authorities have no jurisdiction," she observed, for once openly puzzled.

Annalee was more open in her sentiments. "What a dim bunch of hicks! Ken, maybe they'll put you in Elaine's old cell."

"If they want me around as a witness, I'm easy to find. It's not as if I'm going anywhere. Is somebody running for office or something?" I saw a warning light beginning to glow in Harry's eyes.

"Well, yes, sir," the short one admitted. "Both the sheriff and the city attorney are running this time around." He added eagerly, "It looks like we're going to have some really tight races, especially the sheriff's race. The old sheriff—the one who got voted out last election after the papers said he was corrupt— he wants his job back. This time around, he's the Reform candidate. Sheriff Jamali is running as the incumbent. After we drop you off at the station, we've got to go out and start rounding up campaign pledges."

"For which side?" I asked.

"Both sides. We're career employees."

"Look," I said, rubbing my temples, "I don't mean to fuss, but I am getting real tired of being pushed around. I have almost been murdered three times this month—"

"Four times," Clyde interjected.

"Thank you, Clyde. I have almost been murdered four times this month, and it's making me crabby. Now, if you arrest me, I am going to sue everybody I can think of including that reporter for false arrest."

I had my eyes on Catarina, not the cop, and she nodded. "And," I continued, "with a little luck, I'll collect enough from all of you to fix up my ship and live happily ever after. Now you call your sheriff and tell him what I just said. Okay?"

"Sorry, sir," the tall cop said unhappily. "We've got our orders."

Standing side by side, Harry and Rosalee crossed their arms in unison and stared down at the unfortunate flatfeet.

I explained, "That's what they said at Nuremberg. Catarina?"

Catarina began ticking off points. "I'll arrange for official protests from Commander Hiro and from Ambassador Beaver as representative of the government whose vessel you allegedly took unlawful action against, Beam can get hold of that lawyer you talked to, and I'll ask Bunkie to whip up a press statement. If you think it will help, I'll ask Commander Hiro to accept a voluntary recall to active duty from you. That will give him a little more leverage to spring you."

"Catarina, you're wonderful. You've read my mind. Do that."

"Ken," Rosalee said softly, "do you need any help? Like right now?"

Harry indicated agreement. "I'd be awfully, awfully upset if anybody tried to arrest my buddy here." He tapped the side of his nose. "I was thinking, we ought to keep this friendly. So if anybody draws a gun, I'll make him eat it."

"Now, wait just one minute," the taller one said. "We're police officers."

"You know, this carpet's kind of dirty. We could mop it," Rosalee observed. I had the warm feeling that she was making the offer only partly because it sounded like fun.

"You know," Harry said, tapping his chin and looking the taller cop in the eye, "you'd look real good in a body cast."

The two cops looked at each other, obviously not happy with the turn of events.

Catarina shook her head slightly.

"No," I said. "Thanks, Harry. Thanks, Rosalee. I think we'll try diplomatic means first, but I really appreciate the offer. Well, at least I'm packed for the occasion. All right, kids, if you really want me, I'm yours." I held my hands out for the bracelets.

They actually did cuff me. We got my duffel out of Piper's trunk, and the poor guy whose job it was to inventory my stuff wanted to die when he saw the extent of it.

I gave them my name, rank, and serial number and asked for my lawyer, Commander Hiro, and Ambassador Beaver, in that order. Somebody must have figured out that the kimchi odor in the air ducts was unusually spicy, because they didn't take me into the back room where they kept the rubber hoses. Instead, they let me keep my clothes and put me in the cell next to Bobo and Ironsides.

"MacKay, what are you doing here?" Ironsides demanded.

"Hoping my stay will be short," I explained.

"Then you're with us," Davie asked with a peculiar gleam in his eye.

"I think that we're going to have to file personal bankruptcy when we get out. I also think that when the banks find out, jail will be the safest place for us," Bobo explained without enthusiasm. "But Davie wants to try a jailbreak."

"It'll be a cinch," Ironsides said, holding up a bent spoon.

"No! Hold it! Time *out!*" I said. "I expect to get out of here legally, with the aid and approval of the local gendarmerie. If you tell me anything about escape plans, I will reluctantly have to turn you in. Besides"—I glared at Davie Lloyd—"I haven't forgotten that the two of you tried to decommission me a couple or three times."

Bernie hung his head. "I'm sorry, Ken. I really feel bad about that." He elbowed Davie Lloyd.

"Yeah, we're both sorry," Ironsides said. He shuffled his feet. "We heard you bought the *Scupper*."

"I did. Hopefully, I'll eventually be able to fix her up and put together a crew." Somehow.

"Ken," Bernie said softly. "About Sasha . . ."

Jail had given Boo-Boo a certain nobility. *De Profundis*, so to speak.

"A ship always needs a ship's cat. I'll make Annalee turn in her barber's shears."

"Thanks, Ken." Bernie assumed a blissful look.

"We had a funeral for Frido this afternoon. That's where they picked me up. It was a pretty nice service," I said clumsily.

"He deserved that, didn't he?" Ironsides said sadly.

"He did," Bernie agreed. He looked at Davie Lloyd. "Ken looks like he's had a hard day. We ought to let him sleep."

I must have had a hard day, because I had an awful time falling asleep. I woke up when I felt someone gently shaking my shoulder.

"What? Is it morning already?" I said groggily. "I'll skip breakfast. If I'm in jail, I ought to be able to sleep in."

"Actually, it's not even dinnertime yet, and you haven't been in here more than a couple of hours," Piper said.

I tried to bury my head under a pillow full of sawdust. "God, when did I fall asleep?"

I heard Bernie answer from the adjoining cell. "Oh, about fifteen minutes ago."

"I don't live right," I groaned.

"You could be doing worse," a gravelly voice said.

I looked up. An older guy with a hooked nose was standing there with a coat thrown over a striped nightshirt.

"This is Sheriff Jamali. You weren't the only one to get dragged out of bed for this," Piper explained helpfully. "Okay, Ensign MacKay, on your feet."

I crawled out of bed and stood at attention.

"Here is a copy of the orders recalling you to active duty, and a copy of the official protest from Dr. Beaver," Piper said briskly, obviously enjoying every minute. "Your duffel bag is packed, I checked the contents against the inventory, and Sheriff Jamali is waiting to release you. You will, of course, release him by signing the legal document he is holding which absolves him of any claim you may have for false imprisonment." She winked. "Having heard of your plight, Sheriff Jamali's brother-in-law, the tailor, agreed to make you a complete set of uniforms out of the goodness of his heart. Catarina took measurements from the clothes you have which actually fit."

"You are free to go, Ensign," Jamali said, smiling. He added, "And if you so much as jaywalk, I will put you in jail for the rest of your life."

"Uh, thanks." I scrawled my signature across the document he was holding, waved good-bye to Bernie and Davie, and followed Piper out to the car, where Catarina was waiting.

"I ought to do this right," I said as Piper unlocked the door for me. I straightened. "Ensign MacKay, reporting for duty, ma'am." I snapped off one of my less sloppy salutes.

Catarina returned it gravely, and I squeezed in beside her. "Your eyes hurt?"

She nodded. "It's still good to see you, Ken."

"Good to see you. Thanks for getting me out."

"You're even on the payroll," Piper commented. "We're coming up on the end of the fiscal year, and we had some use-or-lose money in the budget."

The first thing that they drum into the head of every new ensign is the axiom that money disappears at the end of the fiscal year. If you don't spend all of the money the budget people gave you this fiscal year, they assume that you will only need half as much next year. Thus do the navy's auditors reward economy and thrift. It does make running a navy somewhat expensive.

"How did you ever sell this to Hiro—excuse me, Commander Hiro?" I asked, polishing up my military etiquette.

"I emphasized the moral and practical reasons for doing so," Catarina told me.

"The moral reasons, I understand. Practical?"

"We've managed to keep a surprisingly tight lid over events on the *Scupper*. Whoever set up the smuggling scheme may not know what happened. He—"

"Or she—" I interjected.

"He, she, or it may think that the drugs are still hidden on board," she amended. "There are rumors flying."

"Some of which you glued feathers to. Go on," I said.

"With you free—"

"I may be contacted," I finished for her. "I shouldn't ask this, but did you have anything to do with my getting jailed in the first place?"

I could see Piper shaking her head through the rearview mirror, but she was grinning.

"Only indirectly," Catarina said candidly. "Lydia Dare must have fastened on to some of the rumors. She's not especially discriminating."

"Even for a reporter," I admitted. As we rolled around to the front of the police station, I noticed Lydia standing out in front with a microphone in her hand and a camera on her. "Lieutenant Piper, could you slow up for a minute?"

As I rolled my window down, I heard Lydia Dare saying, "And so begins the first day of the Ken MacKay watch. With that vicious desperado finally behind bars—"

"This is too good to miss," I said. "Mother, may I?"

"Well, it fits in with the plan. Go ahead," Catarina said.

As Piper slowed the car, I hopped out and walked up right next to Lydia's mike. "Hi, Lydia, how's tricks?" I exclaimed. "Listen, I just stopped by to let your viewers know that everything's been cleared up, I'm back out on the street, you're still getting sued, and I'm still not going to give you an interview."

As I walked away, I heard her sputtering into the mike. "This must rank as another stunning example of corruption in high places in this city!"

I climbed back into the car. "Am I going to be helping Catarina with her investigation?"

"Not immediately," Piper said. "Catarina thinks that the political trouble with the Macdonalds in Kopernican sector is getting worse. You were in logistics, right? Depending on what orders come through on the mailship, I may need you to do some things."

"What trouble?" I asked.

The Macdonalds were the first advanced nonhuman species mankind had come across, and they were the most nearly human in a number of ways, which made them pretty obnoxious to deal with. They had been a wizened-looking bunch of pastoralists when the first ship ran across them, which is supposedly how they got their name, although I've never figured out why. The Contact/Survey Corps was specifically formed to manage humanity's contacts with the Macdonalds and to uplift them, which is something the Macdonalds have yet to forgive us for.

"War and rumors of war," Piper explained. "The Macdonalds want a few extra planets of their own, and they've started making noises about their 'biological destiny.' The Navy has been quietly moving a large part of the fleet out that way in the hope that the diplomats will screw things up so we can beat the tar out of them while they're still small enough to whip. It could get serious."

"I did a tour in intelligence out that way," Catarina volunteered. "Macdonalds look and think a lot like humans. Unfortunately, their leadership isn't very sophisticated—their societies changed technologies without necessarily internalizing too many cultural changes. They're still pretty much barbarians at heart, and they tend to judge us by the Contact boys. It will be pretty hard to convince them not to get too greedy.''

''Wonderful,'' I commented as we drove past the Atlantic Hotel.

I cleared the polarization on my side, squinted up at the building, and pointed. ''You can see my old room from here. I should ask whether Clyde knows I'm out.''

Catarina nodded. She looked tired, but her eyes had a little hint of a smile. ''He has accommodations waiting for you. Your quarters allowance will cover it.''

Just then, the window of my old room blew out in a sudden explosion. The glass fell and shattered on the street. The fire alarm went off. From the yelling, I deduced that the people inside the hotel were a little excited. ''Not much of a bomb,'' I commented as calmly as I could. ''It was probably Elaine. She always did go for flashy touches.''

I noticed Piper was staring at me wide-eyed.

''You know, for a while there I was beginning to feel neglected,'' I said in the calmest voice I could manage.

''Ken,'' Catarina explained, ''has a certain talent for winning friends and influencing people.''

Piper shook her head. ''Ken, when you want a drink, I'm buying.''

Clyde had an inflatable sleeping bag waiting for me at his place. I rolled it out under a table as far from the window as I could get and went to sleep.

Once upon a Mailship

The following morning, I pinned insignia on a set of my new tailor-made fatigues and reported to Piper for duty. She was busy putting things together for the mailship and barely glanced at me when I walked in.

Mankind has yet to come up with a method of long-distance communication that operates faster than lightspeed, and mailships are the glue that hold civilized planets together, as well as places like Schuyler's World. Even in places that qualify as pestholes, the arrival of the monthly mailship is an occasion for great joy and great sorrow. In addition to ordinary mail, a mailship's electronic memory comes bearing documents, pictures, banking records, and a month's worth of television programming at a time. Unfortunately, mailships also facilitate monthly reporting, which was what Piper and I were going to be busy at.

I needed to touch base with Wyma Jean, so Piper waved me to a desk and told me to go ahead. Bunkie, of course, had anticipated my need to call and had me set up. I was just getting ready to put the call through when Catarina walked in the door wearing civilian clothes. "Good morning, Lieutenant," I said cautiously.

Catarina smiled. "No need to be formal. Just remember to try not to give Commander Hiro a heart attack. Are you calling Wyma Jean?"

"Yeah. Cheeves is already on his way up in the shuttle, and I need to tell her what's going on before Fast Eddie gets here." Bunkie gave me a high sign to tell me we had a connection, and

147

I switched on the phone. "Hello, Wyma Jean. Good morning, it's Ken."

"Hello, Ken, you douchebag," she replied.

Wyma Jean was sitting in the command chair in a ratty kimono with her hair up, finishing off a carton of ice cream.

"Oh." I was momentarily at a loss for words. I couldn't remember starting off a conversation that way with a woman I wasn't married to. "Uh, how's it going, Wyma Jean?"

"Boring. The damned cat is on a hot streak. She keeps winning. I think she cheats. How did the auction go?"

"Uh, yeah," I said. "I guess you've heard I'm the proud purchaser of the *Scupper*."

"You are?" Spooner sounded surprised. "Oh, well. Good for you." She waved the spoon for emphasis.

"You're not mad? I figured you were mad at me for buying her."

"Oh, that had nothing to do with it. You're a guy—all of you are worthless scum-suckers," Spooner said in a perfectly normal tone of voice. "The more I know about men, the better I like cats."

"Uh, one second, Wyma Jean." I put the phone on mute and leaned out of the picture. Catarina had drawn the blinds in the other room and seated herself at a terminal. "Catarina, what do women take for PMS?"

"Are you talking about Wyma Jean?" She shook her head. "I don't think that's it. You know that Clyde's taken up writing poetry, don't you? Bad haiku mostly."

I shuddered briefly and took the phone off mute. "Wyma Jean, now that I own the ship, I'd like to exercise my option to renew your contract. I'll figure out how to pay you somehow."

She looked startled for a second. "That's okay, Ken. I know you haven't got any more money than the rest of us. We can work something out if you ever get the ship fixed."

"No, I'd rather start paying you now since you're up there working, if that's all right with you. It'll make me feel better. How's everything else going?"

"Things aren't going bad. You find any lattices so we can eventually move this piece of junk if we somehow find a full crew?"

"No. We're still working on it. There's none to be had here. I'm sending out an order with the mailship. Dr. Beaver, the !Plixxi* ambassador, thought that maybe Dennison's World had some to spare."

"I figured you'd order some, so I told Fast Eddie to make sure he delivered the order."

"Oh, you've heard from Eddie?"

"He says he's about twenty light-minutes out," Wyma Jean affirmed.

Mailships were flown by fourth-generation expert systems, and Fast Eddie was the artificial personality construct aboard mailship Foxtrot Echo 7. A human pilot trained each artificial intelligence aboard well enough to operate independently, which left space for a passenger, although the accommodations were not exactly up to QE3 standards. For short hops, such as Cheeves's trip to Dennison's World, a mailship was fine for any dwarf-sized person who didn't eat much and didn't mind sensory deprivation. I personally had never ridden one and didn't plan on starting soon.

"What did Fast Eddie have to say?" I asked guardedly.

"The usual. 'Well, shush my mouth, it's Wyma Jean, the little gal with the celestial knockers. Say there, honey, you want to fire up my solar panels?' Little pervert!"

Eddie was pretty eccentric, even by mailship standards. Most of the mailships in this sector had been trained by Big Jake Bauer. Unfortunately, that meant that most of the mailships in this sector talked like Big Jake Bauer, and Fast Eddie was no exception.

Peeled out of his shell, Big Jake Bauer was about half Bernie Bobo's size, with a deep bass voice and the metabolism of a frog. That made him a perfect mailship pilot on papers like account ledgers, a fact that Big Jake exploited with merciless regularity. Big Jake habitually wore size-four boots and a ten-gallon hat, and he spent most of his time between planets watching shoot-'em-ups. As a result, there were about fifty mailships in service that habitually called out to orbiting traffic, "Whoa, watch it there, little doggie!" Most of them had also picked up some rudimentary ideas about how to respond to the choice expletives they received in reply.

Unfortunately, Fast Eddie was better at being Big Jake than Big Jake was.

"Did Eddie include any details?" I asked Wyma Jean.

"It's not funny, Ken," Wyma Jean said, rubbing her neck. "That's twice he's done this to me! It's embarrassing to get propositioned by a computer program whenever we match orbits."

"I know, Wyma Jean, but the poor little ship doesn't know any better. You've got it better than Davie Lloyd, though. Eddie always tells him, 'Mine's bigger than yours, pardner.' "

"That really makes me feel a whole lot better," she said sarcastically.

I figured it was time to change the subject. "Wyma, I called to say that the shuttle will be matching orbits with you in a few minutes. It's carrying a passenger for the mailship, a Rodent named Cheeves. He's the number-two man at the !Plixxi* consulate and a real nice being. He's headed back to Dennison's World to try and straighten out our diplomatic problems with the Rodents. The ship we helped to blow itself away was carrying a Rodent prince, one of the sons of their planetary ruler—"

Wyma Jean whistled. Apparently, she'd missed that part.

"—so I'd like you to roll out the red carpet for him. I thought it would be better for him to wait aboard the *Scupper* than in the space station."

Eddie would be orbiting for a day or two while people downside composed immediate replies to whatever priority mail he was carrying, and it was marginally cheaper to let Cheeves board the *Scupper* and wait for Fast Eddie there than to put him up in the space platform. Although the space platform did have a place about the size of a small bedroom for transients to wait, Schuyler's World left the systems shut down to save money, and Cheeves wouldn't be waiting long enough to make it worth starting them up.

"Okay, Ken. No problem," she assured me.

"I think you'll like Cheeves. Let him have whatever he wants, within reason. Fast Eddie say anything worth mentioning?"

"There's a war alert. The Macdonalds are acting up. A lot of the fleet is deploying out that way, and it might be serious this time. You ought to mention it to Catarina and the other Navy people."

I thumped my head. "Oh, I forgot to tell you. I'm with the navy now. They called me into active service."

"Oh, that explains the funny clothes. I thought you just got tired of blue. God, they must really be desperate. Why you?"

"It's a long story that has to do with the local politics down here. I'll explain some other time. You need anything else up there?"

"No, I'll be fine as long as you didn't forget the skim milk. Thanks for asking, Ken. You're okay, even though you're still useless male slime."

"Thanks, Wyma Jean. I'll talk with you later."

Bunkie cut the connection. I walked over to Catarina's workstation. "Uh, Catarina, about our problem—if I talk to Clyde, will you talk to Wyma Jean?"

"If I say yes, what's in it for me?" she asked mischievously.

"Dinner," I said promptly. "I'll buy, with, uh, Lieutenant Piper's money."

"Yeah, count me in," Piper said without looking up from her desk. "Get Clyde to pick the place. He can't boil water, so he knows most of the restaurants in town."

"I'll do that." I looked down at Catarina. "Well?"

"You knew about the haiku, didn't you?" she said, tapping away at her terminal.

"No. When Clyde locked himself in the bathroom for about three hours, I knew there was something going on, but I figured it wasn't something I wanted to know about."

"You're right about that."

As I sat down and tried to make sense out of the paperwork Bunkie had laid out for me, Commander Hiro opened the door and walked in, and we all stood at attention.

"At ease. Continue what you're doing. Ensign Mickey, welcome aboard!"

"Thank you, sir. I'm happy to be here." As a rule, Navy offices are nicer than jail cells.

"Good, good." Hiro nodded his head up and down as he talked. "Where are you staying now?"

"I'm staying with Petty Officer Witherspoon, sir."

Hiro's brow furrowed and he stopped nodding. "You're rooming with an enlisted man? That sounds like fraternization. That's hardly proper, is it?"

Piper looked up from her desk. "It's all right, sir. He's a reserve officer."

"Oh." Hiro nodded his head firmly in apparent satisfaction. "Well, anyway, Ensign, I just want you to remember that no matter what calumnies that news-media person heaps upon you, you're still Navy. Navy reserve, but still Navy for all that."

"Thank you, sir."

As soon as he disappeared into his office, I stuck my head up. "Calumnies?" I asked.

Piper looked up again. "You hear the news this morning?"

"I've been trying very hard not to," I admitted. "Is it about me?"

She nodded. "Our intrepid newsperson decried the bombing. She wants your underworld contacts brought to light."

I rubbed my temples. "I didn't know you had an underworld here."

Piper didn't bat an eye. "We don't, but it sounds good, doesn't it?"

"Right." I looked to see if there was enough room to crawl under the desk. "What have the police figured out about the bomb?"

"Let's just say that we have a bomb squad as of this morning, and they're looking into it. Makes you want to take up a life of crime, doesn't it?" She tilted her head. "Nobody was hurt. I saw the pictures. Your room was a mess. Looks like somebody packed a pipe with black powder and nails."

"That'll do the job," I said, thinking back to the short course the Navy had given me on demolition for fun and profit.

I picked up the top piece of paper in front of me, which was last quarter's command expenditure report, and started trying to make sense out of it.

Piper tilted her head. "Oh, Bunkie?" she called. "You'd better get in here. Ensign MacKay's eyes are beginning to glaze over. He may need some help getting back into a military routine."

It was sad, but true, and the rest of the day was singularly uneventful.

Clyde is one of those people who think that sushi is Japanese for "gesundheit," and the restaurant he picked for dinner was Zack's Famous Grotto of Fine Fish.

The place was sort of a local landmark. Every three months it would fold and somebody would buy it and change the name. This month, it was a hot-rock restaurant, one of those places where they give you raw vegetables and meat and a hot rock to cook them on. As Catarina put it, it's the kind of place where you can have your steak and heat it through. It was one of the two or three nice places in town where they handed out napkins, and it sounded all right to me. I'm usually not too particular as long as poshint'ang isn't on the menu.

It was only a few blocks away on Second Street. When we got there, a little after six, the hostess hitched up her gown and put us in a nice little corner booth. Piper and Clyde sat on one side, and Catarina slid in beside me.

While everyone else was studying the menus, which were shaped like little stones, I looked around the room. The decor was mixed: they had fake palm trees at one end and a fake fireplace at the other. There was a live band clustered around the palm trees playing "hot New Orleans jazz"—they were okay, although the guy with the accordion kept losing the beat.

The waitress working the room eventually found us. For obvious reasons, nobody ordered the fish. I ordered the veal francine, which came out as tender little slivers of meat served with vegetables and three secret sauces which looked an awful lot like mustard, ketchup, and horseradish. Catarina asked for a vegetarian platter, and Clyde and Piper got the chicken.

Flipping my morsels of veal onto my rock, I cooked them up and bit into one. Then I looked around to see if there were any dogs in the room. "Uh, this really doesn't taste like veal," I said, setting down my chopsticks.

Piper spoke up. "It probably isn't. I should have warned you that they don't have very many cows here."

"Oh," I said. Poshint'ang is Korean dog stew.

Piper poked at my rock with her chopsticks. "It's probably gerbil. They grow them big as chickens. Actually, they look an awful lot like miniature Rodents." She picked up one piece of meat and turned it over. "It looks like you've got a couple of thighs there."

Clyde started giggling. "You should have ordered the chicken!"

Catarina stopped eating. She put her elbow on the table and rested her chin on her hand with a little half smile on her face. She and I both looked at Piper, who cleared her throat. "Well, the chicken isn't exactly chicken either. They have a couple of iguana ranches not too far from here."

Clyde stopped giggling. "Uh, Lieutenant. Are you telling me I'm eating lizard?"

"I thought you knew," Piper said defensively. "I thought that's why you picked this place."

Clyde turned a delicate shade of green and hurriedly left the table.

"Iguanas are herbivorous. They're actually much cleaner animals than chickens," Piper said to nobody in particular. She grilled a sliver and popped it into her mouth.

"I didn't notice a vegetarian platter on the menu," I remarked to Catarina.

"I just told them that I was on a special restricted diet, which is perfectly true, and I mentioned that if I ate any meat or fish I would probably get violently ill and sue them. They were very understanding. I plan to leave a large tip."

I shrugged. "You want to pass Clyde's plate over here? It seems a shame to let it go to waste." I speared a couple of pieces. "I was planning on talking to Clyde about Wyma Jean. I guess that now is not a good time."

"Probably not. He seems to have other things on his mind," Catarina agreed. While Beam and I were finishing off Clyde's dinner, she stood up and took some money out of her belt purse to leave on the table. "Ken, Beam, I have some work to do tonight, and I really should get to it. Don't wait up for me." She crooked her little finger and flexed it. "Good night."

I looked at Piper. "And that was . . . ?"

She nodded. "A microwave."

"Well, that was the quickest dinner-date I've ever been on,"

I said, realizing about three seconds too late that I'd just set myself up for more abuse.

Piper chewed some vegetables and winked at me.

After we paid the waitress, we pried Clyde out of the bathroom and called it a night. By then, I was feeling sympathetic tremors. I guess you shouldn't mix gerbil with your iguana.

When I crawled into the office the next morning, Catarina was out, but there was a note on my terminal which said that a Mr. Ted E. Baer had called about lattices and wanted me to call back. I dialed the number, which turned out to be the number for an animal-husbandry station. After a long and tedious discussion, I found out that they didn't know anyone named Ted E. Baer, they didn't know anything about lattices, and today was the local equivalent of April Fool's Day.

Everybody in the building except Hiro was in on it.

Piper and I finished our reports, Hiro chopped off on them, and we wired them to Fast Eddie, who took off for Dennison's World with Cheeves. Mission accomplished, we took the afternoon off, so I changed out of my uniform and stopped by the Rodent embassy to see how Bucky was faring.

He answered the door wearing a yellow smoking jacket, knee breeches, a pink ascot, and enormous red carpet slippers.

"Bucky, are you all right?" I asked, allowing concern to edge into my voice.

"In the pink, friend Ken! How good of you to come! Come in, come in!" He appeared enormously pleased with himself.

I stepped inside, momentarily at a loss for words.

"Care for a honeyball?"

"Uh, no, thanks." I gestured toward what he was wearing. "About your clothes . . . you look different."

"Oh, yes. What do you think? It's me!" He did a little pirouette.

"Well, yes," I admitted.

"Cheeves would positively flinch if he saw me wearing these. You won't tell him, will you? I so hate to upset him."

"My lips are sealed," I told him solemnly.

"What a charming phrase."

"Sure. Why the, uh, clothes?"

"These are just a few favorites of mine that I couldn't bear to part with, so I hid them in the back of the closet. Cheeves is a dear, but he's so particular about what I wear. I think he feels it reflects badly on him if I'm not dressed suitably. He doesn't come out and say anything, mind you, but you can sense his disappointment." Beaver pushed aside some dishes so that we could find a place to sit down. "I pulled some of the old things out. What do you think?"

"Clyde's got a dashiki you might want to borrow."

"I shall consider it. Oh, did you know that Cheeves has taken an interest in your attire?" Beaver asked, planting himself on the divan. "He confided in me just the other day that his greatest ambition is to place you in matching socks."

"I have matching pairs of socks," I protested. I pulled up my pants legs. I had on one black sock and one blue one, and I was sure I had another pair just like it somewhere.

Beaver tugged at his whiskers. "Perhaps it would be nicer if you had matching socks on at the same time."

"I'll have to work on it," I mumbled.

"That's the spirit, Ken! As Bucky says, 'Every defeat requires earnest application to remedy.' "

"Uh, right."

"Friend Ken, I was just about to make an excursion to the Prancing Pony. Would you care to join me?"

"You mean in public? Uh, right. I have a few errands to attend to—how about if I meet you there a little later?"

"Capital! I'll be waiting for you."

I went back to Clyde's place and called some people to install deadbolts, motion sensors, and a surveillance camera on credit, which appeared to be a good idea. I couldn't find Clyde, so I took a quick look at his wardrobe to restore my self-esteem and went to find Bucky at the Prancing Pony.

When I got there, Dinky was trying his hand at Chopin and Annalee McHugh was working the bar. Both of them were presumably aware that God had intended them to do other things. Annalee greeted me with a scowl. I gave her a casual wave. Spotting Clyde, I went over and sat down with him.

"Oh. Hello, Ken. Bucky told me you'd be here."

"Where is he?"

Clyde blinked a couple of times. "I think he's in the bathroom. You know, the funny one with the round door. I think that's where he went."

"Right. What are you drinking?"

"Pink squirrel." Clyde shifted one shoulder. "Bucky liked the name."

"It figures." I looked up at the mushroom baskets gently swaying in the current from the air ducts. "You want to talk about Wyma Jean?"

"No," he said, slurring his speech a little. "Of course not. She thinks, excuse me, she thinks I lied to her just to get her in the sack." He waved his finger. "That wasn't the only reason. I mean, I like her. Excuse me, love her." He seemed to sober up. "She's got me pretty upset."

"No problem. Look, I'm pretty sure you two could patch it together somehow."

"No way."

"I thought you got along pretty well. I remember you were teaching her thieves' cant."

"That's another thing she blames me for. Excuse me. I pretty much made it up as I went along."

"How imaginative?"

"Uh, I think I told her a caboose was a fat lady in a tight dress. She thinks I made a fool of her." He took a very deep breath. "I've been working on some poetry."

"Catarina told me."

"I've got a couple poems finished. Want to hear them?"

"Not really," I admitted.

" 'Leaves falling softly/Quickly presaging winter/Frost rimes windowpanes,' " he rattled off.

"I need to think about it. What was the other one?"

" 'Morning cherry twigs/Icicles melting brightly/Thin frozen fingers.' That's my best one."

"Look, Clyde, I don't mean to criticize your taste in romantic poetry, but how is this going to help you mollify Wyma Jean?"

"Don't you see, the winter images, the frost and the icicles, represent blighted love, and . . . and . . ."

"Oh, yeah. I didn't catch that the first time around," I said quickly. "Why not go with some Shakespeare?"

"She'd think I was faking that, too," he said, disconsolately.

I looked around the room to see if there was any woman in the place who could take Clyde's mind off Wyma Jean, but the Prancing Pony usually leaves something to be desired in that respect. The last time Harry tried a wet T-shirt contest, his patrons voted to have the contestants wear more clothing.

A familiar shadow blotted out the sky. "Hey, Admiral."

" 'Lo, Harry. How're they cooking?"

"All right, I guess." He reached out and spun a limewater in front of me. "It's on the house. I feel like doing something for the navy."

I looked over at Clyde, who was beginning to drift. "You can start by not feeding him any more pink squirrels. What's been wrong with you lately, Harry?"

"I don't know, Ken. I'm getting tired of tending bar. Night after night, you see the same faces, you toss the same people out on the street. I told you I was in the navy myself once, didn't I?"

"Only about a million times."

"I heard from Clyde that there's going to be a war with the Macdonalds."

"Could be."

"That's where I should be," he said eagerly. "Instead, I'm here. Tending bar."

"Lighten up a little, Harry. You're a good bartender. That's worth something, isn't it? I've never seen anybody bounce a drunk the way you can."

"But it's not what I want to do anymore, Ken," he said, very softly.

The pleasant sound of splintering chairs drifted to our ears from the corner of the room, and McHugh yelled out, "God damn it, Harry, will you quit jabbering and get over here before these two bozos murder each other?"

Dinky started playing "When the Saints Go Marching In." Harry rose from his chair with a thoughtful look and wandered off to wreak mayhem.

Bucky sauntered over, tiptoeing past the struggling combatants. "Friend Ken, you were able to come after all!"

"Hi, Bucky. What kept you?"

He seated himself and tugged at his whiskers. "I seem to

have misread the signs and walked into the wrong restroom facility. I expressed my most sincere apologies."

Clyde lifted his head.

"Peculiar anatomy your human females have," Bucky observed.

McHugh shouted, "Who ordered the extra-large Tropical Surprise pizza?"

Bucky raised his paw. "Over here, please." Annalee slid the thing in front of us and departed. "Ken, would you care to join us?"

"What's on that thing?" I asked politely.

"Let me see, papaya, guacamole, heart of palm, Japanese mushrooms, crushed pineapple, bell peppers. Friend Clyde, did I omit anything?"

Clyde laid his head back down on the table. "And anchovies."

"Oh, yes. I forgot about those."

"I'll try one piece." I managed one bite. The anchovies weren't anchovies. Nibbling politely at the crust, I said, "Well, I hate to eat and run, but I really have to call it a night."

I left Clyde a set of keys for the deadbolts and found out that pizza with guacamole affected me about the same way iguana did.

The next morning was Saturday, and Catarina called to ask about Clyde and woke me from a reasonably sound sleep. I explained about the pink squirrels and asked her about Wyma Jean.

"I spoke with her. It was not a particularly productive discussion."

"Should we be meddling like this?"

"What else are friends for? Oh, by the way, Wyma Jean is pretty annoyed at you for telling Cheeves he could take the cat."

"Cheeves took the cat? I didn't tell him to take the cat."

"That's what he told Wyma Jean."

"As far as I can recall, the subject never came up. Maybe he just likes cats. I hope not. He seemed okay."

"Wyma Jean was afraid he might hurt Sasha."

"I wouldn't worry. Cats almost never get what they deserve. I wonder if it was a spur-of-the-moment thing on his part."

"I don't think so. Wyma Jean said he brought a carrying cage."

"It sounds pretty strange, but he'll be back next week, so it shouldn't be a problem. I'll ask Bucky what he knows. I just wish we'd stop accumulating mysteries faster than we can dispose of them."

"I'll second that," she said.

"Anyway, I was thinking that if you and Beam didn't have plans, maybe we could get together."

"Thanks, but I've really been pushing myself, and I really need to rest. Tonight, if you're interested, there's a Catholic church with an evening mass over on Seneca Street. I plan on attending, and I've talked Beam into coming."

It had been a few years since I'd seen the inside of a church. "Well, okay, as long as you're sure they won't have to rededicate the place if they have us both in there together."

"Trust me. I don't plan on vanishing into a pile of dust. How about if we meet you at six-thirty in front of the church?"

"Six-thirty it is." I thought for a second and told her, "Somehow, I didn't think of you as the Catholic type."

I heard her chuckle. "I used to be an occasional Lutheran, but I converted. Recently. Talk to you later."

"Bye."

After I checked Clyde for vital signs, I spent the day looking over the paperwork on the *Scupper* and working through some projections on runs. Then I grabbed something to eat and met Piper and Catarina for mass. It was pretty nice. They had a woman deacon doing the service, and she did a dynamite sermon. She was hell on sinners, of which Schuyler's World apparently had an inordinate share.

After it was over, Catarina managed to excuse herself with indecent haste and left me standing there with Piper in front of the church.

Piper stared at me uncomfortably. "Ken, Catarina still thinks that somebody might take another crack at you, so she asked me to walk you back."

"Thanks, Beam." As we headed down the street, I asked, "How far is Catarina going with this religious kick?"

"I don't really think it's a 'kick,' Ken. Catarina hasn't said much about it, but one thing she did say was that being a vampire tends to make you take the long view on things. You also have to remember that the Catholic Church is a pretty diverse organization. I know she hasn't made her mind up about what to do when the navy kicks her out, but I get the feeling from talking to her that some of the contemplative religious orders provide the right kind of physical environment for a vampire, and a few of the smaller ones may have a lot more experience with vampires than they let on."

That jolted me. "Hold it, are you hinting that Catarina's thinking about becoming a nun?"

"I obviously don't know anything, but it's at least a possibility. When you think about it, Father Damien ministered to the lepers, and he was a leper. I would think that the best person to minister to vampires would be another vamp. And it's not as if Catarina would have to make her mind up right away. She could spend a year or so and see what kind of vocation she has for a religious calling."

I looked at her. "Beam, what is going on with Catarina?"

"What do you mean, Ken?"

"Well, I'm not real sure what I mean, but I mean about me and Catarina specifically. It feels like she never has time for me anymore. I know she's working nights and that's got to be part of it, but it just doesn't seem like she's interested. You're the only person I know she talks to. What gives?"

Piper colored very slightly. "Well, I'm not sure how much I can say . . ."

I stopped and leaned my back against a handy awning to make my point. "Beam, look. You're the only person I can think of who can give me a straight answer on this."

She stopped next to me and hesitated. "Let me tell you what I can. Catarina's navy through and through. She's pretty broken up about having to leave. She really doesn't want to talk to people right now."

"Well, I understand that, but I really thought for a while there that I wasn't just 'people' to her. Right now, I feel a considerable distance between the two of us. About two parsecs' worth, which even I would notice.''

Piper hesitated again. ''Well, that's part of the problem. Be realistic and try to look at this from her point of view. Where's the future in letting anything develop with you? I mean, she's regular navy, and you're not. You're going to have a ship, and she's about to get medicaled out and be a groundhog for life . . .''

''She's a vamp, and I'm not,'' I interjected.

''There's that, too,'' she admitted. ''Look, Ken, let it lie for now. Let Catarina get her thoughts sorted out.''

''It doesn't look like I have too much choice, does it? Do you think she's letting this vampire thing get to her? I mean, I've looked in her closet, and everything she owns is black.''

''No.'' Piper shook her head. ''She's always dressed like that.''

When we got to Clyde's place, I thanked Piper for getting me there and went on in. Clyde was waiting up for me.

''Hi, Clyde. What's up?''

''Well, I talked with Wyma Jean again.'' He was hanging his head a little, which didn't look promising.

''What did she say? You don't look too happy.''

''Well, she said she forgave me, and she understood why I had to do what I did. That's the good part. Lieutenant Lindquist must have talked with her. But she also said that we'd have to be just friends.''

'' 'Just friends'? She said that?'' I looked at him. ''That's the absolute kiss of death.''

''That's about what I thought,'' he said dejectedly.

A Guarded Response

Piper called me in to work Sunday morning. The Fleet had sent a requirements survey with Fast Eddie to see what Schuyler's World could supply in the event that war did break out with the Macdonalds. Piper and I spent four days on that. It turned out that from the navy's point of view, factoring in distance and tooling-up costs, Schuyler's World was absolutely worthless. Some of these things you realize instinctively, but it's always nice to have objective evidence.

The remainder of the week was pretty quiet. I got out to see the tourist attractions around Schenectady, including The Wonderful World of Miniature Horses, and I stopped looking under my sleeping bag.

Fast Eddie was coming back from Dennison's World, and I was hoping he'd bring Cheeves with a contract for some lattices, which would go a long way toward solving my more immediate problems. He wasn't due in until Friday, which is why it surprised me when Bucky called me during the middle of the night on Thursday.

"Hello, friend Ken?"

"Oh, hello, Bucky," I said groggily. I looked at the clock. "Hold on. Let me get into some clothes and switch the visual on." I threw on a T-shirt and some pants. When I switched on the video, I saw that Catarina was with him. "What gives? It's not even morning yet."

"Friend Ken. Fast Eddie has arrived earlier than expected,

and I have both good news and bad news. The good news is that there are spare lattices on my world which can be shipped here.''

"That's great. Thank Cheeves for me. By the way, where is Cheeves?''

Beaver's whiskers twitched. He made a little coughing noise in his throat, folded his hands over his round, little belly, and turned to Catarina.

"That leads us to the bad news,'' she said.

"They want cash up front, right? Oh, hell, I thought that might be a problem.''

"Not exactly, Ken,'' Catarina said, looking at Beaver out of the corner of her eye.

"Well, yes,'' Beaver said, rubbing his hands together briskly. "But as Bucky says, 'In times of adversity, we must all pull on the rope together.' ''

"Bucky, what—is—the—problem?'' I asked.

"Well, it seems that your destruction of the ship was reported to my father by several of my demi-brothers in a most hostile manner, and deprived as he is of my sagacious counsel, he has reacted in a most belligerent manner,'' Beaver explained.

Catarina interpreted. "Bucky's doting daddy wants you and the rest of the *Scupper*'s crew strung up by your heels, and he's sending an invasion fleet to do the stringing and make hash out of this planet generally.''

"In my capacity as ambassador, I must state that at least one of those two objectives is excessive under the circumstances,'' Beaver added.

"Where is Cheeves?'' I asked stupidly.

"I regret to say that my father has forbidden Cheeves to return and has ordered him to advise my demi-brother Genghis, who will be leading the punitive expedition. Cheeves expresses his regrets,'' Bucky stated. He reached up with a handkerchief and wiped a tiny tear from his eye.

"The invasion fleet will consist of two armed merchantmen, a light cruiser, and one or more troop transports,'' Catarina explained.

"My demi-brother Genghis was quite attached to my departed demi-brother Adolf,'' Beaver observed. "He sent a message to the effect that he has personally sworn to execute you in a most revolting manner.''

"The two armed merchantmen are similar to the one that attacked us,'' Catarina added in a quiet voice. "They probably mount a pair of missile launchers and twin twenty-millimeter cobalt lasers.''

"But you just said something about a light cruiser. Who in hell gave them a light cruiser?'' I asked politely.

"We did, of course. It's an obsolete Phoenix class. The Rodents purchased her as scrap. It was turned over disarmed to them, but they've refitted a lot of weaponry to her, and I'm guessing that she carries six missile launchers and eight laser cannon in twin mountings. Commander Hiro is jumping up and down at the prospect of repelling the invaders at cutlass-point.''

"With eight navy personnel, including me, and no ships?'' I had a really horrible thought. "Do we have any antiship weaponry at all on this dirtball?''

"Oh, I'm sure something will turn up,'' Beaver said.

"Commander Hiro wants to call out the planetary reserves. You and Clyde get dressed and report in to Piper.''

"Clyde must be in the bathroom. I hear him composing,'' I said automatically, thinking about other things.

Catarina smiled, one of her real solar flares. "You tell Clyde that if he doesn't get his tail in here, he's going to be decomposing.''

"Aye-aye, ma'am,'' I said automatically. A few seconds later, I started to wake up. "Please tell me this isn't happening.''

"Well, if you insist. This isn't happening,'' Beaver told me solemnly.

When I arrived, Piper and Bunker were both there trying to make sense out of what Fast Eddie had to say. "Hello, Ken— you might as well listen,'' Piper said, waving me to a seat.

Fast Eddie was pontificating. "Friend, you got problems. Seems like most hombres have the same kind of problems all over . . .''

"This is serious. Skip the editorial comments, Eddie, or I'll pry you loose and stuff your circuit boards into a video recorder. What happened?'' Piper asked.

"Well, all right, pardner. No need to be hostile. Long about

Monday, I sashayed on in, gave them varmints the stuff, and then rode circuit for a spell waiting for them to figure replies to all the express mail. There must have been something in it that bothered them. Most goldarn chittering you ever did hear on the airwaves. Don't know what it was about, though. Never paid much mind to what tenderfeet think. Anyway, when my time was up, I flat-out told them I had to git. You know how it is—neither nebula dust nor comets nor darkness of space shall keep the postman from his duly appointed rounds, and all that. Well, sir, do you know what they did? Those lily-livered skunks shot at me, and they didn't even say 'Draw.' Well, I'll tell you, I gave them what-for. The next time I mosey on down to that planet to deliver mail, why, no TV for those buckaroos!''

Fast Eddie could pass the Turing test; he's as stupid as anybody I know.

"Hell and damnation," Piper swore. "Thanks, Eddie." She waved to Bunkie to cut the connection. "Bunkie, call up the naval movement schedules. Let's get them decrypted and see if we can get a navy ship here in time.''

It took us about an hour, and there was nothing moving even close to Schuyler's World. "No good. No ships," Piper said. "Ken, take my car and drive over to the armory. The Civil Guard here is pretty much low-grade dogmeat, but see what they've got to offer—how many men and whether they've got anything that can shoot at a spaceship. Their emergency number is disconnected, but somebody ought to be in there by now. Go, move it!''

Bunker whispered directions, and I went out the door to Piper's car. The Schenectady Armory was about twelve blocks away, and I made most of the lights. The building looked deserted, but the door was open, so I walked on in.

"Hello, is anybody here?''

"In here," someone said from one of the outer offices. "Can I help you?''

I went and pushed open the door. A sad-looking guy with a lot of forehead showing was sitting in a chair with his feet up, doing the crossword puzzle. His eyes widened when he saw my uniform.

"Oh, hi. I thought you might be looking for the fire station across the street." He swung around and stood up. "I'm Roger Kimball. I'm the full-time civilian technician here. The one and only technician—it's a pretty small armory." He stuck out his hand and pumped mine. "Are you here on business? This is kind of exciting. You're the first official visitor I've ever had."

"Pleased to meet you," I said. "I'm Ensign Ken MacKay, and I'm a reservist with the navy here. We have got a major problem. The Rodents have declared war, and they're invading this planet next week. The navy doesn't have a whole heck of a lot to stop them with, and I got sent over to see what you fellows have. Men, weapons. That sort of thing."

Kimball whistled through his teeth. "That is a real problem," he admitted.

"There really isn't very much time to waste. What can we count on calling up from the Civil Guard?"

"Ensign, I'm not sure you'd believe me if I told you. Hold on a minute." He reached over and punched a number into his phone.

"Hey, Bubba? This is Rodg. Can you break away and come over to the armory for a few minutes? I have a navy officer here I need you to talk to . . . That's right, a real officer . . . He's really from the navy . . . He says the Rats have declared war and are going to invade us next week . . . Yeah, Bubba, I *know* how many birds you got to look at this morning, but it's important. Just get on over here *now* . . . Thanks, Bubba. Give my love to Esther and the kids . . . Bye, Bubba."

He hung up the phone. "Corporal Briscoll's on his way over. He's a chicken inspector on the morning shift. He'll be over here in a minute—he only works a block away. He's secretary for the local guardsmen's union."

"Your Civil Guard's got a union?" I asked dubiously.

Kimball nodded. "Believe me—we've got a union. Pull up a chair. Can I get you some coffee?"

"No, thanks. I'm not in a coffee mood. What does the Guard have here?" Just about every planet has a Civil Guard. Mostly, they're considered planetary organizations—the planetary governments use them for disaster relief and things like that—but they are also part of the Confederation Reserve Forces, and Confederation government officials can call them into service to fight wars and things like that. Most Civil Guard outfits drill once a month and get together to train for a week or two in the summer.

Kimball looked at me. "Well, on paper, the Schuyler's World Civil Guard consists of one independent combat infantry company based out of this armory—the 536th 'Weekend Warriors.' "

"Who's in command, and what do you mean, 'on paper'?"

Kimball pursed his lips. "That's kind of tough to say. Colonel Sheen is in command, if anyone is. We're a little short on officers. We're rated for four."

"That's not very many officers to have a colonel in command," I commented.

"Colonel Sheen is essentially a political appointee," Kimball said evasively.

"Well, I take it you don't have a full complement of officers. How many do you have, and if Colonel Sheen isn't running things, who is?"

"Well, actually we don't have any other officers right now. They all resigned last year, and the governor and the legislature haven't been able to agree on appointments. The governor and the legislature really don't see eye-to-eye on most issues. The election ought to settle things one way or another. Oh, hello, Bubba." He waved at the fat man who waddled in the door. "This is Ensign MacKay from the navy. This is serious. The Rats are going to invade us next week, and he wants to know what the Guard can do."

Corporal Bubba was carrying around a second stomach and smelled of chicken. "Gee, that's a problem."

I was getting tired of hearing that line. "How long would it take to assemble your company?"

"Oh, gosh, sir. You'd have to send written notification to the union. That would mean a change in working conditions," he said uncomfortably.

"Well, assuming we did that, how long would it take to assemble your company?" I asked. "You do have a company here."

Kimball decided to save him embarrassment. "We've had to reorganize the Civil Guard company as a squad."

"The other guys sort of quit," Bubba admitted.

"When the legislature decided to annoy the governor by passing a bill to unionize the Civil Guard, they made it a closed shop," Kimball explained. "This did not go over well with the officers and a lot of the rank and file. The governor and the legislature really don't like each other very much."

"How many Civil Guardsmen do you have left, Corporal?" I asked.

"Eleven—or is it twelve? I forget." Briscoll scratched his head.

"Eleven," Kimball said firmly.

"The other two hundred quit?"

"The goddamn fascists quit just so they wouldn't have to pay union dues," Bubba said. "I mean, why shouldn't we collect dues from them? If they filed a grievance, we'd have had to represent them the same as if they were brothers in good standing. Blood-sucking toadies to exploitive oppressors is what I call them. Well, good riddance to them, I say. They weren't good union material anyway. Uh, begging the ensign's pardon, sir."

"Well, eleven of you is better than nothing." I rubbed the bridge of my nose. "How long would it take to assemble your squad?"

"What do you mean? Like, where would we serve?" Briscoll asked.

"Best to hit the Rats before they enter atmosphere, so if we can get hold of some space weapons—"

"Nope. No. No can do, sir," Briscoll said, shaking his head. "Not out in space. It's not part of our contract."

"The legislature passed a rider to the union bill which provides that the Civil Guardsmen don't have to serve off-planet, which means they can't be compelled to leave the planet's surface," Kimball explained. "Unless, of course, the planet is invaded."

"Besides which, we are on strike until our demands are met!" Bubba said fiercely. "We're going to show those blood-sucking monopolistic capitalists a thing or three. The pay's lousy, the working conditions are terrible—why, do you realize that we don't even get overtime? It's . . . it's . . . it's sheer exploitation of the working class!" He shook his fist. "We will overcome!"

"How long have you been out on strike?" I asked.

"What's it been, five months now, Rodg?"

"About that," Kimball agreed.

"We aren't going to do nothing until our legitimate demands are met," Bubba said firmly.

"Does that mean that you wouldn't report if the navy called you up to defend your planet?" I asked mildly.

"What, and cross a picket line? No way, sir! My mother didn't raise no scab!" he retorted. He looked at me suspiciously. "Is this some kind of ploy to interfere with our right to demand redress of our grievances?" He jabbed his finger. "Well, if it is, you can tell them from me that it won't work! Labor will never bow its head to the dictates of the Master Class! Uh, begging the ensign's pardon, sir."

There didn't seem to be very much else to say. "Thank you, Corporal. You're dismissed," I said politely.

"Uh, right, sir." Bubba tromped out.

I noticed he was limping a little. "What's wrong with his leg?"

"Bubba has a moderate handicap," Kimball said dryly.

I shut my eyes and opened them. "This is a combat infantry company."

"The legislature passed a bill applying the Civil Rights for the Handicapped Act to the Civil Guard. Unless the Civil Guard can show that Bubba is incapable of performing his duties and reasonable accommodations can't be made for him, he gets to stay on. With the strike, no one is sure what Bubba's duties are, least of all Bubba."

"I know. The governor and the legislature don't see eye-to-eye."

"Corporal Briscoll is actually one of the moderates in the union," Kimball volunteered. "We probably should have given him written notice before asking him over here, but I doubt he'll file a grievance over it. As for getting the Guardsmen to serve, the union wouldn't dream of exploiting this little crisis, but, ah . . ."

"Right," I said.

"I thought it would be easier if I showed you," he said apologetically.

"All right, what next? Can you get Colonel Sheen on the phone?"

Kimball nodded and punched in another number and motioned me around to where I could see. A girl answered.

Kimball asked her, "Doris, this is Guard business. Can you put Harvey on the line? It's important."

She nodded pertly, and the screen blanked. A moment later Colonel Sheen came on.

Sheen looked like a colonel—tall, aristocratic, frosted hair around the temples. The effect faded when he opened his mouth.

"Gee, Rodg. I wish you wouldn't call me early in the morning like this."

"Can't help it, Harvey." Kimball pointed to me. "This is Ensign MacKay from the navy. He's here on official business."

"Oh, my God!" Sheen put his hands to his mouth. "Nobody told me about any inspection!"

"No, sir," I broke in. "I'm not here to inspect your command. The Rodents have declared war. They are going to invade this planet next week. I need to know what the Civil Guard can do."

"Gee, that's a problem," Sheen said. "But I don't know what I can do." He sounded like Bernie in one of his less decisive moments.

"Sir, I've already talked to Corporal Briscoll. The question is whether we board him out or bring him up on charges."

"Oh, gee. I couldn't do that to Bubba. Why, he buys two half gallons of milk a week," Sheen said feebly.

"Colonel Sheen runs a corner grocery store," Kimball explained with a blank expression.

"Sir, I think we have to write off the current personnel in the Civil Guard then. But the Rats are going to invade, and we need men to stop them. Mr. Kimball tells me that there are a lot of former Guardsmen around who have resigned within the last week. I think we can rely on some of them. I need you to call them and get them to volunteer, and I also need you to get the governor to sign an emergency decree."

Sheen was visibly distressed. "I . . . I couldn't do that. Why, those men would be strike-breakers. I mean, the legislature would never approve. Couldn't we wait until after the election?"

"Sir." I stared at him. "The Rodents are coming next week."

"I . . . I don't know. Rodg, I need time to think. Let me call you back. Tonight or tomorrow . . ." The screen abruptly blanked.

"How long did he serve on active duty?" I asked thoughtfully.

Kimball scratched his head. "A couple of months as a lieutenant, I think. I should tell you that the legislature passed a bill forbidding the governor from exercising his emergency powers unless they pass a joint resolution approving it, and the legislature's not in session. They call it the War Powers Act. I'm thinking that even if you could talk them into calling a special session, they'd have a hell of a time getting a quorum, what with the campaigning and the legislators in jail."

"That's fine. I'd just like to know who's going to explain this to the Rats." I eyed Kimball. "Are you any better off for weapons?"

"In a word, no." He stood up and went over and opened up the vault to the arms room. He waved an arm, pointing out the contents. "When the M-20 rifles were declared obsolete, the legislature sold most of them off as sporting weapons. The gun clubs made a big deal about it. The legislature declined to appropriate money to replace them." He grinned. "For some reason, sector naval headquarters moved most of the heavy stuff out and didn't make replacing any of it a priority."

I went over to the door and looked inside.

"I have about thirty rifles and a thousand rounds of ammo for them, and I've got a fifty-millimeter mortar that I don't have any ammo for," Kimball said. "Other than that, I'm pretty well strapped."

"That's really not going to be much help in stopping spaceships," I observed, and sighed. "Is there anything you can think of that the Civil Guard can contribute?"

"Well, there's me. I have dual status as a reservist and a civilian technician. And I'm a pretty good ordnance tech, if you can find me something to work on. However, I'd just as soon you didn't call me up if you don't have anything to shoot with."

"I understand." I shook his hand. "Thanks, I'll let you know."

I drove back and found Piper. "How'd you make out?" she asked.

"Not very well. The Civil Guard here is pretty much defunct, and there's nothing but a few rifles in the armory. There's a tech who's pretty sharp. How did you make out?"

"Not well." Piper brushed a stray lock of hair from her eyes. "We've double-checked, and there's no navy vessel passing close enough to Schuyler's World for us to divert here in time to help. We're going to send off the mailship, but barring a miracle, it'll be at least three weeks before the navy can respond. We've also been blessed with the presence of Lieutenant Commander Stemm, the Naval attaché to Dennison's World, who came with Fast Eddie."

"You sound like you know him," I commented.

"I sure do. Off the record, he's an ambitious son of a bitch. Fortunately, he had a rough trip over on the mailship, so we won't have to worry about him for a day or two until he recovers. Let's go meet Catarina for breakfast. Maybe she's got some ideas. I don't."

We met Catarina in the Atlantic Hotel's restaurant, where she was finishing off a Bloody Mary without the vodka. "What would you like?" she said. "In light of recent events, I'm buying."

"I'll go with the eggs Benedict," I said. "Beam?"

Piper agreed. "The same. Did you talk to Dr. Beaver?"

Catarina nodded. "He's hoping everything will turn out for the best."

"Well, do you have any ideas? We can't run—the only ship we have is the *Scupper*, and to run her through a black hole in her present condition would be a messy way of committing suicide. And we can't fight because we don't have anything to fight with. Will they accept a surrender? Without executing us on the spot, I mean."

"Bucky thinks not," Catarina said quietly. "Genghis apparently enjoys that sort of thing." She looked down at her watch. "Commander Hiro has called a staff meeting for nine o'clock. He and Bucky are talking right now. He still wants to fight."

"I wish I knew how," Piper said.

"I think it's called the Tinkerbell theory of planetary defense," I interjected. "Maybe if we all wish hard enough, we can make it happen. Can I have the vodka from your Bloody Mary with my eggs Benedict?"

Hiro opened officers' call wearing a sorely troubled look. He and Bucky had been talking. Apparently the more he heard about demi-brother Genghis, the less he liked.

I shut the door as the junior member present and Hiro began. "Lieutenant Commander Stemm, who arrived on the mailship, is still indisposed. At Lieutenant Lindquist's suggestion, I have asked Dr. Beaver to be present despite his status as envoy of an enemy power." The lines in his face stood out, and he looked like he hadn't gotten enough sleep. "It is a little irregular, but I can't think of anyone who is going to complain under the circumstances. You all are aware of our situation. Do any of you have suggestions?"

I nudged Piper, and she shrugged.

"Well," I said, "I've got one idea, although maybe it's not a popular one. First, we pile all of us into my ship. Now the *Scupper* isn't fit to travel, but there are another seven planets in this system and enough moons and other orbital junk so that we could hide her and make rude noises at Genghis and his invasion fleet until the navy can send some real ships. What does everyone think?"

Bucky had on a bright purple jacket with a frayed collar and a candy-cane-striped waistcoat. He blinked his eyes and made a polite noise in his throat. "I regret to say that I believe my demi-brother Genghis would land his soldiery and take the citizens of Schuyler's World hostage so that he could then threaten to shoot them if you did not immediately surrender. My demi-brother is somewhat lacking in chivalry."

"Which means he probably would shoot them. It was just a thought," I said.

"Does anybody have any other ideas?" Hiro asked heavily.

"I should mention that I fear for the consequences if my demi-brother's soldiers are permitted to invade," Bucky said. "They might not wish to return home."

"I don't understand. Why wouldn't they?" Hiro asked. It

seemed a sensible question, considering this was Schuyler's World.

"I suppose it has much to do with our planetary psychology," Bucky said. "It is sort of a small dream with each of us to become a gentleman farmer and own our own little patch of soil to grow Brussels sprouts on."

"Brussels sprouts?" I asked.

"Tasty little morsels, aren't they? I can't think why you humans don't grow more of them."

"Maybe it's an acquired taste," Catarina interrupted. "Anyway, are you saying that the invasion force has been promised land here?"

"Oh, undoubtedly." Beaver nodded firmly. "Why else would they want to leave home? It was all in Cheeves's message."

Piper almost choked.

"Cheeves sent a message?" Catarina asked very softly. "May we see it?"

"Oh, certainly." Beaver slapped the pockets on his waistcoat. "I have a printout here somewhere."

"Look," I said, "forget the message for now. Unless we find some space weapons, we're dead. Right now, we're just going around in circles."

"Wheely?" Catarina said under her breath with a perfectly straight face.

"Mickey is right," Hiro said. "We need weapons. The navy has never given up a planet without a fight." He paused. "I'm not sure anyone has asked us to before, but it would set a terrible precedent." He slapped his hand down firmly on the table. "There has to be something we can do. We need weapons."

"Oh, how unfortunate," Beaver said. His whiskers twitched. "Cheeves did say that the invasion fleet would arrive next Friday, which gives us a week to look. I can't think where you could find any, unless of course there are some in the cargo Adolf was supposed to pick up at the spaceport."

"What cargo?" Piper and I asked in unison.

"I believe that it is manifested as agricultural machinery," Beaver said. "Cheeves apologized in his message for not seeing to it before he left. Although I can't think why anyone would be shipping agricultural machinery to my planet . . ."

Piper and I were out the door before he could finish. We left Catarina behind to explain to Commander Hiro.

When we got to the customs area, we found a woman with pigtails that were that funny blond color you associate with too much bleach. She was eating a sandwich and reading a bridal-fashions magazine.

Piper leaned on her terminal and asked her where the stuff consigned to Adolf's ship was located.

"Hey, I'm on my break!" the woman protested.

"I'm Lieutenant Piper from the navy, and this is an emergency. Your planet's about to be invaded, and we need to check that cargo." She pointed a thumb at me. "Ensign MacKay here is a desperate man."

"Oh." The girl swallowed what she was eating and pondered this. "I can't tell you stuff like that. I guess you'd have to ask the customs inspector."

"Where is the customs inspector?" I asked, moving her out box aside and sitting on the corner of her desk.

"It's only a part-time appointment, you know. I guess he's working his regular job," she said, staring up at me. "I'm pretty sure the stuff you want is up there, on the space platform, you know?" She pointed at the ceiling.

"Makes sense," I agreed. "It would cost too much to send it down just to shuttle it right back up."

"Let me check." The girl punched up some data on her terminal. "It's there!" she said triumphantly.

"Thanks, you've been a great help," Piper assured her, grabbing my sleeve.

"Now what do we do?" I asked.

"Where's the shuttle pilot?" Piper asked the girl. "I'm going up to check it out."

The girl shrugged expressively.

"Every time I've seen the California Kid, he's off taking a siesta," I said, pointing out the door at the hydrogen tanks. "I'm sure he's over there somewhere, but he'll need to fuel up. Kimball, the technician at the Civil Guard armory, would be the perfect guy to go with you. Let me give him a call."

Piper nodded and pulled the girl's terminal around so she could scroll up Adolf's manifest.

"Wow, this is exciting," the girl said. "Is there, like, a hidden camera in here or something?" She waved. "Hi, Mom!"

I grabbed the phone off the desk and called Kimball, who said he'd get a space suit and some tools and head on over. The girl pulled out a compact, touched up her makeup, and pasted a bright smile on her face. Then she began minutely examining the corners of the room. She waved again, a little more uncertainly.

The shuttle pilot nicknamed the California Kid wandered through the door.

"We need you to fuel up," I said. "Your planet is about to be invaded, and Lieutenant Piper here needs to get up to the space station."

The Kid nodded. "Sounds radical." He walked out in the same unhurried fashion.

"Is he in on this, too?" the girl behind the desk asked.

"Have you ever read Tamarkin's *Demographics of Colonial Migrations?*" I asked Piper. "Somewhere in there he describes colonists as 'offscourings of society and their diseased progeny, instinctively seeking places where their only competitors are other misfits.' "

Piper looked at me. "How else would a ship like yours make a living?"

"Right," I said, "I'll wait here for Kimball while you go get packed for the trip."

Piper took off for her car while I leaned over and reassured the girl behind the desk. "It's okay. It really is an invasion."

While she headed off for the ladies' room to have a nervous breakdown, I called up Catarina to tell her the plan.

Her image on the screen nodded without very much enthusiasm. "Commander Hiro may be a little giddy right now, but *if* Beam finds weapons up there, and *if* we can get them working, we still have Genghis coming at us with a Phoenix-class cruiser." She grimaced. "Out of a misplaced sense of honor, Bucky has volunteered to accompany us as an observer."

"Oh," I said.

"Had it occurred to you that the only two places we can mount weaponry are the space platform and your ship?"

"No," I said slowly, "but the thought would have come to

me eventually. And if it's okay with you, I'd just as soon change the subject. You know, in all the excitement I forgot to ask you whether you've figured out who masterminded the drug smuggling?''

Her face tightened. "Possibly. Can anyone there hear you?"

I listened for the water running in the ladies' room and turned down the volume on the phone. "No."

"A few weeks ago, the Second Bank of Schenectady had four six-figure bearer accounts."

"Hold it. What's a bearer account?"

"In essence, it's an account without a registered owner. Anyone who presents proper identification can claim it."

"That doesn't sound very honest," I commented.

"It's a very nice way to give dirty money a quick rinse and soak," Catarina agreed. "The banks don't pay interest on deposits, so they like the idea. There are five or six other planets I can think of where it's legal."

"Why bearer accounts? Didn't Davie and Bernie get paid off in jewels?''

"Davie and Bernie did. I wouldn't recommend the idea. Have you ever tried to fence hot jewels?''

"No. Not easy?"

"Not easy. There's not much of a market for them most places, and isotope analysis makes them easy to identify. If your paymaster gets annoyed with you, he or she can reduce the value very easily by leaving accurate descriptions with the local authorities. Bearer accounts are a better way to exchange payment. Well, two large ones got cleaned out."

"Whoever did it can't get very far."

"He already did." Catarina sighed. "It was Cheeves."

"Cheeves? You're kidding! Are you sure?"

"How many meter-tall Rodents are there on this planet?" she asked. "I have him on camera."

"Why Cheeves?"

She sighed again. "I don't know. It may have been the money. That's always a good motive. There's another thought that's even less appealing—Cheeves is Bucky's first cousin. He isn't that far out of the line of succession."

"That doesn't make any sense. If Cheeves isn't on our side, why would he tip us about weaponry in Adolf's shipment?"

"Ken, what would you do if Piper didn't find any weapons up there?"

I thought for a moment. "Even with wrecked lattices, the *Scupper* has a fifty-fifty shot of making it through to Brasilia Nuevo."

Catarina looked very tired. "Ken, Commander Hiro wants to fight it out if we can find anything to fight with. That's what the navy is for. But I'm not going to kid you—I don't care what Adolf has stashed away up there, the odds of our coming out of this are a lot less than fifty-fifty."

"Are you suggesting that Cheeves is setting us up?"

"It's possible," she conceded. "Why don't you do a qualitative analysis on the situation?"

"Well, let's see." I ran my fingers through my hair and thought for a minute. "There are what?—three probable outcomes: Genghis blows us away and causes Bucky to meet with an accident thanks to the information that Cheeves supplied, we blow Genghis away thanks to the information that Cheeves supplied, or all of us blow each other away."

"All three outcomes result in Cheeves being richer, closer to the throne, and at least arguably in the good graces of any and all survivors," Catarina postulated.

"I don't like the way this is starting to sound," I whined.

Catarina blew me a kiss and signed off.

Kimball drove up about fifteen minutes later with a flight bag and a chest of tools that was almost as large as he was. He pulled up in front of the customs shack and stuck his head out the window. "Can I leave this parked here?"

"Sure. Are you sure you got enough stuff?" I was trying not to stare at the tool chest.

Kimball gave me a funny look. "I brought a toothbrush and an extra change of clothes. Did I forget something?"

"No, you're fine," I conceded.

Piper showed up, her eyes sparkling, about twice as excited as I'd ever seen her get. I made introductions. "Ken, have you talked to Commander Hiro?" she asked.

"No, but I called Catarina."

"Good." She nodded to Kimball. "Okay. Kimball and I will see what's up there. If it turns out Adolf left some weaponry we can use, we'll try and install it, either on your ship or on the platform itself. We'll call you and let you know if we need anything. Don't forget to let your ship know what's going on." She transferred her keys from her right pocket to mine. "Here, take my car."

"Right." I winked at her. "We'll all see what we can do here with a hope and a prayer."

"Why don't you do the hoping and let Catarina do the praying?" She gave me a quick slap on the backside. "Wish us luck! Come on, Kid!"

Kimball and the Kid obediently fell in behind her. Piper was obviously psyched—weaponry does that to some people. I watched the shuttle take off, then drove back to the office.

Catarina was waiting for me as I walked in the door. " 'Operation Hope and a Prayer' is well and truly launched," I told her. "Piper and Kimball are on their way."

" 'Operation Hope and a Prayer'?" Catarina smiled.

I caught myself before she had a chance to respond. "No. No. Have I set myself up for a wicked line?"

She nodded primly.

"How bad? Real bad?"

Catarina kept nodding.

"I still think a pun is the absolute lowest form of humor. How about if I walk outside, and walk back in, and we both pretend this conversation never happened?"

Catarina turned her head demurely. "Do you remember the night we met?"

"I remember perfectly," I deadpanned. "You wore blue. The Germans wore gray."

"Louie," she said, "I think this could be the beginning of a beautiful friendship, although it might be a very short one."

We briefed Hiro, and Bunkie called up the news media while the rest of us brainstormed. It was a lot of storm and not much brain until Piper called in to say that she and Kimball had dug up two missile launchers with twenty reloads, two shipboard target-acquisition systems, and fifty hunter-seeker active mines. They were already starting to mount one of the launchers on the station loading platform. We told them to put the other one in the *Scupper*'s Number One hold in the middle of the racketball court.

Clyde and Bunkie started working on logistics. Catarina and I broke away to try and come up with a plan for a decent minefield. We knocked off for Leopard Milk and cookies—neither of us appreciated experiments with the local pizza—and went back to work until about midnight.

The next morning, the first thing I did was scroll up the newspaper to see what kind of coverage they'd given the invasion, and the second thing I did was hunt up Bunkie.

"Bunkie! What gives? There's nothing in the papers about the Rats!"

"Oh, the story is in there, sir," Bunker said, "look on page three."

"What do you mean, page three? This is an eight-page newspaper, for God's sake." I flipped down to page three.

Bunkie shrugged one shoulder. "Sir, we're competing with an election and a dog who plays the accordion by tapping on the keys with his paws. Reporters tend to be a little skeptical about anything that the government reveals voluntarily, so I expected them to downplay it a little bit."

I stared at her. "You mean, unless some reporter overhears it through a keyhole, we don't make page one?"

"That's about the size of it, sir. You haven't studied public relations, have you?" She patted her terminal. "I've prepared a news release for Commander Hiro stating that we have the situation well in hand, and there's absolutely nothing to worry about. That ought to bring them running."

Catarina pulled me away to help find crews for the missile launchers and watch-standers for the *Scupper*.

When I counted the jobs, I ran out of fingers. When I counted the people we had, I had a few fingers left over. "Just hypothetically," I asked, "what if we did it by the book?"

Catarina stared at me cross-eyed. "At a minimum, we'd need two shifts. Beam said the launchers are AN-33s, which means a crew of two plus someone else to man the acquisition system. That's twelve people, plus two people in command, two executive officers, six watch-standers for the *Scupper*, and two people for communications down here. Call it twenty-four people at a minimum.''

''Let's see, counting Kimball and McHugh—she's in the reserves—we've got seven,'' I thought aloud.

''The two Marines, Sin and Trujillo, have some shipboard training. That makes nine. If we pushed it, we'll need four or five for the space station, eight or nine more to run the ship, and Bunkie down here. The missile launchers don't have to be manned continuously, and we only have to keep one person conning the *Scupper* until Genghis shows up and we go to action stations.''

''After that, things will be over with quickly, one way or another.''

''We need Spooner and Dykstra if we can get them to volunteer. I'll take care of that—it isn't something I'd ask you to do. We probably have a few naval reservists on the planet—Bunkie can check the records. As soon as Clyde gets back, I'll send him out to round them up. Maybe some of them have something resembling the qualifications we need.''

I nodded. ''What about training?''

Catarina gave me a tired and dispirited look. ''We'd better call Beam. She's more familiar with the AN-33 systems than I am.''

Bunkie, of course, already had the call ready.

Piper appeared on the screen with a smudge of lubricating oil on either cheek. She pulled a rag out of one of her side pockets and wiped it away while she listened to Catarina.

She thought for a minute. ''Well, the usual training courses for these systems is about five months. By the time we get everything mounted, I figure we'll have about five days. If nothing goes wrong. Of course, something always goes wrong.''

''We may have to shorten the course. No weekends off,'' Catarina said with a ghost of a smile.

''The instruction manuals are all written in Rodent, but we won't have time to read them anyway,'' Beam said agreeably.

''Do you need more people up there now?''

''Not yet,'' Piper said judiciously. ''There's not enough room here to swing a small cat. Tomorrow, Roger and I ought to start working on the ship. Send Clyde and maybe one or two other people.''

"They'll be there." Catarina thought for a moment. "We need to start laying mines by the day after tomorrow at the latest.''

"One slight problem there." Piper grinned. "Ken's ship doesn't have a friend-or-foe identification circuit for the mines to recognize—it's not what you'd call top-of-the-line as warships go. I wouldn't recommend that we get close to them after we lay them. Talk at you later!''

She blanked the screen. "Does this mean we have as much chance of being blown up by our own mines as the enemy does?'' I asked Catarina.

Catarina wrinkled her nose. "Not really. They have more ships than we do.''

Hiro reconvened his council of war, and Catarina briefed him on the status of things.

Hiro stroked his chin. "We are honor-bound to protect this planet and uphold the navy's reputation.'' He asked with the faintest note of doubt in his voice, "Do we truly need to call up reservists?''

"Yes, sir,'' Catarina said. "Unless we can find some reservists with at least rudimentary gunnery training, we have no chance whatever.''

She carefully avoided saying what our chances were if we did find the reservists we were looking for.

"Well, as Napoleon said, 'The morale is to the material as four is to one.' We have that in our favor,'' Hiro said, trying to convince himself that we could take on a Phoenix-class cruiser and a couple of armed merchantmen with morale alone. He paused and added reflectively, "It's a shame Napoleon wasn't a navy man.''

Beaver woke up with a start. "Did somebody mention my demi-cousin Napoleon?''

Hiro turned to him. "Dr. Beaver, has Genghis had any military training?''

"Oh, dear! I'm afraid that I can't tell you very much. We were never very close—we had different mothers and that sort of thing. I believe he enrolled in one of your command and general staff colleges by correspondence, but our family never discussed grades," Beaver confided.

Clyde said gloomily. "Commander, I hate to ask this even hypothetically, but shouldn't we consider the possibility of surrendering?"

Hiro had difficulty following. "Well, Witherspoon, if Genghis sued for peace, I'm sure we'd accept."

"Sir, I was thinking more along the lines of our surrendering to Genghis, if we could get good terms—maybe a promise to spare the *Scupper*'s crew. Purely to spare the civilian population the hardships of war, of course."

"Dr. Beaver?" Catarina asked while Hiro digested this little bit of heresy.

"I do wish Cheeves were here," Beaver said. "Genghis was always appallingly violent as a child, and I fear that he would hardly be likely to accept any surrender conditions. I am sure that he is looking forward to this, and he would be so disappointed. He could hardly go home without at least landing ground forces and conquering the planet."

I suppose it would be a bit much to expect from somebody who picked the name Genghis.

"In that case, the navy can hardly surrender, can it?" Hiro said firmly. "I wonder if Lieutenant Commander Stemm could tell us what tactics Genghis will employ. Has anyone seen him since he arrived?"

"Lieutenant Commander Stemm had a very rough journey here aboard the mailship, and he is still recuperating," Catarina said, far too quickly.

"Lindquist, what have you and Ensign Mickey worked out as a plan of defense?"

"The Rodents' primary objectives are *Rustam's Slipper* and the city of Schenectady. If we orbit the *Slipper* over the city, the space platform can provide it with supporting fire. I expect Genghis to make his approach from out of the sun. The solar wind will degrade our sensors enough to give him an additional advantage—that's textbook. I recommend laying the mines in a standard stacked triple-vee along that axis," Catarina told him.

"You don't think Genghis will try a diversionary landing elsewhere on the planet, do you?" Hiro asked, pursing his lips.

"Sir, ninety-eight percent of this planet's land surface is un-inhabited. As Ensign MacKay aptly pointed out when we dis-cussed the matter, if they land out in the sticks, it might be a while before anyone notices."

Clyde spoke up, "Uh, ma'am, what if they decide not to come at us out of the sun? If this guy Genghis took the command correspondence course, he ought to figure that we'd defend against the textbook solution."

"Clyde, we only have so many mines. If Genghis doesn't use a textbook approach, the best we can do is give him a failing grade on his exam and ask him to do the problem over."

"I hope stupidity runs in that family," Clyde said glumly. Nobody else present had any other thoughts to contribute.

"Well, darn it! We're just going to have to do it!" Hiro pounded his fist on the table with more enthusiasm than most of us felt.

"As Bucky says, 'It's always darkest just before the dawn, which often has a silver lining,' " Beaver said cheerfully. As we broke up, he confided, "Bucky really didn't say that, but I felt it was appropriate anyway."

Hiro laid a hand on my arm. "Mickey, I just wanted to make sure you understand." He searched for words. "I've been in the navy for twenty-one years. I knew that this was going to be my last duty station. But just once . . ."

He broke off the sentence without completing it, patted my arm awkwardly, and left. I've seen people who retired long be-fore they filed the papers, and—all things considered—I figured I was lucky that Hiro hadn't gone that way.

Clyde and Bunkie had turned up four reservists, and Catarina and I sat down to screen them.

McHugh was the first. Bunkie brought her in and sat her down across the table from us.

McHugh started off breezily, "Oh, hello, Ken. Hello, Lieu-tenant Lindquist. Does this have anything to do with your in-vestigation? The woman who called me didn't say."

"I understand that you quit working for Harry," I said, evading her question.

"Harry is a pig! I can't stand that man." McHugh narrowed her eyes. "What's going on?"

"The Rodents are invading us," Catarina said with some small show of compassion. "We need to recall you to active duty."

It was the first time I'd seen Annalee lose her composure. "Oh, shit . . ." she said weakly.

"We need you, Annalee," I said.

"We're primarily looking for people who can operate the AN-33 missile launcher and a Gremlin detection/acquisition configuration," Catarina explained, tapping McHugh's file, which said she was familiar with both.

"I've worked with the Gremlin a little," McHugh said warily. "I thought the AN-33 was obsolete." She knitted her brows. "Where are you getting launchers like that?"

Catarina and I exchanged glances. "We picked up two that were on their way to the Rodents. We're mounting one on the space platform and another on the *Scupper*. We also have some mines," I told her.

"And what have the Rodents got?" McHugh insisted, beginning to fidget.

Catarina shrugged. "A Phoenix-class cruiser and a couple of armed merchantmen."

"Shit. Shit! It's not fair. It's just not fair!" McHugh wailed. "It's just not fair!" She folded her arms in front of her and started pounding her head on the table.

Bunkie walked in without being bidden and gently helped McHugh up. "Come on, we need to get your records updated," she said, leading an unresisting McHugh away.

"Well, that was easy. I hope they all go that well," I told Catarina.

"The day is young," she said confidently.

The next reservist through the door was someone named Halsey. He came through the door wearing full dress uniform. As Bunkie led him in, I said incredulously, "Harry, what are you doing here?"

"Petty Officer Harold W. Halsey, reporting for duty." Harry stopped in front of us and snapped off a nice salute. "I am proud to bear arms in my planet's defense."

Catarina leaned over and whispered in my ear, "Take off your jacket and roll up your sleeves." Some saliva went down the wrong pipe. Catarina pounded me affectionately on the back. "Harry, why don't you sit down? Somehow I had the impression that you were no longer in the reserves."

"Thank you, ma'am." Harry obediently lowered himself into our little chair, which trembled slightly. "I'm still in, ma'am. I'll be navy blue until the day I die," he said with a perfectly straight face.

"We need people who can operate the AN-33 missile system and Gremlin detection gear," I said, pulling his file away from Catarina.

"Sir, I cut my teeth on AN-33s, sir."

I stared across the table at him and waved his qualifications printout in the air.

"Well, maybe I didn't exactly cut my teeth on AN-33s, but I flossed them a little. Honest, Ken, I can help," Harry said helplessly. He hunched over and looked at me, crushing his cap in his hands. "This means more to me than you'd believe."

I looked at Catarina and shrugged. "Harry, did Bunkie tell you what the odds against us are?"

He nodded.

"Thank you, Harry," Catarina said. "We'll let you know in a couple of minutes. Please wait outside."

After Bunkie led him off, I turned to Catarina. "Catarina—I mean Lieutenant—what do you think?"

"I think Harry is a genuine patriot, and he bleeds navy blue. I suppose tending bar does get a little tame for him at times." She tapped the personnel folder I was holding. "According to this, he does know a little fire control."

I leafed through. "He was only on active duty for a year or so. He was kicked out for what sounded like aggravated assault, but his discharge sheet seems to have gotten wiped off the system somehow. How did he ever get into the reserves?"

"He may have forgotten to mention a few things," Catarina said. "Did you read his last fitness report?"

"How bad is it?"

"He maxed out in enthusiasm, which pulled the rest of his marks up to what you would expect from slime mold. There's only one written comment: 'This sailor will spend the rest of his life pushing on doors marked Pull.' "

"Can we afford not to take him?" I asked.

"No," she said briefly, closing the file.

A minute later, I got an even bigger surprise when Seaman 1/C Disler reported.

"Dinky, I should have guessed. What are you doing here?"

Dinky looked almost as surprised to see me in uniform. "Sir, Harry talked me into joining about a year and a half ago, sir. He made it really sound like fun."

"Dinky, I thought you were married and had kids," Catarina said, cutting to the point.

"Yes, ma'am. I am married, and I have two lovely daughters." Dinky's eyes glowed with pride.

"Dinky, I really don't think we should take you if you have a wife and a family. I know you want to do your duty, and I know you want to be with Harry, but what we're engaged in is pretty close to being a suicide mission," Catarina explained gently.

Dinky hesitated and looked confused. "But ma'am, you can't do that! Uh, Ken, sir. Can I speak to you in confidence, I mean, in private?"

Catarina was accommodating. "I have to leave for a moment. Ensign MacKay, please take charge."

As soon as the door closed behind her, I told Dinky, "Okay. Make it good."

"Well, sir . . ." Dinky hesitated. "Have you ever met my wife?"

"No," I admitted, puzzled.

"Sir, she looks an awful lot like Harry. With Harry joined up and the bar closed, she'd expect me to stay home nights. Under the circumstances, sir, I really think I want to be out there defending my planet. I know I've never served on active duty, but Harry's taught me fire control, and we really work well together. I won't let you down, sir."

"Well . . ."

Dinky looked me straight in the eye. "I realize that we don't have much of a chance of stopping the Rats, but sir, understand that death holds no terror for me."

"Thank you, Seaman Disler. We'll let you know in a few minutes."

Dinky saluted and left, and Catarina reentered.

"We've got to take him," I told her.

"What did he do, sing 'The Marines' Hymn'?"

"No, but we're lucky the Foreign Legion doesn't have a recruiting office here. I can honestly say that I won't be able to sleep nights if we don't take him."

The last reservist was retired Chief Petty Officer Chandrasekhar, who had spent his entire career running a mess hall. We made him our chief of logistics and put him to work making box lunches.

Catarina called Rosalee Dykstra and Wyma Jean. Wyma Jean volunteered, even after Catarina explained the odds. I asked her about Rosalee. Catarina smiled. "Rosalee is a pacifist."

"Hold it. Rekey the data," I said. "Rosalee's favorite pastime is assault and battery."

"Oh, Dykstra's genuine, Ken. She's like most pacifists I've met. She doesn't believe in violence, except when it's absolutely necessary. Rosalee is just a little fuzzier than most pacifists about defining the exact parameters of when violence is absolutely necessary."

"Okay, Dykstra's out. How do we divide up our people?"

"Our best chance is to put our best missile team on the space platform and use the *Scupper* as a tethered goat to lure the Rodents in. I'd like to put Sin and Trujillo there with Beam and Kimball."

"Lindquist Sahib, you mean you're going to stick the Marines up there under a woman officer? They're going to pitch a fit. Actually, I'm surprised nobody thought of volunteering me for the assignment."

The Marines have a proud tradition of absolute chauvinism that goes back several centuries.

Catarina coughed delicately. "Actually, I did, and I asked Sin and Trujillo who they'd prefer to serve under. Sin sort of shuffled his feet and said, 'Begging your pardon, ma'am, but we'd just as soon have a real officer, even if she is a woman.' "

I reflected. "I'm touched. Deeply touched. I keep thinking back and trying to recall if I've ever had amnesia because I have to believe that somehow, somewhere, I've done something so horrible that God would want to do this to me."

"Trust me. God has a sense of humor."

"I don't mean to be critical, but Harry and McHugh are going to mix like gunpowder and sparks, and Clyde and Wyma Jean are likely to get along about half as well."

"Ken, the big children aren't going to have very much time to think about their personal problems. And if the launcher on the space platform doesn't score a first-round hit before Genghis realizes it's there, they'll have even less time."

"Point taken. Whatever happened to Lieutenant Commander Stemm?"

"Commander Stemm showed up dehydrated and severely disoriented from watching a week's worth of Fast Eddie's Westerns. He checked himself into the hospital on arrival. I have a friend there, and Stemm is under what people refer to as heavy sedation."

"You don't sound very high on him."

"Bobby Stemm?" Catarina's nostrils flared slightly. "No. There are people who make you realize the blessings of being shorthanded." For a second, I thought she was describing half the planet.

Six Days Thou Shalt Work,
and Do All Thou Art Able;
and the Seventh the Same,
and Pound on the Cable

Things started hopping on Sunday. While we were getting ready to send people up, the newspapers reacted exactly the way Bunkie had predicted. As soon as they found out that we had called up reservists and commissioned the *Scupper*, they brushed aside our coy assertions that nothing was amiss. The papers came out with banner headlines that read "War!" Bucky added fuel to the fire by closing down the embassy and refusing to issue an official statement.

None of the candidates for election had any statements to make. Apparently the early opinion polls were all over the place.

After Catarina and I got back from mass, Bunkie ushered us in to take an urgent conference call from the Schenectady Chamber of Commerce. Commander Hiro arrived a moment later.

"Bother," he said. "Do I have to talk to them, Lindquist?"

Catarina nodded.

"Bother." Hiro took a deep breath. "Put them on the screen, Bunkie."

About a dozen people appeared on the big screen, jammed together so that we could see all of them. They were all wearing nearly identical suits, and they were all smiling. Two of them were women.

The man in bangs in the middle opened by saying, "Hi, I'm Buddy—Buddy Shishekli. You know, 'Buddy's Convenience Shoppes'?"

Hiro nodded politely.

"A few of us happened to get together to discuss things, and we're so very happy we could touch base with you to discuss our mutual interests. Right now, there are rumors circulating that the Rodents are preparing to present a hostile takeover, and we feel that this might have an adverse effect on the overall economic climate.''

Commander Hiro made a pleasant noise in his throat.

''Commander, I have to tell you that this hostile takeover that the Rodents want to drum up financing for comes at a really, really bad time, market-wise. I don't know if you've been following trends, but our banking industry has developed some weaknesses recently.''

Hiro looked at him blankly. ''Say that again?''

Shishekli took a deep breath. ''Commander, you're a hard bargainer, and I'll lay it on the line for you. I want to personally assure you that both our banks are sound institutions that are strong, strong boosters of the local economy. This hostile takeover, coupled with a soft real-estate market and an apparent downturn in retail sales, might have a really, really severe impact on them.''

Hiro quickly said, ''Thank you. Excuse me one moment, please.'' He blanked his screen. ''What did he just say?''

I cleared my throat. ''Sir, he said that the local banks are stuffed to the ceiling with unsecured sweetheart loans to friends and neighbors, and that going to war will cause their unsuspecting depositors to hide their money in mattresses and cause all of those bad loans to pop out like mushrooms. After that, both banks go under, and everybody concerned goes to jail.''

Hiro nodded firmly. ''Thank you, Mickey.'' He turned the screen back on. ''Sorry to be away. Please continue.''

The next guy to launch was a stiff fellow with a waxed mustache named Mahmoud who introduced himself as manager of the local J-Mart.

''Commander, we have some little financial disequilibrium here. I've heard some people say that we've been a little overambitious in our growth objectives . . .''

J-Mart provides Schenectady with its upscale shopping. There's a joke to the effect that when God calls all the poor people to heaven, he's going to start by flooding J-Mart.

When Mahmoud ran out of breath, Hiro politely disengaged and placed us on mute. "Mickey, did he say anything?"

I stopped polishing my nails and looked up. "Not yet."

"That's what I thought." Hiro flipped us off mute. "Is there something else, Mr. Shishekli?"

"Certainly, Commander," Shishekli said smoothly. "Now, we also feel that we should stress the negative cash flow situation across the board. We're not talking R-word numbers yet . . . ."

"Recession," I translated.

"But long-term corporate prospects are not good. There are a couple of high-stakes mergers on the table that might be impacted by any negative publicity. It occurs to us that it might be a real mistake for you to try to block this hostile takeover by the Rodents. Interest rates could go up, many of the businesses that depend on the seasonal business would be hit hard by any loss of consumer confidence, and a lot of us feel that the extra buying power that these Rodents would generate could rebound the economy, really move the indicators, if you know what I mean."

A thin, hatchet-faced woman wearing three layers of makeup broke in in a bright, bubbly voice. "We at Mary Keye think that's absolutely right. We're looking at a real opportunity for explosive growth if we can just turn this corner. We've crunched some numbers, and we think that a good buying surge from the Rodents in the touristry niches would do the trick. All we need are some positive vibes from you for us to jump on targeting the short-term opportunities here."

Apparently noticing that Hiro was beginning to nod off, Shishekli jumped back in. "Commander, I can see you're a bottom-line man. To come right to the point, all of us here feel that we need your help in avoiding any event-induced pressure on the money supply. Now, when the rubber meets the road, can we count on you? That's what we'd like to know."

"Thank you. One second, please." Hiro blanked his screen.

Catarina looked at me, and I shrugged. "They asked us not to fight. Christmas sales have been lousy, the shopkeepers are getting antsy, and they figure that having a few hundred invading Rodents in town buying up souvenirs would be real good for business." I shrugged again. "I didn't understand the part about the rubber in the road."

Hiro digested all of this. "Does this mean I can shoot them for treason?" he asked hopefully.

"Treason requires two overt acts, and besides, we'd have to have a trial," Catarina explained tactfully.

"Hmmm." Hiro pondered this. "Can I tell them to pound sand?"

"Why don't you tell them that the idea has snap to it, but you need to run some long-term projections through the accountants and run the idea up the flagpole to see if anyone salutes," Catarina said smoothly.

"That almost sounds military," Hiro mused. He flipped on the screen. "Well, the idea has snap to it, but I need to run some long-term projections through the accountants and run the idea up the flagpole to see if anyone salutes."

"Commander, I feel that we have had a really productive exchange of views, and we'll wait to hear back from you," the industry spokesman said with evident relief.

"Thank you. I certainly enjoyed sharing thoughts," Hiro said, switching off the phone. "I really wanted to tell him to pound sand," he added wistfully.

"Sir, you did, but it'll take them a few days to figure that out," Catarina told him. "Fortunately, there are a couple of two-story buildings in town that they can jump off of."

"It's nice to know that the people here appreciate what we're doing for them," I observed.

We got Spooner to dock the *Scupper* at the space platform so that Piper and Kimball could start militarizing the ship, and Bunkie dug up an old simulator program for the AN-33 launcher system and started training our two launcher teams, which were Sin and Trujillo and Harry and Dinky. While they fiddled with their joysticks, the rest of us started accumulating the things we needed to make the space platform livable, including a portable rest room.

By midafternoon we were ready for another shuttle run, and sent up Hiro, Catarina, McHugh, Clyde, Harry, and Dinky.

Catarina talked me into staying behind to keep an eye on things downside, which was probably a polite way of saying that my talents wouldn't be missed for the time being.

The rest of us worked through lunch on Monday—an eggplant-curry concoction that Chandrasekhar whipped up—and I was looking for a quiet corner where I could take a nap when Bunkie called me over to the window.

I went over and wiped away some of the smudges that the cleaning crew had left. "What the heck?" I said to no one in particular.

The Civil Guard, all eleven of them, were marching down the street in uniform carrying signs proclaiming a strike. They stopped a couple of meters in front of the door, where they set up a picket line. A couple of them started singing "The Red Flag":

> "Then raise the scarlet standard high!
>   Within its shade we'll live or die.
> Tho' cowards flinch and traitors sneer,
>   We'll keep the Red Flag flying here!"

The signs read BETTER BENEFITS and RODENTS ARE OUR ALLIES AGAINST MILITARIST EXPLOITATION OF THE WORKING CLASS. The pedestrians in the street ignored them completely.

Attracted by the noise, Chandrasekhar stepped out of the galley, smiled inscrutably, and went back to stirring his rice. Trujillo and Sin spilled out of Catarina's office and joined Bunkie and me by the window.

"We could have the police arrest them for trespassing," Bunkie suggested.

"The court will let them off with a twenty-dollar fine and some free publicity," I lamented aloud. "This is not something they covered at Woolmera. Does anyone have any suggestions?"

Asking the question was an obvious mistake.

Sin longingly pressed his face up against the glass. Sin was Korean and appropriately named for a marine. Trujillo, the more apelike of the two, tugged at his mustache. "Begging the ensign's pardon, sir, but Sin and I had a couple of good friends in the Guard before the wimps took it over. Sir, could we, uh . . ."

Sin started twitching. Trujillo hooked his right hand in Sin's belt to keep him stationary and gently tugged my sleeve with the other.

I was about to say the proper thing when a couple of the Guardsmen switched to singing "Joe Hill," slightly off-key, which offended my aesthetic sense.

"This requires careful thought," I temporized, stroking my chin. "Bunkie, you have access to their personnel records, don't you? What if I called them into active federal service?"

Bunkie stiffened at the thought, but said, "Of course, sir."

"Just hypothetically, what could we do with them?"

Bunkie eyed me with a measure of respect and tapped on her terminal. "Seven discharges for ineptitude and four on medical grounds, sir."

"About how long would it take for us to process them?" I asked innocently. Trujillo and Sin stared at me intently.

"If they request a board, fifteen days," Bunkie said. "Eight seconds if they waive the board."

"Bunkie, please print out waivers." I looked at my Marines and glanced down at my watch. "Gentlemen, please ask the people out there to sign them. Since we're all probably going to get ourselves killed next week, you have five minutes beginning when I step away from the window."

I peeked. I noticed that a few of the pedestrians pitched in and helped Sin and Trujillo out. They came back with a pile of waivers, including a few signed by persons who were not members of the Civil Guard, and two waivers signed by my friend Bubba, who apparently couldn't run very fast. By the time that Lydia Dare and the police rolled up, Schuyler's World no longer had a Civil Guard. I gave the police sergeant in charge a bottle of Hiro's sake that looked suspicious, Chandrasekhar presented Lydia with some radishes cut up to look like flowers, and we declined comment.

The police helped Lydia leave when she started screaming imprecations. As Lydia and the cops drove away, Bunkie turned to me and said, "Sir, I don't think Lieutenant Lindquist could have handled it any better."

I nursed that small glow of pride until the next contingent of visitors arrived.

A large, muscular woman threw open our door and came in leading two little girls by the hand. She casually shoved Trujillo out of her way and rumbled, "All right, where is he? Where is my husband hiding?"

She had more of a mustache than Trujillo, and she looked a little bit like Harry. "You must be Dinky's wife. We just sent him up to the space platform," I mumbled, as Bunkie pressed herself unobtrusively against the wall and edged her way out of the room.

"Silly man." Dinky's wife gave me a contemptuous look and her eyes narrowed. "What would he be doing up there? If he's in here, I'll find him. Here, watch my darlings!" She stalked off to search Hiro's empty office.

Her two daughters looked at me without smiling.

"Uh, hello," I said awkwardly.

The taller of the two blinked. "You must be Ensign Ken."

"That's right," I said.

The short one blinked twice. "Mommy says that Daddy's left us." We listened to Mommy shift the furniture in Hiro's office. "Mommy says that he's abandoned his family and run away to join the navy and isn't ever coming back."

The taller of the two looked up at me. "Can we run away and join the navy, too?"

I looked to see to if Mommy was out of earshot. "Give me a call on your seventeenth birthday—if your dad signs the papers, you're in."

The short one nodded to her sibling. "See? Daddy said he was nice."

Mommy emerged flushed and disheveled. "He isn't here," she said accusingly.

"He's up in space," I repeated very carefully.

She pointed her finger at me. "You tell him just wait until I find him! Come on, children."

I shut the door behind them. "Whew!"

Bunkie, Sin, Trujillo, and Chandrasekhar appeared, looking slightly pale. Bunkie sniffled and wiped her nose. "Sir," she said, "I just want you to know that that was a beautiful thing you said to those children. I don't think you're half as nasty as everyone says you are."

"Thank you, Bunkie," I said. "I am truly touched."

Chandrasekhar took advantage of the momentary silence to

ring the dinner bell and pass out foam plates loaded with what looked like large pastries. Sin and Trujillo began chowing down with enthusiasm. Bunkie wrinkled her nose.

I broke a corner off mine. "What is this, a calzone? Where's the pepperoni?" I asked Chandrasekhar.

Chandrasekhar was short and dark, with a round and surprisingly youthful-looking face. Having been plucked out of a well-deserved retirement, he was obviously taking his reactivation philosophically. He tilted his head and looked at me very severely. "This is a roti, sir. It is filled with dhal and sweet potato and other healthful things. Dhal is a very tasty pea puree."

"Chief Chandrasekhar runs a vegetarian restaurant," Bunkie explained.

"I also have a very healthful salad for you," Chandrasekhar said.

"You wouldn't possibly consider buying some meat, would you?" I asked very tentatively.

"While it is against my moral precepts to eat meat, I would never dream of imposing these precepts on other persons," Chandrasekhar told me. He added, "It might be very, very hard to find any, however. Unless meat is very, very fresh and very, very well prepared, it is completely impossible to eat."

For those among us who were slow learners, Bunkie explained, "Chief Chandrasekhar's restaurant is going to hell every day that he's away."

"I was thinking about eating out tonight," I said hastily.

"Sir, the persons who run these restaurants are friends of mine. I would not want them to feed you something by mistake which might disagree with you. Lieutenant Lindquist requested of me that I watch over your health very carefully," Chandrasekhar said. "Truly it would be better for you not to stray."

"Are you trying to tell me that I'm going to eat rabbit food until the day you take that uniform off?" I asked.

Bunkie stared at the ceiling. "Sir, the chief is losing *a lot* of money."

"Truly, it would be better for you," Chandrasekhar said, disappearing into the galley to bring out seconds for Trujillo.

I put away about half of my roti, gave everyone a two-hour break, and decided to take a walk.

Bunkie cautioned, "You'd better stay close, sir. We don't know what kind of crazies may be roaming around out there."

I refrained from pointing out that most of them had already dropped by and headed out the door. On impulse I walked over to Catarina's church.

I went inside and leaned against a pew. While I was silently contemplating the altar, a heavyset man came out of one of the side doors. "Hello, I'm Father Yakub. Can I help you?"

Father Yakub could have been a young Father Christmas. He had dark blue eyes under bushy eyebrows, and a thick, black beard.

"I'm Ken MacKay," I replied, a little embarrassed. "I'm a friend of Catarina Lindquist. I've been in here for some of your services. Last week, I remember you had a woman doing the mass."

"Deacon Mary Robb. Mary gives a dynamite sermon, doesn't she?" Father Yakub smiled, exposing a row of even, white teeth. "You're a friend of Catarina's? Why don't you come on back?

"Catarina said that you might be stopping by," Father Yakub said as we entered the sacristy.

"She must know me better than I do," I said. If she did, I was really in trouble.

Father Yakub started heating some water for coffee. "Would you like to tell me why you came?"

"Well, now that you mention it, the Rodents are probably going to kill me next week unless somebody else does the job first, so I guess I was thinking about squaring things with God, just in case."

"We prefer to call it 'reconciliation.' "

"Whatever. Do I tell you my sins?"

"Only if you want. Pull up a chair."

"Don't I have to kneel in one of those little boxes, with incense? Like in the movies, you know, 'Bless me, Father, for I have sinned'?"

Father Yakub chuckled and handed me a cup of coffee. "That went out with high-heeled shoes. You have a seat, I give you a cup of coffee, and we talk. Cream and sugar?"

"Black coffee, please. I must be getting an ulcer—cream upsets my stomach. Father, is this okay? I'm really not a Catholic."

"It can't hurt." Father Yakub extended his index finger in the direction of the ceiling. "The Big Guy or Gal in the Sky doesn't mind, and I get paid the same either way. Besides, our sister in Christ Catarina says you need all the help you can get."

We went through everything I could think of, which took a while because I kept reminding Father Yakub of things he did when he was nearly as young and almost as dumb as I was, which kept reminding me of more things to confess. As I wound down, I looked at him critically.

"Is something else troubling you, Ken?" Father Yakub asked, stretching.

I thought for a moment. "I guess this wasn't quite what I expected." I thought a little longer. "Since my present occupation involves trying to blow away hordes of invading Rodents who are likely to be in a better state of grace than I am, I expected you to be, well, a little less accepting."

"Ken, the Church eschews violence and prays earnestly for peace, but the fullness of God's plan calls for us to demonstrate an acceptance of the things of this world. In short, you get a lot of different opinions within the Church about the morality of engaging in warfare. If you want total nonviolence and a loving repudiation of war, try the Franciscans up the street. Speaking unofficially, give our misguided Rat brethren hell."

He stroked his chin. "Let's see, for your penance . . . how about five Hail Marys, five Our Fathers, five hours of community service sometime next week if you get out of this alive. Let's see, we've got faith covered, we've got love, what about charity? . . . Okay, sometime in the next week or so, slip a wink to some homely girl. That should cover the bases." He winked. "Catarina said that there was hope for you yet."

He traced out the sign of the cross. "I absolve thee . . ."

Father Yakub was my kind of priest.

When I got back, Bunkie grabbed my arm. "Sir, you're just in time. Do you know Lieutenant Commander Stemm?"

"He's the one who came in on the mailship. Why?"

She moved her head in the direction of Hiro's office. "He's

here. I'm setting up a call to the ship now." She looked in the direction of Hiro's office and whispered, "He wants us to surrender. You might want to sit in on this, sir."

"I think I will. Never a dull moment around here," I said feebly. I went in and found myself a chair in front of the viewscreen.

Bunkie patched us through. Commander Hiro and Catarina appeared, looking grim. Catarina was still wearing coveralls. The skin was stretched taut over her face, and I could see she was tired. She smiled briefly when she recognized me. "Hello, Ken. Where's Stemm?"

"He's in Commander Hiro's office as far as I know. I haven't seen him."

"A little one-upmanship to put us on the screen first," she commented. "Stick around, Ken. You have as much right to be here as anyone."

Stemm strode in a few seconds later and casually took a seat. He was tall and blond with a hairline mustache. He looked like he stepped off a recruiting poster, and I disliked him on sight.

"Ah, Lieutenant Lindquist, how nice to see you again. Commander Hiro, I recognize. This call is not being recorded." Then he noticed me. "Who is this other officer? Is he cleared to hear this?"

"This is Ensign MacKay. Of course he's cleared. He's cleared for Top Secret and below," Catarina lied with a perfectly straight face.

"Ah, so this is the infamous Ensign MacKay. Ensign, do you have any idea how much damage you've done?"

Catarina elbowed Hiro in the ribs.

Hiro started slightly, then narrowed his gaze on Stemm. "Stemm, can we get on with this? We're very busy here."

Stemm coughed. "I regret that I was not here earlier. I was placed under sedation on my arrival. Fortunately, a nurse—Nurse Clarkin—noticed that the medication prescribed for me was improper." He eyed Catarina.

She smiled sweetly and said very, very softly, "Shame they didn't dose you with strychnine."

"Commander, did you hear that?" Stemm demanded, jumping up.

"Hear what?" Hiro asked.

"Commander Stemm, calm down. Perhaps you could still use some medical attention," Catarina said agreeably.

"That won't work, Lindquist. I had the hospital give me a full medical evaluation," Stemm snapped, pricked beyond endurance. "I expect to be filing some charges."

"Pity," Catarina said without explaining.

"Why don't we get to the point, Stemm? We're expecting the Rodents to attack, and we have a lot of work to do," Hiro said.

"Commander Hiro, that's just my point. You cannot expect to resist that attack." Stemm seated himself, recovering his urbane demeanor. He held his hand up. "I questioned your personnel closely upon my arrival." He peered intently at Hiro. "You have to avoid provoking the Rodents at all costs. The Macdonalds are preparing for war. A defeat here would be absolutely disastrous! If the navy divides its strength to deal with the Rodents, the Macdonalds will attack. That is what is at stake, not this loathsome ball of mud we are on." Stemm leaned forward. "We have never fought a space war before. If you fight here and lose, the consequences would be incalculable." Then he leaned back and sneered. "And what do you have to fight with? Two obsolete launchers and a ship that ought to be broken up for scrap, a spacegoing honey barge. I know what orders Captain Crenshaw would give you."

I resented the crack about a honey barge.

Hiro's face turned gray. "Am I being ordered to surrender?" he asked woodenly.

Catarina broke in, hardly troubling to conceal her opinion of Stemm. "Do you have these orders in writing?"

"Of course Captain Crenshaw didn't put them in writing," Stemm said sarcastically.

"Too bad. Well, Captain Crenshaw's not here." She tilted her head to look at Hiro. "Sir, I don't see that anything's changed. I can't imagine Captain Crenshaw expecting us to surrender without putting up a fight."

Stemm sucked his breath in. "Captain Crenshaw obviously could not foresee that particular eventuality, but you really don't understand what's important here, do you? Can you even begin to imagine the magnitude of the harm that you would precipitate by losing a hopeless and completely irrelevant battle here?''

''Unless Lieutenant Commander Stemm has something else in his bag of tricks, I think we've been through all this before, sir,'' Catarina said, looking at Hiro.

Hiro nodded. ''I am afraid that what you have to say does not alter my decision, Commander. My sense of duty compels me to act as I see fit until I receive orders to the contrary through proper channels.''

I almost started clapping.

''That will be too late! Prince Genghis will be here in a week!''

''That's certainly a possibility,'' Hiro agreed. I saw a smile flicker across Catarina's face.

Stemm blinked his eyes a few times. ''I had not expected to have to use this,'' he said reaching into his pocket, ''but I have here written instructions from the ambassador on !Plixxi* forbidding you to open fire on any Rodent ship so that you will not sabotage her efforts to resolve this matter through diplomatic means without any appreciable amount of bloodshed.''

He placed the letter under the overhead camera. The computer automatically slapped the top two-thirds of the document up on a split screen and focused the camera to make the printing legible. ''Please read paragraph two,'' Stemm suggested.

Since it was my blood that was involved, I got up and peered over Stemm's shoulder before he realized what I was doing. ''Uh, sir, this letter isn't signed.''

''What? Why isn't the letter signed, Stemm?'' Hiro knitted his brows.

Stemm began looking around the room, although I'm not sure what he expected to find. ''There wasn't time for the ambassador to sign it, but the letter expresses the spirit of her instructions—''

''Let me try and understand this,'' Catarina interjected. ''The ambassador didn't sign the letter, and you don't have anything authorizing you to sign the letter on her behalf.''

''No, not actually,'' Stemm began.

''Look,'' I said, ''I may just be a dumb reserve ensign, but the last time I checked, the navy's never lost a war and never started one by surrendering a ship. I don't know much about the Macdonalds, but I'd like to think we have a better chance of staying out of a war by convincing them that whipping us doesn't come easy."

"I'll second *that* . . ." Catarina whispered loud enough to hear.

"I agree," Hiro said forcefully.

"This is complete madness. You won't have heard the last of it," Stemm sputtered. He cocked his head. "Commander Hiro, I have heard an even more disturbing rumor that one of your officers is a vampire. It would be utterly inappropriate to have a vampire aboard a navy vessel."

Catarina and I looked at Hiro, who colored slightly. I saw her nostrils flare, and I'm sure Hiro saw it as well.

"Now, see here, Stemm," Hiro said gently. "There was a game we used to play. We called it 'count the stripes.' Now let me see, on your sleeve I see one—two—two and a half stripes. And on my sleeve I see one—two—*three* stripes. Now it seems to me that the last time I checked that means that when I tell you to get bent, you say 'yes, sir' and you get bent. I like that. Get bent, Stemm."

Stemm stood up stiffly. "I shall report this to Captain Crenshaw at the first opportunity, sir."

"Lindquist, thank you for your support," Hiro said heavily. "You too, Ensign Mickey. If you would please excuse me a moment." Looking older and exhausted, he left his seat.

I looked at Catarina and blew her a kiss. "Wonderful performance."

"Ken, I've been wanting to say a few things to Stemm for a long time. I think that you're right—as long as we put up a good fight and bloody Genghis's nose, it doesn't matter whether we win or not." She smiled radiantly. "Except, of course, to us."

I returned her smile as well as I could manage. "And I love you for it. When am I coming up to join you?"

"Actually, we're coming down to join you. Bunkie showed me this." She held up a printout covered in elegant, squiggly, illegible script. "A messenger handed it to Bunkie while you were out. It's an invitation from the mayor of Schenectady for all of our officers to attend an election-eve reception late tonight.

Apparently Mayor Feldman works on the principle that if you can't beat them, join them.''

"You mean we're going to play dress-up and go to this thing?'' I asked.

"Why not? We have to send the shuttle down to pick up Lieutenant Commander Stemm so he can leave with Fast Eddie.'' She smirked. "We might as well hobnob with the politicians. Show them that good old navy sangfroid. Like the Duke of Wellington's ball on the eve of Quatre Bras. The politicians will feel a whole lot better if we come. Besides,'' she added, "they're serving food.''

"Say no more. I'm your man.''

"Also, Commander Hiro's wife has been here for three years and I'm sure she'd love it. She may not have very much time to spend with her husband over the next few days.''

"I understand,'' I said.

"See if Lieutenant Commander Stemm needs any help in getting out of here at the first opportunity, then climb into the mess whites the sheriff's brother-in-law made you and get Bunkie to trim your hair.''

"Right.''

I found Stemm in Hiro's office, moodily swiveling Hiro's chair back and forth. "Sir, is there anything I can do to help you on your way to Brasilia Nuevo with the mailship?''

"No, Ensign,'' Stemm said bitterly, staring at the wall. He swiveled some more. "Ensign, how long will it take the mailship to get to Brasilia Nuevo?''

I calculated swiftly. "About a week and a half,'' I said, tacking on an extra two or three days for good measure.

Stemm exhaled deeply, his face lined with resignation. "A week and a half with Fast Eddie,'' he breathed, and glared at me. "While I watch horse operas in a glorified coffin, you silly idiots will be dragging the navy's good name into the dirt!''

"Look at the bright side, sir,'' I said cheerfully. "If we pull this off, it'll be the first war that ever came in on time and under budget.''

"My God! And they let people like you wear the uniform and pose as officers? What is the navy coming to?'' Stemm held his head in his hands. "You're dismissed, Ensign.''

I paused by the door. "It's all right, sir. After the war's over and everything's safe, we'll go back to the way things are usually done." I shut the door, whistling "The Yellow Rose of Texas."

An hour later, cleaned up and snugly encased in my mess whites, I bid a fond farewell to Fast Eddie, who had Stemm tucked away in his saddlebags and was ready to ride.

When our data flow stopped, Eddie said piously, "Ken, I'll be moseying along, now. Best of luck with those ornery varmints." He paused in his transmission. "You know, I seen all these mines you're putting in."

Eddie was programmed to understand about mines.

"Now, I'm almost ashamed of myself for asking this, but you aren't planning on dry-gulching them Injins, are you? That's hardly fitting for the boys and gals wearing white hats."

"Not a chance, Eddie. We're going to shoot it out fair and square," I assured him solemnly. "At high noon."

"Thanks, Ken. I feel better. I always knew you were a straight arrow. Happy trails, then, cowpoke. Tell Wyma Jean to have a pair of big squeezes for me! Until we meet again!"

It occurred to me that Eddie was lucky the missile launchers weren't hooked up if Wyma Jean was anywhere near the trigger.

Bunkie cut the connection and came over to inspect me. "You'll do, sir," she announced. "Have fun at the party."

I touched the gold braid on my shoulder. "I feel like a lizard ready to shed its skin."

"Stick to waltzes, sir." She raised her head. "I hear a car pulling in. That must be Chief Chandrasekhar with Commander and Mrs. Hiro and Lieutenant Lindquist now."

I stepped outside and put my hat on.

Bunkie followed me out. "One minute, sir."

I turned around and leaned over so she could adjust the angle. "Much better."

"Thank you, Bunkie."

"Don't mention it, sir. I'm used to working with reserve officers."

Catarina gave me a demure look and made room for me in the backseat. Hiro was sitting in the front with his wife next to him. As we pulled away, he turned around to make introductions. "Ensign Mickey, this is my wife, Evangeline. Evangeline, this is Ensign Mickey. He's a reservist and a little unpolished, but good material for all that.''

"Charmed, I'm sure," Evangeline said. She had piled-up hair and one of those iridescent gowns with a feather fringe.

"My pleasure, ma'am."

The mayor was holding his reception at the Atlantic Hotel by necessity, since it had the only ballroom in town. As Chief Chandrasekhar stopped the car, I saw what looked like two sets of feet poking out of the shrubbery. I got out and turned to Hiro. "Sir, I'm going to be a minute. Why don't you go on in and I'll join you."

"All right, Mickey," Hiro agreed.

"Sir, I'll wait here and go in with Ensign MacKay as my escort," Catarina said.

While Hiro took his wife by the arm and led her in, I went over to see who the feet belonged to. As I might have expected, it turned out to be Harry and Dinky lying side-by-side in the bushes nursing a sick bottle.

"Sshhh!" Harry admonished, holding a finger to his lips. "We smuggled ourselves down on the shuttle. Lieutenant Lindquist doesn't know we're here."

"What are you two doing here?" I asked quietly.

Harry sat up, holding the bottle upright with one hand and Dinky with the other. "Sir, we're going to disgrace ourselves or die in the attempt!"

"No," Dinky rejoined, "we came so I could see my kids. Harry's going to call and lure my wife out of the house while I slip inside."

"And if your wife finds you?" I asked.

"Then like Harry says, we die in the attempt," Dinky muttered, swaying slightly.

"What are you doing *here*?" I asked.

"We talked to the chief before we left. Chief was going to give us a lift as soon as he let you off. We were waiting for him. You're not going to give us away, are you, sir?"

"Never saw a thing," I said, walking back toward Catarina.

"Bunkie'll watch over them," Catarina said.

"You knew they were coming down, and you let them?"

"Wouldn't you?"

I paused for a few seconds of soul-searching. "Having met Dinky's wife, I'd probably be making the phone call for him."

"Shall we go in?" She extended her arm for me to grasp.

We were late enough to miss the receiving line, so we dropped off our hats and went inside to mingle. I met half a dozen local notables, including the guy who owned Mall World and the president of the bank that was trying to fleece me for everything I owned.

It reminded me of the wedding feast of Cana. The wine they were serving came in jugs, and they were waiting for Jesus to show before they passed out a better vintage.

I made a beeline for the food table, looked over the hors d'oeuvres—most of which I couldn't identify—and settled for a handful of crackers. As I was standing there, a young woman came over and touched me on the elbow. "I recognize you. You were on the news."

She wasn't exceptionally pretty, but she had a front porch like a cantilever bridge, and I get nervous when people stand that close.

I stepped back a pace. "Pleased to meet you, ma'am. Ensign Ken MacKay at your service."

"Christine," she said. She had on a white scarf and one of those simple white dresses, cut low off the shoulder, that probably cost more than I ever expect to earn. She had thick auburn hair and wore a gold chain, gold earrings, and more makeup than I care for.

"I'm not half as bad as the reporters would have you believe."

"What a shame," she said, smiling.

I didn't realize that she was moving forward every time I stepped back until I felt the hors-d'oeuvres table in the small of my back.

"The battle you fought sounded so exciting."

"All in a day's work," I tried to make a joke out of it. "You know how dangerous it is to fly into black holes."

"No." She laid her hand on my arm. "Tell me all about it."

I blinked, momentarily at a loss for words. Then I told her three stories, all of which may have actually happened to somebody else.

"But that's enough of talking about me. What do you do?"

"Oh, things," she said. "I have my hobbies, and my interests."

She noticed I was staring in the general direction of the little jewel she had suspended from the chain around her neck, and she held it up for me to see.

"This is my crystal. I use it to focus my psychic energy."

"Oh," I vaguely recalled seeing ads for crystals. For $69.95, you, too, could master the secrets of the universe.

"It has healing powers." She let the crystal fall and reached up and used both hands to straighten my tie.

"Oh. I may need your help about the middle of next week," I said, trying to keep the conversation alive and idly wondering if she did resurrections.

"You will?" Her eyes brightened and her voice softened.

"I'm sorry, that was a dumb thing for me to say."

"No, Ken, don't say that. I can feel your aura drifting on me. Try to loosen up. We were so close. Do you like children?"

"Oh, I guess they're all right in small doses, although I still think King Herod got bad press." It occurred to me to check whether she was wearing a ring. She was not.

She touched my arm again. "Ken, don't be so rigid. We're so close. I can feel it."

With the table pressing into the small of my back, I said, "Yeah, I've noticed that, too."

She half closed her eyes. "Are you really a pirate?"

A man with an angry look on his face started walking toward us at a rapid pace.

Christine took a quick look over her shoulder. "I think my father wants to talk with me. I'll find you later." She blew me a little kiss.

Her father took her by the hand and jerked her away with an angry look in my direction.

I stayed where I was for a few minutes until I saw a familiar figure wandering my way. "Dr. Beaver! How have you been?"

"Friend Ken!" Bucky scooped up a handful of canapés and stuffed his face. "I must say, these little spinach things with caviar are superlative. Your friend, Miss Christine, the one who is so apparent, all of the females are complaining about her. Is she really a floozy? Everyone is saying so. What is a floozy?''

"It's a little tricky to explain." As far as I was concerned, between Genghis and Bucky, human-!Plixxi* relations were going downhill fast.

"Then we shall speak of it another time. I must go pay my respects to Mayor Feldman, but I shall return. Have you met the mayor?''

"No. I missed the receiving line. I don't know anything about the local politics. Is he a liberal conservative, or a conservative liberal?''

Bucky tilted his head. "That is hard to say. He seems to switch. I could ask. Oh, there is someone I absolutely must talk to, but I shall certainly find you later. Ta-ta!'' Bucky waddled off in the direction of the punch bowl.

Catarina must have been watching, because she slipped up beside me and put her arm in mine. "Just remember, as Bucky says, 'A clean mind and a strong heart weather every storm.' ''

"What would one out of two get me?''

"What thoughts are running through your mind?''

"You're the second person to ask me that. Right about now it's beginning to hit me that there is a substantial likelihood that when Genghis gets here, we are going out in the proverbial blaze of glory.''

Catarina pulled out a handkerchief to hide her smile. "As Commander Hiro enjoys pointing out, it beats retiring and having to sell life insurance for a living.''

"Or entering a convent," I said in a neutral tone of voice.

She appraised me coolly. "Beam squealed. It's one option. A blaze of glory is another." She smiled and began twirling her handkerchief. "You look nice in your dress uniform.''

"It's the one you had Sheriff Jamali's brother-in-law make for me under duress. The shoes feel about a half size too small.''

"The trousers also look a bit snug.''

"Not a bit,'' I assured her.

"What are your plans for the evening?''

"Ah, have you met Miss Christine whatever-her-name-is?'' I asked, trying to figure out what to do with my hands.

Catarina nodded. "I met her briefly. She puts up a good front. Go on."

"Well, she's been making sheep's eyes at me, so I thought I'd get sloppy drunk and do something about it."

"Ken, I hate to say this, but she's been making sheep's eyes at everything else in trousers."

"I realize this. But the opportunity might not recur, so I thought I'd give it a try. I never would have believed it, but that line about black holes really does work."

"As a pickup line, it's marginally better than 'Do you like children?' " Catarina said amiably. "Did you have a particular plan in mind?"

"Well, I'd rather not get grass stains on my uniform. I'm hoping I can talk her into a motel."

"You're going to hate yourself in the morning."

"I know, but I figure that won't last long, under the circumstances."

"I'd also prefer to have you sober. We're going to need to spend as much time shaking down as we can," Catarina said solicitously.

"It might not work the other way," I said after reflection.

"Not exactly your type of girl?"

"Hmmm. Catarina, can crystals focus your psychic energy?"

"Nooooo," she said. "Why?"

"In that case, she has meringue upstairs." I tapped my forehead. "She's working off spun sugar, egg whites, and lots of air pockets. So I guess the answer to your question is no."

"Are you sure that I can't talk you out of this?" she asked, coiling her handkerchief around her ring finger.

"Afraid not."

"Okay," she said and lost control of her handkerchief, which slipped out of her fingers and fluttered away. "Oops!"

"I got it," I said, and squatted down to grab it before it reached the floor. It was a serious mistake.

I stood up stiffly. "Here!" I handed her back the handkerchief. Then I moved a few steps closer to the wall and assumed a parade rest position.

Catarina waited a moment or two and then moved in next to me and slipped her arm back into mine.

"Shall we dance?" she cooed.

I shook my head solemnly.

"Trousers a little too tight?"

"Not any more."

"Can Miss Christine sew a stitch?"

"I doubt it. I seem to have altered my plans for the evening."

"Why? You weren't planning on keeping them on anyway."

"It's the principle of the thing."

"How long are we going to stand here by the wall?"

"Until we have a power failure or everyone else leaves. You realize that God is going to punish you and the sheriff's brother-in-law for this." I thought for a minute. "How old is Miss Christine, anyway?"

"Fifteen or sixteen, I think."

I shuddered. "I think maybe I ought to call it a night. You want to see me to the door?"

"I'm about ready to quit myself. I have a change of clothes out in Piper's car. I'll run you back, and we can both change and take a walk somewhere. There are a few things I need to talk to you about."

"Good plan." We edged out the door sideways, and Catarina left me to get Piper's car. While I was waiting, the Mall World guy came by. He must have been hitting the punch because he kept singing, "It's a Mall World After All," over and over and over.

Catarina headed out to Clyde's place to change. On our way in the door, I grabbed the mail and tossed it in the trash. Catarina rescued one really thick envelope. She opened it and started reading while I went into the bedroom and threw on denim pants and one of my less obtrusive shirts. When I came out, she was still reading.

"Aren't you going to change?" I asked.

"In a minute." She handed me the document she was holding. "This changes what I was planning to say to you."

She walked into the bathroom and shut the door while I immersed myself in the details of yet another legal complaint against me.

"Catarina! What is a temporary restraining order?" I yelled through the door.

"It means the bank is asking the court not to let you do something because it will cause them irreparable harm."

I read a little further. "What do they mean they want the court to prohibit me from leaving the planet's surface?"

She stepped out wearing slacks and a cotton blouse. "It means the Second Bank of Schenectady doesn't want the court to let you leave the planet's surface. This latest suit is on behalf of the people left holding the mortgage on your ship. I think they're arguing that if the judge lets you leave, you'll flee the jurisdiction or get yourself killed, and they're afraid that if you do, they'll have trouble collecting the money they claim you owe them. I have some chocolate out in the car if you're still hungry. Last one out the door is a groundhog!"

I was a groundhog. As we drove off, I tapped the piece of parchment. "According to this, my hearing is set for tomorrow afternoon in front of Judge Osman. If Osman grants this, how long can he keep me on the ground?"

"Until the bank gets their case against you settled." She grinned and shook her head.

"You have got to be kidding."

"No, I'm not, and neither is the bank. If Osman grants this, the California Kid isn't going to fly you up unless you take over his shuttle at gunpoint."

"I have the distinct feeling you don't want me to take over the Kid's shuttle at gunpoint."

"No, I don't think it's a good idea," she said judiciously. "It could lead to problems."

"Why isn't everybody else named?"

"Probably because McHugh and Spooner have already flown the coop, and nobody else is going up."

"It occurs to me that there is a war on, and it might be inconvenient for the navy not to be able to move me. Isn't there a federal law covering this situation?"

Catarina paused. "Actually, there are two, wherein lies the problem. One law that's been on the books forever says that Confederation law preempts local law, and the navy can move you. Now, some of our people aren't very good about paying their phone bills, so Parliament passed another law to keep the navy from rotating service personnel until they settle their debts.

Unfortunately, the staffer who drafted it was in a hurry, and left out a few small considerations, like the possibility that we might want to go to war. The navy is still working on getting it fixed.''

"I know. You're going to tell me that this is my tax dollars at work. Let me get this straight. I have to hire a lawyer—''

"I'll loan you money.''

"And I've got to go to court, so I can persuade Judge Osman to let me go and get myself killed with you and Hiro.''

"That's a fair summation.''

For at least half the year at Schenectady's latitude, Schuyler's World enjoys long twilights. Tonight was no exception. There was plenty of light to see by, and you could almost make out the stars. It was like being under a bright full moon on Earth. We stopped at the Ijamsville municipal park and pulled a blanket out of the car, along with the half-kilo chocolate bar Catarina had brought to nibble.

She straightened the blanket and motioned me to sit. "I owe you an apology for keeping you out of a motel.''

"But you're not going to apologize because you know I really didn't want to go through with it anyway.''

"Correct.'' She peeled the wrapping off the chocolate bar, took a bite, and handed it to me. "Ken, I'm not handling this right. I meant to straighten out our personal relationship before we got up to the ship. Now it doesn't look like you're coming up with me.''

"Catarina, look,'' I protested between bites of chocolate, "that's my ship up there, and the people on board her are my friends, especially you, although that may say something about me. You need me up there. Nobody knows how to fly that ship better than I do, and you're short of people to begin with.''

"Ken, don't do this to me.'' She took hold of my wrist. "The *Scupper* is hopeless as a warship, and using her to decoy Genghis into the minefield and then into a line of fire from the space platform is probably going to get her atoms spread over three parsecs. I want you to stay here, and if Osman rules against you, you'll stay alive. Don't make this hard.''

"Catarina, I'm in this up to my neck! If I'm not up there with you, Genghis is going to come looking for me.''

"Ken,'' she said gently, "if Genghis blows your ship away,

he is going to assume that he blew you away with it. And if I speak with Genghis before we start shooting, I intend to foster that assumption.''

"Oh," I said, swallowing.

We sat there without saying anything for a few minutes, watching the chocolate shimmer in the twilight. Half the fun of eating chocolate is the abstract holographic patterns they transfer onto the candy when they cool it. I broke off a chunk and handed her back the bar.

She started picking apart a fallen leaf. "This is a really awkward way to say good-bye, isn't it?''

"Of all the gin joints in all the towns in the world, you had to walk into mine." I shook my head. "How long have you known you were a vamp?''

"About five months now." She shredded the leaf, exposing its delicate veins before discarding it.

"I really messed up your career by making it public, didn't I?''

She shrugged. "It would have come out eventually.''

"How do you feel? About being a vamp, I mean?''

"If I don't eat right and avoid doing things to shove my endocrine balance out of whack, it's like being on a roller-coaster ride." She grinned. "But like anything, you discipline yourself and come to terms with it. Or you don't.''

"Despite the thing with the cookies, I still have trouble seeing you as Count Dracula.''

She got serious. "I think that the vampire legends have more to do with the way corpses decay than they do with McLendon's Syndrome. In Slavic legend, vampires have ruddy faces—'bloodred as a vampire'—so Bram Stoker got that part of the story wrong. Harry looks more like a vampire than I do.''

"Explain the part about the corpses," I said, finishing off my chocolate and looking around the forest for more.

"Well, for one thing, rigor mortis is a temporary condition, so after a period of time, bodies get supple again and a fair amount of blood stays liquid inside. As gases from decay build up, the corpse bloats and forces blood from the lungs out the mouth and nose. Dead bodies are funny—if the temperature and humidity are right, they won't decay for a fairly long time.''

"So that somebody's dead body looks like it's been out for a stroll drinking blood. Go on."

"Well, another thing, the skin shrinks away from a corpse's fingernails, which makes them look like they've been growing until they finally fall off."

"I remember reading somewhere that corpses also make noises."

"As any pathologist will tell you, when you force a stake into a corpse, you compress the corpse's chest cavity and force air past the glottis." She smiled, recollecting. "You wouldn't believe the sick jokes that pathologists make in books they write for other pathologists to read."

"If you think the jokes are sick, they must really be bad."

"I'll take that as a compliment. Anyway, I resent being thought of as a vampire. Vampires are supernatural creatures. There is nothing supernatural about having McLendon's, although there's a lot that isn't pleasant. What are you thinking?"

"I'm thinking about how impossible it would have been to have a conversation like this with my ex-wife." I stretched my feet past the end of the blanket and wiggled my toes in the funny grass. "People who get married usually deserve what they get, I guess. I must have been pretty obnoxious when she latched onto me."

"I thought about getting married for a while." She looked past me into the twilight.

"Oh?"

"I don't know how much Beam let slip, but I went with one man for eight years. I figured out I had McLendon's a few months after I was exposed and broke up with him. After that, I put in for deep-space duty." She wrapped what was left of the chocolate.

"It seems to me that after putting eight years into it, having McLendon's would be something that you could work out," I said, putting my foot right into it.

Catarina looked at me directly. "Ken, there were other, serious problems with the relationship. Think about who I caught McLendon's from and try subtracting five months from eight years."

"Sorry. That was stupid, wasn't it?"

Her voice softened. "I should be apologizing to you."

"No problem." I took her hand. Then I noticed something crawling in the grass at my feet. "What's that?" It looked like a moving cow patty.

Catarina tilted her head. "It's a velvet frog. I think the locals call them 'flops.' "

The flop sprouted eyes and leaped onto my shoe, where it began doing vigorous push-ups. It broke the mood.

"They're not particularly bright," Catarina said delicately.

"Or discriminating." I stood up away from the blanket and swung my foot to propel the flop into the middle of next week.

"Most people here don't wear brown shoes."

"I'll make a note of that." I pointed at something purple flying a wobbly course overhead. "What's that?"

Catarina grabbed my arm and jerked aside as a stream of green slime splattered onto the turf where I'd been standing. "It's a dumbat. They mostly live on leaves and berries, except the berries ferment this time of year. They get drunk eating them and fly into buildings and pedestrians."

The dumbat was flying in a shaky circle and came back around my way. I sidestepped left to let the little fellow go by, which apparently confused him. He veered left, tried to pull up with a startled look in his eyes, and bounced off my chest. He ended up flat on his back and lay there.

"A dumbat, huh?"

"What else would you call something that flies around half-drunk?" Catarina asked.

"Marine aviation. Seriously, they don't bite or anything, do they?" I picked the little guy up and cradled him in both hands. "He's kind of cute. I hope he's all right."

The dumbat looked at me and yawned. I thought for a second. "Can they eat Earth-type foods?"

Catarina nodded. "I think so." She flipped me a piece of chocolate.

I popped it into the little dumbat's mouth by way of repara-tion. He chewed it up contentedly and swallowed. Then he twined his claws into my sleeve, shut his eyes, and went to sleep.

"Hey! Let go!" I tried to pull the dumbat loose, but he had

a tight grip and it looked like he was out cold. It also looked like I was either going to keep him or sacrifice my shirt.

"You've made a friend. I'm impressed."

"Can you potty-train them? Maybe I could give him to Wyma Jean to replace the cat." I thought for a minute. "No. Bad idea. Forget I suggested it. The cat was enough trouble, and the cat couldn't fly. As soon as Dumbo here wakes up and I can figure out how to unhook him, he goes."

She started laughing softly.

I grimaced. "I'll bet you're thinking that not only are the people here not worth fighting over, but the fauna isn't either."

"Oh, absolutely." She laughed until tears ran down her cheeks, and then her smile faded. "Ken," she said gently, "I can stay a little while, but then I have to catch the shuttle back."

"And you're trying to tell me that you don't want to make this too hard."

"It seems like the best idea," she agreed. "Even if we both live through the next few days, we'll end up going our separate ways."

"Can I come visit you in the convent?"

"We'll scandalize the good sisters." She smiled.

We threw the blanket in the trunk and headed back to Clyde's place. As we pulled up, I saw two vehicles parked out in front.

"Slow up," I told her. "I want to check this out."

She stopped about a block away. I gave her a hug, and she let me out. I watched her drive away. As I walked up to the first car, I saw a familiar brown felt beret with artificial flowers. I rapped on the window. "Dare, what are you doing here?"

Lydia rolled down her window. "I saw you leave the reception. You're supposed to be inside. Where's the girl you were with?"

"You followed me." I didn't try to hide the disgust I felt. "Well, as you can see, there's no girl." I pointed to the dumbat on my arm. "He's the only friend with me at the moment. Now, please get out of here before I call the cops."

She huffed, and she puffed, and she finally drove away.

There were two men sitting in the second car. One of the two got out. "Hey, buddy, you got a light?"

"Sorry," I slapped my pockets reflexively. "I don't smoke."

"Hey, aren't you Ken MacKay? I saw you on TV."

"I am, and you may have."

"Good." He pulled a pistol out of his pocket. "Move it. Get in the car. No tricks, now!"

Obviously, if any of this had been in my horoscope, six or seven people would have called to warn me, and I never would have gotten out of bed.

I got in the backseat, and the guy with the gun got in after me. "Take us back to the trailer, Larry."

"Right, Joe."

"Okay, Joe, what's all this about?" I thought for a second. "You wouldn't happen to have a girlfriend named Christine, would you?"

"Naw! Christine, what kind of a name is that?" Joe lit a cigarette. "Relax, this isn't personal. This is just business. Mind if I smoke?"

"Yes, I do mind," I said coldly.

"Jeez, you're touchy!"

"Wouldn't you be?"

Larry turned his head around, still steering the car. "He's got a point, Joe. Don't you read anything about secondary smoke? It's very unhealthy."

"Larry, will you drive the car?" Joe said in an exasperated tone of voice as he snubbed out his cigarette.

We pulled up to a trailer on a lot next to a frame structure with a jaunty red neon sign. The top line flashed out, LITTLE NELL'S SPORTING HOUSE. The next line said GIRLS! GIRLS! GIRLS! The bottom line read, 10% OFF WEDNESDAYS FOR SENIOR CITIZENS.

Dumbo the dumbat was still hanging onto my arm, half-asleep. As I got out of the car, I shook him free, whispered, "Go get help!" and tossed him into the air. He landed with a thump.

Larry opened up the trailer and Joe motioned me with his pistol to follow him inside. I don't like trailers—the best thing I can say about them is that they attract cyclones, which keeps them from multiplying. Larry disappeared into the bedroom and returned a moment later. I gingerly sat down on a fuzzy orange couch. "What's the smell in here?"

"What smell?" Larry asked, scratching his head. Joe was dark and round; Larry was tall with sandy hair and what people generally refer to as a vacant expression.

"It's probably the garbage," Joe observed. "The garbagemen are on holiday, and there wasn't any pickup yesterday. I think they get Ramadan off. You want something to eat?"

"No, thanks. I'm not hungry." Ramadan lasts about a month. I eyed the two of them. "I don't believe we've been introduced."

"I'm Larry," the tall one said. "This is Joe. We're from the Mob."

I stared. "The real Mafia isn't going to be very happy with you two."

"Hey! Watch what you say," Larry said. "Joe here is a real Sicilian."

Joe chimed in. "Yeah. If you don't button your lip, we're going to drive you down to the river and let you take a walk in some cement overshoes."

Spacers tend to watch a lot of old cinema stuff, including material so ancient it's been colorized, so I'd seen any number of bad gangster movies. Apparently, these two had, too.

"You don't have a river. What is going on?" I exclaimed wearily.

Joe looked at Larry uncomfortably. "You're the captain of the ship that's going to fight the Rats, and you're interfering with our business, MacKay."

"Yeah, our girls are all complaining," Larry added.

It was Joe's turn. "Yeah, you got all the businessmen in town worried sick. They're all going home to their wives, for Christ's sake. The last couple of nights, business has been terrible. Do you know what the rent is on this place?"

"Yeah. We're as patriotic as the next guys, except when it interferes with business," Larry concluded.

"I take it that's your establishment next door," I said.

"Yeah. Neat place, isn't it?" Larry responded. "We got the neon stuff from an antique store."

"How is kidnapping me going to improve your business?"

"We called the papers to let everyone know we got you. After everybody reads about it, they'll know there won't be any war, and things will pick up in a day or two," Larry explained.

"And what do you plan on doing with me?"

Larry and Joe exchanged looks. "We're still working on that, but we were figuring on ransoming you after this Rat thing blows over. There's a hot tip that you scammed a bunch of drug money. It said so in the newspapers."

"Hold it, kids. Let's get this straight." I used my fingers to count off. "First, don't believe everything you read in the newspapers. Anybody over the age of four ought to know that. Second, the navy commandeered my ship, so there's going to be a war with the Rodents whether I show up for it or not. Third, if I don't show up, the Rodents are going to come looking for me, because they are not very happy with me at all."

I gave Joe and Larry a few seconds to let that sink in. "Last," I said, "I haven't got any money. I especially don't have any drug money. The only thing I own is a wrecked ship, which the Rodents are trying to turn into scrap metal and the bankers are trying to take away."

Larry's face fell, and Joe furrowed his brow. Then he brightened. "I get it! The bankers want you, and the Rats want you. We could sell you to the highest bidder!"

"Wrong, Joe. The Rats want me dead, and the bankers will probably also want me dead when they find out I haven't got any money. I would add that the Rats are on their way, and if I'm not around to help protect your planet, business might even get worse."

"That is a problem," Joe agreed. "We got to think."

"You ought to. This was your dumb idea," Larry told him.

Joe looked up and took Larry casually by the collar. He slapped him once. "Don't say stuff like that, pal."

I saw Larry clench his fists, but he didn't say anything. A little chilled, I asked, "You seem a little new at this. Have you two ever done this kidnapping thing before?"

"Sure, we have!" Joe said indignantly, after a slight hesitation.

"Lots of times," Larry volunteered.

"How many times?"

"Seven," Larry said, at the same time Joe said, "Five." They looked at each other.

While I considered asking them to split the difference, somebody knocked at the door.

"Who the heck could that be?" Larry pulled out a pistol of his own and let go the safety. He opened the door and Lydia Dare walked in with Dumbo clinging to her sweater, followed by a cameraman. She shoved her microphone in Joe's face. "Hello, I'm Lydia Dare from the *Schenectady Post-Dispatch*. Are you the persons who kidnapped the notorious pirate, Ken MacKay?"

"Gee, Lydia Dare. Can I get your autograph?" Larry asked.

"I seen you on TV," Joe said. "Yeah, we kidnapped him. How'd you find us?'

"I just followed this little guy here." Dare gestured to my dumbat, which was hanging upside down on her free arm.

Dumbo launched himself, flopped on my shoulder, and opened his mouth wide for a handout. Dumbats may not major in plasma physics, but they know a soft touch when they see one. I looked in my pocket and found that Catarina had stuffed it with what was left of the chocolate and a check for the lawyer. I broke off a piece of chocolate and stuffed Dumbo's beak.

"She knows our hideout!" Joe exclaimed. "We got to shoot her!"

"You can't. I'm a reporter," Dare said arrogantly.

"These two kidnapped me and are trying to figure out what to do next." I pointed to Dumbo. "Did he actually lead you here?"

"I went cruising when the call about you came in and spotted your dumbat sitting on the steps outside with his mouth open. How's that for good investigative reporting?" she said smugly.

"You wouldn't have happened to have notified the police, would you?"

"Of course not!" Her eyes blazed with righteous fire. "This is a *scoop*." The cameraman gave me a pitying look.

"Okay, Dare. No cops, no interview." I folded my arms and turned around so my back was facing her. I jerked a thumb. "If you want a story, why don't you interview these two?"

"Just for that, I will!" Dare said, outraged.

"Hey, I want to go first!" Larry said.

"Hey, who's supposed to be in charge, here? I should go first!" Joe responded.

I turned my head around in time to see the cameraman roll his eyes.

After a slight hesitation, Lydia made a Solomonic decision and let Joe and Larry both go first, alternating questions.

I listened for about ten minutes, and while everyone else was otherwise occupied, I quietly borrowed Larry's keys and walked out. Locking the door behind me, I pitched the keys into the weeds, found a pay phone next to a Lucky 7 store, and called Bunkie to pick me up.

It was comforting to know that organized crime on Schuyler's World was on a par with its other institutions.

When Bunkie pulled up, I introduced her to Dumbo and got her to drive me back to Clyde's place. Then I roused Sheriff Jamali from a sound sleep and asked him to send his minions down to pick up Joe and Larry. Parking my dumbat in the bathtub with a blanket, I went to sleep.

The next morning, I called Father Yakub for some spiritual guidance. I explained the events of the previous evening, and he gave me another absolution for sins I had intended to commit and asked me to try and keep my nose wiped for a few days.

He also told me to pray, in order to become closer to God, and to hire a good lawyer.

"Sounds like good advice, Father. However, the only lawyer that I can get on short notice is Jimmy Omura."

"I might pray a little harder," Father Yakub ventured after some reflection.

I couldn't help asking. "Father, don't take this the way it sounds, but you seem like an awfully sharp guy—"

"To be living on Schuyler's World?" His image on the telephone screen grinned impishly. "I assume by that you mean I can get through doors and around corners without backing and filling."

I nodded. "It seems kind of unusual," I said limply.

"Ken, my son, the Church in its wisdom decreed that its children on colonial worlds should receive the finest shepherds available, because, praise le bon Dieu, they need more shepherding than most."

I called Omura from the office and spent an hour going over the details of the case while Bunkie fed the documents he needed into the scanner. We arranged to meet in front of the courthouse.

As I signed off, I noticed Bunkie looking at me out of the corner of her eye.

"Bunkie, I know the courts here interpret the law here a little loosely, but I think I can beat this temporary restraining order."

"Sir, I don't mean to comment on your private life, but there may be more to this than you think."

"Oh?" I sensed I wasn't going to like what I was about to hear.

Bunkie stared down at my shoes. "Sir, the, uh, mayor's office has called here three times. They would like to speak with you. Apparently Mayor Feldman saw you leave his reception early in a, well, furtive manner, right before his daughter left."

"Is the mayor's daughter named Christine?"

"Yes, sir. The mayor's not real happy."

"How old is she, anyway?"

"Ummm." Bunkie clearly didn't want to answer the question. "Fifteen, sir."

"Bunkie, how do you hear all these things?"

"Just around and about, sir."

Chandrasekhar was singing as he cut up the radishes, and it gradually registered on me that he was singing an old marching song I'd learned at Woolmera.

> "The wedding was—a formal one
> Her father had—a white shotgun
> The wedding was—a formal one
> Her father had a! . . . White shotgun!"

The song is a sad commentary on the perils of mixing with sweet young things who are impressed by black holes.

"Bunkie, I'm beginning to think that I may have some difficulties with Judge Osman. Do you have any suggestions?"

She thought for a moment. "Sir, I think that everything will depend on the quality of the testimony you present in your favor,'' she said very carefully.

"Good point. Can you call up Piper and have her send Clyde back with the shuttle?''

She nodded. "Consider it done, sir. And sir, about your pet?''

"Right. He's in my office, and I don't know what to do with him. He's actually kind of cute. I'm surprised that people don't try to make pets out of them.''

"Sir, I imagine that the blanket you have him wrapped in is going to need cleaning,'' Bunkie said diffidently.

"Uh, right.'' We walked into my office and surveyed the dumbat in question. Dumbo had polished off four bananas and an apricot for breakfast. He opened one eye blearily, then yawned and went back to sleep.

"Well, I really can't keep him.''

"I'll take care of it for you, sir,'' Bunkie said, deftly picking him up.

"Uh, Bunkie, what do you plan on doing?'' I asked, a little squeamish.

"Get him stewed and dump him in the woods.'' She shrugged. "It works with blind dates.''

"Thanks, Bunkie.''

"No problem, sir.''

I went back and packed up my stuff, just in case, and then I went down to the courthouse. Clyde was sitting in the back, waiting for me.

The three lawyers on the other side and their clients refused to make eye contact with me. When Judge Osman walked in, he recognized me immediately. "Ah, another crew member from *Rustam's Slipper* appearing before me in my courtroom. How pleasant.''

It was shaping up as one of those days.

The bank presented its case first. Basically, they argued that I owed lots of people tons of money, both in my own right and on behalf of everyone else they could think of to drag in, and while invasions come and go, business was business. If the court let me take the shuttle up to my ship, there was a high probability that I would not return, except possibly in small pieces when it next rained.

Then Omura stood up to refute the bank's case. Somebody may have had to dress him that morning and point him in the direction of the courtroom, but his arguments were brilliant. He demolished the bank's case, point by point.

He established that Confederation law precluded enforcing a civil court order which would cause a military officer to miss deployment, and that granting the bank's motion for a temporary restraining order would destroy the foundations underlying the Confederation's commitment to its own defense. He cited case after case showing that going up into the atmosphere to fight Rodents was not leaving the jurisdiction within the meaning of the rule. Since the "irreparable harm" the bank was complaining of consisted of me getting myself killed, he commented acidly on the bank's failure to prove that this wouldn't happen anyway the minute the Rodents showed up.

Omura then proceeded to point out that the bank could produce no evidence suggesting that I wasn't simply a salaried employee of Davie Lloyd Ironsides right up to the moment that the navy's seizure of the ship extinguished the bank's lien on the vessel; and he finished off with an offer of proof, consisting of Davie Lloyd's documents, to show beyond a doubt that the bank had no underlying cause of action against me.

He concluded with a rousing argument invoking the golden thread of the common law, the rights of man, God, mother, and the flag. The two or three court-watchers in the gallery clapped when he was finished, and the cameraman from the *Schenectady Post-Dispatch* caught it all on video.

Magistrate Osman glanced at the documents on his bench and frowned. "In light of all the issues, I shall need to hear further testimony. This court will recess for twenty minutes." He rapped his gavel.

As I stood up, he fixed me with a beady eye. "Mr. MacKay, although I wish to assure you that this has absolutely nothing to do with this proceeding, I am aware that there is a very eminent personage who is at this very moment sifting facts to determine your relationship with his daughter. This was very, very naughty of you!"

"I will keep that in mind, Your Honor," I said, taking a deep breath.

Since law hadn't worked, it was time to try chicanery. "We need to put Clyde on the stand," I told Omura.

Omura scratched his head with a pen tip. "I don't understand. His testimony is hardly relevant to these proceedings."

"Just play along." I scribbled down questions to ask on a sheet of paper. "As a friend of mine would say, 'Trust me.' "

When court resumed, Clyde took the stand. He was wearing his dress uniform and looked sharper than anybody who knew him would believe. After he took the oath and identified himself for the record, Omura bowed slightly and asked him, "Petty Officer Witherspoon, please explain what brought you and Ensign MacKay to this planet."

The bank's lawyer bobbed up. "Objection, Your Honor! What has this got to do with anything?"

"Petty Officer Witherspoon's testimony is essential to show the nature of Ensign MacKay's mission to this planet," Omura said, trying to read my notes. "Your Honor, you can hardly rule on this motion without understanding the navy's operational constraints."

Osman gave the bank's lawyer a what-have-you-gotten-me-into-now look. The lawyer threw up his hands. "We withdraw the objection."

"Counsel, aren't you skipping some foundation questions?" Judge Osman asked in a very small voice.

"It will all become clear, Your Honor," Omura said with a flourish, which was as close as he could come to admitting that he didn't have a clue either.

"Ensign MacKay was assisting Lieutenant Catarina Lindquist and me," Clyde said smoothly. "We were investigating an interstellar drug-smuggling operation that involved money laundering and corruption of local political figures."

Omura reached into Clyde's gym bag, pulled out a purple dashiki, and asked, "Do you recognize this garment?"

Clyde grinned. "Yes. That was my working costume during sting operations."

Osman may not have recognized Clyde, but the dashiki was something else. His face turned a nice shade of gray.

"What, if any, sting operations did you conduct?" Omura asked.

"Objection, Your Honor! This line of questioning is totally irrelevant," the bank's lawyer protested, much too late.

"Boy, shut up and sit down!" Osman barked. He added soothingly, "The witness will please be so kind as to answer the question. There is no need for him to go into any of the extremely fine, sordid details, however."

"Yes, sir." Clyde's eyes were dancing. "In the course of our investigation, we handed out marked money to at least one judicial official to alter the outcome of a case. I got some *good* pictures."

The guy from the *Post-Dispatch* was taking in every word.

Before Osman could say anything, Omura commented quickly, "Your Honor, before we continue this line of questioning, I need to have the witness discuss the money laundering."

"A couple of big bearer accounts were being used to fund the Rodent drug-smuggling operations that Mr. MacKay broke up," Clyde interjected without being asked.

Osman duly chastened him for speaking out of turn while one of the bank officials in the front row clutched his chest.

"Your Honor, may we have a five-minute recess?" the bank's lawyer requested, looking at his clients.

"Your request will be honorably granted," Osman said, mopping his brow with a handkerchief.

As soon as we resumed, the bank's lawyer requested a sidebar. Omura and I went up to the judge's bench.

"Your Honor, we would request a closed session, given the, uh, sensitivity of the testimony," the lawyer requested.

"Opposed, Your Honor." Omura scented blood somewhere.

"Well, Your Honor, it's like this," I said breezily, speaking out of turn. "I'm still part of a navy criminal investigation team. If I can't be up there fighting Rats, I guess I've got to stay down here pursuing corruption and violations of the banking laws."

"Gentleman and learned colleagues in the law, I believe that I feel I have heard enough evidence to render a decision in this matter," Osman said hurriedly. "It is very, very obvious that if Mr. MacKay wishes to do his bounden, patriotic duty, we should not let trivial matters of law stand in his path to glory and honor."

"Your Honor, my client has instructed me to ask if we could

withdraw our request for a temporary restraining order.'' The bank's lawyer looked around nervously. ''In fact, we are willing to withdraw our lawsuit, without prejudice.''

''With prejudice,'' Omura said.

''Granted without prejudice,'' Osman said, rapping his gavel. ''This hearing is adjourned. Now please leave my courtroom.''

As soon as everybody in the gallery started moving, Osman blinked at me. ''Mr. MacKay, may I be so kind as to offer you one slight bit of friendly-intentioned advice? I would hint and suggest to you that you should consider departing, if that is your intention, with the swiftness of an eagle chick. And while I may be straying from my role of judicial impartiality, good luck, Mr. MacKay. Any man who wishes to go and get himself killed as much as you do deserves the opportunity.''

I saluted. ''Thank you, sir!''

As soon as we got outside, Clyde went to get the car. I shook Omura's hand and stuffed Catarina's check into it. ''Thanks, but I guess this means no law review article.''

''Oh, I haven't given up hope just yet, Mr. MacKay,'' Omura said solemnly.

''This wouldn't have anything to do with that 'without prejudice' business?'' I asked suspiciously.

'' 'Without prejudice' merely means that the bank can refile their lawsuit whenever they like,'' Omura assured me as Clyde pulled up.

''How nice.''

The two guards on the shuttle looked dumbfounded when I showed up waving my court order.

''We've been told not to let you aboard,'' said the shorter one of the two as he attempted to read the document upside down.

''We're going to have to call the sheriff,'' explained the other one.

''By all means. Do hurry.''

While Clyde went on board to wake up the California Kid, I walked over to a bench and sat down.

Jamali drove up a few minutes later and greeted me with a radiant smile as he stepped out of his car. ''Mr. MacKay—or should I call you Ensign MacKay?''

''Ensign MacKay, if you please. When do I board? I'll even

forgive your brother-in-law for the stunt with my uniform if it'll hurry things along."

"Such impatience in the young." Jamali said philosophically. "We must first dispense with the amenities."

"All right," I said agreeably. "Are you having any luck bribing the voters, and have you recaptured Elaine?"

"I prefer to think of it as permitting the citizens to observe my fitness as a candidate." Jamali seated himself beside me. "As for your shipmate, Allah has willed otherwise. In Schenectady, an extra psychopath or two is not especially noteworthy," he said with an air of indifference. "Did I by chance see you with a young woman at the mayor's reception?"

"Christine. The mayor's daughter. It's possible."

"Charming girl. Now I gather your purpose in departing so abruptly is to defend us from the Rodent hordes."

"Yes, I'm going to go get myself killed as soon as your boys there let me through. Would you care to see the court order?"

"Ah, such youthful fire and impetuosity. No, I admit defeat. You may depart forthwith."

He reached into a pocket and pulled out a box of cigars. "Even though you are not a voter, to show that there are no hard feelings, allow me to present you with a cigar for you to savor as a token of recompense while you wait for your shuttle to be fueled."

"Thanks, but I don't smoke."

"Everyone should indulge once, and you may not have other opportunities." Jamali pressed it into my hand.

"Well, why not?" I accepted a light from him and coughed a little as I got the thing going. "Thanks," I said, wondering why people who weren't brain-dead would do this on a regular basis.

Jamali smiled. "Adieu, then, Ensign MacKay. May Allah guide your footsteps." He exchanged a few words with his men and then drove off.

I was looking for a good place to ditch the cigar when the taller cop walked over. "Excuse me, Ensign MacKay? There is an ordinance against smoking in public, sir."

"That's fine. I was just looking for a place to put this thing out."

He clarified. "Sir, I am going to have to arrest you." He slapped the cuffs on my wrist.

"Hold it! Sheriff Jamali gave me this cigar."

"Yes, sir. That's what he told us," the policeman said apologetically.

I was still yelling, "Clyde! Get hold of Bunkie and get me sprung!" when the paddy wagon came and hauled me off.

I briefly renewed acquaintances with Davie Lloyd, Bernie, Larry, and Joe. Joe didn't want to talk to me—a fact he explained at some length. When the cops had arrived, they had refused to believe that he and Larry couldn't get the door open. It had taken all of Lydia's eloquence to keep the constabulary from shooting the place full of holes, and the lock was easily going to cost twenty dollars to fix.

While periodically calling for the duty officer to fetch Sheriff Jamali, I amused myself by rattling the metal seal on my court order against the bars, pretending it was a tin cup. Since the fine for smoking in public was ten dollars, the duty officer was bright enough to figure out he had a problem and call Jamali.

He brought the phone over to my cell. "Sir, would you please speak with the sheriff?"

The viewscreen showed Jamali sitting in his car wearing an even bigger grin. "Ensign MacKay, how pleasant to renew our relationship."

"I want out. Now."

"Ah! Frank and open speech. How endearing," he said.

"Please shorten the small talk. I have a shuttle to catch."

"Therein lies the problem," Jamali admitted. "The mayor will be greatly distressed if you depart, and who am I to stand in the path of true love?"

"An elected official about to get sued," I said grimly. "True love?"

"Your beloved Christine. One must observe the proprieties," Jamali said complacently. "You are slightly more respectable than the last two gentlemen for whom Miss Christine has conceived an attraction, and you have placed the mayor in an awkward public position." He lingered on the word conceived.

"My hands, unfortunately, are tied." He spread them to demonstrate. "As your Saint Paul said, 'It is better to marry than to burn.' "

"Sheriff, most people I know do both. Let me try to explain."

I related my story, and Jamali stroked his chin. "I think her father suspects as much. The little dove is not speaking, and this is sufficiently unusual as to excite comment. However, I am sure that any omission on your part can easily be rectified. To salvage his daughter's reputation, the mayor has made it known that an engagement is in the offing—if you will allow me a play on words, two engagements are in the offing if Rodents are indeed on their way—and it would not improve his chances of reelection if you were to depart hastily. As we speak, he is conducting a poll to discern what effect you would have as a prospective son-in-law. The results of the first poll were inconclusive."

I had the distinct impression Jamali was enjoying our discussion very, very much.

It was time for what the infantry calls final protective fire. "Look, Sheriff—"

"Please, call me Ragheb. You will say that you have a court order. I have my orders, as well."

"Ragheb—with my demonstrated proclivity for mayhem, do you really want me around here long enough to end up as the mayor's son-in-law?"

Jamali stared at me in silence for a moment and burst out laughing. "Mr. MacKay, you continue to display unexpected talents," he said wiping his eyes. "Tell my henchmen to send you back to catch your shuttle, and may God go with you."

"Thanks. Could you, uh, try to square things with Christine?"

"It shall be as you desire," Jamali said, stroking his beard. "I shall find her a nice biker. Now, give the handset back to my worthless underling."

The duty cop listened to his boss for a minute, saluted, and then brought a car around to take me back to the shuttle. As the Kid was beginning his preflight check, I stepped through the door and slung my bag in the bin over my head.

"I thought for a minute you were going to miss the party," Clyde said.

"Wouldn't miss it for the world—not this one, anyway," I said grandly. "Let's go, Kid. Time to take her up, again!"

The California Kid gave me a glazed stare. "Up, down. Up, down," he muttered to himself. "This job is beginning to be like work." He looked back down at his board, perplexed. "Dude, what're you packing? We are totally overweight. You have got some gnarly kilos here."

"Hold on." I walked back, opened up the lockers, and said to the two young ladies inside, "Sorry, girls. We used up our quota for stowaways this month."

"Darn," said the older of Dinky's daughters.

"I'll tell your father you said hello," I said, escorting them out.

"Like, wow! How did you know they were in there?" the Kid said in amazement as they made their departure.

Clyde burst out laughing.

A second or two later, Dykstra walked on board, slammed her bag into a locker with force, and strapped herself into a seat.

"Hello, Rosalee," I said, lifting my eyebrows.

"Hello, Ken. Just shut up, if you don't mind."

"Okay," I said as the Kid fired his engines and took us up.

Clyde said tactfully, "Rosalee, I think I can speak for Ensign MacKay when I say we're glad you're here."

"Thanks, Clyde," Dykstra said. "Now, just shut up about it."

Iron Ships and Wooden Men; or, The Good Ship Pinafore

Catarina and Bucky were waiting for us at the entry port when we got to the *Scupper*. Catarina embraced me wordlessly, which made up for a lot of the trouble I had getting there.

With Hiro's approval, she had already revised our operational plan, which she explained as we walked toward the bridge.

Standard navy doctrine was to lead with small craft, and Catarina was convinced that Genghis would send his armed merchantmen in ahead of his light cruiser. Catarina and I would maneuver the *Scupper* while Hiro commanded our little "flotilla" from one of the jump seats. Harry and Dinky would operate the missile launcher in Number One hold, with Annalee to operate the acquisition system. Clyde and Rosalee would take care of damage control. Piper had Kimball, Sin, and Trujillo on the space platform.

If we could lure the Rodent armada into the minefield and take out one or both of the smaller Rodent ships in the confusion, we'd make the fight a fairer one and give Piper and her merry men an opportunity to shiver Genghis's timbers by putting a missile or two into his cruiser. Spooner and the Kid would hang around the general vicinity in the shuttle in case there were survivors.

Harry, Dinky, and Annalee had about three days left to train, and Catarina had them practicing almost without a letup. I made the mistake of asking how they were doing.

She slapped on the intercom, and we stopped in the corridor for a minute to listen to the three of them.

"Marking, marking . . ." Annalee coaxed.

Tracking a simulated target, Annalee's acquisition system marked it with a twisting "cone," which was a mathematical construct consisting of points in space where a launched missile would intersect the target's projected flight path close enough to guide itself the rest of the way and hit.

"Lost, lost, marking, marking. Get ready! Marking . . ." she continued.

"Got her!" Harry shouted. "Firing one and two!"

Even though I knew that they hadn't actually fired any missiles, I instinctively braced myself.

Annalee shrieked in outrage. "Don't shoot yet, you half-wit!"

"Reloading one and two," Dinky said laconically.

There was a pregnant pause. Then Harry replied. "What's wrong, honey? Somebody steal your broom?"

"Goddamn pig!" McHugh hissed after a few seconds of silence. The simulator buzzed twice to show two clean misses.

The two of them started to argue. "All right. Back to work," Catarina called out. "Give it another half hour, and then you can break."

"It's just about dinnertime, isn't it?" Harry said innocently. "Who's slopping the little piggies here?"

"Belay that, Harry," Catarina growled. "You too, McHugh."

"Aye-aye, ma'am," a chastened Harry said, and McHugh said something that might charitably have been construed as concurrence.

"Ma'am, I don't feel so good," I commented as we walked toward our cabin.

"We haven't even started maneuvering yet," she commented. "When you and I start twisting the ship around, we'll really test their reflexes." She looked at me. "Beam has the better launcher crew. She has to hit that cruiser before the cruiser even realizes she's there."

"I see."

Catarina read my expression and punched me very lightly on the shoulder. "Go get changed, and we'll get started."

I unpacked, slipped into my coveralls, and went up to the bridge.

As I took my seat and began checking the panel, Catarina mentioned, "Beam brought a bucketful of microrobots aboard to see what was wrong with the ship. The worst problem we found was in the right secondary control node. The ceramic wiring running through there is corrupted, which is why we've been having so many problems with the lower drive and the starboard impeller."

I whistled. "How did that happen?"

Catarina looked embarrassed. "Bernie's cabin is laid over that node, and Beam found a bubble under Bernie's bed where there's a split in the seam between the wall and the deckplates. Bernie's cat has been using the split as a part-time litter box. The cat urine interferes with the superconductivity of the ceramic wiring."

I started choking.

"Everything running through that node needs to be replaced," she said in a matter-of-fact tone. "Unfortunately, we don't have the time or the materials to do the job."

The situation defied comment, but I thought of something to say anyway. "You know, it just occurred to me that if Bernie's cat hadn't been screwing up the wiring, the ship probably wouldn't have been bucking like a bronco when Davie Lloyd was holding a knife to Frido's throat. That means—"

"Yes. In a manner of speaking, the stupid cat did kill Frido." She smiled. "Shall we try some combat maneuvering?"

We warned everybody aboard we were going to stop the spin and ordered them to strap down where they were. Commander Hiro and Bucky both showed up to observe. Catarina had control. The next four minutes were pretty wild as she put the *Scupper* through her paces: half loops, reverse thrusts, Immelmanns. Then a red check light went off inside my head. "Cut thrust," I yelled a second or two before the problem showed on the board.

Catarina heard me and chopped back, too late. The starboard impeller hiccupped and cut out. The ship yawed, which is a polite spacer way of saying that she started flipping cartwheels.

Catarina slowly brought her under control to a rest position as the starboard impeller finally resumed functioning.

I shut the intercom off so we wouldn't have to listen to any comments from the cheap seats.

"Oh, I say," Bucky said, his tiny eyes glistening, "that was fun! Can we do it again?"

"I suppose we have to rate this as a qualified success," Hiro said with a feeble attempt at levity.

"It's no go," Catarina said, her face paler than usual. "Even for basic maneuvers, I have to fly this ship well past her tolerances, and she's not holding up."

"What are you saying?" Hiro asked.

"I'm saying that if we fight this ship, we can't count on lasting the first five minutes," Catarina said somberly.

"Wait a minute," I said, "I can tell you when she's going to blow. Let me fly her." Catarina knew combat maneuvering, but I knew the *Scupper*.

Hiro winced. His body language said, Why me, Lord?

"Ken," Catarina said gently, "I know you know how to fly this ship, but your military specialties are what?"

"Navigation and fleet logistics," I admitted.

"I may be rusty, but you haven't even had the rudiments of small-ship combat maneuvering. You don't have the instincts. At close quarters, a second or two hesitating over whether to turn or roll will cause us to eat a missile. You can't fly her. I have the training, but any combat maneuvering I do will take this ship well past the red line where she's unreliable."

"But, modesty aside, I'm probably the only person alive who knows this ship well enough to fly her at the edge and still bring her back more or less in one piece." I thought for a minute. "Unfortunately, you're right about my instincts. If my instincts were worth anything, obviously I wouldn't be on the ship to begin with."

There was a brief silence which Bucky graced with an observation. "Oh, dear. This is a dilemma, isn't it?"

"We need a solution," Catarina said. She looked at me slyly. "I suppose we'll both have to fly her, won't we?"

Hiro raised his eyebrows. I did the same.

She sketched the idea through. However awkward, what made sense was for her to start a maneuver and have me follow through just under the *Scupper*'s breaking point once I understood what she was trying to accomplish. It sounded stupid. It was also the best thing we could think of. While everybody else ate dinner, we modified the yoke that gives one pilot or the other control and then tried the system out.

It didn't work. We spent the first twelve hours or so fumbling it good until we started to get each other's rhythm. We ended up taking the arms off the command seats and moving them together until we were touching so I could feel what she was going to do without having to think about it.

I wouldn't recommend it as a way to fly a warship, and I wouldn't advise trying it with someone you don't like.

We ran into a few unexpected glitches. Harry found out, with disagreeable consequences, that frictionless toilets don't work the way they're designed when the ship is rolling. That's one of those things the navy doesn't mention when they talk about hazardous duty pay, and it marked the first time in weeks that I saw McHugh smile.

We finally quit practicing when Catarina and I were too tired to see straight, but it looked like Operation Rat Patrol was still on target. We turned the ship over to Clyde and Dykstra, went back to our cabin, and split a carton of Leopard Milk to celebrate.

"I'm too tired to sleep," I told her. "You want to put something on the video?"

"Oh, I don't know. All right."

"I forgot to pick up new disks. Did you bring any?" I sorted through the selections.

"No, I was too busy. I asked Harry to find some. Why?"

"Well, what would you like to see?" I turned the monitor around so she could see what was new in the ship's library. *"Teenage Student Nuns from Hell, Mutant Vixens from Hell,* or, best of all, *Teenage Mutant Student Vixen Nuns from Hell?"*

By unanimous vote, we settled for Humphrey and Ingrid, ably supported by Paul Henreid, Sydney Greenstreet, and Peter Lorre.

The next morning, we practiced for about four hours and had Dinky, Harry, and Annalee practice launch simulations while the ship was maneuvering. The ship only misbehaved twice, and

Harry and McHugh never actually came to blows, so we chalked it up as a success.

Hiro had arranged for us to call Bunkie daily to follow events on Schuyler's World, so while Spooner ran the ship, Catarina and I gave her a call.

"Hello, Bunkie. What's going on?" Catarina asked.

"The newspaper articles about the invasion are beginning to sink in," Bunkie's image said primly. "Some of the people who quit the Civil Guard when it went union have come by and asked if they could help. I let them form themselves into a platoon and issued out about thirty rifles. Mayor Feldman is a little upset. He thinks that what I did was illegal and provocative, and he wants me to call the rifles back in. I told him that I'd have to ask Commander Hiro. I think he's still a little mad at Ensign MacKay. You want me to ask for the rifles back?"

"No," Catarina answered. "He can ask the police to recover them if he really wants them called in."

"He's already announced that he's going to do that," Bunkie said. "I can get you odds of seven to five against the police."

"How's the election going?" I asked.

"They're still busy with the usual flurry of last-minute ballot-box stuffing," Bunkie said, shrugging.

I got the impression that voting in Schenectady mostly depended on who had physical possession of the polling place. "Is the mayor's administration beginning to take the invasion seriously?"

"I think so," Bunkie said cautiously.

I said injudiciously, "Well, that's good."

"Well, maybe not that good, sir," Bunkie said. "As soon as the polls closed, the mayor's press agent announced that they were closing City Hall for renovation and that the city government would temporarily work out of the school gymnasium over in Possum Leap."

"Possum Leap?" I asked.

"It's a little place out a ways on the Hicksville Road, just inside the city limits," Bunkie explained.

Catarina looked at me out of the corner of her eye with a crooked smile on her face.

"Come on, Bunkie, nobody on a planet like this would name

a town Hicksville." I searched for the proper way to express my thoughts. "It hits too close to home."

"No, sir," Bunkie insisted. "You're wrong there. A guy named Hicks—Tewfiq Hicks—was one of this planet's founding fathers." She thought for a minute. "There's a Hicksville, a Hicksdale, and a Hicksburgh that I know of."

"Oh," I said, very quietly.

"Sir, would you like me to explain about the possum of Possum Leap?" Bunkie asked in that neutral tone of voice that navy other-ranks reserve for ensigns who don't know what they're talking about.

Catarina interceded. "No, thank you, Bunkie. Any other reactions to the invasion news?"

"A few things, ma'am," Bunkie said impassively. "The souvenir shops raised their prices, and the Associated Civil Liberties Union held a press conference to announce that they were filing a lawsuit to have the war declared unconstitutional as a violative of the Rodents' due-process rights. The editorials are split about fifty-fifty."

Catarina nodded.

"Anything else newsworthy?" I asked.

Bunkie reflected for a moment. "The Society of Herpetologists wrote an open letter to seventeen religious denominations asking them to correct the unfair characterization that serpents get in the Book of Genesis, but other than that, I can't think of anything. How are things going up there, sir?"

"Well, Bunkie, I'm wondering if our squirrels can take their squirrels, if you know what I mean," I said candidly.

"Good job, Bunkie. Keep us posted on what's going on down there," Catarina added briskly, signing us off.

We had twenty minutes before we were ready to get started again, so Catarina sent me back to see how Harry and Dinky were getting along in stores.

"Hi, how are we doing?" I asked incautiously as I stepped inside.

"Ready to waste those 'Phers, sir!" Harry stood to attention and saluted emphatically.

"Furs?" I asked politely, returning his salute. Sometimes I'm slow on the uptake.

"No, sir! *'Phers!* That's what we call 'em," Harry insisted.

I looked at Dinky, who made small placating gestures. "Which we?"

"You know, sir. Us fighting men." Harry shrugged. "Well, me and Dinky, here."

"Because they wear fur?" It occurred to me that Harry was taking this fighting-men stuff far too seriously.

"Naw. 'Cause they're Gophers, sir!" Harry said in disdain.

Dinky tossed in his half centime. "I thought you said it was because they were furry!"

Harry fixed him with a fierce look. "Well, it's not!" He pulled out the pistol he was wearing—it was one of those big 12mm Osoros—and began fiddling with it.

My experience with pistols is that the accuracy drops off markedly if you're not actually touching your target with the barrel, and that this is true of the 12mm Osoro, except more so. The Osoro has to be the weapon of choice for a shoot-out in a crowded elevator.

"Harry, could you please put the pistol away?" I asked.

Apparently having a sixth sense for this sort of thing, Catarina walked in the door, took in the situation at a glance, and laid her hand on Harry's arm.

"Ah, it's okay, Ken—I mean, sir," he said abashed, holstering his weapon. "I'm just a little nervous."

"That's all right. We all are," I told him. "We'd just prefer it if you didn't flash pistols around on the ship."

I saw Harry's eyes go wide. "You're not prejudiced against pistols, are you, sir?" he asked timidly, looking at me and Catarina.

"Oh, no. Of course not," I said, following Catarina's eyes.

"I just thought that calling them 'Phers would help morale, sir." He hung his head and started rubbing his toe against the deckplates.

"Harry," I said before Catarina could get a word in, "if your morale improves any, we're going to have to tie you down." I slapped him on the shoulder.

Harry smiled sheepishly. "Sure, sir. And thanks, for everything." He headed back up to his battle station in Number One hold.

"Tie him down?" Catarina pondered.

"Ma'am, with all due respect, if you say one word about rope, I'm going to hang myself," I said, rubbing the sting out of my hand where I'd slapped Harry.

"Knot a word. Furthest string from my mind," she assured me.

"Harry's doctor was right. Acting out his fantasies like this is very therapeutic for him," Dinky volunteered unexpectedly.

Catarina's eyebrows came alive.

"What do you mean 'his doctor'?" I asked.

"You know." Dinky gestured ineffectually. "His psychiatrist."

"Harry is seeing a psychiatrist?" I hoped I wasn't hearing what I was hearing.

"I thought you knew." Dinky thought for a minute. "Sir, if you were Harry, wouldn't you be seeing a psychiatrist? When I saw some of the other people on board, I didn't think anything of it."

Catarina cleared her throat. "When you put it that way, I'd have to be the first to admit that not everyone connected with this operation is rated for a full charge."

"Harry isn't—dangerous or anything, is he?" I asked.

"Oh, no," Dinky volunteered. "The doctor just says that he's subject to fits of depression. I think he was going to try gene therapy if this didn't work. I'd better go up and help him get ready."

As soon as Dinky left, I looked at Catarina. "Are wars always like this?"

Her eyes twinkled. "Now you know why we try and avoid having to call out the reserves."

We spent another four hours practicing, and Harry and Dinky actually improved. Encouraged by—or despite—McHugh's waspish comments, they brought their simulated shooting average up close to the Mendoza line, which is a batting average of .200.

Improvement, of course, is a relative thing; and sitting next to Catarina shoulder to shoulder and hip to hip for four hours at a time was as good a way to improve my blood circulation as any.

When we were done for the day, we turned the ship back over to Rosalee and a mournful Clyde. While Catarina was using the shower, I went to find Bucky, who was billeted in Bernie Bobo's old room. I rapped on his door. "Dr. Beaver, can we speak?"

"Certainly, friend Ken! Please, come in and be at home!" He was sitting on his bunk finishing off one of Chandrasekhar's boxed vegetarian delights with more enthusiasm than was seemly.

I sat down at the desk and came straight to the point. "Look, Bucky, you really don't need to be up here." I searched for the proper words. "Friendship is friendship, but we are probably going to get killed up here. You are going to get yourself killed along with us to no purpose."

"Friend Ken, friend Catarina and Commander Hiro have already discussed this with me. You don't understand," Bucky said sadly. All pretense of playacting dropped away from him. "My demi-brother Genghis is coming here to do his utmost to displace me as a threat to his accession. Although Papa does not realize this, he intends to kill me. If I am located on the planet, he will merely extend the scope of his activities to insure my demise. In accordance with the principles of Bucky, I wish to limit the involvement of unfortunate bystanders."

"Oh," I said.

He tugged his whiskers. "Except in matters of succession, we are not a fierce people by nature, friend Ken. Although my misguided demi-brother has imbibed some exceedingly unfortunate attributes from your culture, I truly believe that if I am aboard your ship, he will be satisfied with destroying it and will spare Schuyler's World the ravages of war. As a last act of allegiance to my father, I wish to avoid any harm to the unfortunate beings on the planet below us. I fear that your navy would hold it against my people." Then he spoiled it by quoting Bucky. "'Duty should encompass practicality whenever circumstances permit.'"

While I was trying to pry my foot out of my mouth, Catarina knocked on the door and asked to join us.

"Hello, Bucky. How is everything?" Catarina asked, seating herself cross-legged on the floor.

"Oh, most excellent. I was feasting on one of Mr. Chandrasekhar's culinary masterpieces and engaging friend Ken in a discussion about silly political matters.'' Bucky's whiskers drooped, which gave him a wistful look. "I was just thinking that after the present unpleasantness resolves itself, friend Ken will be the captain of his own starship. How exciting! It seems so fortuitous for him.''

"Catarina had more than one hand in the decision. I'd like to think she decided I was a little better suited for the job than anyone else,'' I said modestly, looking at her and daring her to contradict me.

The corner of Catarina's mouth dipped slightly. "We have an old saying, 'In the land of the blind, the one-eyed man is king.' ''

"Do you, really?!'' Bucky exclaimed eagerly. "That is uncanny! We have almost the exact same expression in our lovely language. Let me see, it translates as, 'In the country of the witless, the half-wit is crowned.' ''

I said, "Thank you, Bucky, for sharing that with me.''

"Bucky, speaking of kings, I've been meaning to ask you, just what is your father's title?'' Catarina asked.

"Oh, I suppose that you would translate it as 'the Poobah,' '' Bucky said airily.

I exchanged looks with Catarina. "The Poobah?''

"Yes. It is queer that you should ask. When I was very young and first began studying your speech, I asked my grandfather that very question, and he told me that he had selected 'Poobah' as the best approximation. Very impressive-sounding, is it not?''

"Yes,'' I allowed.

Bucky finished off the last crumbs of his roti and twitched his whiskers. "Strange, my grandfather said something at the time that I didn't understand. He said that he wanted a translation that would not unsettle humans, and that 'Poobah' sounded friendlier than the other choices he considered. Can you imagine?''

Catarina managed a nod.

"A fascinating topic.'' Bucky stood up from his bed and dusted off his paws. "But, having dined, I must perform my ablutions. Friends, I shall return momentarily.''

As soon as I heard the shower running, I glanced at Catarina.

"I'm just glad the old boy's dead. Otherwise we'd probably be speaking Rodent."

Beaver came back in a few minutes later, dripping water. "Has anyone seen my blow-dryer?"

A wet Rodent smells like a couple of wet Labrador retrievers, and the vents on the *Scupper* weren't designed to handle the load. My stomach did flips, and Catarina turned two shades paler than pale.

"Ah, no," I said, "but we haven't eaten yet, and I'm afraid we really must go."

"How regrettable," Bucky lamented. "Until tomorrow!"

Catarina decided to skip supper and call it a night. As we paused by her door, she gave my hand a quick squeeze. "A small coin for your thoughts."

"I'm just wondering if there's some tactical wrinkle that we haven't thought of," I said, lying through my teeth.

"I put in a suggestion box in case somebody had an idea."

"And?"

She shrugged. "Somebody suggested installing a pasta bar." She gave my hand another squeeze and disappeared.

I quieted the queasy feeling in my stomach with some fruit and called it quits a little later. As I crawled into bed, it occurred to me that it had been at least a week since somebody had tried to kill me. Then I heard footsteps outside my door, which I'd forgotten to lock.

About the only thing that somebody hadn't tried was the direct approach—machine-gunning me in my bunk.

I rolled out, landed chest-down on the floor, and scooted into the storage space underneath my bed. Then I remembered I was hiding underneath a waterbed, which probably meant I'd drown if somebody did spray the room with lead.

"Damn," I mumbled to myself as the door opened.

Clyde stepped inside. He slowly drew Harry's pistol. "Sir? Where are you?" Then he spotted me and holstered the gun. Curiosity got the better of him. "Sir, Lieutenant Lindquist asked me to look in on you. What are you doing down there?"

I thought for a second. "The mattress was too hard."

He gave me a funny look. "It's a waterbed."

"Hard water." It dawned on me that if anybody aboard did

mean me harm, they'd at least wait until the Rodents had a shot at it.

"Sir, are you sure you're all right?"

"Just fine, Clyde."

"Well," Clyde said, shaking his head, "have a good night, sir."

The next morning while I was shaving, I remembered that McHugh's half coin was still hidden behind my mirror. A little sheepish, I fished it out and stuck it in my pocket to return.

Before we started practice, Hiro, Catarina, and I called Piper to check on her status.

"We're doing fine over here," Piper explained. "Kimball hogs the bathroom every morning, but otherwise everything's running smoothly."

"Have you encountered any problems?" Hiro inquired.

"I let Trujillo and Sin split an extra roti every time they rack up ten hits in practice, sir," Piper said jauntily. "If Genghis doesn't show up on schedule, we may need an emergency re-supply. Signing off!"

I turned to Catarina and Hiro. "How's our gunnery practice going?"

Catarina increased the volume on the intercom.

"Take that, you weasel! How'd you like another dose of hot lead! Rat-tat-tat-tat-tat!"

"Harry, why don't you let Dinky take the next simulated launch?" Catarina directed.

"Ah, I'm hit, men!" Harry shouted. "They got me! I can't see! Dinky, you take over for me!"

"Voyage of the Damned," McHugh muttered loudly.

Hiro's face indicated great pain. I couldn't make out what he was saying to himself, but it had something to do with "reservists."

"Maybe we should keep practicing until we get it right," Dinky said mildly.

McHugh grunted. "I'm glad I didn't make plans for Christmas."

"Before you practice maneuvering, we should contact Bunkie," Hiro told Catarina with his eyes still closed.

Bunkie filled us in on the latest news. "Sir, there are a few small problems now that people are starting to realize that Genghis is due tomorrow." She was trying to make it as palatable as possible. "Somebody started a rumor that the brewery in town was going to cut back to one shift, so there was some rioting until things got sorted out."

"Any new lawsuits?" I asked.

"Just one, sir," Bunkie explained. "The Associated Civil Liberties Union filed, requesting an injunction against any Rodent invasion."

"Oh?" I said. "That's interesting."

"They voted two-to-one to file the suit. I understand the woman who got outvoted quit, and they're looking for new members. I think they got disconcerted when I leaked the news about the firepower the Rodent cruiser was packing and the betting line against us hit fifty-to-one. They pretty much said at the press conference that as long as they had a lawsuit against us and a lawsuit against the Rodents, they had their bread buttered both ways."

"Why the sudden change of heart?" Catarina asked mischievously.

"Off the record, ma'am, downtrodden, underprivileged aliens stop being downtrodden and underprivileged when they land in your neighborhood and start running down property values. One more item: the legislature scraped together a quorum and passed a nonbinding resolution condemning the Rodent invasion and asking us to peacefully disarm them."

"When we finally get hold of Cheeves and start rattling the skeletons in his closet, I expect a few of the local politicians to fall out," Catarina commented. "Thanks, Bunkie. Let us know if there are any new developments."

"Yes, ma'am," Bunkie said. She looked at all of us. "Best of luck."

With a couple of breaks, we spent the next eight hours practicing tight turns without having too many breakdowns. I got a better feel for what Catarina was trying to accomplish, no pun intended, and Catarina got a better handle on the *Scupper*'s more obvious quirks and shortcomings.

After dinner, I hunted up McHugh and gave her back her coin.

"Annalee, I found this a while ago, and I think it belongs to you. I forgot I had it. Souvenir?"

"Sort of. It's my good-luck piece. Fat lot of good it's going to do me now." She looked at me directly. "I wish I had sense enough to hop into the lifeboat and get the hell out of here. But I just can't shake six years in the navy."

"I guess it affects us all that way," I said lamely.

I left her kicking the bulkhead, saying, "I'm stupid! Stupid! Stupid! Stupid!"

I headed off to Bucky's room to help Catarina, Clyde, and Harry teach Bucky how to play poker. To shorten a long story, we taught Bucky how to play, and I acquired a great deal of sympathy and a smidgen of respect for the Contact boys. The only thing that saved us was the fact that he wagged his tail whenever he got a particularly good hand.

I also spoke to Clyde about Wyma Jean. Catarina had originally billeted Clyde in Rosalee's cubicle, but when Rosalee had changed her mind and joined us, she bumped Clyde back into Frido's old cabin. That made the common area between Spooner's room and Clyde's room the second minefield in the star system, and Clyde was a little wistful about it.

"It still bothers you, doesn't it?"

"Well, yes," he admitted. He grinned. "But, as Bucky says, 'I worried about whether my shoes matched until I realized I wasn't wearing any.' "

"I gather that I'm not the first person to give you a little pep talk."

"No, sir. You're the fourth."

After I left Clyde, Catarina and I sat on the sofa in our common area and turned on the TV to catch the news from the two Schenectady stations.

Channel 1 was running a special on "Military Unpreparedness and Expensive Weapons that Don't Work." It turned out to be one of those balanced discussions of the AN-33 missile system where they find the one guy in the universe who thinks that the thing is a complete piece of junk and cut to him every five seconds.

Channel 2 had a roundtable discussion of the invasion, which was kind of interesting. One woman called for a peace vigil in the hope that we would turn the plowshares we were going to fight with back into plowshares, while somebody from the Keep Schuyler's World White, Black, and Yellow Committee called on us to whip the Rats back to their holes and carry the war to total victory on !Plixxi* by Saturday noon at the latest.

Then we talked until I fell asleep. Unfortunately, I didn't stay asleep long. Catarina shook me awake.

"Let me go back sleep. Tell Genghis I surrender," I mumbled.

"Ken, Bunkie's on the line. We have real problems. Lydia Dare got the California Kid to talk. She knows where we planted the minefield, and she knows about the launcher in the space station. She's planning on breaking the story live tomorrow morning."

"That's freedom of the press for you—you can't hide anything from them." I figuratively scratched my head. "Wait a minute, is she going to try and broadcast this before Genghis shows up?"

"Genghis is going to get a detailed, slashing, no-holds-barred exposé of what passes for our battle plan," Catarina said grimly.

"Well, we just have to tell her not to run the story," I said.

She stared at me. "Ken, are you awake yet?"

"Ah, right." I made a battlefield retreat. "We can tell her to delay running the story."

"Are you sure you aren't the one who's thinking about entering a convent?" Catarina shook her head. "Come on, we have to find Commander Hiro."

Clyde and Bucky joined us as we assembled in Hiro's bedroom. After Clyde explained the problem, Hiro asked, "Are we certain that the Rodents will be listening in?"

"Even if they're not monitoring, Lydia wants to interview Genghis, so she's planning on broadcasting the segment live from Genghis's flagship," Catarina explained. "If we don't stop her, we're going to have to take our chances on surviving the trip to Brasilia Nuevo. Once Lydia spills her guts, our chances of doing significant damage to Genghis drop from pitiful to nonexistent." Frustration lined her face.

Hiro adjusted his nightcap. "This complicates matters. Does anyone have any suggestions?"

"What if we launched a commando raid and took her prisoner?" Clyde suggested.

"I don't know," I reflected, recalling my previous encounters with Dare. "It would be tough to gag her. Couldn't we just shoot her instead?"

"We'd pretty much have to strip the ship to pull off a raid, and we're short on time to plan and execute it properly," Catarina pointed out.

"Could we fire a missile at her?" Hiro asked hopefully.

"No good," Catarina said. "It would take at least a couple of days to modify our ship-to-ship missiles to hit ground targets."

"There might also be adverse publicity," Bucky added thoughtfully.

"What if we simply order her not to make the broadcast?" Clyde asked.

Catarina formed a crooked smile. "That's prior restraint of free speech, and we're talking about a reporter. We'd have less trouble with the courts if we simply shot her."

"We've got to keep her out of the newsroom tomorrow," I said, thinking aloud. "The only way to do that would be to dangle an even bigger story in front of her nose."

"Keep going, Ken, you're on a roll," Catarina said.

"I am? Somebody help me out."

"I think that it is very newsworthy that one of my officers is a vampire," Hiro said unexpectedly.

" 'Vamp Leads Navy into Battle.' Sir, I like it," Clyde said.

"Clyde, go pull out a copy of my report and delete all the names," Catarina directed. "That'll keep Dare busy for hours trying to figure out who is who. How do we plant it on her?"

That was my cue. "That, my dear Lieutenant Lindquist, is a job for professionals. I've got just the guys in mind."

After we arranged the details with Bunkie and sent her the edited version of Catarina's report, I called Jamali and told him I was dropping the charges against Joe and Larry.

"Why should I release them?" he questioned, stroking his beard, "and why do you always bother me in the middle of the night?"

"Sheriff, it's a harebrained scheme to keep the long arm of

the news from complicating operations tomorrow." I shrugged.
"As for calling you in the middle of the night, it's probably
force of habit."

"All right, in the interests of what I presume is planetary
security I shall do so, on one condition. If your scheme works,
I want you to call me—in the afternoon—and give me the details
to cherish the next time Lydia abuses me in print."

"Done," I said promptly.

The next step was to explain the terms and conditions of their
release to Joe and Larry.

"Here's the deal," I told them. "Tomorrow morning, you go
over to Clyde's apartment at eight o'clock sharp. You've got the
address, and the key will be in the door. You call Lydia and tell
her she's got to meet you there in person at eight-thirty to do the
deal. Now on the computer in there will be a read-only copy of
an official report. You can't print it out, you can't copy it, and
it will vanish like smoke if you try. That means you've got to
negotiate price with Lydia before she reads it all, otherwise
you've got nothing to sell her, *comprende*?"

"Why does he sound like he's selling us a used car?" Larry
complained.

"Quiet!" Joe said as he tried to get his notes straight. "How
did we get this stuff again?"

"When you kidnapped me, you found the key and a computer
file access code in my pocket, and you figured that it was something big," I explained patiently.

"Oh. Right!"

"Now, you're going to tell Lydia that this is the official clas-
sified report of events aboard *Rustam's Slipper*. You're going to
tell her it's proof that one person on board the ship is a vampire.
I get the first thousand she pays you and half of anything you
make over a thousand, so make sure you see the color of her
money before she reads it. And keep her there a while dickering
or she'll get suspicious. I'll contact you later about paying me
my share." I crossed my fingers. "Any questions?"

"I still want to know why you can't sell this to her directly,"
Larry said.

"He works for the government, dummy!" Joe's indignation
boiled over. "Dare is never going to believe something like this

coming from him. She's a reporter! That's why he needs us!"
He sounded happy. He had obviously figured out what he was
going to do with my share. "It's free money!"

"Well, jeez, I was only asking," Larry said. "I mean, it just
seems a little odd that some reporter's going to believe a couple
of small-time crooks like us instead of some high-powered navy
guy."

I shrugged. "You got to play every game by the rules."

After they had the details straight, I signed off.

It seemed a little incongruous that the fate of human civili-
zation—at least my share of it—depended on whether a couple
of petty hoods remembered to get up on time, but if it came
with a night's sleep attached, I wasn't going to argue.

As I went to bed, one of Piper's lost little microrobots came
wandering out from under my desk on six tiny legs like miniature paper clips. It waved its sensors at me to see if my wiring
was shorted. "Do you have days like this, too?" I asked it.

In the Words of General Custer, "Will You Look At All Those Indians!"

While Cheeves had told us what day Genghis was planning on arriving, he hadn't told us what time, so Catarina woke me early enough to attend to a lot of last-minute details.

The first thing on my list was to put Spooner on board the shuttle. Clyde thought she was in the galley. It turned out she was—locked in a passionate embrace with Harry.

"Excuse me," I said, "but we're real pressed for time here, Wyma Jean."

"Oh, ah, sure," Spooner said, a little flushed.

"Ken, this isn't what you think," Harry said, zipping his coveralls a little tighter.

"I'm sure it's not, Harry." I said in my most authoritarian manner, "Wyma Jean, meet me by the lock. In ten minutes." I shut the door behind me.

Clyde joined me by the lock to see Spooner off, which apparently didn't violate the terms of their joint cabin occupancy agreement but did make my job a little delicate.

"Clyde," I asked as we were waiting, "what do you and Spooner have in common. I mean, besides a difference in sex?"

Clyde had dark circles under his eyes. "I've been asking myself the same thing. I guess I follow my heart."

"Off of cliffs and in front of moving trains," I started to say, but checked myself as Wyma Jean arrived.

"Goodbye, Ken," she said. "Thanks for everything." Then she solemnly stepped up to Clyde and shook hands with him as the Kid pulled up.

She disappeared onto the shuttle. "Ken, sir, maybe I would like to talk to you after all," Clyde said.

I stared at him. "Clyde, are you sure? There are at least four different things that can happen over the next few hours, and three of them would obviate the need for our discussion."

"Uh, right."

I grabbed something quick to eat and reported to Catarina on the bridge. Under Hiro's approving eye, we warmed up and then tried a few simulated launches out of practice maneuvers. Whatever effect Wyma Jean may have had on Harry's hormones, she didn't help his shooting eye much.

In the middle of a reverse thrust, Bunkie cut in. "Commander Hiro, Dare is going for the honey pot."

"Good job, Bunkie," Catarina said, easing us out of the maneuver. "Secure from action stations. Let's take a break."

The *Scupper* came to a rest position and we resumed spin. "Where is Dare now?" Catarina asked Bunkie.

"She's in with the two guys you found. I'm jamming the telephone frequencies and watching her on the security camera. The two guys are pretty good—they're spending more time arguing with each other than they are talking to Dare."

"That's natural talent. It sounds like things are under control. What else is going on down there?"

"Ma'am, things are getting a little crazy. So far this morning, I've gotten in four hundred and seventy-one reports of Rodents warships and other unidentified flying objects, including one that landed in somebody's bathtub. I've also received two hundred and ninety-one photos of clouds, meteorites, and animals jumping over fences." Bunkie looked harried. "It's like Elvis's Second Coming out there. People are afraid that the invasion may hold up their welfare checks."

"Do the best you can, Bunkie," Catarina told her. "Keep us posted."

As Catarina cut the connection, I looked at her. "I just thought of something. We expect Genghis to show over the next five or six hours. What if he's late?"

"Then we have problems with Dare," Catarina responded. "And if Genghis is late by a couple of days, we have worse problems. This is a small planet and the media is stretched just to cover the election, so for now we only have Lydia to contend with. As soon as the election is over—"

"The other reporters will be swarming over us like flies on fresh manure," I finished for her.

Bucky arrived a few seconds later carrying a steaming mug of honey-water. "I was just thinking," he said. "It is possible that we are overreacting. Papa has had nearly a week to come to his senses and recall my demi-brother."

I looked at Catarina. "I wish he hadn't said that. My luck being what it is, the odds on Genghis showing up within the next five minutes just went from one in ten to about ten to one."

Catarina nodded and flipped the intercom back on. "Annalee, I need you to make an especially good search."

"Did I say something?" Bucky asked.

"Ken keeps bumping up against unfavorable chance deviations," Catarina explained.

McHugh was monitoring the Gremlin. "Commencing full search beginning with the most likely sectors," she said crisply. "Oh, shit! Ships approaching. I can barely make them out."

"Rodents!" Hiro exclaimed, his eyes alight with the fire of battle.

"All hands to action stations," Catarina called out, pulling up the picture Annalee was seeing.

At a nod from her, I opened up a channel to Piper and Bunkie. "Four ships approaching at extreme detection range. It looks like Genghis is here."

Two small Rodent merchant ships were leading, one after the other, with the Phoenix-class cruiser and a passenger liner trailing them astern. The liner was obviously being used as a troopship. This was shaping up to be what military people call a "target-rich environment." We didn't have to look very far to find something worth shooting at, and we didn't have to look very far to find something shooting back.

Catarina ran her hands over the controls. "They're heading straight for the second vee in the minefield," she said calmly as we eliminated our spin and moved to interpose our ship between the Rodent ships and Schenectady below.

There was a squawk from the loud-hailer. "The light cruiser

signs herself as *Nemesis*. She's trying to communicate," I commented.

Hiro and Beaver were sitting in the jump seats. Although Bucky was busy trying to strap himself in, Hiro was perched on the edge of his seat. "Ensign Mickey, please put the cruiser on. Try and get full video if you can. Dr. Beaver, stand by."

"Sorry, sir, the best we can do at this distance is audio, with about a one-second transmission lag." I flipped on the loud-hailer. "*Nemesis*, this is Confederation Navy vessel *Rustam's Slipper* acknowledging."

The Rodent flotilla slowed its approach. *Nemesis* responded, "*Rustam's Slipper*, this is Cheeves. Is Dr. Beaver present aboard your ship? If so, may I speak with him?"

"That does sound like Cheeves," Hiro exclaimed. He picked up the little microphone attached to the jump seat and spoke into it. "Cheeves, this is Commander Hiro, aboard *Rustam's Slipper*. Dr. Beaver is aboard. Go ahead and speak with him, Doctor."

"Cheeves, what a pleasant surprise to hear from you. I had given up hope altogether," Bucky said.

"It is very pleasant to speak with you, sir. I feared that I would not be afforded the opportunity," Cheeves responded.

"How are things over there?" Beaver asked.

I could have answered that. The three lead ships were still closing on us slowly, leaving the liner behind them, well out of range. At a nudge from Catarina, I opened up the intercom to let everyone else on the ship listen.

"Sir, I regret that your dread father had already made up his august and Imperial mind by the time of my arrival, and although I pleaded your case as forcefully as I was able, he declined to change it," Cheeves explained. "As you are aware, your demi-brother Adolf was your father's favorite offspring, and his unfortunate demise moved your father greatly. Your dread father is much sorrowed."

"Indeed, Cheeves," Bucky sympathized.

"Sir, I was constrained to comply with his wish that I accompany the expedition and advise your demi-brother Genghis, although with heavy heart. I reported to your demi-brother the feeble condition of the vessel you are on and the somewhat questionable caliber of her personnel. I earnestly hope I have not caused you inconvenience. Is there any way that you could remove yourself from *Rustam's Slipper* prior to its destruction?"

"You switched sides, you sawed-off little gopher!" Harry exclaimed.

Bucky drew himself together. "Pardon me, this is a private conversation," he said icily.

"Belay that, Mr. Halsey," Hiro said. "Please continue, Doctor."

"Uh, Cheeves, I say," Bucky said. "These humans are my friends. I volunteered to accompany them. Would you now have me show the white feather and abandon them in their hour of need?"

"Of course not, sir. I merely felt that you might find it acceptable to view the conflict from a slightly greater distance."

"I appreciate your solicitude for my welfare, as ever, Cheeves, but I really don't see how I could leave friends Ken and Catarina bereft of my counsel, so here I must stay, for better or worse."

"I feared as much, sir. To touch upon a difficult subject, I had hoped to fully explain my conduct to you, and it does not appear probable that I shall have the opportunity to do so. I can only offer my deepest regrets."

"That is not necessary, Cheeves. I am convinced that your motivations are fully honorable. As Bucky says, 'One's friends, one must trust.' "

"Thank you, sir. I am deeply touched by your confidence. I fear I must now bid you adieu, inasmuch as the ship's commanding officer, Captain von Tirpitz, informs me that the moment of your destruction has arrived and wishes to speak with you on behalf of your demi-brother Genghis. Farewell, sir."

"Ta-ta, Cheeves," Bucky said, wiping his eyes with a handkerchief.

Catarina cut in. "Hold it a moment. Cheeves, what about the money?"

"I regret that whatever explanation I could provide you must await a more suitable moment," Cheeves said firmly. "Captain von Tirpitz wishes to speak."

"Worthless humans, prepare to die!" a higher-pitched voice said.

Somehow, when you're keyed up and expecting to get fried, you don't expect remarks like that from somebody who sounds like he's on helium. I giggled.

Von Tirpitz had a complete and total sense-of-humor failure.

There was a great deal of squeaking from *Nemesis*. "Oh, I say," Bucky exclaimed. "Such language!"

Hiro reproved me mildly. "Ensign Mickey, please." He said to von Tirpitz, "*Nemesis*, this vessel is an armed Confederation warship. If you have something to say, say it. Otherwise, prepare to be fired upon and destroyed."

"Humans!" von Tirpitz said. "We have hung out a flag of truce as a sign of parley in accordance with Admiral Genghis's noble and beneficent instructions. Our Supreme War-Leader informs me that he will accept one of your officers aboard this ship to discuss terms of surrender. If you surrender promptly and abase yourselves, some among you will be permitted to keep your short and brutish lives."

"One moment," Hiro said, and Catarina turned off the loudhailer.

"They're asking for a parley. That's a hopeful sign. Lieutenant Lindquist, can we get the lifeboat out there and back?"

"Yes, sir. It's small, but it has enough range," Catarina said, hinting delicately that the lifeboat was too small to trigger our mines and tip our hand, so to speak.

"I don't think that they expected us to be armed. Maybe they'll leave after a show of negotiations," Hiro said optimistically.

I had forgotten to shut the intercom off. Someone up in Number One hold said in a very unmilitary fashion, "The man is obviously playing bridge with a pinochle deck."

Hiro wisely ignored the comment. "Lieutenant Lindquist, Dr. Beaver, can we trust Genghis? It would be very awkward to have to maneuver without all our personnel aboard."

"I believe so," Beaver answered. "Among my people, parleys are considered sacred, since we !Plixxi* much prefer talking to fighting and do far more of the former than the latter.

Since we have adopted your custom of a flag of truce, I have never heard of one being dishonored."

"I doubt it's a ploy. I'm not sure they think they have anything to lose," Catarina said grimly. "But, remember, we can't stall Dare forever."

"True. All right," Hiro said. Catarina switched on the loud-hailer. "*Nemesis*, halt in your present positions. I will send an officer empowered to discuss the disarming of your ships and the repatriation of your personnel," Hiro told von Tirpitz.

There was a shrill noise on the other end that sounded like laughter. "Your conditions are accepted! Send your officer!"

As I broke contact with *Nemesis*, Bucky said, "I must say. This von Tirpitz is quite rude. I don't know where Genghis finds these hooligans of his."

"Mickey, are you willing to volunteer to go?" Hiro asked. "As long as there is any hope of persuading Genghis to simply leave, I feel that it is our duty to sit down and smoke a peace pipe with him to try and bury the hatchet."

Beaver reacted. "Commander Hiro, I can see that burying the hatchet might make it hard to find if you didn't mark the spot beforehand, but smoking a peace pipe? Wouldn't that lead to emphysema?"

Catarina stared at the ceiling. I spoke up loudly. "Uh, Commander, the Rodents over there are a trifle annoyed with me on a personal basis—I remember something about ritual castration—so sending me might not be conducive to the successful completion of negotiations."

"Can't be helped, Mickey. I cannot command the force from a lifeboat, and I can't send Lieutenant Lindquist. Even though she's attached to the combat services, she is an intelligence officer, after all, and it would be a major intelligence failure to allow her to fall into Rodent hands should they prove treacherous. It just isn't done in the Regular navy." Hiro's tone of voice was one usually reserved for half-wits. "You are the only other officer on board. You're protected by a flag of truce, so you shouldn't have anything to worry about."

"All right, sir," I told him. Catarina was chewing her lower lip into hamburger. "Any ideas?" I asked her under my breath.

"Take the lifeboat. Drape it in a bedsheet. Go out a little slow to make them think that the boat doesn't have any speed, and come back quick. Keep your discussion short. As soon as Channel Two notices Genghis's ships overhead, they're going to start looking under rocks for Lydia.'' She waited until Hiro turned his head and then kissed me softly. "Godspeed."

"Ken, I shall accompany you," Beaver said loyally. "I shall prevail upon my demi-sibling to see the sweet light of reason."

"You'd better not. You're a target, too. If you go, Ken will need someone to stay with the lifeboat to keep Genghis from tampering with it," Catarina cautioned.

"I'll go! I'll go! I can stay with the lifeboat," Harry volunteered promptly. Hiro acquiesced.

Crammed together in the little lifeboat with Bucky and Harry, I found the long ride over to Genghis's flagship seemingly interminable. Even Harry was subdued. As the lifeboat passed the stubby cylinder of a floating mine, I asked Harry, "What's this thing under my seat?" I asked Harry.

"What thing, sir?"

"This box."

"Oh, it's a case of emergency rations I threw in, sir," Harry said. "They might come in handy. You never know."

As we closed in on the long, lean hull of *Nemesis*, I confided to von Tirpitz that we had Bucky aboard. I could tell I had his attention.

I figured out why when we boarded. When Bucky appeared, von Tirpitz had twenty side-Rodents there to greet him in style. Some of them were still buckling their crossbelts on.

The Rodent in charge gestured with what looked to be a ceremonial bread knife, and the honor guard presented arms with a flourish. I noticed they were all carrying modern FN rifles. Bucky twitched his whiskers appropriately. "The pomp is always so tiresome," he confided.

A chubby Rat in oversized epaulets bowed stiffly. "I am Captain von Tirpitz, Your Rotundity." He gave me a poisonous look. "I was not made aware of your coming. Permit me to give you a tour of the unrestricted areas of my ship."

"That won't be necessary," Bucky said loftily. "I must see my demi-brother Genghis."

"That will not be possible. Our Supreme War-Leader left instructions that he is indisposed."

"Of all the nerve—where is Cheeves, then?" Bucky said with a hint of anger in his voice.

"Cheeves is also indisposed. Permit me to give you a tour of the vessel."

Bucky leaned over and whispered to me. "Friend Ken, my presence here is wasted. My demi-brother refuses to see me. It is up to you." He allowed von Tirpitz to lead him off.

A smaller Rodent wearing a lieutenant commander's stripes came up to me. "You are Ensign MacKay? Please to follow me."

He led me back to a huge cabin decked out in shimmering tapestries, striped animal skins, and swathes of gauzy fabric. It bore an obvious resemblance to what Mad King Ludwig thought a Moorish harem should be. The Rodent three-striper immediately left, leaving me alone with Genghis and a brace of guards.

The Supreme War-Leader, draped on a divan, was a lean, scrawny-looking Rodent with drooping side-whiskers and eager, burning eyes.

He sat up and rubbed his paws together. "Ah, Ensign Ken MacKay—may I call you Ken?—I was hoping you would come. I wanted to see you in the flesh. Before I destroyed your ship, of course." He made a gesture. "Oh, don't worry about my guards. They don't speak English."

"Nice digs," I said, looking around at the tapestries.

"It is nice, isn't it? It has that look of burnished, barbaric splendor. The little interior decorator I found was worth every penny."

"Right. Shall we get down to business? I hope Cheeves mentioned that Adolf managed to put a missile into his own ship while he was trying to waste us, so strictly speaking, I'm not sure we're responsible."

"Oh, Cheeves said something of the sort. He is a gem, isn't he?" Genghis guffawed. "Sorry, little joke there. You know, 'gem,' as in emerald?"

"Uh, right."

"In any case, Cheeves is truly a Rodent of vision. I intend to make him my grand vizier when I have taken power. I shouldn't be telling you this, but if it were not for his assistance with the financing end of things, I wouldn't have been able to pull this off. I have plans, Ken, big plans.''

He broke into a rousing chorus of ''For I am a Pirate King.'' The song sounds better sung by a bass.

''Let's get back to Adolf,'' I said.

''You wish to discuss Adolf? My weak, venal, and exceptionally stupid demi-brother? I made use of him, but it would have been very awkward to keep him around after I succeeded to the throne. I am actually rather grateful to you for disposing of him. Although I personally can't say that I care whether you live or die, I did promise Papa that I would blow you to atoms, so there is nothing further to be said on the subject. Hopefully, I'll be able to recover your corpse from the wreckage of your ship so that I can flay the hide off you and turn you into a blanket. It'll go well with the draperies, don't you think?''

I sighed. ''Well, now that we've disposed of that issue, let's assume that you do blow our ship away—will you leave Schuyler's World alone?''

''I wish I could,'' Genghis said apologetically, ''but we've been showing the troops these pictures all week.'' He opened a little drawer in the side of the divan and rummaged around until he found a stack of photos to hand to me.

''They look like gerbils,'' I said, thumbing through them.

''They also look remarkably like baby Rodents. We didn't even have to touch them up much. We've been telling the boys all week that the people down there fatten them up in concentration camps and eat them. If you look through, there's a really nice photo of a roasted gerbil with a grape stuck in its mouth. Really good propaganda, isn't it? I rather think I outdid myself there. Anyway, the troops are wild, and I couldn't very well bring them back without a little sack of the city, could I? We promised them they could stay a few days and survey homesteads.''

''I guess that disposes of my second point.'' I thought for a few seconds. ''Genghis, you do realize that *Rustam's Slipper* is armed and we're going to do our level best to make you pay. You also realize that the navy is on its way.''

Genghis made small noises of amusement. ''How unfortunate for you that your navy will not arrive in time.''

''True, but irrelevant. You're not going to get away with this. When the navy does arrive, it's going to come to !Plixxi* and clean your clock.''

''Oh, but there you're wrong, Ken! The navy is not going to come clean my clock, at least not immediately. They're going to be busy with my friends, the Macdonalds, for quite a while yet,'' Genghis said with a certain malicious glee. He went over to a little six-legged table and picked out a cigar, lit it, and blew smoke in my face. ''While your politicians are negotiating with the Macdonalds, your navy won't be able to divert ships. I come home a conquering hero, and my darling daddy either abdicates in my favor out of joy or has an accident. When your navy arrives in force, I shall surrender. I'll have what I want, which is my father's throne. My friends, the Macdonalds, will have what they want, since your politicians obviously won't want to start a war with them while I'm pillaging defenseless planets. And in a few years, after everyone forgets, we'll do it again. If I pull this off for them, the Macdonalds are going to give me real warships.''

He pulled the cigar out of his mouth and held it under his nose to savor the aroma. ''And of course—oh, rapture—when I blow your ship into tiny fragments, I also dispose of my darling demi-brother Bucky. You can't imagine how embarrassing it is to have an overgrown boy scout as your nearest kin.''

I was running out of points to make. ''You don't really think that the Confederation is going to let you stay in power after you sack Schuyler's World?''

''Ken, you miss the sublime beauty of my scheme. Nobody's going to know I was here. You and the people with you will be the only witnesses, and you won't be witnesses for long. When your diplomats come, I will have a different name and will be a newly enthroned and very peaceably inclined ruler who had nothing at all to do with my father's militaristic policies, don't you see?'' Genghis took another puff on his cigar. ''It's all quite brilliant, if I do say so myself.''

''And the people on Schuyler's World?''

''What's a few peasants among friends? Actually, you should thank me for improving your species's breeding stock.''

"So what am I here to negotiate?" I asked.

"Oh, nothing. But as the villain in this piece, I have to boast to you what my plans are now that I have you in my power. It's in all your literature. And besides, it's fun." He ground out his cigar on the tabletop and looked down at his watch. "Oh well, time is money, as my grandfather used to say. How about if I give you a twenty-minute head start to get back to your ship." His whiskers twitched and his upper lip curled a little, exposing his front teeth. "It's been a pleasure doing business with you, Ken. Ta-ta, now!"

Bucky and Harry were waiting for me when I got back to the lifeboat. The sideboys were still there, but I noticed they were wearing less clothing. One of them was practically undressed.

As I strapped myself down and we took off, I pushed my feet under my seat and a little light went on in my head. "Harry, what happened to the crate of emergency rations I was sitting on?"

"Well, sir, I decided we really didn't need it after all," he said circumspectly.

"Harry, what was in that crate?" I asked in a mild voice.

"Ummm, mostly honey."

"What else, Harry?"

"A few books, maybe."

"What kind of books, Harry?" I turned around to look at him.

"Lab studies about white rats." He saw the expression on my face. "Sex studies. In color."

"Harry, you didn't!" Bucky exclaimed.

"Harry, you weren't trading stuff, were you?" I asked.

"Oh, no, sir! I gave some of those Rodents some gifts, and they gave me some gifts." He beamed from ear to ear. "Like this tunic." He pulled one out. "Ain't it a beauty?"

"It looks like it would be a little tight on you," Bucky observed.

"Harry, these Rats want to chop us into chutney, and you're trading with them for souvenirs?"

Harry knitted his brow. "Sir, is something bothering you?"

"Never mind, Harry."

Catarina moved the *Scupper* toward us. We didn't have time

for normal lifeboat-recovery procedures, so I moved in close, whipped the lifeboat's nose around, and matched speeds. Catarina was ready for me. The lock opened and the cargo arm came out and hooked us by the nose to ease us the rest of the way. Clyde and Rosalee were waiting.

"Not real promising, huh?" Rosalee commented, reading my expression.

"Battle stations," I told her, undoing the faceplate on my space suit and running toward the bridge.

Commander Hiro was pacing the bridge when I arrived. "Did your mission meet with success, Mickey?"

In the viewscreen, I saw the winking lights of the truce flag disappear, and *Nemesis* fired off two huge missiles at extreme range. The two lead Rodent ships began moving toward us to take us in a pincers movement while *Nemesis* kept us occupied with long-range fire.

"Perhaps not," I said, flipping on the intercom. "Prepare to maneuver."

"Hey! They're shooting at us when we're out of range," Annalee complained.

"They are out of our range. We are not out of their range," Catarina corrected. "Hard maneuvering. Cutting spin, now! Everybody close the faceplates on your suits and get strapped down."

"Can I shoot? Can I shoot?" Harry asked.

Hiro went over to help Bucky into his jump seat.

"Sir, I need you to strap down, too," Catarina told him. I could feel her preparing to shove the ship's nose down.

"In a second," Hiro assured her.

Bunkie called us. "Dare is still in with Joe and Larry. She doesn't know the Rodents have arrived, but I can't stall her much longer. I've been jamming the phone calls to her from her station for the last twenty minutes, and they're about to send a car over and drag her back."

"Good work, Bunkie. We'll take it from here," Hiro said. He turned to us. "Engage the enemy more closely!"

I took control to firewall the old girl. "Sir, will you kindly strap yourself down, now!" Catarina said to Hiro.

Both impellers kicked in raggedly, and I heard a loud thump.

"Oh, dear," Bucky said.

Out of the corner of my eye, I saw Hiro drift by with his eyes shut and a lump the size of an egg on his head. Catarina snagged him by the ankle and pushed him in Bucky's direction.

The two missiles slid past us. "I am taking command," Catarina said quietly. "Bucky, please grab Commander Hiro and try to get him strapped down."

As the two smaller Rodent ships darted toward us and penetrated the outer edges of the minefield, we powered forward.

"*Nemesis* is hanging back," Catarina called out in a clear voice over the loud-hailer so that Piper could hear her. "We are engaging the other ships."

I felt her shrug. "We need to make them hit some mines," she said casually so that only I could hear. "Otherwise, we're probably dead."

"Tracking, tracking second ship. Keep your fingers off that firing button, you stupid chauvinist pig! Contact's twisting. Tracking, tracking. Contact's too faint, I'm losing it!" Annalee called out.

"Engage with one missile at maximum range. Fire as soon as you acquire a target," Catarina told her.

"Harry, tracking. Follow the little bouncing ball. Tracking, good long contact! Mark! Fire!" Annalee said.

I had that little thrill you get just before you expend a piece of ordnance that consists of fifty thousand moving parts all manufactured by the lowest bidder.

Harry hit the firing button. Two missiles leaped out of Number One hold.

"Oh, crap! I only meant to fire one missile. Reload! Reload!" McHugh yelled to Harry and Dinky.

Both Rodent ships dodged nimbly out of the missiles' flight paths. The missiles lost acquisition and sped off harmlessly into space.

"You missed, damn it! You missed! Reload, reload!" McHugh shouted helplessly.

As the second ship jumped aside, a mine identified it and erupted into life. It struck the Rodent ship just forward of the engines and ruptured them. The engines went up, causing the

ship to engage in a little energetic disassembly. The lead ship
kept coming.

All of us cheered.

A second later, one of our missiles exploded.

"I don't know how you two did it, but you just shot down the
television satellite," Annalee said in utter disbelief.

"War *is* hell," Rosalee commented. Rosalee liked her soaps.

"Reloaded. Ready," Dinky announced, but *Nemesis* and the
remaining Rodent merchantman both fired, and it was our turn
to dodge.

"We're bracketed. This is going to get rough," Catarina said
as we hauled the ship's nose around. The smaller Rodent ship
turned itself over and disappeared below our firing arc.

"Pinging! Pinging!" McHugh yelled to tell us that one of the
missiles had locked on to our image.

"Oh, dear," Bucky said.

"Make it good, Ken," Catarina ordered as we wrestled the
ship around and doubled back on our course.

The missile lost acquisition and skipped on by. That left *Nemesis* clearing mines with her laser, and the smaller Rodent ship
on our tail closing fast.

Mounted as it was in Number One hold, our launcher could
cover an arc of about two hundred degrees from side to side and
about ninety up and down. With the Rodent ship behind us, it
wouldn't bear.

"Oh, boy, we've got them now!" Harry said.

"The smaller ship's launching," Annalee said desperately.

Catarina and I tilted the *Scupper*'s nose and dodged to the left,
guessing right but losing momentum in the process.

The other ship closed on us.

"Harry, Annalee, we can't hold this. I'm going to roll the
ship and pivot. Fire as you bear," Catarina called.

As we turned to meet the Rodent vessel, McHugh said,
"Harry! Mark. Mark, damn it. Mark. Fire!"

Harry fired. One missile misfired; the other one missed. As
he and Dinky struggled to reload, the Rodent ship dodged nimbly aside and closed in the dead zone behind us where our missiles couldn't reach.

"What do we do?" I asked as we zigzagged to throw them off.

"Usually, warships have to trade speed for agility. We should either out-turn her or outrun her," Catarina said. As we weaved to keep from straying inside the Rodent ship's cone long enough to eat a missile, we rapidly discovered that she could fly faster and turn tighter than we could. "Unfortunately," she said, "we can't do either."

That made us what the navy likes to call a "BFT"—Big, Fat Target. The Rodent ship took position below and behind us where she could plaster us at will. In a straight stern chase, we were dead, quickly. If we bobbed the wrong way, we were also dead. Flying the ship by instinct, Catarina pulled the nose around and used the impellers to slip left, left, left again, then right. Each time, I caught her movement and forced the *Scupper* to respond. The board started lighting up like a Christmas tree. With her superior speed and agility, the Rodent ship skillfully maintained her position close behind us, methodically herding us into the planet's gravity field and cutting us up with her lasers while waiting for us to make a mistake so she could sink a missile.

Meanwhile, *Nemesis* was still busy clearing mines, although at the moment it didn't look like she'd be needed.

Catarina faked reversing thrust, then sped up. The Rodent merchantman reacted, lost a little distance, and quickly recovered its position. Her lasers began turning the wheat in Number Three hold into popcorn.

"Ken," Catarina said calmly, "I can't shake her. The only gamble left to try is to reverse thrust and hope she sails on past. That will give her a perfect launch as she goes by, and if she outguesses me and drops her speed immediately, she'll put two or three missiles into us before we build up thrust."

The chase brought us closer to the space platform. "Piper," I said.

"No! We can't!" Catarina said. Piper had orders to stay concealed until *Nemesis* came into range. "Piper has to surprise *Nemesis*!"

"Missile launched. Pinging! Pinging!" McHugh yelled. "Do something!"

Catarina and I desperately reversed thrust and somehow the missile slid by. That left us wallowing with no forward momentum.

"We're losing power," I said.

As the Rodent ship lined us up, two missiles leaped toward her from the space platform. Piper broke transmission silence. "Is this a private fight or can anyone get in it?" she asked dryly.

The Rodent ship suddenly forgot about us and maneuvered desperately.

One missile missed. The other punched a hole in her side and ripped a thirty meter gash. The Rodent lost power and began drifting, spreading a trail of metallic debris.

There was another round of cheering. "That's two!" Harry said. Catarina nodded, and I commented to Piper, "Thanks, Beam. As Eddie would say, 'You headed them off at the pass!' "

After that, we were a little too busy for chitchat. As Catarina tried to pull us out of the planet's gravity well so we could build momentum, the ship skewed sideways.

"She's not handling," I said, trying to pull her in.

"We've lost the starboard impeller!" Catarina shouted over the whine of abused machinery.

"She's packed it in," I said as the ship began spinning like a top.

Von Tirpitz may have been a hood, but he knew his business. Before we could regain control, he fired one missile at us to keep us occupied and moved in to plaster the space platform.

Piper and her crew made a fight out of it. She tilted the platform with her emergency jets and launched twice. The cruiser fired six shots to her two. Four antimissiles obliterated Piper's missiles. The other two ship-killers impacted on the platform and half of it disappeared. The plastic tubing that acted as the station's umbilical cord to Schuyler's World ripped free and hung in space. Broken pieces spun off in all directions.

As Clyde and Rosalee struggled to repair the damage, *Nemesis* turned her attention toward us.

"The busted Rodent ship is launching a lifeboat," Annalee commented.

"So is the space platform, so somebody there is alive," Catarina said.

"Well, at least we've got the odds in our favor," Harry added optimistically.

"Oh, dear," Bucky and Dinky both said.

Bunkie called us. "Lydia Dare is about to start broadcasting. I tried shooting her tires out, but I missed."

"No problem, Bunkie. We have other things to worry about."

Moving at an exaggerated crawl, we aimed ourselves at *Nemesis*.

"Marking, marking," Annalee coaxed.

Harry fired.

Nemesis wasted three antimissile missiles knocking our efforts out of space and then put a shot into Number Five hold, where it exploded just inside the ship's skin and ripped the hold apart. The engines shut down to keep from exploding. We lost power and the lights dimmed.

A few seconds later, Lydia finally came on the air and started broadcasting the details of how we planned to pull off the biggest upset since David decked Goliath with a sucker punch in the opening round.

McHugh came on over the intercom. "Goddammit, MacKay! You got us out of this predicament the last time, think of something! We got any shit left?"

I turned to Catarina. "We're holed badly and listing. We have no thrust, and the impellers aren't working. In short, we can't run, we can't fight, and we can't hide. What does the master plan call for at this point?"

The hulking mass of the *Nemesis* slowly moved toward us, carefully staying where our missiles could never reach.

"To tell the truth, I was hoping you had a few ideas."

"I regret that I, too, have nothing to contribute," Bucky chimed in. "I am exceedingly sad that our brief but fruitful comradeship will come to an end."

Harry punched in over the intercom. "We're not moving!"

"Why don't you get out and push?" McHugh snapped back.

"While I believe in miracles, I understand that God's timing is a little bit off now that they've started making Him file environmental-impact statements," I commented. "Piper?"

"I just hope she got out alive," Catarina said grimly. She turned to Bucky. "Bucky, you get in a lifeboat and get out of here. We'll tell Genghis you're in it."

"Mistress Lindquist, I thank you for your excessive solicitude on my behalf, but I feel that I must share your fate. I believe that my demi-brother would be more likely to fire on a lifeboat I was in than a lifeboat I was not in. I truly believe that one of his objectives is to remove me from the—I forget how it goes, is it the picture or the frame? In any event, he would like to succeed my father, and as we Rodents say, there's only so much swill in the trough." He sighed. "I feel that I somehow failed with him." He meditated for a moment. "But remember, Ken, death is a truly wonderful adventure. Did I ever show you a hologram of my fiancée?"

He passed it over. Female Rodents, I discovered, look like miniature schnauzers.

We figured out why Genghis was prolonging the agony when he showed up a few seconds later on the viewscreen. "Vile enemies of Rodentdom! You are toast! Prepare to die!" He twirled his whiskers. "Has a nice ring to it, doesn't it? Want to throw in the towel, demi-brother? Throw yourself onto my non-existent mercy?"

"As Bucky would say, I would like to say once more how pleased I am to be dying in company with such good friends," Bucky said.

"I think I'm going to toss my cookies," McHugh responded sullenly over the intercom.

Bucky looked up quizzically. "Tossing cookies? Is this an athletic event?"

I whispered to Catarina. "You know, just once I'd like to tell Dr. Beaver what I think of ol' Bucky."

She shook her head. "No, no. Don't forget, Ken. As Bucky says, 'You should endeavor to leave this life with a clean heart and good deeds to be remembered by.' "

"Well, there's one more I had in mind." I leaned over and kissed her.

It was apparently Dinky's turn to use the intercom. "You know, I have a feeling in my bones that we're going to get out of this okay."

"Have you considered a transplant?" McHugh responded.

"This is such fun. Any other last words?" Genghis inquired, cocking his head. "Please maintain screen contact to the very end. I want to assure my father that I personally witnessed your destruction." He smirked. "And you, dear demi-brother, ta-ta! Bye-bye! Bridge, *fire!*"

"Folks, I think the fat lady's doing her warm-ups," Clyde said.

A long minute passed.

"Where's the bang? I'm still waiting to hear the bang," Genghis observed. He looked at us. "You're still there. Bridge? Why are they still there? Bridge, fire!"

Another long minute passed.

"Oh, drat! Excuse me one moment," Genghis said. "I need to go check up on things. There seems to be something wrong with my bloody ships today."

At that moment, a swarm of lifecraft moved away from *Nemesis*'s sides.

Catarina and I looked at each other. "Cheeves!" we said simultaneously.

Bucky was the first to react. "Cheeves is indeed a true friend," he intoned sonorously.

McHugh's voice floated in over the intercom. "Ken, you louse! Since we're going to die any minute now, I want to tell you exactly what I think."

"Annalee, everybody, I think we just won," I said.

I heard a muffled squawk from the intercom.

"Now that we've won, I'd like to know how," I continued. "What is going on over there?"

Catarina stared into the screen, then punched on the loudhailer. "Let's see what's on the mayday frequencies."

We listened to chittering on several bands. "Hold it," I said. "Go back. That sounded like English!"

She was already tuning it in. "The signal's weak."

". . . *Slipper*, come in. Please come in *Rustam's Slipper* . . ."

"Quiet, everybody!" Catarina ordered. "This is *Rustam's Slipper*. Please identify yourself."

"Ah, Miss Lindquist. How happy I am to hear your voice! I trust things are well with you, Dr. Beaver, and Mr. MacKay."

"Cheeves, we're fine. What's going on over there?"

"I have made certain adjustments to this ship's system of controls and have cut power to both the bridge and to the ship's weapons systems," Cheeves said. "I trust this meets with your approval."

"Quite, Cheeves," I said.

"Unfortunately," Cheeves continued, "I was forced to dispense with the ship's safety systems. The ship's computer informs me that the engines are unbalanced, and that if I do not restore normal fuel controls and adjust the damping, whatever that might be, the ship will blow up underneath me in approximately thirty-six point two minutes. I do not know how to do this and am somewhat loath to restore controls. I felt it prudent to advise the ship's crew to abandon ship under the circumstances."

"Cheeves, we're coming after you. Where can we find you?" Catarina asked.

"That is very . . ." Cheeves started to say. Abruptly, the connection died.

Catarina shifted frequencies. "Spooner, bring the shuttle around immediately. Cheeves has wrecked *Nemesis* for us, and we're going after him."

As soon as Spooner acknowledged, Catarina got on the intercom. "We're going to abandon ship. McHugh, check out the lifeboat. Commander Hiro is injured and unconscious. Witherspoon, Ensign MacKay, and I are going to board the shuttle and rescue Cheeves. Evacuate everyone else."

"You want invitations engraved? Move it!" Annalee shouted over the intercom.

Clumsy in free fall, Annalee and Harry piled through the door to carry Hiro off. "Here, Ken. Take my pistol," Harry said, pressing it into my hand.

"Thanks, Harry." I made sure it was on safety and stuffed it into the thigh pocket on my suit.

Harry fished around in his pocket. "Here, you'd better take this, too."

"Uh, thanks again, Harry. What is it?"

"It's a sock full of marbles. You use it to cosh sentries. Like this! Wham!" Harry proceeded to demonstrate and almost turned a somersault.

"Uh, thanks, Harry." I slipped it into another pocket.

Catarina grinned. "I have a service pistol, and so does Clyde. There's Spooner and the Kid now."

We got to the lock just as the Kid docked. Clyde was carrying an assault rifle in addition to his pistol.

Spooner's face lit up as we climbed aboard the shuttle. "Ken, where's Harry?"

"Harry's fine. We put him aboard the lifeboat," I told her, wrapping one arm around Clyde so he couldn't aim his rifle.

Catarina whispered instructions into the Kid's ear, and we pulled away with the equivalent of squealing tires.

"I've never been aboard a light cruiser before. Where should I look?" Clyde asked her.

"You won't. You're rear security. Ken and I will do the searching," Catarina said, looking at her watch. "We'll have fifteen minutes at most to find Cheeves. If we're not back by then, button up and take off before *Nemesis* goes off."

She got on the loud-hailer. "*Nemesis*, we are here under a flag of truce to pick up survivors from your ship. Do not fire. Repeat, do not fire." She looked at me. "I wish I'd remembered to ask Bucky how to say that in !Plixxi*."

"Uh, right."

We sailed past the stricken cruiser's lasers and missile launchers to dock. As we touched, someone on board *Nemesis* opened the lock, and Catarina and I got out. Immediately, a couple of dozen Rodents scampered past us and threw themselves at Clyde's feet.

Inside, *Nemesis* was no longer the taut ship I remembered. There was discarded equipment and other debris all around.

"We're going to have trouble finding Cheeves. We'll have a better chance if we split up," Catarina said. "Clyde, give us fifteen minutes starting now!"

She gave my arm a squeeze. "You know your way to the main cabin—you head that way. Stay to the main corridors, and if you don't spot Cheeves in ten minutes, come running back. Whatever you do, don't get lost!"

"Uh, right," I said.

"Okay." Catarina reached down to pick up a discarded sword and pushed it into my hands. "Here, take this!"

"Uh, thanks." I was a walking arsenal.

I went jogging down the central corridor. Ahead of me, a trio of Rodents poured out of one cabin, chirping horribly. I fumbled for the sword hilt, then relaxed as they ran past.

Behind me, a squeaky voice said, "We meet again. The gods are kind."

I turned around, saying, "I'm looking for a fellow named Cheeves, about so tall. Have you seen him?" I found myself facing Genghis, who was holding a small chain saw.

"Vile human, this is all your fault. Prepare yourself to die!" Genghis said hoarsely.

"I'd like to meet the guy who did the language tapes for your planet." I reached into my pocket and pulled out Harry's pistol. "Don't move or I'll shoot. And why are you holding that chain saw?"

"They are used as antipersonnel weapons in all your finest films. I shall drink your blood, Ken MacKay!" He fired up the saw and waddled toward me.

I pulled the trigger. Nothing happened, of course. The chamber and the magazine were empty; Harry had forgotten to load the thing. "This isn't supposed to happen," I muttered, and heaved the pistol at Genghis's head, which was probably the smartest thing I could have done whether the pistol was loaded or not.

Then I took off running. I figured out that you run faster if you drop the sword you're carrying. There was a long, straight corridor ahead of me, full of doors. One door facing me opened, and a Rodent holding a rifle timidly stuck his head around, his whiskers twitching.

I slammed the heel of my hand in the middle of the door as I ran by, which put it in the middle of the Rodent's face.

"Sorry," I said, "I'm in kind of a hurry."

Behind me, over the roar of the chain saw, I heard Genghis panting. "I will carve your ribs from your backbone, and spread the Blood Eagle!"

"Why are you chasing me, you idiot? You know this ship is about to blow up, don't you?" I yelled irritably.

"It couldn't have been that fool brother of mine who planned this! You did this to me!" Genghis wheezed. "It was your fiendish mind that devised this evil plot, Ken MacKay. Turn, and look at your doom! I will be requited if I can but reach into your rib cage and clutch your pulsing heart and liver." Genghis sounded like he was in the same lousy physical shape I was in.

"You have obviously been reading too much science fiction!" I replied.

The corridor made a sharp bend, and as I rounded it I felt a sharp pain in my side. "Dear God, if you get me out of this, I swear I'll play racketball three times a week," I muttered.

Leaning against the wall to catch my breath, I heard Genghis's footsteps coming closer. I reached into my pocket and pulled out Harry's overstuffed sock of marbles. Counting to three, I took the sock and emptied the marbles out in Genghis's path.

"Oh, no!" I heard Genghis shout. A second later, he came flying into view and slammed into the wall muzzle-first. The chain saw hit the deckplates and spun around a few times.

I bent over and turned it off. "Fun's fun," I told Genghis, "but the ship's about to blow up, and I have work to do."

Genghis shook his head and rose to his knees. He pulled out a long, ornate-looking dagger. "Vile human, prepare to suffer pain!"

"Obviously, I am not doing this right," I commented.

Suddenly, Genghis's head froze and his whiskers twitched. I saw his nostrils flare. Behind me, I heard a deep, resonant growl, and a familiar, rank odor filled the air. Genghis dropped the dagger like a flash and scooted back up the corridor.

I turned. Peering out from around the corner ahead of me, I saw the head of a cat the size of a grizzly bear. The cat bared its fangs and reached out a huge pink tongue to lick its whiskers. The image shimmered.

The cat looked suspiciously like Sasha Louise.

It meowed, a high bass rumble. Then the holographic image faded, and the real Sasha Louise poked her furry little head around the corner. She was followed by Cheeves, who had a clip on his nose and a fair-sized camera arrangement hooked to a strap over one of his rounded shoulders. He tucked away his can of Cheez Whiz.

"I do hope you weren't inconvenienced by our tardy arrival, Mr. MacKay." He bowed slightly.

"Shuttle. Starboard bay," I croaked. "Double-parked."

"In that case, it would be prudent for us to make haste. I would highly recommend the path to our left."

Sasha Louise took off at a dead run, and we followed her as fast as Cheeves's little legs would carry him.

"Nice toy you have."

"Quite," he agreed. "Excellent engineering, if I may say so. The image resolution is quite superior. I believe it's Japanese. The cheese, sir, is as effective as you portrayed it."

"Uh, right. What made you decide to use Sasha?"

"There is a large feline sort of creature, fortunately extinct, that figures prominently in !Plixxi* fairy tales—quite unpleasant and dependably disagreeable. It was very similar to the hirsute tabby depicted in such an unfavorable light in 'Bucky Beaver Meets Bun Rabbit.' I felt it would be advantageous to have dependable means of disrupting the ship to order to obtain access to its controls.

"In providing my intelligence summary to Admiral Genghis, I mentioned that Miss Lindquist was a vampire, a fact which featured prominently in her report. Naturally, the crew was curious and to explain what a vampire was, I had translations of *Dracula* prepared. I arranged for a few minor alterations in the story. I had the Count himself turn into a giant cat, rather than into a bat. I trust this meets with your approval."

I had to smile. "Changing the story on them?"

"Sir," Cheeves said stiffly, "Mistress Lindquist weighs approximately fifty-two kilograms. Even if she changed her appearance, she would still possess the same weight if the physical laws governing conservation of mass and energy are to hold true. As I understand it, most bats are much smaller."

"Smaller?"

"Smaller, sir. They weigh at most a few hundred grams, and a fifty-two-kilogram bat, even with Mistress Lindquist's personality, would be quite improbable. I felt this to be a serious defect in an otherwise admirable tale. As you may perhaps be aware, sir, one of the seminal vampire stories is a charming little tale called 'Carmilla,' by a Mr. J. Sheridan Le Fanu, which much influenced Mr. Stoker. Mr. Le Fanu's vampire transformed herself into a large sooty-black animal of lithe restlessness resembling a monstrous cat, and I felt that he was likely to be accurate about such matters.''

"I bow to your scholarship, Cheeves.''

"Moreover, it was far easier to obtain a cat to impersonate Miss Lindquist on short notice than it would have been to obtain a bat.''

I shook my head. "Cheeves, you're unbelievable. Well done.''

"Thank you very much, sir, I am most gratified. It seemed to me to be the most suitable way to resolve the contretemps. However, if I may be so bold, sir, that pale green shirt of yours with the checkered collar . . .''

I took a deep breath as we turned another corner. "Consider it done, Cheeves. Give it to the deserving poor.''

"I shall endeavor to find someone suitably color-blind. And about the blue plaid, sir—''

"Not the blue plaid!'' We turned a final corner.

"Yes, sir. I strongly recommend it.''

"Okay, Cheeves, it's gone. You are enjoying this, aren't you?''

As he trotted along, Cheeves brushed his whiskers in what may have been the Rodent equivalent of a wink. "I strive to stay in character, sir.''

"One more question. The book, the cat, I presume the rattle of chains over the intercom, an announcement that the ship was about to blow up—is that all you did to convince the crew to abandon ship?''

"There may have been a few discreet bribes in addition, sir,'' Cheeves admitted.

We saw the shuttle door ahead of us. "I've got Cheeves! Where's Catarina?'' I shouted to Clyde.

"She was here a second ago. She went to find you.''

The Kid stuck his head out. "Like, dude, you know, we've got to blow this place, before this place blows.''

"No, not for another three minutes and fifty-seven seconds,'' Cheeves said as he stopped and consulted his pocket watch.

"Catarina!'' I shouted. It sounded thin in the almost empty ship. I turned to Cheeves. "Quick, switch that thing on. I need an amplifier.''

He caught my idea immediately. "Full volume, I feel, is called for," he said, fiddling with the dials.

"Catarina," I bellowed, the echoes pounding around us. I motioned to the Kid. "Start the shuttle, I'm going after her."

"No need—dumb as hell—I'm here," Catarina announced, breathless. "Let's go!"

"A most excellent idea." Cheeves shut off the sound on his hologram projector.

But as we crossed the threshold, a familiar voice said, "Not so fast. I turned to see Genghis holding Sasha Louise under his arm with a sword under her chin. "Surrender yourselves or I will slit your accomplice's throat."

"I would scarcely advocate it, sir," Cheeves said, and disappeared into the bowels of the shuttle.

"I'm out of here," Catarina said, and followed.

"Genghis, I wouldn't want to disillusion you, but cats cost twenty-four cents a pound at the animal shelter," I said. I pressed the button to close the hatch.

As I was dogging it, I heard a squall of pain from Genghis, and Sasha came darting through the narrowed opening. She gave me a dirty look and started licking her paws.

The shuttle was packed with Rodent refugees. "This is a happening place," the Kid said as we took off.

"Are we going to make it?" Spooner asked.

"I would rather not venture a guess at this juncture," Cheeves said.

I turned to Catarina. "Catarina, haven't we done this before?"

"Two or three times," she agreed.

"Right. I've said everything stupid at least once, and I meant it."

"Right." She smiled.

I looked at Cheeves. "Cheeves, !Plixxi* family politics get pretty violent, don't they?"

"Quite vigorous, sir. Even in this enlightened age, it is customary to reduce the number of potentially disgruntled heirs."

"Out of curiosity, who is the heir apparent now that Genghis is out of the running?"

"That would be Dr. Beaver."

I looked at Catarina. "Do you think maybe we've been had?"

"I've suspected it for some time now."

"Would you officer types mind getting back to worrying about the Rodent ship blowing up?" Spooner asked, white-faced.

The Kid had the outside monitor pointed directly at the receding figure of the *Nemesis*. All of a sudden, *Nemesis* quietly blew up.

I counted to twenty.

"I believe that it is customary to cheer," Cheeves said, and we did.

When the noise died down, I turned to Catarina. "While we're thinking about it, maybe we ought to do something about the troopship."

"Good point." She reached over and flipped on the loudhailer. "Commander of unidentified Rodent ship, this is Lieutenant Lindquist, commanding Confederation navy vessel *Rustam's Slipper*. The remainder of your fleet has been destroyed. Please land your ship at the Schenectady spaceport and surrender her to the authorities there so that we can process her personnel for repatriation back to !Plixxi*."

We waited a few minutes. "And if they don't?" I whispered.

Catarina shrugged. "We take chalk and scrawl rude graffiti on the hull."

A moment later, the Rodent ship responded. "We will comply with your orders."

"I don't know if my nerves can take much more of this," I commented.

"Ken, your hand is bleeding!" Catarina said suddenly.

"Apparently Admiral Genghis injured you," Cheeves said. "I believe that this would qualify you for a wound stripe."

I looked at the thin line of blood on my left hand. "I hate to say this, but I think the stupid cat just bit me."

"What about the money, Cheeves?" Catarina asked as we led the Rodent ship down to the spaceport.

"It is a convoluted story, Mistress Lindquist. Approximately one year ago, Prince Adolf gratuitously complained about some unexplained financial reverses. Dr. Beaver magnanimously volunteered my services in sorting matters out. I discovered that Prince Adolf wished to make discreet, delayed payments to unnamed individuals. On his behalf, I established bearer accounts, accessed through the use of special tokens.''

Catarina listened quietly.

''My suspicions were aroused when Prince Adolf asked me to manufacture duplicate tokens. It appeared unscrupulous, in that Prince Adolf would be able to withdraw the money even after ostensibly surrendering control of it. I complied with his wishes. However, inasmuch as Prince Adolf is notorious in family circles for losing items like cuff links, I manufactured a third set, which I stored in the consulate safe in the event they were needed. I then informed Dr. Beaver of my suspicions. As I had no firm evidence of wrongdoing, however, Dr. Beaver declined to allow me to pursue the matter further.

''While making plans for my departure, I concluded that I might have unexpected travel expenses and felt it would be remiss of me not to take possession of the funds as a representative of my government. I intend to make a full accounting to Dr. Beaver when circumstances permit.''

''Cheeves,'' Catarina finally said in admiration, ''you were born to be hung.''

As we made our landing approach, I asked her quietly, ''What happens to you and me now?''

''We enjoy life for a few days. Then you work on getting your ship fixed up somehow. After all, I'm going to need a ride out of here.''

''Sure. It shouldn't be too much trouble scraping up a crew.''

''It won't be good-bye, Ken. At least, not yet.''

''But you're telling me that it would be easier all around if we didn't see very much of each other,'' I said, listening to the shuttle descend.

''Why don't you take a few days off?'' she suggested. ''I'll write out a three-day pass.''

''I guess. It would be fun to go to the beach and soak up some sun and surf. I feel like absolute hell right about now.''

''Get that bite looked at first.''

When we touched down, Clyde and I were the first ones out the door. I guess I expected confetti and a brass band waiting on the ramp. Instead there was a cameraman from the *Post-Dispatch* and about five or six people, including Bunkie, Harry, and Commander Hiro with the van. Commander Hiro had a bandage wrapped around his head.

My disappointment showed. "I wouldn't let it bother you, sir," Clyde said. "I think we're competing with a truck-pulling contest."

"I didn't expect a ticker-tape parade, but I thought I'd see a little more than this," I admitted. I noticed the vendors were already out hawking "Operation Rat Patrol" T-shirts with a slightly recognizable picture of me on the front.

The man standing at the foot of the ramp frowned. "Hello, Mr. MacKay, is it? I'm Smith, from Customs and Immigration. I have had numerous reports come in that undocumented aliens have been landing in small lifecraft." He touched his badge. "You are the owner of record of the ship up there, and I was wondering if you knew anything about this."

I made sure Catarina wasn't in earshot. "I have no idea where they're coming from," I piously told Smith. "There's about twenty we picked up in the back of the shuttle and a few more about to land in a ship. Do your duty."

"Why, thank you, Mr. MacKay," Smith said, walking past me.

Clyde blinked. "That transport's full of dope-crazed Rodent assault troops."

I nodded. "They started it."

Another guy pushed past the cameraman. "Mr. MacKay?"

"That's me."

He seized my hand and pumped it. "Good job! Give them hell!" He reached into his pocket and handed me a thick envelope. "You're being summoned. The persons holding the mortgage on your ship have commissioned the law firm of Schmarbeck, Schneider, Schwartz-Uppendieck to file a lawsuit against you. Good luck with it."

I stared at his back as he walked away. Catarina appeared at the shuttle door. "Is that Lydia's car I see?" she asked.

I shuddered. "Please, anything but Lydia."

She sighed. "All right, I'll do the interviews. Ken, go ahead and get everyone else into the van."

I pushed through the T-shirt vendors and went over to salute

Commander Hiro. "Hello, sir. You missed a great battle." I let a little worry seep into my voice. "Who else made it out?"

"It's amazing, Mickey," Hiro said wistfully, returning my salute. "Everyone is accounted for. Our Marines, Sin and Trujillo, are severely burned, but they are receiving treatment. I understand we owe a great deal to Cheeves."

Cheeves bowed low.

"I need to go back and figure out how to write this up," Hiro said, mopping his brow.

Spooner threw herself into Harry's arms—literally. Harry's big, but he's not that big. I thought for a minute he was going to go over.

As we drove off, they started necking in the back of the van. Clyde said to me quietly, "I would just like to know—"

I patted him on the shoulder. "Trust me, Clyde. It's the sleaze factor. Some people have got it"—I looked at Harry in the rear-view mirror—"and some people don't."

"Sir, perhaps Mr. Witherspoon should consider alternatives," Cheeves said, giving me a meaningful look.

"Right," I said. I took a piece of paper and a pen from him, scribbled down Bunkie's name and phone number, and handed it to Clyde.

Riding Off into the Sunset

Commander Hiro confirmed my three-day pass. Clyde and I got out at his place, and I got to use the bathroom first. I polished off a bag of cookies in the shower and collapsed in bed, roughly in that order. I woke up when I heard the telephone ringing.

"What is it, Bunkie?" I asked groggily.

"Sir, you have an appointment over at the hospital."

"How long have I been asleep? What appointment?" I tried to crawl under my pillow.

"Forty-five minutes, and you need to have your hand looked at. I also need to get a physical on you before I take you off active duty status," Bunkie explained. "Then you can go on pass."

"Isn't this kind of sudden?"

"Well, sir, we don't have *that* much use-or-lose money in the budget, and I have a few more reservists on the payroll than I'd planned on," Bunkie said spryly. "Please get yourself dressed and report to Room One-twenty-one at the hospital."

Room 121 was white and painted with little pastel happy faces everywhere, except on the nurse who was waiting to examine me.

"Mr. MacKay, I am Nurse Clarkin, and you are fifteen minutes late."

"It's been a busy morning," I muttered. I opened and shut my eyes a couple of times. "Don't I get to see a doctor?"

"What makes you think the doctor would want to see you?

All of you spacemen are disgusting animals. Now shut up and stick out your tongue."

She checked my pulse, my temperature, and my eyes, ears, and throat. She took some blood work and commented, "It's such a shame the navy is lowering its standards."

She condescended to stick a proper bandage on my thumb and made me take something to fight the inflammation. "Well, you appear to be mostly alive."

"Thanks, Nurse Clarkin. Look, I'm starving. Is there some place around here I could get a hamburger or something?"

"Hamburgers are full of nitrites and other carcinogens. No wonder you are such a pallid, pitiful specimen." She shook her head. "If you eat anything that unsavory and nauseating, you may have a reaction, and in your condition, I won't answer for the consequences."

"Nurse Clarkin, do you have some kind of a personal problem?"

"I do not answer personal questions from strange men. Now step down and breathe in," she said icily.

That was when I found out that nurses have very cold hands.

"I can't do anything more with you," she announced finally. "The treasurer's office will mail you the results."

"Thank you," I said politely. I immediately went looking for a burger place and found one right outside the front door. After I ordered a burger and a beer, I figured out why they called it a "burger" rather than a "hamburger" and ended up throwing most of it away.

Cursing Nurse Clarkin's soul, I had a salad and a milkshake instead.

On the way out, I scanned the newspaper headlines. "MacKay Does It Again!" and "Ensign Blasts Rodent War Fleet" they read, which I suppose was about the best I could have expected, given Catarina's sense of humor. Apparently Lydia Dare had finally finished digesting Catarina's report, because as I was standing there, the headlines on the screen changed to read, "Local Vamp Wins Rodent War, Saves Planet" and "Rodent Blood Shed—Is It Snack Time?"

I was wide awake when I got back. Clyde was still blissfully snoring, so I grabbed a towel and a bathing suit and asked Bunkie to pick me up and drive me to the beach.

The beach turned out to be an unprepossessing stretch of gray sand littered with kids cheerfully playing ball and building sand flophouses. Staking out a space away from the tourists in aloha shirts, I lay down on my towel and closed my eyes, thinking that a little rest and sunshine would put me right.

It wasn't something that a little rest would cure. When I woke up, instead of sand, I saw hospital happy faces and Nurse Clarkin.

"Had a nice nap?" she crooned.

I was completely wrung out, and my head hurt. "I haven't decided whether I'm dead or alive," I answered truthfully.

"I'm not surprised."

I looked at her. "I hope I'm not dead. This might be permanent. What happened?"

She sniffed. "Spirituous liquors are the Devil's tools."

"What's wrong with me, anyway?"

"I will check on your prognosis and discuss it with you later after you have had a chance to adjust to your surroundings." She ostentatiously ignored the electronic notepad on the bed that would have told her everything she wanted to know.

"Tell me the truth, Nurse. Does anybody else work in this hospital, and what is this thing in my arm?"

"That's a glucose drip. Don't play with it. You're dehydrated. You have a sodium imbalance accentuating your natural hostility."

"I'm not hostile! I'm hungry and also uncomfortable." I hefted my pillow right-handed. "This pillow here feels like a sack of sand," I said, thinking of something other than sand.

"Complain, complain, complain! That's all you patients ever do. What do you think a hospital is for? If you're hungry, I have a nice dinner right here for you."

She whisked it under my nose. I'd forgotten that hospitals purchase leftover food from airlines and prisons.

I poked a turgid sprig of broccoli. "Are these things vegetables? What happened to the food?"

That earned me a real sniff. "In addition to my other duties, I am the hospital nutritionist."

Apparently, the damnable things were steamed for precisely ninety-seven seconds so that they wouldn't lose nutrients. I spent the next ten minutes listening to my stomach send me messages while Nurse Clarkin expounded on the horrors of overcooked vegetables. I never realized what Freud was getting at until she started explaining the intense disdain she felt for limp carrots.

I held out as long as I could and finally broke. "Look, Nurse Clarkin, how about if you just bring me up a handful of cookies? I'm dying for a cookie."

"Sorry, you don't get any dessert if you don't clean your plate. The wholesome meal in front of you has the exact nutritional balance for a weird person like you."

"Nurse Clarkin, don't you have a boyfriend to ventilate on?"

"How would you like to be wearing a catheter?"

"Look, why don't you just give me my clothes, and I'm gone."

"You're not going anywhere. The doctor said you need bed rest, and I can't release you. If I gave you your clothes, you'd just wear them, and that's against hospital regulations. Besides, your mother dresses you funny." She looked down her long nose at me. "There are some people who have been waiting to visit you. Now that you're awake, I'll tell them that they can see you."

She flounced out and slammed the door, leaving me with a plateful of cold veggies.

I flipped the tray aside and considered life's cruelties. About twenty minutes later, Annalee McHugh came through the door.

"Oh, hello, Annalee. Thanks for stopping by. I was hoping Catarina would spring me out of this dump. They won't give me my clothes."

"You shouldn't need them."

"Whatever you do, don't get yourself admitted. The food they serve here is poison, and they don't give you enough of it. I'm so mad that I can't even see straight, and I'm dying for a chocolate chip cookie."

"Funny, you should say that, Ken. Dying is just what I had in mind."

I really wasn't paying attention. "What, I realize that Schuyler's World is a hell of a place to get stuck, but you never struck me as the suicidal type."

"Not quite, Ken." She pulled out a pistol and smiled. It wasn't a pretty smile to see. "I was thinking more about homicide. All right, thief. What did you do with the money?"

"What money? You mean, for the *Scupper*? It's going to be months before the navy pays up."

"Don't play games with me, Ken. You used my half coin to clean out my account. What did you do with the money? I want it back!" McHugh demanded.

"McHugh, will you talk sense and quit playing with that thing? I don't know what you're talking about."

"Don't act stupider than you are. I want my money. You got ten seconds."

A little light finally dawned. "Oh. So *that's* what that coin was for. I was wondering." I thought for a moment. "Cheeves cleaned out the bearer accounts at Second Schenectady, and I haven't gotten around to asking him what he did with the cash."

The pistol drooped. "You're telling the truth, aren't you?" McHugh said in disbelief.

"I'm glad we got that straight, Annalee. Now will you help me get this thing out of my arm? I want to sneak down to the kitchen in this place and steal something real to eat. I'd really like some chocolate."

"How about lead, instead?" She pointed the pistol at me.

"Come on, Annalee. I'm feeling really lousy right now, and I really don't have time for this. Are you telling me that after what we've been through together, you'd shoot me?"

"In a heartbeat."

It finally occurred to me that she was serious about all this. "I suppose you're going to tell me how you planned this," I said, hoping she would explain instead of just shooting me the way any normal criminal would.

"Sure, I'll fill in some of your surmises. Ironsides and Bobo were my tools from the beginning. They were childishly easy to manipulate." She chuckled macabrely.

She told me: The deals. The treacheries. The betrayals.

I tried to remember what I was supposed to say next. "How long have you been running the stuff, Annalee?"

"A few years now," she answered, the amusement ringing

in her voice. She had her eyes slitted, watching me. "One or two more shipments would have put me over."

"Was it worth it, Annalee? I mean, really?" I asked, thinking about how starved I was.

"You bet your ass, Ken!" she said, selecting a target.

"Just explain one last thing. People saw you come in. How do you expect to get away with this?"

She leveled her pistol at my midsection. "I told the people at the desk that I was Elaine O'Day."

"Oh. That makes sense." I tried to think of one last thing to ask her, since my head was hurting and I really didn't want to have to deal with this. "Annalee, why are you doing this?"

"Let's see. You screwed up an almost foolproof smuggling scheme. You cost me the *Scupper*—I bought up half of the ship's outstanding debt and would have owned her free and clear in a year or so. You made me serve on the same damn ship as Harry. And you let Cheeves clean out my bearer account with every centavo I managed to save because you were so damned stupid you forgot to give me back my coin. Is that enough, or should I mention other things?"

"Sorry about the coin—I was preoccupied."

She pounded on the bedrail with the butt of her gun. "It's not fair! It's not *fair*."

"Annalee, if you're not careful with that thing, it might go off."

McHugh caught her breath and aimed the pistol again. "Ken, that's the whole idea. So long! I'm going to enjoy this!"

That was the last straw. By this time I'd had it with the horse manure that went on in this flimsy excuse for a hospital, so I picked up the tray of veggies with my left hand and flung it at her gun hand, then followed up by whipping the pillow around and bouncing it off her head.

The pistol went off, the bullet bounced around the room a few times, and Annalee went down like a sack of potatoes. After I ripped the stupid IV out of my arm, I found the pistol. Obviously, it was cheap local manufacture, so I bent it a little so she wouldn't try to hurt someone. Then I went downstairs and tore up the kitchen until I found some chocolate chip cookies.

Then I fainted, which seemed to be becoming a habit.

When I woke up, Nurse Clarkin was standing by my bedside. "Had a little fainting spell, did we?"

"I guess so. Where's Annalee?"

"The doctor called the police and had her taken away. I'm sure she's in jail right now. She tried to shoot you with an automatic, didn't she? Silly woman—it must come from eating animal flesh."

She stuck her hand down her blouse and pulled out an enormous muzzle-loading horse pistol. "Now, if she really wanted to shoot you, she should have used one of these."

"I knew it, I've finally cracked." I looked her up and down. "It looks like you're pointing a pistol at me."

"And it's loaded with a silver ball cartridge, Spawn of Satan—I melted down some earrings. I saw your lab tests. You didn't think we would *notice*, did you? Well, we're trained professionals here!" She pulled the hammer back to a full cock position.

I was still a couple of nickels short of a quarter. "Nurse Clarkin, I have had a really rough week, and I'm having trouble concentrating. What were you not supposed to notice?"

"That you were a vampire," Nurse Clarkin said agreeably, turning her body sideways and adopting a shooter's stance. "Percussion cap pistols have their uses, but I have always been partial to black powder flintlocks. There's such a sense of history about them, don't you agree?"

"Oh, sure. Wait a minute. Are you serious about me being a vampire? Huh! That must be why I passed out on the beach."

"You got that straight, sport," she said levelly. "Your guilt was even published in the newspapers."

"Oh, my Lord, that's right! We left the names out of Lydia's copy of the report, and Lydia read it wrong." I put my head in my hands. "What a mess!"

Then I recollected that Clarkin was pointing a pistol at me. "Wait, let's backtrack here for a minute. What did you mean by 'my guilt'?"

"That you are a foul fiend in human form; an accursed, undead drinker of human blood; that sort of thing." She waved the pistol negligently. "It's in all the literature." She gave me an odd look. "Now, did I remember to bring my mallet and stake?"

"I don't like where this conversation is leading," I admitted. "You don't really want to go through with this, do you?"

Nurse Clarkin looked at me with glittering eyes. "It's God's Will, Limb of Lucifer."

I heard a knock at the door and Piper's voice. "Ken, are you decent? Can we come in?"

"Please do!"

Piper and Catarina opened the door and walked in, clutching their visitor's passes. Piper had a gym bag under her arm.

Nurse Clarkin turned to them. "I was just about to shoot this vampire with a silver bullet."

Catarina's mouth twitched.

I pointed at the pistol and mouthed silently, *Would you please do something about this?*

"I'm sorry, nurse," Catarina said softly and very gravely, "but this is a navy matter."

"You'll just have to wait your turn to shoot him like everybody else," Piper threw in.

"Darn," Nurse Clarkin said. She stuffed her horse pistol back down her bosom and stomped out of the room.

"You wouldn't happen to know if I'm on drugs?" I asked.

Catarina sat down on one end of the bed. "Yes," she said without elaboration. "How do you feel, Ken?"

"Like I died."

"You almost did." Catarina looked up. "I wonder if your nurse remembered to take her pistol off full cock?"

"I hope her belt's tight," Piper said. "What she's got isn't going to hold that pistol up."

There was a muffled report and a little yip a short distance down the corridor.

"Sounds like a misfire to me. That's why they switched over to percussion caps," Piper commented.

"Changing topics, what happened to me?" I asked.

"When you didn't come back after your physical, I tried to call you and got a little worried when you didn't answer. Bunkie said she took you to the beach, so I sent Beam down to check on you. She scraped you off the sand with an acute case of skin poisoning."

"I don't remember being out there that long."

"You weren't," she said gently. "Seriously, you're lactose-sensitive now, and your system reacted to the milk in the milk-shake you drank and whatever else you put away before Beam found you. Along with the sun, it threw your body into shock, and I wasn't sure you were going to come out."

"Oh."

"You looked dead as a fish by the time I got to you," Piper volunteered.

"When the lab results came in, they confirmed our suspicions. Beam and I decided we ought to break the news to you." Catarina pursed her lips for a minute. "I gather Nurse Clarkin spoiled the surprise. Anyway, welcome to the club."

It took a few minutes to sink in. "Yeah. So I'm a vamp. It figures, I guess. That dentist really liked my teeth."

"Regrets?" Catarina asked.

"Well, I remember somebody saying, 'I don't regret anything that doesn't add to my waistline.' So what are we going to do?"

She smiled. "Just rest, Ken. Try and get your strength back. Things will work out somehow."

"I know. 'Trust me.' " I nodded my head up and down, and it even worked. Then I looked from Catarina to Beam and back again. "So why are the two of you smiling?"

"What makes you say that?" Piper asked, turning her head so I couldn't see her expression. "We've been out shopping."

Something clicked in my mind. "You went shopping?"

Catarina widened her smile, which was not a good sign. "We thought we'd get you a get-well gift." That was Piper's clue to reach into her bag and pull out a cardboard box.

I looked from one of them to the other. "I'm not going to like this, am I?"

"Go ahead, Ken. Open it," Beam said.

I pulled the lid off. "It's black. It's clothing." I held it up. "It's a cape. A cape. That's it—just cape it up, guys."

"Sure, Ken," Piper said, laughing. "We found it in a novelty shop. I want you to know we looked around for a set of plastic fangs, but we couldn't find any."

"Yeah, right. Beam, can Catarina and I be alone for a minute?"

Piper stepped outside. "I am going to get even," I pointed

out to Catarina. "For the cape, anyway. Somehow. I don't care how long it takes me, I am going to get even."

Then I started laughing, too.

Catarina leaned over and kissed my cheek. "Ken, I've talked to the doctor, and he's willing to release you to us as soon as you feel up to walking. Piper's going to stay here and bring you over as soon as you're ready. The sector commander, Captain Crenshaw, is over in Commander Hiro's office. I'll phone her. She's going to want to see you as soon as you feel able. Don't keep her waiting."

"How did Crenshaw get here so quick?"

"You've been out for six days," Catarina said. Then she was gone.

Piper came back in, dumped some extra clothes for me out of her bag, and parked herself in a chair. "Are you up for checking out?"

"Whew! Give me a few minutes, here." I flipped on the monitor in the room and sorted through my mail. Buried in the garbage was a little message from Bunkie. "Call Squirrel McNutty about lattices."

I showed it to Piper. "I thought April Fool's was over a couple of weeks ago."

She punched up Bunkie's number on the phone and her image appeared. "Oh, hello, sir. How do you feel?"

"Only slightly dead. I have a message here to call Squirrel McNutty about lattices. Didn't you guys wear out that joke with Ted E. Baer?"

Bunkie lost her composure ever so slightly. "Sir, I don't know how to explain this, but that message is on the level. McNutty is a Rodent who turned himself in as a prisoner-of-war. It turns out that Squirrel McNutty was the boon companion of Woody Chuck in a Bucky Beaver story. He says Cheeves asked him to bring some lattices along." She paused for a minute. "Sir, if this one turns out to be animal husbandry, I'll take the heat."

"Thanks, Bunkie," I said sheepishly.

Catarina called a few seconds later. "Ken—I just wanted to mention that Elaine was waiting in the lobby for me to turn in my visitor's pass. The police took her bomb away and have her in custody."

There was a small explosion, which rattled the windowpanes.

"It sounds like the police bomb squad is getting in some OJT," I observed.

"You'd better leave quietly out the back entrance. A minute ago, the lobby was crawling with reporters," Catarina cautioned.

Piper and I slipped out the back, and she drove me back to the office, where Captain Crenshaw was waiting for me.

Captain Crenshaw was a large black lady with grizzled gray hair and crow's-feet around her eyes. As I walked in and blinked at the light, she was sitting behind Hiro's desk stroking Sasha Louise. Lieutenant Commander Stemm was standing behind her.

"Have a seat, Ensign," she said in a voice that was intended to be friendly.

I sat down. Then I looked at her oddly. "You're not going to tell me that that cat is one of your secret agents, are you?"

"No." She let Sasha Louise jump down. "This is a cat. Not a particularly bright animal, even as cats go. Why?"

"Never mind, ma'am."

"Are you sure you're fit to be up, Ensign?" she asked with obviously feigned solicitude.

"I'm fine, ma'am. What did I miss?"

Crenshaw smiled. "You missed a lot of the hoopla. Your girlfriend, Christine . . ."

"Who? Oh! Go on, ma'am."

"As I was saying, your girlfriend Christine has gotten most of the publicity so far. She's a lot more photogenic than your shipmates. One of the local reporters got a real nice shot of her holding a dumbat a few seconds before the dumbat lost it."

I closed my eyes. "Ma'am, you're not going to believe this—" I started to say.

"That's right, but it doesn't matter," Crenshaw said briskly. "You're not on the hook. She's signed up to model for a local outfit called Mall World, and I understand she's going to host a game show."

I silently thanked the Lord. "How are Sin and Trujillo doing?"

"They're doing fine. We're going to send them on the talk-show circuit."

"And Commander Hiro?"

"He'll make captain out of this as long as he understands he's supposed to retire after we promote him."

"How thoughtful." I looked at Stemm. "Have a nice trip?"

Stemm glared. "Fourteen days' worth of Roy Rogers and the Cisco Kid!" His mouth tightened, and his voice cracked ever so slightly. "I can't wait to see you court-martialed!"

I looked at him, then said to Crenshaw, "Ma'am, I may not have had the advantages of an education paid for by the taxpayers, but I'm not stupid. Would you please explain to Lieutenant Commander Stemm why you're not going to court-martial me?"

Captain Crenshaw looked down at Stemm. "Bobby, I left some suits out in the shuttle that need pressing, why don't you go take care of them? Take the cat with you."

Stemm gave her a stricken look and left the room, shutting the door behind him.

"How did things go with the Macdonalds?" I asked.

Crenshaw smiled like a big cat. "The Macdonalds? As soon as we got word about your situation from Commander Stemm, we accidentally blew away the first Macdonald ship we spotted. We sent the survivors back with a very nicely worded letter of apology. The Macdonalds were very understanding, and the situation there is defused, no thanks to you. I thought that two destroyers would do the trick here. As it turns out, we didn't need them after all."

"No thanks to you, ma'am. I don't mean to be impertinent, but you could have left us with a little bit more to work with."

"I deserved that, didn't I?" she said briskly. "Oh, and sorry about your illness. Damn shame, that. Not duty-related, of course, so navy disability is completely out of the question."

"Yes, ma'am. I'm sure my lawyer will be happy to look into that for me."

It was Crenshaw's turn to glare at me. "How did you get to be a vampire, anyway?"

"Ma'am, I guess it happened the usual way. I must have forgot to wipe the toilet seat before I sat down," I said stiffly.

"Ensign," she growled, "I am the *deus ex machina* that has to figure out how to clean up this mess. I am old enough and mean enough to recognize sarcasm when I hear it, and I think I've heard enough out of you.''

"Sorry, ma'am. Why am I here?"

"Oh, I just wanted to go over your testimony before the Naval Estimates Subcommittee. I'm sure they'll all want to hear about your splendid little action here."

"Big bucks in it for the navy, huh? This war will need a lot of editing before it gets into the history books. What happens when the committee members find out you had a couple of vamps running things at the time?"

Captain Crenshaw looked exceedingly pained. She coughed slightly and said in a very different tone of voice, "That was the part I thought we ought to go over."

"Oh. Good. For a minute there I was beginning to wonder which one of us was rattlebrained." When her eyes started bugging out, I asked her, "Does that really work? I mean that husky-voiced, sweet-young-thing type of approach?"

She looked at me cross-eyed, and then she laughed. "Every damn time, at least up till now. Hell of an inconvenience, that affliction of yours!"

"Ma'am, tell me about it."

She leaned over the desk. "All right, young man. We are going to have to ship you back to Earth for slaughter. This is the first space battle in fifty years, and I doubt there's any way to keep you from testifying short of stuffing you in a sack. As much as it pains me, I'm even going to have to make a hero out of you."

"Why me?" I protested. "Why not Catarina or Piper? They outrank me—don't they have to share in the blame? Or what about Hiro? This was his idea, anyway."

"Hiro was inconsiderate enough to knock himself out and mention it in his report. Piper was operating the launcher on the space station." Crenshaw grinned. "Nobody is ever going to fall for that particular trick again, and if we give Piper the lion's share of the credit, every legislator is going to want to buy the navy an orbiting missile launcher to station on a space platform in his district. The universe will be a whole lot safer if the navy keeps a few ships instead."

"And Catarina?" I rejoined mildly. "You know that none of this would have worked without her?"

"Lieutenant Lindquist submitted her resignation before this all blew up, and she announced to the press that she was a vamp. I don't know if anybody's mentioned it to you, but the reporters covering the Macdonald crisis hired a cruise ship and headed over here when that fizzled. There must be three hundred of them floating around underfoot at the moment."

I gaped, and Crenshaw smiled. "Unfortunately, Lindquist was inconsiderate enough to tell the assembled multitude that your ship handling was the hottest thing since sliced bread in a vacuum pack, which ties my hands. Her sense of humor leaves a little bit to be desired at times."

"I'll agree with that."

"Anyway," Crenshaw continued, "we're going to have to take Lindquist off active duty before the hearings start, which is damnably inconvenient."

I started rubbing the bridge of my nose. "Captain, I'm not sure you realize that half the planet must know I'm a vamp by now."

"Not exactly, MacKay. Now that your friend Miz Dare understands that Lindquist was the vamp who wrote the report, she's running a retraction. Right now, the only people who know you're a vamp are your shipmates, my officers, and one nurse. As of ten minutes ago, the nurse was responding to therapy nicely."

She drummed her fingers on the desk. "Obviously, we're not going to be able to keep this a secret forever, but I think we can keep things quiet until after the hearings."

"Ma'am, there must be fifty reporters looking into the story right now."

"Ensign, by the day after tomorrow, you will be old news and they will all be gone. Now that we've announced it, half of them are skeptical about Lindquist being a vamp."

"Ma'am," I said, exasperated, "what about my little trip to the hospital?"

"Oh, that worked out beautifully. Publicly, we told everybody that you took a sword cut wrestling with Prince Genghis and probably fainted from lack of blood."

"I got scratched by a cat."

"No problem. We have containment on two levels. We told

everybody privately that you had a nervous breakdown. Apparently, you've been acting a lot nicer than usual, so people who knew you figured you were due."

"And the lab results?" I ignored the obvious retorts.

"A couple of reporters put two and two together and figured out that we submitted her tissue cultures under your name in case they tested positive. That's old news, too. All we have to do is get you off this planet relatively quickly."

"So I don't get lynched by Lydia's readership before they read her retraction," I finished for her. "Now comes the interesting part."

"All right, young man, just what does the navy have to do to keep you from blurting out exceedingly inconvenient facts?"

"Ma'am, I'm a spacer. I want to stay in space."

"Can't help you there. That's not a navy matter. The Guild'll pull your license and boot you out as soon as the news leaks that you're a vamp. The navy couldn't let you sign on to a ship without telling them that you've got McLendon's, and who would take you on if they knew?" Crenshaw was a big woman, and nobody would mistake her for a grandmother.

"Well, ma'am, I was hoping to run my own ship. I kind of like the idea, now that I've had a chance to try it. Captain MacKay—it has a certain ring to it. And I might add that if I got infected while I was on active service and can't space, that sounds like a one-hundred-percent navy disability until and unless you can retrain me. And I'm not very trainable."

Crenshaw smirked. "MacKay, let's be serious about this, shall we? How are you going to get that piece of junk of yours repaired, and how are you ever going to get it reregistered?"

"Well, first of all, the navy commandeered my ship and owes me standard rates plus money to put it back in the condition it was in before it got shot up the last time, which is another thing my lawyer will discuss at the proper time. It also occurs to me that the Rodents are a little short on spacecraft at the moment."

"MacKay, I don't mean to pry in your personal affairs, but apart from the fact that it may take you a long time to see any government money, hasn't it slipped your mind that you have had entirely too much to do with the fact that the Rodents are short of spacecraft?'' Her expression said, *You have about one more minute to make your point before I throw you out.*

"Ma'am, Ambassador Beaver has assured me that !Plixxi* is due for a change in government. I suspect that a new !Plixxi* government would be interested in hiring and registering my ship, and they might even compensate me for the original combat damage.''

"All right, sailor.'' Crenshaw met my eyes. "Supposing you can manipulate your Rodent friend, what deal do you want from me?''

I took a deep breath. "Ma'am, you want me to forget about being a vamp long enough to testify. I want you to forget about my being a vamp long enough to get me back here and get the *Scupper* repaired and reregistered under Rodent merchant colors, at which point I will cease to be a navy problem.''

"I seriously doubt *that*. Out of idle curiosity, how do you propose to crew this rust trap of yours?''

"Oh, I ought to be able to find a few people willing to sign on. I imagine some of my old shipmates would say they've seen worse, and I could probably get some Rodents if I had to.''

"And is there any little thing else you want?'' Crenshaw asked casually.

I took another deep breath. "Just this. Lieutenant Lindquist is navy through and through. I know she doesn't want to get out. Now, I know there's no way you can assign her to a navy ship, but there has to be something the navy can give her to keep her in space. So she's part of the deal. She keeps her commission and you assign her to my ship undercover.''

I saw Crenshaw start to utter a really biting remark and hesitate, so I jumped in. "And to cap the deal, I'll resign my Wavy Navy commission.''

Crenshaw looked at me for a long minute. "No way you get to resign, son. I have the feeling I am going to want all the hooks known to mankind into you. Now tell me, does this crackpot notion belong to you or to Lieutenant Lindquist?''

"Ma'am, this one's mine. Believe me, if Catarina had cooked this up, it would be a hell of a lot smoother.''

"And if I agree, I suppose the next thing you'll want to discuss is compensation for your ship's hire and the combat damage." Crenshaw folded her arms.

"Ma'am, we can discuss that later. As far as I'm concerned, if the navy gets too chintzy, as long as I have a missile launcher aboard I can always run up the Rodent flag and do a little self-help," I told her lightly.

"Blackbeard you're not, but you already know that if we have to put you up in front of a subcommittee, we'll make sure you get paid fairly. All right, what happens if I say no to this silly scheme of yours, Ensign?"

"Well, ma'am, as Bucky says, 'In times of utmost adversity, desperate actions are sometimes necessary for the general good.' "

"What in hell is that supposed to mean, MacKay?"

"Ma'am, it means on Earth I squeak like a rusty wheel. Also, I lean across the desk and bite you on the neck," I said, leaning across the desk.

The lady was tough. "Son, genetic predisposition for McLendon's Syndrome is what, three percent of the entire population? You ever seen a black vampire?"

"Ma'am, for the last month or so, I have been hitting on lower probabilities than that. You don't get a deal without Catarina."

Crenshaw grinned and shook her head from side to side. "MacKay, you'll do. Lindquist? You out there?"

Catarina opened the door and came in. That's when I figured out I was really in trouble.

Crenshaw looked at me. "All right, MacKay, did my lieutenant put you up to this, or did you come up with this harebrained notion on your very own?"

My mother always taught me to tell the truth when I get confused. "Ma'am, I can honestly say this one was my very own."

"Lindquist," Crenshaw said, "your insubordinate subordinate here has just threatened to foul up his testimony before the subcommittee, commit piracy, and bite me on the neck unless I agree to let him operate his ship for the Rodents and ship you on board her with a covert commission. Do you know anything about this?"

"It sounded so much nicer when I said it," I murmured inaudibly.

"Captain, this was Ken's idea. This is the first I've heard of it."

"Hrumph. I would have sworn he didn't have enough sense to pour water out of a boot, and his mother dresses him funny . . . Did you want to say something, MacKay?"

I shook my head.

She looked back at Catarina. "It isn't polished enough to be your handiwork, so I suppose it's his. I suppose that in a myopic way, his mind is just as evil as yours is, and if so it would be a shame to waste it on honest pursuits. If you want him, he's all yours."

Crenshaw turned her head and fixed one beady eye on me. "Congratulations, young man. Don't let your head swell, but you probably just became commander-in-chief of the Rodent navy. It's a hell of a lot cheaper than letting them have another cruiser."

Catarina rapped her ring against the desk for emphasis. "Ken, I thought you should know that Captain Crenshaw was my Tac Officer at the Academy."

"Uh, yeah," I said.

"Catarina, why don't you take your fire-breathing young ensign aside and put the finishing touches on his concoction."

Something wasn't tracking. "Huh?" I said.

"Captain Crenshaw had me listening in on the intercom. She felt it would save time all around," Catarina explained. "So how about this: I resign my commission for health reasons and accept a civilian intelligence appointment. You hire your ship out to the navy—"

"We buy you cheap," Captain Crenshaw said helpfully.

"—And I stay on as your controller. The navy pays your expenses for purely navy missions."

"Keep lots of receipts," Crenshaw added.

"Do I get any say in this?"

The two of them looked at me. "Of course not. This is the navy."

Catarina shrugged and tossed her hair. "I feel kind of responsible for you. And if it doesn't work out, I can always try the convent."

"Some choices are better than nothing. I assume that makes me—"

She nodded. "Better than nun."

I took a deep breath and finished for her. "You'd find it too convent-ional. It's not something you'd want to make a habit of."

Crenshaw shook her head. "God help those Rodents!"

"And we all live happily ever after. Think we can get a crew?" I asked.

Catarina smiled. "I looked into that. Clyde's interested if he can get a license. Wyma Jean is, too."

"What about Rosalee?"

"Rosalee is in. She said, 'It wouldn't feel right if the captain on that ship wasn't a bloodsucking son of a bitch.' "

"That's four watch-standers," I said. "That's a start. Should I ask about the lawsuits chasing me around the galaxy?"

"Omura and I fixed a few of them. When the J. T. Pollard Fertilizer and Feed Company found out you used their guano for your smoke screen, they agreed to drop the suit and pay you five thousand if you'll appear in an advertising video."

"It's a deal as long as I get to hold the feed bag and don't have to wear it," I said quickly.

"As for the others?" She shrugged. "Think of it as your public duty to keep lawyers off the welfare roles."

I looked at Crenshaw, who was trying very hard not to laugh.

"Ensign," she said, "I am going to tell you one secret that had better not leave this room. We broke the Macdonalds' code six months ago, so we knew Genghis was going to invade—"

"But—" I said.

"—two months from now. That's why I sent Catarina. I will leave you with one thought to ponder. If you hadn't involved yourself, Genghis would have invaded this planet on schedule, and I would have blown away his ships and guaranteed my own career and Naval appropriations for the next twenty years. Unfortunately, the best military plans rarely survive contact with the people who get to carry them out. There's a moral in there somewhere. As you reflect upon this, Ensign, I trust you will grow in wisdom. Because if you don't, Lindquist is under orders to beat it into your pointy little head."

"Yes, ma'am," I said, standing to attention.

Crenshaw left the room. "Come on. Let's find Cheeves and get the details fixed," Catarina said.

Cheeves was waiting for us outside. "Cheeves, Bucky offered to reflag the *Scupper* as a !Plixxi* merchant vessel, or will, about ten minutes after you suggest it to him. Tell him I accept."

Cheeves bowed very slightly. "Very good, sir. I will convey these auspicious tidings to His Rotundity, and I will have the necessary papers sent to your residence for signature."

"Thank you, Cheeves. Now, off the record, what is there that I should know?"

Cheeves twitched his whiskers. "Sir, a number of the survivors from *Nemesis* and the other ships have not been captured, and there are reports of random violence—bands of armed marauders are entering gerbil farms at night and opening all the cages. These survivors apparently feel themselves too shamed to return to !Plixxi*. Dr. Beaver intends to ask Captain Crenshaw to allow them to remain if they agree to lay down their arms."

Catarina looked at him thoughtfully, and I remembered that a couple of the Rodents on the shuttle looked a little like schnauzers.

"Sir, I should also mention that as I was leaving !Plixxi*, Dr. Beaver's demi-brother Cain was fomenting a rebellion which might occasion some difficulties. But nothing above your ability to handle, I trust."

"Uh, right, Cheeves," I said. I then plugged my fingers in my ears so that I wouldn't hear the inevitable pun.

It eventually worked out. Harry sold his bar and bought in. Bucky looked sharp in his robes of state when we got him to recommission the old bucket, and I'm still dodging lawsuits.

I even talked to a reporter once. I said, "In your face."

When all was said and done, the one thing that annoyed me was the actor they got to play me in the TV movie. He was a forty-five-year-old homosexual, and when I saw what he looked like in plastic fangs, I wanted to change my name.

And whatever happened to actresses like Ingrid Bergman? The woman they had playing Catarina could barely stuff her cleavage into coveralls. And they never did get the bar scenes right.

About the Author

Robert Frezza was born in 1956 at Bolling Air Force Base and grew up around Baltimore, Maryland. He graduated from Loyola College in Baltimore with a B.A. in history and was commissioned as a second lieutenant through the ROTC program. He then went on to the University of Maryland Law School to learn a trade and avoid ending up as a second lieutenant in infantry in Alabama.

After serving on active duty for three years in Germany as a captain in the Judge Advocate General's Corps, he went to work for the Army as a civilian attorney. He was formerly the Deputy Chief of the Personnel Claims and Recovery Division of the U. S. Army Claims Service and is a graduate of the Army Management Staff College.

A third-generation Baltimore Orioles fan, he enjoys reading, theater, and arguing military history. He lives reasonably quietly in Glen Burnie, Maryland.

this! Wham!" Han proceeded to demonstrate and almost

Somewhere behind the dark, slim girl the light of the world pushed piercing fingers into the earth. But here, an hour's walk into the depth of the Unending Cave, the only light was a single candle illuminating an old witch-woman's face. Seen by daylight, it would have been an ordinary face, wrinkled by sun and wind, gap-toothed as old mouths are, and surmounted by thinning gray hair like any crone's in the town. But here, in the earth's very gut, in the home of all secrets, it was a terrifying sight.

If I survive this, the girl reminded herself, I will be a witch, and I will fear her no more. She will be only an old woman. If I fail, it won't matter. I won't remember a thing.

"Outsiders call us witches, child," the crone murmured. "What are we?"

"We are children of a far star," the girl Illyssa recited in singsong. "Our minds entwine. Our thoughts reach out and speak with tongues of flame."

"High, green hills surround and hide us. What do we fear?"

"We fear black abominations, slavers and herders of men." The memorized words flowed. This was the easy part of her catechism; the real test would follow. "We fear the False Church, their tool," Illyssa continued. "Priests who are their eyes and ears on Earth, and soldier-priests who hunt us for the black masters."

"We are hunted," the hag stated. "Are we wild pigs, then, or hares? Are we playthings or food?"

"We are star-wolves and raveners," the girl replied, her voice tremulous with the frightening impact of her words. "We are far-wanderers, dark-space rovers marooned on this isle. The black ones would use us as dogs in their harnesses, leaping and running their errands from star to star."

"What holds us here, planet-fallen?"

"The One Man was lost, and with him the Merging and Melding, keys to the stars. The Seed and the Flower do not breed true. The Ship lies beneath waters and the slavemasters circle above."

The old woman lit a dark cheroot from her single candle. "Enough, child. I am sure you can recite all the Responses word for word. But do you *understand*? Do you *believe*? Or are you no more than any village girl, a child of these mountains?"

"I am a child, Grandmother," the girl said in ritual singsong. "I am an unbeliever, unfit. Do with me what you will."

"Do you *want* to understand, to believe?" It was no ritual question.

Illyssa's eyes sparkled with anger. "I want to know what is *real*," she said. "I want to believe what is *true*. If the Tales and Responses are history, I want to know that. If they're only madness of old women, I want to know *that*, too."

The hag sighed. "I can't show you Ferosians, child. I cannot give you the True Flower to eat, either, and I can't take you through the corridors of the Ship. How will you *know*? What are you willing to risk for your assurances?"

The girl slipped back into singsong, unable or afraid to put her wishes into plain words. "I wish to eat the False Flower, and to speak with the minds of my ancestresses. Then I will believe. I have seen the simpleminded ones, now only wombs to birth and breasts to nurse, and I will risk becoming as they are."

The old woman responded with a sad, slow shake of her head. "Then risk it you shall. Have you said your farewells to your mother and father?"

"I have."

"Then we begin. When you emerge from this chamber, be you brood mare or witch, your parents' child will be no more."

* * *

Washington—(IPS)—The House of Representatives narrowly passed the New White House's favored anti-emigration bill, which prohibits designated Nationally Valued Persons (NVPs) from boarding any non-government owned spacecraft. Citing the recent departure of the entire faculty and many students of the Midland Technical Institute, ferried from the rooftops of the flooded campus to a waiting Faroseen ship, President Tuthill stated that "we cannot continue to permit the heart and brains of this nation to be excised, and still expect its body to function."

—April 12, 2260, *International Weekly*, Geneva.

West Wind's mast bobbed wildly as the young man descended to her deck, swinging a blue canvas sack ahead of him. It hit the smooth, bleached deck with a thump.

The boat's owner regarded him with wary neutrality. At first glance, the old fisherman thought, the lean, large-boned fellow looked out of place in ordinary traveler's clothing. His ice-blue eyes and narrow, distinctly northern nose hinted at noble birth among the foggy, heavily forested coastal bogs and islands. Omer mistrusted men of noble birth, especially those with thick wrists more suited to broadswords than teacups, with skin weathered to rich bronze, not pale. The times were unsettled. The only honest enemy was the sea. There were too many goings-on and intrigues for a man to let his guard down.

"Don't you remember me, Om?" the younger man asked.

The fisherman took another look. His yellow-gray, bushy eyebrows rose in surprised recognition. "P'fesser!" he exclaimed. "I never saw you so—no scholar's robe, no dirt on yer face. An' tha' beard, it ages you." He stretched out a leathery hand.

"You've only seen me in summer," Yan said. "I shave then, because of Michan's burrowing mites, but now that the digging's done, I'm like anyone else, I'm afraid." His faint smile faded. "At least I was."

"And what are you now?" the boatman asked. "You look to be well worn by the road."

Yan hesitated. How much did he dare tell? He'd picked the *West Wind* because Omer had worked for Lazko, ferrying supplies to the archaeological dig and artifacts back to Nahbor. But what did he really know about him? Eyes can't peer into a man's soul. "I've left the university on . . . on extended research. I go to New Roster. Will you take me there?"

"New Roster? Aya, it's a long sail. Nearly to th' other end a' the Reach."

"Will this be enough?" Yan held out copper and silver coins, a generous offer. "I must leave immediately."

"Aya, I'll take you there," Omer agreed. "And for that sum, you get meals, too. Is that all your gear, P'fesser? No crates or boxes? How can you do research wi'out your tools?"

Omer's words were casual, but Yan sensed falseness. I'm paranoid, he thought. He's only curious. The old man stared past him as if bidding the quaint, silvery wood buildings of Wain good-bye. "Well, then, cast off tha' line," he said gruffly. "Na—just toss it on th' dock. Now push us away." Yan pushed at a piling with a foot, unbalancing as the boat slipped sideways. He caught a tarred stay with one arm and a leg, then dangled over the water until he could get his other leg back on board. He barked his shin, and as he bent to rub it, he missed seeing what Omer had seen: a gaunt figure emerging between two shanties, robed and hooded in cloth the color of wet ashes, squinting at them over the low-angling sunlight that glared off the *West Wing*'s wake.

"Can I help with anything?" Yan asked.

"You paid your passage." The fisherman's words came from aft, over the cabin roof. "Help any more than that, and you'll be bruised all over." Yan grimaced at the hoarse laugh that followed. Shrugging, he climbed aft and settled against the mast to watch the shoreline recede.

The brown-robed priest scurried unhappily back to his waiting carriage. He would have to report that his quarry had escaped again. His driver, an acolyte and his current playmate, cringed and tightened his buttocks when he saw his superior's red, angry face. *He* would suffer the priest's rage. It already promised to be a most unpleasant day.

There was nothing productive for a landsman to do on a small boat rocking gently on nighttime swells. Observing Yan's fidgety unrest, the fisherman chided him. "It's a long few days to New Roster, Yan Bando. The sea's no place for a man who's na' at home wi' his own thoughts."

Did he know something was wrong? Had he sensed Yan's unease? The scholar was no accomplished dissembler, and he knew it. "I'm comfortable enough with my thoughts," he replied, smiling to cover his anxiety, "but only when I have a pen in my hand and paper before me."

"Aya. Always the p'fesser, eh? Then let's make a light for this airy study a' yours." He went below, returning with a contraption of glass and prisms. "A chart lamp. The glass magnifies the candle's light a bit."

Yan thanked him. What could he do now? He didn't want to bring out the notebooks. There were too many odd-looking pages of edge-punched paper spewed from the Library's machines, and photocopies with letters too small and regular to have been written by human hands.

With considerable dexterity he fished new, creamy sheets from his bag, and using the hard book-covers within for a desk, he picked up his thoughts where he'd left them in Wain.

The wreck of the alien ship itself was only one sad relic of a long trail of events that led further back in time. Philosophically, Yan suspected his troubles had begun when the first rudimentary cell divided in Earth's ancient seas; as an antiquarian, he was constrained to begin with the artifacts and events recorded in the books he'd saved from the fire.

By earthly standards of any age, the alien ship was enormous, thirty by two hundred meters of gray, pitted metal, like seven lengths of sewer pipe bolted together at the flanges. A conical trailing segment was tipped with a slender, pointed mast, and the leading end was a forty-meter sphere with a large depression in its forward surface. Four metal-mesh dragonfly wings a hundred meters long stretched from just behind the bulbous "head."

Yan, a careful observer, had noticed different degrees of pitting on adjacent sections, worn corners on pentagonal bolt-heads, and scarred lips on connecting flanges. He had deduced that the ship was no more than a conjoining of interchangeable modules: control, cargo, and drive. Hardly a "ship" of space, it was really a "train." Its odd pentagonal bolts and mixed four-

and fivefold symmetries were clearly not of human design or manufacture.

Within, the leathery remains of a human crew were scattered on makeshift wooden couches in holds and hallways, their shriveled eyes still facing equally makeshift instrument panels. Colorful sheaths of corroded cable ran everywhere, secured to walls, floors, and ceilings with roughly welded staples and twists of wire. They ran through ventilation ducts, down hallways, in and out of once-airtight doors. Most of them originated within rudely cut openings in the vessel's gray metal and terminated at improvised crew stations, where branched tangles of colored wires ended in rough, hand-fabricated controls. In the forward control room, a huge machinelike pilot's seat made to enclose an unimaginably alien pilot stood abandoned, disconnected from the cable nerve net of the ship.

Imagine their surprise when those far-traveling men and women first gazed on the planet their ancestors had left long ago. No satellites had spun about them, no signals had greeted them. Below, no electric-bright city lights winked. Yan suspected the outlines of continents their slave ancestors might have recognized were changed beyond recognition. No polar icecaps would have glared. Could they have guessed how seas had risen, continents twisted and plunged, in the half millennium since their kind had left Earth as slaves of alien Ferosin? Earth must have seemed void of intelligent life to them. Could their instruments have seen towns linked only by muddy tracks where mules and donkeys, oxen and barefoot men, shared the rutted ways?

How long did it take them to decide their course of action? Did they have fuel to return home to some far world? Would they have been welcome there? Only desperation could have forced them to land; their great ship was never intended to breach the atmosphere of a world. They had surely expected to have been met in orbit, but no one had come. No one had answered their signals. For all they could have known, they had been alone. It must have been a bitter dose, Yan thought, when they decided to take it. Once landed, they were trapped on a world so primitive that men had forgotten how to reach their own looming moon, had forgotten even that their ancestors had once stood on its surface. They could never again have seen the stars except as they winked from Earth's thick veil of air and cloud.

Perhaps they had hoped Earth's primitives could be taught the secrets they'd learned on some far world. Perhaps they'd intended it, but Yan knew it had not happened. The world would have been far different from the place of rude, dirty towns, of dusty roads and torchlit streets, that *he* knew.

There was a terrible inertia to ignorance. Without the scientific mindset that linked cause and effect, without understanding hypothesis, proof, and disproof, Earth folk might have worshiped those ancient spacefarers or slain them as witches, but they would never have let them change the world.

Yan Bando, fugitive, was in no position to change anything, but he would still be able to supplement his knowledge with bits and pieces, to collect data and record them. Perhaps some wiser reader of his notes would find the key to change, and would turn humanity back into the channel that had almost led to the stars. The long diversion into dust, disease, and ignorance could yet end. Yan was determined to continue observing and scribbling, collecting a morsel here, a bit there, his small contribution to a future that might or might not be . . .